Books by Robert Bidinotto

Fiction

Hunter (Dylan Hunter #1)
Bad Deeds (Dylan Hunter #2)
Winner Takes All (Dylan Hunter #3)

Nonfiction

Criminal Justice? The Legal System vs. Individual Responsibility
Freed to Kill

WINNER TAKES ALL

A Dylan Hunter Thriller

ROBERT BIDINOTTO

Chester, Maryland

WINNER TAKES ALL: *A Dylan Hunter Thriller*
ROBERT BIDINOTTO

Copyright © 2017 by Robert Bidinotto.
All rights reserved.

This is a work of fiction. Names, characters, places, and incidents are the product of the author's imagination or are used fictitiously.

Published by
Avenger Books
P.O. Box 555
Chester, Maryland 21619

Trade paperback edition: December 2017

Published in the United States of America

Cover design by **Allen Chiu**
http://www.allenchiu.com

Formatting and layout by **Polgarus Studio**
http://www.polgarusstudio.com/

*To my patient, loving, supportive, and long-neglected wife,
Cynthia,
and to the other brilliant and beautiful ladies in my life:
Katrina, Doria, Enid,
and, of course, Luna.*

*Also to my family, my friends, and the fans of
Dylan Hunter:
You are far too many to name,
but far too important ever to forget.*

My love and gratitude to you all.

"I have never been able to conceive how any rational being could propose happiness to himself from the exercise of power over others."

—Thomas Jefferson

PART I

ONE

"You sneaky *bastard...*"

Arnie Wasserman whispered the words, even though he was the only person in the office of his apartment. He leaned closer to his computer screen, staring in disbelief at what it had just revealed.

He knew enough now to be scared.

Multiple browser windows stood open, a diagonal stack descending across the screen. They displayed corporate financial statements, IRS Form 990 reports from foundations and nonprofit organizations, and lists of donations and grants.

Superimposed across them hovered a transparent "mind map" chart: a bewildering spider web of lines linking the names of the groups, corporations, and individuals. His previous keystroke had just caused all those lines and names to shift positions.

And at the very center of that web, the mouse cursor blinked on the name of a single individual.

Now he understood why the man had threatened him on the phone this morning . . .

"I have placed some inquiries about you, Mr. Wasserman," the man had told him, his voice cold and clipped. "You do investigative work—not magazine features, as you pretended during your call to my secretary. So let us not play games. What, precisely, is your interest in my charitable activities?"

Realizing he couldn't bullshit the guy, Arnie had cut to the chase. He told him he wanted on-the-record responses to three questions about contributions passing through the man's foundation.

"And what questions would those be, Mr. Wasserman?"

The man had listened a moment, then interrupted in the middle of Arnie's third question.

"You will soon regret you ever poked your nose into my business."

He had said it softly, each syllable precise and distinct.

Then he was gone . . .

At that instant, Arnie knew he was on the right track.

But now, staring at his computer screen, he knew a lot more.

He knew he was looking at a conspiracy.

He knew who was involved.

He knew exactly what they were after—and just how high the stakes were.

And—except for *them*—he was the only other living person who knew about it.

That last realization sent a small, cold shiver through him.

2

The man closed the door behind him, locked it, then flicked on the light switch.

The spacious study within his opulent Watergate apartment was his sanctuary in the city. His architect had provided him a cherry coffer ceiling and built-in cherry bookcases. The latter were crammed with hardcover and leather-bound volumes of history, political science, law, economics, and reference works. A massive, intricately tooled desk, also cherry, dominated the center of the room.

He went there, reached under the desktop, and pressed a hidden latch. A side panel, disguised by ornate carving, popped open. Kneeling, he pulled it wide. Inside was a tall, narrow safe with a keypad lock. He tapped in seven numbers and opened its door.

On a stack of six narrow shelves rested items no one else knew about.

Four false passports and matching drivers' licenses.

A Sig-Sauer P220 Carry in .45 ACP, and two loaded eight-round magazines.

Emergency cash—$25,000, in mixed denominations. A burst transmitter. A half-dozen cheap "burner" phones and batteries. An encrypted satellite phone.

He removed a burner, inserted a battery, let it power up. Then thumbed in a phone number and texted an eight-digit numerical code to it. By pre-arrangement with the recipient, the code meant: "Call me immediately on my satellite phone."

He purged the phone's history, removed the battery and SIM card, and returned it to the safe. Then took out the sat phone, powered it on, and waited in his red-leather office chair, near the window. The phone chirped three minutes later.

"Just got your message, sir," said the man on the other end.

"Thank you for being prompt. Let me get right to it. A certain journalist is about to create significant problems for me. The threat he poses must be . . . mitigated."

"Great!" The voice was eager. "And I gather this 'certain journalist' is—"

"No. Not *him*. This is another. An impetuous freelancer. He is making inquiries that seriously jeopardize my interests. I believe he will go public with his information at any time. And that cannot be permitted."

"Oh." The man sounded disappointed. "All right. Tell me about him."

He did.

"So, how soon would you like me to take care of this, sir?" Ray Lasher asked.

"Before the end of the day," said Avery Trammel.

3

By the late afternoon, Trammel could no longer stand the confinement of his study—not while awaiting the outcome with the reporter. He decided to do his waiting out in the fresh air, overlooking the city.

Bringing the satellite phone, he locked the door behind him, then proceeded down the hall. He reached the large, lavishly appointed reception parlor—site of many Washington social events. He heard laughter in there—his wife's voice.

From the entrance, he saw Julia was with two others, seated on the plush leather sofas before the fireplace, scrapbooks of her film roles spread on their laps. He noticed she had brought out and displayed her two Academy Award trophies on the mantelpiece; they stood at either end, like golden sentries, their color matching the hand-painted fluting and capitals of the flanking Corinthian pilasters.

He tried to slip past, but she spotted him.

"Oh, there he is! Hello, dear—we were just discussing you. I want you to meet Nikki Epstein of the *Post*, and her photographer, Bill Standish. They're putting together a Sunday feature about—"

"Hello," he interrupted, stepping into the room and forcing a smile. "My apologies, Julia. I would love to visit. However, I must return an urgent international call, and the reception for this thing"—he waved the satellite phone—"is poor in my study. Please excuse me."

Her smile faded as he nodded at them.

From the wine cellar off the foyer he selected a good bottle, a glass, and an opener. Then he headed up the stairwell to the private rooftop terrace of his penthouse. He left the items he had brought on a glass-topped table, then threaded through the thicket of potted plants and flowers, to the wall at the roof's edge.

Trammel gripped its cold brass rail.

Fourteen stories below, the Potomac River flowed, a waxen mirror of the slate sky. Across its expanse, the bare, ashen fingers of trees on Theodore Roosevelt Island groped for a fugitive sun. His gaze drifted south, past the pallid Carrara marble of the nearby Kennedy Center, to where the gray arc of the Roosevelt Bridge linked the nation's capital to Virginia. A chill March gust stung his cheeks and knuckles.

The past month had been catastrophic. All that he had been working toward, for decades, now stood at risk.

Avery Trammel was not a man given to superstition. Yet he had a disquieting feeling of foreboding about his phone confrontation with the reporter—the sense that it signaled some sort of turning point.

4

Arnie suddenly realized that daylight was waning. He got up from the computer screen and went over to flip on the overhead light. It revealed the glittering cluster of framed awards hanging nearby on the wall.

For a moment, he stood there, seeking reassurance from them. His journalism degree from the University of Missouri. His FOI Award from Investigative Reporters and Editors. His finalist nomination for a National Magazine Award. And the other, lesser-known ones. These recognitions reminded him of just how good a reporter he was.

But this story—it was much bigger than anything he had ever tried to handle.

From this point, he would have to proceed far more cautiously. The sooner he could get this information into print, the safer he would be.

Returning to his desk, Arnie composed a brief, cryptic email to his contact at the Center for Advocacy Profiles, the main outlet for his investigative reporting. No details—these days, you never knew who was intercepting your email. He said only that he had a huge story about the Currents Foundation and had to discuss it with them at their next weekly meeting.

He hit the *send* icon.

Then immediately had misgivings.

This story was way too big for a small nonprofit outlet like CAP. It was a game-changer. It would affect everyone in the country.

And that made it worth a lot of money.

You have to stop thinking small. You need to shop this one around, to one of the majors . . . Maybe—

He was startled by the sudden ringing of his land line in the living room. He got up and trotted out there, following the sound across the room. He found the phone on the floor, hidden behind a footrest next to the sofa. He leaned over to read the Caller ID screen. His hand moved eagerly toward the receiver—then hesitated.

Sure, Wonk would be the ideal person to confide in. But he couldn't risk revealing too much to him over an open phone line.

He picked up on the fifth ring. "Yes?"

"Hello, Arnold." The voice was incongruously high-pitched for a man whose weight was north of five hundred pounds.

"Hi, Frederick." Wonk didn't like to be called by the nickname everyone used for him.

"You did not answer my text message, Arnold. Are we still on for chess at seven?"

"Oh! It's Wednesday, isn't it? Damn, I forgot. Look, I'm sorry, Frederick, but I can't. Not tonight." He hesitated, then blurted: "I'm working on a really big story."

"I see." The voice was disappointed. "What kind of story?"

"Political. As usual . . . Well, *not* as usual. There's nothing usual about this one."

Arnie settled down on the carpet, leaning back against the sofa. He tried to resist saying more, but felt as if he were on a slippery slope. And something told him he would be safe only if he shared this—at least, as much as could be said on the phone.

"You won't *believe* whose money is being laundered through the Currents Foundation," he said, "and where it's winding up. I mean, this one's a *bombshell*. It . . . has major implications for the presidential race. In fact, I think it's going to blow the whole election campaign sky-high!"

"Really?" Wonk's voice climbed another octave. "So tell me!"

"Not now. Not over the phone. Anyway, I've still got some details to figure out before I draft something. And I've been thinking . . . I may not want to break this one through CAP. I need a much bigger platform. Maybe the *Post* or the *Inquirer* . . . Oh, hey—somebody's at the door. I'll call you right back."

"That is fine. Since we shall not be playing chess, I shall be here all evening."

Arnie hung up, leaving the phone behind the footrest. Puzzled, he rose and headed to the door. He expected no visitors, and the mail had arrived hours ago.

The bell chimed again as he put an eye to the security peephole.

Outside, a big blond guy, chewing gum. A large pizza box resting in his hands.

"Yes?" Arnie called out through the door, watching the man carefully.

"Pizza Rossano." The guy squinted down at a scrap of paper taped to the lid of the box. "Delivery for the Wasserman residence."

Arnie frowned. "I didn't order any pizza."

The guy scowled and looked at the paper again. "Arnold Wasserman, Potomac Village Apartments—right?"

"Yes, that's me. But I didn't—"

"Says here it's from 'a friend.' Doesn't say who."

"But—"

"Hey, look—somebody's giving you a free pizza. If I have to take this back, I don't get paid for the delivery, okay?"

Arnie sighed. *Who in hell . . . ?*

The man outside looked tired and bored. Not at all suspicious. And it *was* free food. He hadn't had anything since breakfast.

"All right. I'll take it, then."

He unhooked the security chain, flipped the lock, and opened the door.

The big guy smirked at him—then dropped the box and rushed him.

TWO

Lasher saw Wasserman's eyes widen as he charged in. He grabbed the little guy's shoulder and spun him, then snaked his left arm around his neck. Positioning the crook of his elbow against Wasserman's throat, he used his bicep and forearm to squeeze the opposite sides of the man's neck, compressing the carotid arteries. At the same time, he pressed his right palm behind the guy's head for leverage. He didn't squeeze hard enough to do any internal damage or leave bruises—just enough to temporarily cut off the blood to the guy's brain.

He felt the scrawny body thrash and squirm for a few seconds, then go slack.

He eased Wasserman to the floor. He was glad it was hardwood: no chance of leaving his footprints on a carpet.

The guy wouldn't be out for more than a minute, if that. Moving fast, Lasher fetched the empty pizza box and the duffle bag he'd left in the hallway, then closed and locked the apartment door behind him. Keeping on his surgical gloves, he yanked off Wasserman's T-shirt. Then lifted him in his arms, like a child, and carried him into the bathroom. He hoisted him feet-first into the tub, holding him upright.

The runt was just beginning to stir and groan in his arms when Lasher leaned forward and slammed the side of the guy's skull down against the faucet and the rim of the tub.

Blood began to flow from the unconscious man's scalp into the tub. Lasher finished undressing him in there, taking care not to get any of it on his own clothes or the rest of Wasserman's, which he tossed onto the floor.

Then he turned the naked guy face down. Put in the drain stopper. Turned on both faucets.

Wasserman's bleeding temple left rose-colored spirals in the water.

Lasher knew how to stage it to look like an accident. He'd done this very thing once before, in London, and had gotten away with it.

He saw a bar of soap and a bottle of shampoo on a rack at the foot of the tub. He took the soap and rubbed it in his gloved hands under the running faucet, to leave its traces in the water. He added in some shampoo, and the churning water began to boil up suds.

The water level slowly crept up Wasserman's bony body. First it covered his small hands. Then it crawled up his cheeks. As water began to enter his mouth, the little man quivered, sputtered, and tried groggily to raise his injured head.

Lasher leaned over and pressed down on the back of Wasserman's neck, holding him under. The thrashing wasn't strong and didn't last long. There were a couple of final spasms. Then nothing. He held the body under the rising water for a full minute, just to make sure.

2

He gathered Wasserman's clothes and shoes, along with the T-shirt from the living room, and left them strewn in a casual heap on the bedroom floor, next to a hamper already crammed with dirty clothes.

Back in the bathroom, Lasher shut off the faucet and looked around slowly. Closing his eyes, he imagined the logical sequence of actions by a man taking a bath.

He fetched a fresh bath towel and wash cloth from the linen closet. He dampened the towel under the water from the faucet, spread a few touches of soap and shampoo on it, and dropped it on the floor next to the tub. He soaked the wash cloth under the faucet, too, grazed it across the bar of soap, and left it crumpled in a ball on the edge of the tub. He replaced the wet bar of soap and damp shampoo bottle on the rack.

Then Lasher removed a white terrycloth bathrobe from its hook on the door and stuffed it over the towel rack, draping it within arm's reach of the tub.

The surface of the water was dead still now, except for the faint, sizzling pops of a few stray bubbles. The pale, naked, motionless corpse looked like an underwater statue. The head had turned slightly to the side, eyes open. He yanked the chain of the drain stopper, set the plug on the edge of the tub, then waited. The gurgling water receded slowly, inch by inch, gradually exposing the guy's skinny, naked back, leaving traces of soap scum on his skin.

Ray Lasher studied his handiwork through the eyes of the cops and the M.E.

Okay, so the guy just finishes his bath. He stands and pulls the plug, then towels off right there, in the tub. Then he drops the towel on the floor, to step on when getting out, so the floor won't get soaked with his wet feet. But before he gets out, he reaches over to grab his bathrobe—then slips, falls, and bashes the side of his head against the faucet and edge of the tub. Knocked unconscious, he drowns face down, before the tub drains.

Supporting that scenario, they'll find mingled traces of soap, shampoo, and blood in the tub, inside his mouth and lungs, and dried on his skin. But the towel and wash cloth won't bear any traces of the blood from the bathwater, of course, because he'd have finished using them before cracking his skull.

No signs of foul play. Just a tragic accident.

As he started to leave the bathroom, Lasher realized he had not turned on the bathroom's light or ventilation blower. He swore at himself as he took care of that.

Just the kind of little mistakes that could blow everything.

3

Worried about time, Lasher walked hurriedly through the living room/dining room area, then the kitchenette, glancing at the walls and tabletops. No landline phone in evidence. He entered the guy's office.

Before touching anything, he used his phone to take photos of the precise layout of the office and positions of desktop items.

Wasserman's mobile phone was on the desk. Lasher spent most of the next half hour going through all recent messages and texts. He deleted any history of calls pertaining to his employer's interests, including references in the address book and calendar.

Next, he copied all files displayed on the screen, plus the past two month's research and correspondence, onto the thumb drive he'd brought with him. Then he deleted the computer files and anything else related to areas of concern. When he discovered Wasserman's cloud-based backup service, he went online and deleted those copies, too.

He rummaged through all scribbled notes and file folders for anything relevant. Retrieved four thumb drives he found in a drawer. Jammed everything of significance into the duffle bag he had brought with him.

Finally, guided by the photos he had taken, Lasher returned each item to its former position.

He hauled the bulging duffle and the pizza box to the front door. Before leaving, he returned to the bathroom for one last look.

He gazed down upon Arnold Wasserman's still, damp corpse in the now-empty tub.

It looked pretty much like all the other corpses he had left behind.

Ray Lasher felt nothing.

Darkness had fallen by the time he pulled into a McDonald's parking lot, three miles away. He retrieved his sat phone from the glove compartment and keyed the sequence of numbers.

4

It was nearly dark now, and Trammel shivered in the cold rooftop breeze. The low overcast above Washington reflected the city's pale, dirty yellow glow. Not far away, the landing lights of aircraft burned holes through the cloud cover and descended toward Reagan National Airport.

He poured his third glass of Syrah from the nearly empty wine bottle.

His fingernails drummed the bowl of the glass. The faint staccato ringing of the crystal mingled with the hum of city traffic.

He did not like having to wait for this call.

Avery Trammel was not accustomed to waiting for anyone.

Abruptly, his satellite phone beeped and lit up.

"Yes?" he snapped.

"It's done, sir," Lasher said.

"Were there any complications?"

"None at all. Don't worry. I know how to do this sort of thing. I was very careful."

"And his records?"

"Exactly as you specified. I have every last scrap of his physical files, thumb drives—all his research. I left nothing relevant in his office or online. You'll get it when we meet tomorrow." The man paused, then added: "Relax, sir. You're safe, now."

Trammel set down his empty wine glass, then released his breath—a long, slow hiss.

"For both our sakes, I hope so, Mr. Lasher."

THREE

". . . And as we all know, it isn't just the politicians we have to deal with. The news media also show a lot more sympathy for criminals than for their victims."

Standing behind the lectern in the hotel's banquet room, Jeri West paused and nodded to acknowledge the murmurs of agreement from the dinner guests. "Yes, we've certainly had our issues with the press, haven't we? But happily, there *are* a few rare exceptions among reporters. And we are fortunate to have an exceptional journalist—and an exceptional man—with us tonight."

The trim, middle-aged blonde peered over the top of her reading glasses . . . right at him.

"Dylan Hunter, would you please join me up here?"

He hadn't known this was coming. As applause burst forth from the tables all around him, he turned to Annie, seated to his right. He saw amusement in her eyes. The others at their table—Morgan and Lila Jackson, and Jeri's husband Bob—were smiling and clapping, too.

"You *knew* about this, didn't you, Annie Woods?" he growled, feigning anger.

"Who—me?" She widened those eyes and batted them innocently. The table candles cast a warm golden glow on strands of her tousled chestnut hair. "Go on—get up there, mister."

Sighing, Hunter slid from his chair, adjusted his tie, and headed to where Jeri motioned him to stand beside her. After the applause died down, she continued, glancing at prepared notes.

"Dylan Hunter is the one reporter we've always been able to count on to tell our side of the story. His investigative articles this past year in the *Capitol Inquirer* cast a spotlight on the horrible crimes caused by excessive leniency in our legal system. They've inspired tougher sentencing reforms in the Virginia legislature. They led to the defeat of H.R. 207 in Congress—a bill that would have opened prison cells nationwide, and sent thousands of violent inmates prematurely back into our communities. Mr. Hunter's exposés even prompted the MacLean Foundation to abandon its pro-criminal agenda, and instead to start supporting victims' rights organizations—including our own."

Another wave of applause washed over him from the nearly two hundred members of Vigilance for Victims. He glanced at Annie; she was beaming.

"Dylan, you've become more than our champion in the press," Jeri continued. "You've become our friend. And for two special people here, you've become much more than that: You literally were their life-saver. I see you've been enjoying dinner with one of them, Annie Woods. But now, the other person wants to express her gratitude—along with our appreciation. I'd like to ask everyone to hold any further applause until she has finished speaking. Susanne Copeland . . . would you please come forward?"

From a table near the back of the room a young, red-haired woman rose, to respectful silence. It was the first time Hunter had seen Susie since the night she and Annie had been kidnapped by Adrian Wulfe. She wore a long, pale-green dress and matching jacket. As she approached, he was relieved to see that she had regained a bit of weight, that her eyes were bright, and that her smile at him was direct and warm. She continued past him to the lectern, paused to take a deep breath, and leaned forward into the microphone.

"Early last Christmas morning, I had to face my worst nightmare," she said, her voice soft yet steady. "I was attacked, for the second time, by the same brutal, criminal monster—this time, in my own home. That monster also lured my dear friend Annie Woods, and then kidnapped us to Annie's house. And we surely would have died there"—she looked at him—"except for the incredible courage of the man standing before you."

She paused an instant before continuing.

"While the police were searching for us, Dylan Hunter somehow figured out where we had been taken. And with no thought for his own safety, he rushed to help us. I was unconscious at the time; but I learned later, from Annie and the police, that Dylan bravely fought and somehow managed to kill that monster—even though he himself was gravely injured and nearly died during their violent struggle."

She paused again and turned to him; her next words barely broke a whisper.

"Annie and I owe you our lives, Dylan."

Susie held up a thin hand to quell spontaneous applause. Clearing her throat, she went on.

"Yes, Dylan Hunter is more than a crusading reporter, and more than a loyal friend. He is a true hero. The kind of real-life hero I'd almost stopped believing in. So, I asked Jeri if I might thank him publicly tonight. But Jeri said I should also thank him on behalf of all of us."

Susie bent behind the lectern, then straightened, holding a dark wooden plaque. Light from the chandeliers danced like sparks along its bronze face.

"It is now my honor to read the inscription on this plaque: *'Vigilance for Victims Annual Media Award—To Dylan Hunter, The Capitol Inquirer—for sensitivity and unwavering commitment to justice in reporting crime victim issues.'* It is dated today and signed: *'Jeri West and Morgan Jackson, Co-Chairs.'*"

She extended the plaque to him. "Dylan, congratulations . . . and thank you!"

Hunter accepted the award—then, seeing what was in her eyes, held it aside and opened his arms to embrace her. He felt the bones of her shoulders and ribs as she hugged him tightly, trembling.

The guests rose to their feet for an even louder round of applause and cheers. Dylan chuckled as Annie gave a shrill whistle between two fingers. She was a vision of bare shoulders, deep cleavage, and long legs, gift-wrapped in a little black cocktail dress. She winked at him. A promise . . .

He and Susie held the plaque between them and posed as a photographer moved forward to snap a few pictures. Then it was his turn to speak.

"As a reporter, I'm supposed to be good with words. But tonight, words adequate to this occasion elude me. My friends . . . while I treasure this surprise recognition, I want to be clear about one thing. *You* are the real heroes. Your daily battle for justice is making a real difference in the lives of thousands. As I said last September, when I met many of you for the first time: My job is simply to chronicle *your* courage. I wish for each of you the triumph of serenity over pain, and the strength to continue your vital work. Thank you for this great honor, and for the greater honor of letting me bear witness to your inspiring example."

Back at his table, the others insisted on passing around and admiring the plaque. While they were preoccupied, he felt Annie's left hand, hidden by the white tablecloth, begin to roam his right thigh.

"That was eloquent, Dylan," she said to him, her eyes mock-innocent. "I'm glad you find this so . . . touching."

He held a steady grin. "Oh, yes, I'm certainly touched, Annie." Imperceptible to the others, his right hand drifted across her own thigh, then roamed beneath her short hemline. "At moments like this, a man can't always openly express what he feels. I'm glad I could rise to the occasion."

She coughed, raising her napkin to her face.

"This is really nice," Bob West said to his wife, holding the plaque aloft. "You outdid yourself arranging all this, Hon."

"Oh, it wasn't all my doing," Jeri said. "Susie helped a lot, and she enlisted Annie to figure out how to get Dylan to show up, without ruining the surprise."

"She was sneaky about it," Hunter admitted. "She told me—on the phone—that this would be a special honor for Susie."

"But it was," Jeri pointed out.

"Well, it was the nicest lie I ever fell for. I'm grateful to all of you," he said, looking at each of them in turn. They responded with answering smiles—except for Lila Jackson. Morgan's wife had seemed preoccupied all evening. Now she stared at her untouched steak, unsmiling and unseeing.

A moment later, Hunter casually leaned close to her husband, a stocky, dignified black man seated to his left.

"Lila seems a bit distracted tonight," he whispered. "Is everything all right?"

Morgan lost his smile.

"Let us chat afterward."

2

At the end of the evening, Hunter finally extricated himself from the last of the departing well-wishers. Annie had given Susie a ride, so outside the hotel portico he walked them to Annie's car, where he paused to hug and see them off. Then he returned to where the Jacksons waited on the sidewalk near the entrance.

A distinguished-looking administrator at Howard University, Morgan Jackson was a tall, stout contrast to his slim, diminutive wife. Both wore long dark coats; his arm draped around her shoulders, hugging her close. Hunter noticed the shadowed stress lines on their faces, deepened by a harsh exterior floodlight.

"Thank you for meeting with us, Dylan," Morgan began.

"Of course. Is something wrong?"

"It's *him.*" Lila's voice was thin and harsh. "They're letting him out!"

"She means Dixon—the man who killed our daughter," Morgan explained. "He's getting out this week."

"This week? But you told me last fall he was serving a life-without-parole sentence."

"He was. But he just won a reversal of his conviction on appeal. The court said the prosecution failed to notify the defense about a piece of relevant evidence."

"What evidence?"

"A psychiatric exam he'd had years ago, when he was in juvenile detention. Some therapist back then thought he may—*may*—have a 'borderline personality disorder.' That means—"

"I know what it means, Morgan. The textbooks say it means he's impulsive, reckless, engages in risky behavior, and is aggressive toward others. In other words, he's just a typical criminal. But labeling common criminality as 'borderline personality disorder' is one more way the psychiatric industry turns cheap thugs into billable hours."

"Even if it's a real mental illness," Jackson continued, "in Dixon's case it was never confirmed by any other psychologist or therapist he's seen since. But the prosecutors during his murder trial knew about it and didn't share it with the defense. So the appeals court threw out the guilty verdict. And now he walks."

"But he did it!" Lila shouted. "There's never been any question it was him! And no question what he did to my little Loretta. He—" She stopped; swallowed hard. Despite the March chill, a slight sheen of perspiration gleamed on her dark forehead.

Morgan lowered his eyes. "There was . . . DNA evidence."

"I see," Hunter said softly.

"It's like I said before," Lila went on. "There's no justice anymore. I don't even know if there's a God anymore!"

"Lila! Don't say that!"

"I don't care. I don't know how I can live with this. I meant it back then when I said I wish those vigilantes would go after him. I hope they'll be waiting for him, right outside the prison gate!"

"I'm sorry, Dylan. Lila's just very upset."

Hunter rested his hand on her forearm. "She has every right to be."

She shook her head. "I don't want you to pity us. I want *justice*. We thought maybe you could write about this in your paper."

"What's his full name?"

"Reginald Marcus Dixon," Morgan answered.

"Do you know when he's scheduled to be released?"

"Friday afternoon. That's what our attorney told us."

He shook his head slowly. "It's already Wednesday evening, so I can't possibly make tomorrow morning's edition. Even if I could, to be honest, a newspaper story at this point wouldn't do any good in reversing an appeals court decision."

Lila's dark, angry eyes softened. Began to well with tears. Stared up into his.

"Isn't there any way to stop this?"

Hunter drew a long, slow breath.

Then squeezed her arm.

"I'll see what I can do."

FOUR

He pulled into the driveway of Annie's big brick Tudor in Falls Church, parking his Subaru Forester to the side to allow her access into the single-car garage. She'd just called from her cell to let him know she was only a couple of minutes away, after dropping off Susie.

He got out and stretched. The March night air was chilly and crisp, the sky clear. A few bright stars winked through the bare branches of oaks and maples surrounding the house. The yellow glow of the lantern-style light above the front door gleamed off the waxy ivy leaves that clung to the brick. In the near-silence of the upscale residential neighborhood he caught the faint sound of whimpering from inside the house. He was about to enter when headlights swept across the yard and the garage door began to rise. She pulled her red Camry inside. He followed, and the door began to descend behind him.

The whimpering was louder now.

"Hear that?" he said as he helped her out of the car. "Your abandoned baby is crying for you."

"What do you mean, *my* baby? Grant gave him to you."

"To both of us, actually. Remember?"

"Oh, right. Our early wedding present."

He felt his smile start to fade but caught himself and forced it back into place.

He unlocked the interior door to the house and led her inside, pausing to deactivate the alarm system. They walked down the hallway into the kitchen.

A small, screened enclosure he'd fashioned a couple of weeks earlier occupied a corner. Layers of newspapers covered the floor there. Inside were a large cardboard box, open on one side and padded with old towels; separate bowls containing water and food; and a furry, honey-colored puppy that *yipped* and wiggled excitedly at their approach.

"Hello, Cyrano. Did you miss us?" Annie reached over the short barrier to pick him up—then recoiled. *"Yuck!* Oh, Cyrano! What a nice, smelly mess you've left for Daddy."

"Great." Hunter surveyed the soiled newspapers. "And he's got himself a bit messy, too. Let me tidy up down here while you run a bath for him."

"All right. But you'd better get out of your good clothes first. And I'll try to see where poor Luna is hiding, too."

"I'm still hoping they'll learn to get along. Luna doesn't like that's she's no longer the center of attention."

"Females are like that, you know." She smiled sweetly, then turned and left.

When he carried the puppy into their bathroom, he found Annie leaning casually against the wall next to the tub. She wore a wisp of a smile, and even wispier black bra and panties.

"I think I'm overdressed," he said.

She eyed him up and down. "You could lose the t-shirt. But the boxers are okay . . . for the time being."

He placed the pup down gently in the shallow warm suds, then stripped off the t-shirt and tossed it into a corner.

"Mmmm. That's better," she said, running a warm, smooth palm across his chest. He leaned in for a kiss, but she turned away coyly to attend to the dog. "First things first. Could you hand me that bottle of shampoo?"

He sighed dramatically and complied. "I see I'm no longer the center of *your* attention."

"Well, then we're even." She squeezed some gel into her hands and began to rub it onto the pup's white chest.

"But everyone tonight agreed I deserve special attention. So I expect you to lather me up like this, too."

"And vice-versa, Mr. Hunter. Perhaps we can share the shower in a little while."

"In that case, I think we should make short work of this mutt, Miss Woods."

They rinsed Cyrano off, then Annie lifted him onto the bath mat. She knelt over him and went to work, drying him vigorously with a thick towel. Hunter sat back against the wall and watched appreciatively as her curves flexed and jiggled.

"Now what are you grinning about?" she asked.

"I think you've just invented a new spectator sport."

"Lecher."

"I can't help it. You bring out my inner perv."

He fell silent for a moment. Then said, "You've seemed a trifle distracted the past few days."

She frowned. "It's not you. Just a lot of stuff coming down on us at work. Which is distracting when Grant and I have been trying to focus on finding the Russian mole."

"You mean, the one I *didn't* shoot."

It got a smile.

"Yeah. *That* one. The one we're sure is still burrowed somewhere inside the Agency. It would be nice to be able to concentrate on just that, rather than worry about office politics."

"So, what's going on?"

She turned and sat facing him. Lifted the bundled puppy onto her lap. Began stroking its head.

"Houk and Burroughs are planning to gut the Ops directorate."

"*What?*"

"That's what I came back to after our month in Pennsylvania," Annie continued. "Grant hasn't told me the details yet, but I can tell he's worried. They've been fighting it out for months in the director's conference room. It doesn't seem to be going well. So I'm worried, too."

"You have every right to be. Mason Houk is the most incompetent

CIA director in thirty years—which is saying a lot. He had zero background in intelligence when our dear president appointed him. Glover gave him the job only because Houk was a loyal political suck-up."

"Burroughs is worse," she said. "Grant despises Houk, but he sees Burroughs as his main enemy."

"He's right. I crossed paths with him back when he was a young analyst, ass-kissing his way up the Langley ladder. Now he's managed to ass-kiss his way right up to number two. Wesley made no secret that he despised Ops and hated 'cowboys' like Grant and me." He shook his head. "For your sake, I hope Grant can beat them, Annie."

"For *all* our sakes . . . Well, I think Cyrano is dry enough, now. Hey, little guy, it's time to go back to your bed."

Dylan took the pup from her. He went downstairs, holding the little ball of fur to his face and talking to him soothingly. He placed Cyrano gently down into his padded box, next to an equally furry stuffed toy dog. He pressed a button on the toy, and it began to emit a heartbeat sound.

"There you go. See? You have company. Now, go to sleep."

He returned upstairs and went into the master bedroom. He found Luna hunched tensely in the middle of the canopy bed, staring uneasily past him toward the hallway.

"Mrrrraooow!"

"Don't worry, you're safe here, girl," he said, stroking her head. "I put the big bad wolf in his cage downstairs."

He heard the shower running behind the closed door of the bathroom. He slipped out of his boxers, then entered.

The bathroom was entirely dark, except for a faint golden glow from the glassed-in shower in the corner. A single ceiling light, dimmed to a soft amber, filtered down through the shimmering veil of spray.

She stood motionless beneath the cascading water like a naked goddess, framed against a rectangle of dark gray marble . . . stood with eyes closed, head thrown back, back arched . . . stood while it flowed through her hair, glistened over the tawny curves of her breasts and hips, streamed down the impossible length of her thighs and calves . . .

He watched, transfixed, for perhaps half a minute, before he could once again breathe and move.

She remained motionless, eyes shut, even as he entered the shower and closed the door behind him. He joined her under the hot needles of spray—moved behind her, pressed against her, wrapped his arms around her, began to run his hands over the soft, slick skin. In answer she moved only her face, turning her head and raising her wet, parted lips to meet his . . .

2

An hour later they lay atop the sheets, wrapped in each other's arms, exchanging slow, gentle kisses. The comforter was somewhere on the floor. So was the cat.

"Poor Luna," he murmured in her ear. "It's been a disruptive few weeks for her."

"It's been a disruptive year. For all of us."

"It has." He squeezed her.

"By the way—how are your baby foxes?"

He chuckled. Out at his Connors Point house, a mother fox had dug a den near the shed in his yard. At dusk the previous Saturday, they had watched her and her five small kits from the breakfast nook window, barely thirty feet away. The vixen—nicknamed Red Mama by Annie—sat on watch at the corner of the yard, while her babies, no bigger than kittens, pounced upon and wrestled each other in the grass. They enjoyed the spectacle until Dylan's neighbors, Billie and Jim Rutherford, let their young golden retriever out of their house. Immediately, the mother fox signaled to her kits; they scrambled down into the den while she leaped into the marsh, hoping to draw the dog away.

"They're already getting noticeably bigger," he answered. "I hope Red Mama can protect them from the hawks and eagles until they're big enough to fend for themselves."

"Nature is so cruel. Everything preys on everything else." She paused. "Like some people."

He kissed her bare shoulder. "Animals don't have a choice. People do."

They fell silent again for a moment. Her words reminded him of the banquet.

"It was nice seeing Susie again," he said. "She already looks a lot better."

"She's bouncing back a lot faster than anyone thought she would. Oh, and she wanted me to tell you she's absolutely thrilled about our engagement."

His hand stopped in her hair. "You told her?"

She drew back to look at him. "I didn't have to. She saw my ring. What's wrong with that?"

"Oh, nothing's wrong with that." He smiled and started running his fingers through her hair again.

She put her head against his chest. "I've been wanting to tell Dad, too. But that's going to be a lot harder."

He didn't respond.

"Dylan, I think we should meet him first. Together. We should get him used to us as a couple."

"That's probably a good idea."

"It will be tough for him to accept that his former enemy will soon be his son-in-law. Even though you *did* save my life."

He remained silent and realized his hand had stopped moving again.

She noticed and pulled away once more, frowning.

"What's the matter? Are you having second thoughts?"

"Of course not."

"You look like something is bothering you."

He was thinking about the big blond guy who had been following him, just two days ago. He hadn't told her about that. He didn't want to worry her. Not until he could figure out what *that* was all about.

And then there was the other thing.

"I guess it's just the banquet tonight. It was pretty emotional for me."

"You seemed to handle the surprise pretty well."

"Not just the surprise. Seeing and hearing all those poor victims again."

She put her hand on his cheek. "You've done so much for so many of them, Dylan."

He kissed her fingers.

But not all of them, Annie.

3

Cyrano had finished doing his business and was sniffing and pawing the pine cones in Annie's back yard when Hunter's phone vibrated in his pocket. He tugged it out and shielded its screen from the glare of the morning sun. It was a text from Danika at the office, relayed through a "spoofing" website to a burner located in a storage unit near D.C., then call-forwarded to his current, temporary burner, which he swapped out frequently. It read: *"Call your editor."*

He checked the time. Seven forty. Annie would be heading off to work shortly.

"Come on, boy. Time for breakfast." He walked over and scooped up the pup.

Back in the kitchen he put Cyrano inside his pen. Then settled into a chair, took a sip of the lukewarm coffee he'd left there, and keyed in Bronowski's line at the *Capitol Inquirer*. He set the phone on the table and let it ring while he buttered a scone.

"Not now!" barked the harried voice over the speakerphone.

"If you feel that way, Bill—I quit!"

"Oh, Dylan. It's you. Sorry. I didn't expect a call-back this soon."

Hunter heard rustling papers and phones ringing faintly in the background. "I'm just lonely. What's up?" He took a bite of the scone.

"Okay, so last night I had this phone chat with Cap Moyer. He's campaign manager for Roger Helm. He told me something that—at least on its face, and if true—sounds like it could be a story. He says this past two weeks the feds started going after Helm's biggest contributors. Investigating and harassing them. He's sure it's meant to intimidate them, make it too scary for them to continue backing the guy. And he says it's working."

"What's that got to do with me?"

"I was just thinking... this sounds a lot like what you just investigated—what the feds were doing to those property owners and that fracking company in Pennsylvania. Politicians and officials conspiring to screw ordinary citizens. That was a big story for us. So I figured you could look into this, too."

Hunter sighed. "Big campaign donors are hardly 'ordinary citizens.' If Glover's administration is targeting the rich cronies of a rich political opponent, why should anyone care? It's just the usual dirty tricks crooked politicians play on each other."

"Not the usual dirty tricks, Dylan. We're talking personal IRS audits, FEC investigations—then, this past week, FBI raids on their homes and offices, seizing computers and records. In the middle of the night, no less. Real Gestapo stuff."

Hunter spotted Annie hovering at the kitchen's entranceway, listening. He put down the rest of the scone.

"Bill," he said, "this presidential campaign is probably the most disgusting in American history. I've done my best to tune it out and ignore whatever these idiots and crooks are saying and doing to each other. Besides, politics isn't my beat. You have good people on staff who handle political stories for you."

"Yeah, but conspiracies involving powerful elites *are* your beat. Nobody here handles that sort of stuff better than you. And let me add, it's not just rich guys being targeted. What the feds are doing seems to be coordinated with nasty street protests by a bunch of nonprofit activist groups against Helm's company and employees, as well as the donors. They're picketing people's homes and businesses, vandalizing cars, threatening violence." He paused a few seconds. "The rest of the press is looking the other way, or parroting the party line about all this. Like I said, it's a lot like what just happened in Pennsylvania."

Hunter remained silent. Annie approached him. Rested her hand on his shoulder.

Bronowski went on. "Dylan, I've been watching politics thirty, thirty-five years. My gut tells me Moyer is right. That all this is coordinated. A desperation move, after Ashton Conn's death, to salvage the election for Carl Spencer. Moyer suspects it's being run right out of the White House—or at least that the administration is involved. Maybe—maybe not. But still, this is banana republic stuff. It would be nice for the country to know about it. And even nicer for us if you were the one to find out."

Annie winked and gave him a thumbs-up.

"Look," the editor continued, "you aren't on staff; I can't tell you what to do. But I'd *really* like you to look into this. Meet with Moyer and Helm and some of the people being targeted. See if you can get somebody at the FBI to talk. Find out what the hell's going on. You can call on people here to help you."

Annie leaned down and whispered, "You need a new project to keep you off the streets." She kissed his ear and straightened, leaving the scent of her perfume.

He smiled up at her. He felt the smile waver as he remembered the Jacksons.

"Okay, Bill. I'll poke into it. The next couple of days I have some loose ends to take care of. But I should be able to get to it right after that."

"Great! Thanks, Dylan. I'll text you Moyer's number when I dig it out of the debris on my desk. But right now I got a paper to put out."

And with that he was gone.

"I'm glad, Dylan. This could be another big story for you," she said, buttoning her long suede coat.

"Well, you saw where my last story led us."

Her fingers stopped.

He silently cursed his stupidity.

"Don't worry, love," he said. "Actually, I agreed because interviewing politicians will be a nice, boring change of pace." He flashed a grin. "And we can both use a month or two of boredom."

She smiled back, tentatively. "That's for sure." She finished buttoning up, then picked up her purse from the table.

"So, Dylan Hunter, just what are these 'loose ends' you have to take care of?"

He rose quickly and pulled her into his arms.

"You're at the top of my loose-ends list, Annie Woods."

"Oh? And just how loose do you want me to be, mister?"

He lowered his lips close to hers.

"Let's decide that back here on Saturday night."

FIVE

It took Lasher a while to negotiate the Thursday afternoon traffic into Virginia. Following Trammel's instructions, he turned his Chevy rental off Braddock Road and onto a narrow country lane. It cut into a square mile or two of forest—an almost-uninhabited island slowly eroding in the encroaching sea of upscale residential neighborhoods.

He reached the long brick wall that enclosed Trammel's estate and continued a quarter mile to where a break in the trees and the wall heralded the entrance. He turned into the driveway, where his progress was arrested by twin gates. In the center stood a stone gatehouse whose wooden roof arched over it on both sides.

A guy in a security guard's uniform stepped out and approached. Lasher lowered his window.

"I help you, sir?" the guard said, his accent matching thick Slavic features. His belt held a walkie-talkie and what looked like a holstered Glock.

"My name is Lasher. I have a three o'clock meeting with Mr. Trammel."

The guard nodded. "He expect you, Mr. Lasher. Your ID, please?"

He handed over a fake driver's license that listed his name as "Raymond Paul Lasher." The guard checked the photo against his face.

"Okay. Drive to house, around circle, to parking area on left side."

Lasher nodded and raised his window again. The guy retreated into the gatehouse, raising the walkie-talkie to his mouth. Seconds later the gates parted slowly on a recessed track. He pulled through and continued along the tree-lined paver drive.

It stood on a slight rise, a massive, two-story mansion of light-brown stone and bow windows. White Greek columns rose beneath the second-floor balcony that sheltered the front entrance. Two expansive wings jutted forward from each side of the mansion.

He continued into the embrace of those wings, circling the central fountain where ornamental elephants spouted arcing streams of water from their trunks. Two more uniformed guards eyed him from the steps of the entrance as he drove by, continuing past the six-bay garage of the far wing, and into the parking area beyond it. He got out and fetched the duffle bag from the back seat. Then walked back along a flower-bordered sidewalk to the waiting guards.

Lasher sized them up. He always sized up the competition. One dark-haired, one blond, both hard looking, all business. Probably Russian—it would fit what he suspected about Trammel. Without a word, the blond guard extended his hand, snapping his fingers for the duffle, while the other stepped forward to search him. He surrendered the bag and raised his arms to comply.

The guy with the duffle didn't search it—probably ordered by Trammel not to look inside, yet still taking no chances that Lasher might have hidden a weapon there. Of course, he knew better than to bring one here—not that he would need any. The blond guy had his hands occupied with the bag instead of putting it down. His dark-haired partner bent in front of him to pat down his legs, instead of doing it from behind. Good God. Taking out these losers would be a piece of cake.

"What are you smiling at?" the blond guy snarled.

Lasher broadened his grin. "I'm thinking Mr. Trammel needs to hire better security, Ivan."

The guy stiffened, dropped the duffle, stepped forward. The one searching him straightened fast and raised a hand to his partner. Then turned to glare at Lasher.

"Lucky Mr. Trammel wants to see you, or you get your smart ass kicked."

Lasher sneered. "You ever want to try, I'll give you a rain check—Boris."

The dark-haired guard's lips tightened. He turned and nudged his sour-faced partner toward the huge double doors. Lasher followed them in.

Then stopped in his tracks.

Standing between twin sets of thick pillars inside the entrance, his eyes slowly scanned the room. It was a beige-marble vault that rose to a domed ceiling. A spectacular double staircase, also marble, swept majestically in twin, mirroring curves to meet on the second floor. There a balcony encircled the room overhead, and its enormous, gold-and-crystal chandelier.

"What you waiting for, smartass?"

The blond guy with the duffle stood between the staircases. Lasher followed him, his clicking steps resounding off the polished marble. He caught glimpses into large, opulent rooms branching off the foyer, then passed through an arched stone passageway. He was in a museum-like drawing room, adorned with fancy upholstered couches and huge paintings of ancient Roman scenes. The guards led him into another room beyond.

2

It was a bright solarium, smaller but elegant. At its far end, a semi-circle of tall windows bowed outward, presenting a panoramic view of the rear grounds.

Avery Trammel stood there, taking in the view, hands clasped behind him.

"Sir," the dark-haired guard said, "your visitor is arrived."

Trammel didn't turn. "Bring his bag upstairs and leave it outside my office door. Then return to your stations."

"Yes, sir." The pair left. Lasher remained near the room's entrance.

"Join me," Trammel said finally.

Lasher approached and stopped beside him. The billionaire stood tall, slim, and erect. He wore a gray cardigan sweater, unbuttoned, over a gray silk shirt and gray slacks—the tones and shades all matched perfectly.

It was only the third time he had been in the man's presence. On the first occasion, four years earlier, they had met discreetly in a hotel room in Georgetown. That was when he had been hired and put on retainer. On the second, it was in the secret townhouse condo Trammel owned near Capitol Hill. A lot of cash had changed hands on that occasion—a bonus for a tricky bit of wetwork.

He followed Trammel's gaze out across acres of meticulously landscaped lawn.

To one side, a small greenhouse. Opposite, an enclosed tennis court. About a hundred meters off, a pond. The afternoon sun revealed orange flickers of koi moving beneath its green surface. In the middle of the pond, a gazebo, bedecked with jaunty floral baskets, perched on a tiny island and linked to the lawn by a small stone bridge.

Trammel remained silent.

"Your home—it's really spectacular, Mr. Trammel," Lasher ventured.

The man turned slowly to face him. Dark brows hooded deep-set, intense, serpentine eyes, whose color reminded him of chips of ice. He had a strong nose above the thin scar of his lips. The tanned skin of his face bore surprisingly few lines for his sixty-four years. The main sign of his age was a hairline that had receded to expose a high, broad forehead, leaving a thatch of white hair. The man exuded an aura of intelligence, power, and danger. Though Lasher knew, abstractly, that he could kill this guy with his bare hands, he always felt uneasy under that unwavering gaze.

"It impresses you, then, Mr. Lasher?"

He nodded. "I've seen some grand homes, but never anything to match this." He offered a smile. "You must really enjoy living here."

Trammel's unblinking eyes held him. Like a cobra's, he thought.

"Do you think that, Mr. Lasher?"

He felt his smile evaporate. "Well . . . I just thought—"

"Do you know what all this really is?" Not breaking eye contact, Trammel swept his arm around grandly, to include the house and the grounds. Lasher caught a flash of something silver in the man's hand.

"I'm . . . not exactly sure what you mean, sir."

The billionaire's lips formed a slow, tight smile that remained a stranger to his eyes.

"Personally, it is a symbol. Practically, it is but a means to an end."

He turned away, moving into the room.

Unsure of what to do or say, Lasher followed.

"From a practical standpoint," Trammel continued, "this estate is, first and foremost, the headquarters for my work. While I maintain offices in many places, I control my interests from here. As for residences, there is the Capitol Hill condominium where we last met. Undoubtedly you have done enough homework to know of our apartment at the Watergate. Julia prefers it to this more isolated home, because its location better fulfills her many social and professional requirements. And we have other residences, here and abroad, to meet our respective needs for privacy or entertaining when traveling."

He continued back into the drawing room. Lasher followed, surprised at Trammel's apparent eagerness to talk so personally.

"A second practical purpose this home serves is to project the appropriate image to various individuals and groups." Trammel didn't elaborate, leaving Lasher to infer the obvious.

"What about the other thing you mentioned—the personal symbol?"

Trammel halted abruptly, turned slowly. Fixed him with that hooded, intense stare.

"I referred to it as 'personal' for good reason, Mr. Lasher."

Lasher fought the urge to swallow.

Trammel turned and stopped at a door within the passageway. He opened it and led him into a mahogany-paneled elevator.

They emerged on the second floor balcony. Trammel led him around to the corridor that ran above the garage. Its high walls displayed dozens of photos: Trammel posing with presidents, kings, foreign leaders, politicians, and—usually in the company of his actress wife, Julia

Haight—A-list movie stars and celebrities.

Halfway down the hallway, they entered a spacious, utilitarian office. Four individuals looked up from their desks and smiled nervously at the sight of their boss. A middle-aged receptionist rose as he entered.

"You have had five calls, sir. Two from the New York office, one from Mr. Boyce in Bermuda—"

Trammel waved dismissively. "I shall return the calls after meeting with this gentleman."

He continued past her to an inner door sporting an electronic touchpad lock. Lasher's duffle rested on the floor nearby. He bent to hoist it while his host tapped in the combination.

3

Inside, Lasher found himself in a huge, beautifully appointed executive suite of dark paneled walls, built-in bookcases, and Oriental carpets.

His employer moved behind his massive desk, where he placed the silver object he'd been carrying. Then eased himself into his high-backed leather chair.

He gestured toward the bag in Lasher's grip.

"I gather you have everything in there?"

"All here, sir."

"Show me." He tapped his desktop.

Approaching, Lasher noticed that the silver item on the desk was an old watch. Trammel spun it absently with his forefinger while Lasher reached into the bag and began to arrange its contents on the desk, explaining each item as he went. Finally, he settled into the guest chair and held Trammel's eyes.

"Trust me, sir—that's everything he had."

"Can we be certain he did not communicate with anyone else?"

Lasher explained all the steps he had taken to be sure about that.

"I've gone the extra mile to cover our tracks," he added. "This morning I called Wasserman's mobile phone company, pretending to be him. I cancelled his account, saying he had moved, and asked that his final bill be sent to a post office box I maintain under a secure alias. I'll pay that bill with a money order when it comes in. That way, no record of his final month's calls will show up at his apartment to raise any questions."

Trammel lifted a brow. "I would not have thought of that. I am impressed, Mr. Lasher. What about his emails?"

"The only relevant one was his very last message, which he sent just before I arrived there, unfortunately. It was to some people he works with."

"At the Center for Advocacy Profiles?"

"Yes. It was brief. He only said he was onto something big concerning the Currents Foundation, and that he'd tell them all about it at their next weekly meeting."

Trammel stopped spinning the watch.

"He mentioned Currents, then?"

"Yes. But no specifics at all. They know nothing. So you shouldn't worry."

"Shouldn't I? That hint may arouse their curiosity to continue inquiries."

"Well, if it becomes a problem, I can always deal with it."

"I shall let you know, Mr. Lasher. I cannot afford to leave any loose ends."

He stood abruptly, indicating the meeting was over. But Lasher remained seated.

"Before I go, sir, there's that *other* loose end out there. Dylan Hunter. Or whoever he really is."

"What about him?"

"You asked me to follow and find out about him. And as I told you, I found a ghost. A newspaper reporter with a fake name and no traceable background. But with the kind of skills you find only in trained operators. In guys like me. We know from the newspapers that he killed a criminal hand-to-hand last Christmas. And we know he's a trouble-maker who targets prominent people. People like you."

Trammel said nothing, but sat again. He scooped up the watch and began to roll it absently in his palm. It was an old relic, unlike anything Lasher could imagine a billionaire would want. Obviously it meant something to him, but Lasher suppressed the urge to ask about it.

Lasher went on. "You told me he poses a much greater threat to your interests than you had imagined. You hired me to protect those interests. Well, if you want me to do that, it would help me to know exactly what kind of threat he poses."

For a moment, the billionaire remained still, a dark, unmoving figure. Then he leaned forward slowly. Placed the watch down carefully. Flattened his palms on the desktop.

"It is not your business to know," he hissed.

Lasher was not easily intimidated, but it took him a few seconds to respond.

"Sir, if I know what he's after, maybe I can stop him. But all I really know about him comes from the articles he publishes in the *Inquirer*. His pieces last year about the vigilante crime spree. And the recent ones about CarboNot. He listed your name as one of the CarboNot investors. That's it, isn't it?"

Trammel eased back into the cushioned black leather chair and positioned his hands on its arms. The king on his throne.

"Only in part. From what you discovered about the man's abilities, I also have begun to wonder if he might have been involved in recent events."

"Which ones?"

"The recent wave of bombings—at CarboNot Industries and several other sites. The destruction of my plane at Dulles. The assassination of Senator Conn."

"But I thought that terrorist group—you know—"

"WildJustice."

"Yeah, them. I thought they were responsible."

"That is the official conclusion. Their leader, Zachariah Boggs, reputedly was a genius, and it now has been confirmed that he was the so-called 'Technobomber' of years ago. However, these recent crimes involved much more than bombs."

"Such as?"

"Such as planting bugging devices, intercepting and redirecting email and phone communications, interference with financial transactions. It was impressively technical, sophisticated, well-coordinated—and I imagine beyond the capabilities even of a supposed genius like Boggs."

Lasher nodded slowly. "But not beyond the capabilities of a highly trained special operator."

"That thought crossed my mind." Trammel sighed. "But that remains mere speculation. As you say, all direct evidence points to Boggs and his group. Nor can I imagine why this 'Dylan Hunter,' whoever he is, would be motivated to commit risky, violent acts against CarboNot and its investors. Including me."

"Still, with so much at stake, why take chances? I can arrange an 'accident' for him, too."

Trammel's eyes became piercing, hawk-like.

"Absolutely not! Given his public prominence, that would provoke too much scrutiny. And we—I cannot afford that. Besides, we already have quite enough on our respective plates."

"With all respect, sir, I think that's a mistake. He already knows a lot about you."

"Very little, actually. After further consideration, I have concluded Mr. Hunter probably poses a less immediate threat than I had thought."

Lasher shook his head. "Look, I have a sense about the guy. He's a pit bull. Once he's after you, he won't let go."

"You may be right. So, I shall not rule anything out. Action against him may well become necessary. But later—and only as a last resort."

"But, sir, I—"

Trammel raised a hand. "Mr. Lasher, I have made clear to you that we must focus on more pressing threats. You are to steer clear of Mr. Hunter. Is that understood?"

Lasher fought to hold his anger in check. He shrugged casually, forcing a smile. "Sure. It's your call."

"Indeed it is," Trammel said, each word spaced and stressed. He stood again. "And now, if you will please excuse me." He pressed a button on his desk phone. "Marnie, would you please escort my visitor out?"

Lasher rose, nodded curtly, and left. The receptionist led him back to the foyer. He trotted down the stairs and out, past the blond guard he had met earlier. They exchanged profane insults as Lasher walked toward his parked car.

But once out of earshot, he muttered to himself:

"We'll see about that, you old son of a bitch."

SIX

It was an intersection on the western outskirts of Baltimore, with a corner gas station and an attached building that housed a sub sandwich shop, a bodega, and a check-cashing store. Diagonally across the intersection stood a Methodist church, and directly across from that a recreational park with several baseball fields. The local elementary school was a half-mile down the highway.

It all looked serene, perfectly normal to any driver passing by or stopping to fill up his tank. But his homework revealed that the gas station and strip plaza had been taken over two years earlier by Reginald Dixon's gang, "Da Lawn Boyz"—named after the nearby Woodlawn area. Not far from Interstate 70, and with a steady flow of traffic and customers, it was the perfect headquarters for their drug-distribution operation.

Driving a nondescript Ford junker, Hunter had followed Dixon and the girlfriend who picked him up at Jessup Correctional Institution. Now he watched their red Camaro turn right, pulling into the gas station. The pumps and store entrance faced the cross street that ran perpendicular to the one he was on.

Hunter drifted to the intersection and halted at the traffic light. The Camaro had stopped near the store entrance. Dixon and the girl emerged into a waiting cluster of eight young men wearing denim and leather over t-shirts and sneakers. After hugs, high-fives, and fist-bumps, four of them followed the couple inside. The others took watchful positions around the perimeter of the store.

The light changed. Hunter turned right onto the cross street and drove slowly past the entrance. Signs in the windows and above the glass door advertised fried chicken, Philly steaks, lottery tickets, and an ATM.

He took another immediate right, onto the narrow, seedy side street that ran like an alleyway behind the gas station and the strip mall. A Dumpster pressed close to the gas station's rear wall, overflowing with trash. A few feet farther along was the station's rear door, closed and presumably locked. Beyond that, a fringe of debris-strewn weeds ran along the cinder-block rear wall of the stores.

To his left, on the opposite side of the street from the stores, stood a pair of vacant, two-story eyesores. Both boarded-up dumps displayed "No Trespassing" signs. An inexplicable mound of dirt was heaped in the yard between them.

The side street petered out into a dead end. He turned around and came back. This was no place to leave his car: too conspicuous, and only one way out.

So he returned to the intersection. Entered the strip plaza's parking lot at its far end, away from the gas station. Backed the Ford into the isolated parking space nearest the street, positioned for a fast departure. Then pulled a road map from the glove compartment and spread it across the dashboard—a visible rationale for his stop.

From behind the mirrored shades he kept an eye on the sentries, while he worked out the final details of the op. Figuring they would almost certainly celebrate Dixon's release with drugs, he'd give them ten minutes—about as much as he could risk without arousing the sentries' attention. Their dulled senses, combined with surprise, shock, and speed, would help even the overwhelming odds against him.

Because conducting a hit on a sunny Friday afternoon, at a busy commercial crossroads—and against a killer protected by at least eight gang members—was insane. Unthinkable.

Which was exactly what he was counting on. That, plus the fact that Dixon and his pals, feeling secure in their own headquarters, would be distracted and probably partying. Closer to D.C., newly freed killers like him were running scared or lying low, hiding from the "vigilantes" who had been targeting them over the past year. But no freed murderer had been assassinated this far outside the D.C. metro area.

And who would expect a lone man to attack an armed group?

This was an enormously risky op, with significant likelihood of things going wrong. But Hunter had weighed other options and none looked good. All required him to stake out this heavily trafficked, highly exposed location for an extended period—either to attempt a sniper shot, or to follow Dixon elsewhere. But undetected surveillance and tailing required a team and a commitment of days. He simply didn't have time to devote to a lengthy stakeout. Besides, a white guy would stand out conspicuously if he hung around here, or tried to tail the gang leader into his African-American haunts.

This was the only time and place where he *knew* Dixon would be—and when the killer would have his guard down. And complete strangers entered this gas station constantly, which would allow him to get close. So, bad as it was, this looked like his best option.

He tilted the interior mirror toward his face. Inspected his disguise. Ragged blond hair sprouted from under the baseball cap. The pasted-on blond goatee hid his cleft chin and changed the shape of his face for any CCTV cameras.

He adjusted the cap's brim farther down over his mirrored sunglasses.

Tightened the Velcro straps on the tactical shooting gloves he was wearing.

Slid his right hand under his unzipped leather jacket. Found the grip of the Glock 26, concealed in its molded IWB holster against his hip. He tugged it a bit, reassuring himself that it would slide out fast and smooth. The Baby Glock's standard magazine carried ten 9 mm rounds; he'd added one to the chamber. For backup, he carried a spare 15-round, interchangeable Glock 19 magazine in a pocket inside his jacket.

Hunter hoped he wouldn't have to shoot anyone except Dixon. He had a code about such things, a code he had settled on over a year ago, when he started taking vigilante actions.

He would kill only individuals he *knew* were involved in acts of murder—or kill in self-defense against criminals trying to kill himself or others. He would use only non-lethal violence against lesser criminals. And he'd never commit a violent act that risked injury or death to cops or innocent people—not even if that inhibition led to his arrest.

Not even if it cost him his own life.

Those were the risks he had to accept for doing this stuff. Because his goal was to seek justice for innocent victims, not to create more of them.

That was his code. And he had to cling to it with fanatical consistency, because he knew his code was the only thing that kept himself from becoming a vicious animal like Reginald Dixon.

Reaching down, he fetched a jumbo-sized beverage cup from the passenger-side floor. A jaunty red plastic straw stuck out of its white plastic lid. It looked perfectly innocuous.

His final surprise for them.

He checked the dashboard clock.

Three forty p.m.

He took a long, steady breath. Released it.

Time to get it done.

Hunter unfolded from the driver's seat, leaving the door unlocked and slightly ajar, the engine still idling. Another calculated risk, but he'd be gone just a few minutes.

Pressing his unzipped jacket closed with his elbows to hide the gun, he carried the drink cup in front of him with both hands as he walked toward the gas station at the far end of the plaza.

2

Isayah "Oz" Johnson was leaning casually against the wall not far from the entrance when a white guy in mirrored shades came around the corner of the building heading his way. Oz straightened, then relaxed when he saw the cracka holding one of those "Big Sipper" cups in his gloved hands. Dude just coming in for a refill.

Oz didn't like how the guy strutted, so cocky-like in his leather jacket and boots. He wanted to say something to the asshole. But Reggie had a rule against hassling customers. *"Bad for business,"* he said. *"And don't need nobody bringing Five-Oh down on us."*

So Oz just glared silently as the gray dude strode past, ignoring him, and reached Jamal, who stood in front of the doorway. Jammies was so big he blocked the whole entrance. Cracka stopped, smiled up at him, and said, "Excuse me, sir."

"Sir." So po-lite. Probably scared shitless.

Jammies grunted and slowly shifted aside, just enough to let the dude inside.

Hunter barely squeezed past the huge, head-shaved thug in the doorway. Inside, he paused to take stock.

A few aisles of overpriced snack foods, groceries, personal necessities, and auto supplies.

DVD rental machine next to the ATM at the wall on the right.

Checkout counter to the left, a skinny Asian kid ringing up cigarettes and lottery tickets for a middle-aged white customer.

Nearby, another Asian guy, older—maybe the father of the one behind the register—wiping down a small sandwich counter, where the carry-out orders were prepared.

In the rear right corner, a tiny alcove for the restrooms.

In the rear left corner, just beyond the sandwich counter, a door marked "PRIVATE." Two young toughs on either side of it, arms crossed, staring at him. Muffled laughter and profanities rising from the room behind the door. That would be Dixon, his girlfriend, and the rest of his gang.

It was obvious the Asians were the nominal owners, but that Dixon's gang had strong-armed them into remaining in place here, serving as a legitimate-appearing front for their drug operations. Serving as slave labor.

No way he would risk their lives, or the lives of innocent customers, just to do this. He had to get them all clear—or forget about it.

He spotted the coffee station at the center of the rear wall. He made his way back there, circling close enough to Dixon's guards to spot the bulges of concealed firearms under their clothes. He counted four CCTV cameras high on the walls; but given the clientele and transactions transpiring here, he was certain they wouldn't be operating.

At the coffee station, he leaned over his oversized drink container, pretending to fill it from one of the waiting carafes. He made a show of adding packets of sugar and creamer, stalling while he waited for the lone customer to leave. Then he proceeded to the sandwich counter.

He nodded at the middle-aged Asian man.

"Hi. I'd like to place an order. Do you read English, sir?"

The man smiled and nodded.

Hunter placed his cup on the counter, then withdrew a small notebook and pen from his shirt pocket and wrote a note. After he finished, he grinned as he handed it to the man.

And watched his eyes widen as he read:

Please stay calm and continue to act normally.
I am an undercover narcotics police officer.
We are about to conduct a police raid here.
Again—please remain calm. Show no sign that anything is wrong.
Now, go over to the other clerk, and show him this note.
Then both of you leave the store at once.

He saw the clerk was about to speak.

"Sorry, maybe my scribbling isn't clear," he interrupted, leaning close. He drew his jacket aside, just enough to reveal the grip of his gun. Holding his smile and pointing at the note, he whispered: "We don't want you to get hurt. Don't show any surprise or fear. Don't look at those other men. Just walk slowly to that young man, show him this note, and then both of you leave the building and keep walking away from here." He dropped the smile. "Do it *right now.*"

The man obeyed, going over to the boy and handing him the note. The kid frowned as he read, then his eyes snapped toward Hunter. The older man tugged at his arm, got him to follow. They moved out from behind the counter and without a backward glance headed outside.

He had to act now, before any more customers showed up.

He put his hands on his hips and stared after the two departing clerks.

"Hey!" he shouted. "Where you going?"

He looked around, feigning confusion. Caught the eyes of the two thugs in the back.

"Did you guys see that?" He picked up the drink container in his left hand and began to walk toward them. "You see what just happened?" Continuing to approach, he half-turned and gestured behind him, toward the door. "I give the guy my order, but then they both just walk out!" He turned back to them as they moved a step away from the door, suddenly wary. "You work here?" he continued. "You mind telling me what the hell's going on?"

Suspicious, the guy to his right started to reach inside his jacket. Hunter leaped forward and snapped a front kick into his groin. The guy went down, clutching himself and wailing. Before the other could react, Hunter had the Baby Glock in his right hand, trained on his face.

"Raise your hands and turn around," he snapped.

The guard stood paralyzed. He raised his hands—then his eyes darted toward the entrance, just as Hunter heard the door hiss open behind him.

"Jammies!" the guard yelled. "This dude—"

Hunter snapped a kick into his groin, too, then hopped to the side and spun to face the new threat just as a shot rang out.

The big guy stood just inside the closing door, legs spread, a double-handed grip on his gun. His shot slammed into the wall where Hunter had been an instant before. Still clutching the cup in his left hand, Hunter fired three times rapidly, one-handed. The first hollow point slug caught the man mid-body, the second in his left shoulder, the third in his jaw, sending a spray of blood against the glass door. The guy toppled backward into it, slamming it open again, and landed across the threshold.

Oz had watched, bewildered, as the two store clerks hustled outside, then broke into a run across the parking lot. Then he heard yelling inside the store. But he wasn't as close to the door as Jamal. Jammies had played college football, and for a big dude he was fast. He had his Colt .45 out and was rushing through the entrance before Oz could even move.

Oz yanked the .38 S&W revolver. Then Jammies's cannon boomed—followed immediately by three more-muted shots in rapid succession. Scarlet gore splattered the closing glass door a second before Jammies's giant body crashed backward against it, smashing it open again. He landed across the entranceway on his back, his shaved head smacking the pavement with a sickening crack. Half his lower jaw was torn loose and hanging.

Stunned, Oz stumbled back. He tore his eyes away from the horror of what was left of Jammies's face, looking around wildly for help.

Where the hell Deuce and Marvel at?

3

Reggie Dixon had done his first line off the grimy surface of the office desk, through a rolled-up twenty. Then Sharleen, already wasted, decided to do a strip-tease. A coming-home gift, she said.

Dixon's hitmen loved that idea. The four of them hooted and laughed while she held his eyes and slowly unbuttoned her blouse . . .

Well, he love that idea, too. And he don't mind them seeing her body—after all, she *his*, not theirs. He enjoy reminding them about things he has but they don't. Of course, Sharleen's body *would* be amazing, 'cause she still just seventeen. Younger the better . . .

As she did her slow striptease to the thumping rap beat from the office sound system, Dixon frowned, remembering the one that sent him to the joint . . .

Well, okay—not *that* young. But how the hell he supposed to know she barely thirteen? Bitches these days, they grow up so fast. That one, that Loretta, she been standing there outside his sister Neema's house, saying she waiting for Neema's daughter Keshia. And she so *fine*, like she at least fifteen, sixteen—least as old as Keshia. So he smile and tell her, Keshia and her mom over at *his* place, and they send him to pick her up and take her there.

So she go with him. And he take her instead to that spot down under the Amtrak bridge. And he drag her out the car and has his fun.

Then he tell her *shut up*—but she just keep screaming and carrying on. So, what he supposed to do then? Let her go to the po-lice? Ruin his life?

Okay, the whole thing a stupid mistake. But that point, *no way* he can let her talk. Only one way out of it. And too bad, too, 'cause she just a kid. But hey—shit happens.

So he use a rock to shut her up.

Just his damn luck those kids up on the bridge see him do it and call the cops . . .

Dixon watched, stirring, as Sharleen undid her last button. She swayed back and forth, letting the blouse play peek-a-boo. She started to shrug it off one shoulder.

He heard a loud voice, then sudden wailing, right outside the office door.

"The hell?" Dixon growled. He nodded toward the guy nearest the door. "Rocks, go see what—"

But then a hole blasted through the wall, throwing splinters and drywall—followed by three more quick shots from just outside the door.

"*Shit!*" Dixon shouted, hitting the floor behind the desk. The others did the same, Sharleen falling atop him, screaming.

Hunter watched the giant crash to the ground outside the front entrance, then spun and gave each of the downed guards a sharp kick to their heads to keep them out of play. He heard yells and commotion from the office. Holstering the Glock, he tried the door knob. *Locked.*

He took a step back, then launched forward onto his left foot, raised his right leg, and stomped near the door knob with the heel of his boot. It took two tries, but the door burst inward.

He jumped to the side to avoid taking any fire from within. Flipping the lid off the cup, he reached inside and lifted out the flashbang grenade. Holding down the safety handle, he yanked out the pin, then tossed the grenade inside the room. He spun away from the door, covering his ears tightly with his palms and squeezing his eyes shut.

When the shots stopped, Dixon shoved Sharleen off himself and scrambled on his hands and knees to the back door. Those behind him continued to yell as he reached up, threw the slide bolt, and turned the knob. The door opened, and he felt Sharleen clawing at his back as he tumbled outside. She landed beside him, still hollering.

He didn't know who was shooting up headquarters, and he wasn't about to hang around to find out. He got to his feet and turned toward the street behind the stores.

"Reggie! Wait!" he heard her squeal. He glanced back. She was on her hands and knees just outside the open doorway. She began to rise when a dazzling flash and thunderous bang knocked her down.

Even though the blast was largely contained within the inner room, the concussion was stunning.

Ears ringing, Hunter drew the Glock again and rushed inside. The ramshackle office was filled with litter and veiled with acrid smoke. A wad of cash and a few plastic baggies with white powder were scattered on an old wooden desk. He immediately saw the rear exit door was open. It took him a few seconds to determine that none of the dazed and moaning individuals sprawled on the floor was the Target. He moved to the rear doorway.

Just outside, Dixon's girlfriend was on the ground, holding her head and howling *"Reggie! Reggie!"*

He squinted out into the sunlight. Saw the Target running across the street, headed toward a dirt-filled gap between the two derelict, abandoned houses. He raised the gun and snapped off a hasty shot. Saw the guy stumble. Heard the girl scream.

Took a step outside for a clearer second shot.

Then the half-opened door slammed back against him.

4

Devon "Deuce" Taylor had been taking a leak next to the Dumpster when he heard yelling, then gunfire inside the building.

Damn. He was the only one of the outside crew not carrying. He couldn't risk it, not with his sheet, 'cause a gun charge would put him away for at least a dime. He started zipping up when he heard the explosion.

The hell?

Deuce hustled around the Dumpster and spotted Reggie back there, running across the street. Sharleen was sprawled outside the back door. Her blouse was open and she was holding her head and screaming. He moved to help her—then heard approaching steps just inside the office. Instinctively he jumped aside behind the half-open door. Two seconds later, a gunshot blasted from the other side of the door.

In the yard across the street, Reggie wobbled on his feet.

Sharleen shrieked again.

The muzzle of a handgun poked out from the edge of the door, leveling to take aim again at his boss.

He shoved the door, slamming it against the shooter on the other side.

Caught mid-stride and off-balance, Hunter stumbled. Before he could recover, a tall, wiry black guy hurtled from behind the door and slammed into him, seizing his gun hand. Hunter hit the ground with the guy atop him, pinning his gun hand. The guy raised his right arm for an elbow strike to his face. Hunter blocked it with his left forearm, but the guy's descending hand clawed at his face, knocking off his sunglasses—then seized a handful of hair . . .

. . . and yanked off Hunter's cap and wig.

It startled the guy for an instant—long enough for Hunter to shoot a hard left uppercut into his chin. The guy's head snapped back, and he sagged, limp.

Hunter pushed the unconscious man off his body and freed his gun from beneath the guy—just as he saw another sentry, just a kid, peek around the Dumpster, gun in hand.

Before the kid could figure out what was going on, Hunter fired a warning shot into the side of the Dumpster. The kid flinched and ducked back. Hunter sent two more rounds into it, to encourage his retreat.

He sat up, looking to reacquire the Target. He spotted him staggering slowly, as if drunk, trying to get behind the mound of dirt between the two houses. Hunter drew up a knee, braced his forearms on it, took careful aim, and fired twice in rapid succession.

The Target's body twitched twice, then collapsed like an empty sack onto the dirt pile.

Hunter rose to his feet. The Target was not moving. He became vaguely aware again of the howling young woman on the ground a few yards away. She was staring at him, cringing in terror, a hand to her mouth as she wailed.

It was only then that he realized she was seeing him without his disguise.

He turned away quickly, and just as he bent to retrieve the wig, a shot buzzed right over his head.

At first Oz had stood paralyzed by the horrific sight of the indestructible Jammie dead at his feet. He ducked beneath the front windows of the gas station. Then he heard an explosion from inside—and seconds later, a muffled gunshot. Then more, sounding like they were outside, around the back.

He suddenly felt ashamed to be hiding while his bros were in a gunfight. Crouching below the windows, Oz scrambled past the doorway and Jammie's body, heading toward the rear of the building. Rounding the corner, he found Little Marvel cringing behind the Dumpster, eyes big and white, breathing hard.

Oz ducked in beside him. "The hell goin' down?" he whispered.

"White mother back here fightin' Deuce," the little guy gasped. "He just shot at me. I think he shot Reggie!" Marvel pointed across the street.

Oz caught sight of Reggie over there, staggering, just as two more loud shots rang out from the other side of the Dumpster. Stunned, he watched his boss buckle at the knees and pitch face-first on a pile of dirt.

Then Sharleen's voice, screaming Reggie's name, over and over.

First Jammies . . . now *Reggie*.

Suddenly, a murderous rage wiped out his fear.

He left the scared Little Marvel hiding behind the Dumpster and stepped out into the open, like a man.

Deuce on the ground, motionless. Sharleen sitting there, shrieking like some bird.

Gray dude, gun in hand, looking toward Reggie. *The cracka!*

Oz raised his .38, aimed down the sights right at the man'head, and fired.

5

Long-ingrained training and habits saved his life.

Already bending as the shot sounded, Hunter instinctively dropped to one knee and raised his gun.

A guy out in the open beside the Dumpster, aiming at him.

Hunter had spent countless hours on firing ranges—civilian, CIA, then military while attached to special ops units. His training at The Farm and Harvey Point had put him through realistic firefight scenarios. He'd had his share of the real thing on missions. And in the past year, he had resumed regular range sessions, practicing quick drawing-and-firing simulations until his responses were automatic and accuracy high.

He knew he had only two rounds left in the Glock, so he fired just once.

Oz was shocked he had missed. He was about to squeeze a second time when Cracka dropped to a knee and spun, blinding fast.

Something punched him in the gut, *hard*, and there was a loud *bang*.

Suddenly he had no wind and no strength in his legs and his .38 was a giant weight in his hands dragging him forward to land on his face. For a few seconds he felt nothing. Then a great, terrible, paralyzing ache started from the center of his abdomen and began to spread. He wanted to scream, but couldn't.

His head lolled to the side. Through half-closed eyes he saw a figure approach, silhouetted against the sun. Dully, some part of his brain told him it was the cracka, and he had a gun pointing at him, and he wondered what it was going to feel like to die.

Hunter stood over the guy, gun aimed and ready. He kicked the .38 out of his reach.

Then realized he was just a kid, not even out of his teens—the same one who had been standing sentry when he first approached the building.

Then he heard a scuffling noise . . . and saw another one, huddled behind the Dumpster.

This kid was even younger and smaller. He had a shaking gun in his hand and tears in his eyes.

"Don't shoot me, man!" the boy pleaded.

Hunter pointed the Glock at the kid.

"I won't, if you drop your weapon."

The kid obeyed.

"Now kick it away from you."

He did.

Hunter stared at him, hard. He had to get out of here and knew he didn't have a minute to spare. But he saw something in the kid's eyes . . . something still human.

Something he felt he had to reach.

"You see what happened to your pals here?"

The kid was crying hard now. He could only nod.

"Your gang is finished. Leave the gun right there. Go home, kid. Go back to your family. Go to school, grow up—and try to make something out of your life."

The boy continued to stare, bewildered.

"Go! *Now.*"

The kid rose unsteadily to his feet and ran.

Hunter holstered his weapon and trotted back to scoop up his sunglasses, wig, and cap. The girl was silent now, curled into a ball on the ground, shaking uncontrollably.

Maybe she would learn something from this.

But probably not.

He jammed the disguise back in place as he ran along the rear length of the strip plaza. Reaching its opposite end, he turned the corner and slowed to a walk, heading into the parking lot. He strolled casually over to the Ford as the wail of a police siren rose in the distance.

He slid in, swept the map off the dashboard and onto the passenger seat.

The clock read three forty-six.

The op had taken six-and-a-half minutes. Too long.

He pulled out of the lot and headed west, away from the intersection. As soon as he was clear of surrounding traffic, he removed the disguise and shoved it all into a waiting plastic bag. The map followed.

He knew his junker would show up on CCTV cameras at the strip plaza and elsewhere. He'd used it on other ops. Now he had to ditch it for good.

He drove back to an isolated commuter parking lot two miles away. He'd left his switch-out car, an old Honda Civic, parked there early that morning, after making sure there were no nearby cameras. Then he'd taken public transportation back to D.C., to fetch the Ford and his kit for the op.

Minutes later he entered the lot and pulled the Ford right next to the Civic, which he'd left a considerable distance from the street and other vehicles. He quickly wiped down the Ford's interior, then got out, taking the bag bearing his disguise and the plastic sheet he'd spread over the seat and floor, to catch errant threads or strands of hair.

Then started up the Civic, leaving it idling with the driver's door open. From its trunk he took a gasoline can and emptied it around the interior and trunk of the Ford.

His final act was to remove from the Ford's glove compartment the small explosive device from the weapons cache at his Maryland house. He looked around again, waiting for traffic to clear. Then set the timer for thirty seconds, placed it on the floor, and slammed the door.

He jumped into the Civic and drove quickly out of the lot.

Fifteen seconds later he saw the flash in his rearview mirror.

That was when he also noticed the red scratches on his forehead and cheek.

SEVEN

Lucas Carver was standing outside his Capitol Hill brownstone apartment as the Cadillac VIP stretch limo pulled to the curb to pick him up. Carver slid inside, into the beige leather captain's-style chair that faced to the rear, toward the luxury vehicle's sole passenger.

Avery Trammel tapped an icon on the control touchscreen near his armrest. The TV screen behind Carver's head—which had been showing a CNN International report about Russia's energy sector—went dark. The screen covered the soundproof partition between the passenger compartment and his driver, Jeffrey. Trammel tapped another icon; the opening chords of Beethoven's Third Piano Concerto rose quietly over the sound system.

"Thanks for the lift, Avery," Carver began, reaching out to shake hands. His smile was perfunctory, and, as usual, didn't reach his pale blue eyes.

Trammel made a brush-off gesture. "It is no trouble at all. I welcome this opportunity to chat again. It has been a while, *Maestro*." The nickname elicited another empty smile. "The last time we saw each other was at the CarboNot meeting."

"That was early February—not even two months ago." Carver ran his fingers through his gray hair. "Hard to believe, isn't it? With everything that's happened, it seems like years."

"Indeed." Images of that day floated into Trammel's consciousness. The towering figure of the energy company's CEO, Damon Sloan, leading the meeting . . . the faces of anti-fracking activists, businessmen, and bureaucrats seated around the CarboNot conference table... Trammel's private conversation afterward with Ashton Conn, during which he pledged his support of the senator's presidential run...

Now, both men dead—victims of a fanatical bomber.

Trammel eased back into the heated leather and studied his longtime ally. Carver had cut his teeth in radical politics at Columbia while majoring in journalism. After graduation, he founded Vox Populi Communications, a political and media consulting corporation. Vox Populi specialized in "image management and narrative control" for progressive politicians, nonprofits, activist causes, even Marxist foreign governments. Carver met Trammel while raising money for his campaigns. Finding themselves to be ideological soul mates, they had worked closely in the twenty-five years since, with Trammel even taking a seat on the Vox Populi board.

"It is still morning, but you appear to need a drink, Lucas."

"I do. Thanks." Carver opened the lacquered rosewood door of the liquor cabinet, scanned the contents, and retrieved Trammel's favorite—the Ardbeg Uiegedail single malt. He reached for a glass from the rack, then glanced up. "How about you?"

"Please. A single ice cube, if you will."

"Sure... Here you go, *Geppetto*. 'To better days.'"

They clinked glasses and sipped as the limo accelerated through the Saturday morning traffic.

Carver swiveled his seat to look outside, brooding silently as they reached Massachusetts Avenue and headed northwest.

"Why so glum, Lucas?"

"Are you kidding? We had *everything* riding on Ash Conn's candidacy. Now we're stuck with Spencer again. Just what we need: an unprincipled candidate with poll numbers in the toilet."

"So it would appear."

"Even with Ash, it would have been an uphill battle. He jumped into the race so late. We had to talk him into it, only after we convinced him Spencer was bound to lose, but *he* had a real chance. And the thing is, he *did*. The media loved him. His numbers and support were growing every day. Avery, just think of what we could have accomplished with Ash in the Oval Office. Our whole progressive wish list." He snorted. "Everything we *thought* we'd get when we elected Glover eight years ago."

Trammel nodded. "True, Gabe Glover has been a great disappointment." He stared out the window. "However, I suspect that, in the end, Ash would have disappointed us, too."

"What do you mean? Ash was a true idealist. I knew and worked with him for years . . . Hey, you don't believe the outrageous smears that ecoterrorist, Boggs, tried to stick on him?"

"It does not matter what you or I believe. It is all speculative—and irrelevant, now that Ash is dead. What is relevant to our present concerns is: Where do we go from here?"

They were moving past the massive white classical facade of Union Station. Three American flags fluttered in the bright sun above Columbus Fountain and the statue honoring the discoverer of the New World. Trammel felt a tinge of irritation.

"Lucas, I am sixty-four years old. This election may be my last opportunity to achieve objectives I have been working toward for a very long time."

"Mutual objectives, my friend. We have the same goals, you know."

Trammel did not reply. He raised his glass to his lips.

"But I don't see how we salvage anything from this mess now," Carver continued. "Spencer has no convictions at all. Which is why he hasn't been able to rally our base against Helm—or even Waller. Just think of how pathetic it is to be trailing in the polls to an *Independent*, let alone the worst Republican candidate in decades."

"True. However, perhaps in his vacuous pragmatism lies a potential opportunity. Carl Spencer is an empty vessel. That means he is waiting to be filled."

Carver swirled his glass. "You mean, by us?"

"If we play carefully the cards we have been dealt."

"I don't see how. Besides, his personal life will catch up with him pretty soon. Spencer portrays himself as the devoted family man, but word is, he's a dog. Can't keep it in his pants."

"Ash had the same problem, Lucas."

"But it never got out, because everyone knew he had an 'open-marriage' arrangement with his wife. So they weren't hypocrites, like Spencer. They both screwed around a lot—hell, I hear Emmalee Conn is more promiscuous than Ash is." He caught himself. "*Was.*"

"That is what I hear, as well."

"So. We're stuck with a candidate over whom we have no influence, who lacks convictions, a narrative, or a following. And he's up against *two* candidates who do have those things." He peered over his glass at Trammel, looking puzzled. "But you don't seem worried, Avery."

"Worry is pointless and self-defeating. I prefer to occupy my mind more productively—in this case, by devising a plan to overcome the liabilities you mentioned."

"You actually think we can transform Spencer into someone he's not?"

"Of course not. But perhaps we can transform him into someone whom we can direct."

Carver chuckled. "Well, if you can pull those strings, you truly *are* Geppetto. So . . . where do we begin?"

Trammel drummed his fingers on his armrest.

"Let us ignore Tom Waller for the time being. Should that ignoramus win the Republican nomination, as now seems inevitable, you have plenty of dirt on him to drop at the right time. Let us focus instead on Roger Helm. As I read the national mood, his Independent candidacy poses the greater threat."

"All right. Helm, not Waller, then. But meanwhile, what are we going to do about Spencer, now that we're stuck with him? How the hell do we turn around his poll numbers?"

"Let that be my concern. Do your job, and leave Carl Spencer to me."

2

The limo continued on Massachusetts, cutting through the heart of the city, then up Embassy Row. They turned onto Wisconsin Avenue, then South Road. The neo-Gothic towers of the Washington National Cathedral arose before them, piercing the pale blue veil of the sky.

By prior arrangement, his limo was allowed to pull up to the main west entrance. Jeffrey hurried around to open their door, and the two of them stepped out under dazzling mid-day sunshine, into the mingling mass arriving for Senator Ashton Conn's memorial service.

Carver stopped to shake hands with a congressman while Trammel weaved through the crowd and mounted the steps.

Avery Trammel was an atheist. But he acknowledged the seminal, inspirational role that the great religions had played in the arts, of which he was a connoisseur and patron. As he stepped through the entrance, he had to pause.

Supported by massive columns on either side, the enormous vaulted ceiling peaked a hundred feet overhead, painted in pastels cast by stained-glass clerestory windows. Before him—warmed by the soft golden glow of suspended Gothic pendant lights—the nave extended the length of a football field, to the Great Choir area and beyond, to the High Altar. Above the murmuring voices of the congregation, Bach's haunting "Air on the G String" reverberated throughout the cavernous space from the pipes of the cathedral's magnificent organ.

He paced briskly down the broad central aisle, sensing heads turning his way from the thousands of seats around him. Avery Trammel never tired of the impact his studied, carefully cultivated aristocratic presence made on people. He strode on, heading toward a distant figure standing near the front of the congregation, waiting for him.

3

It took Trammel a full minute to reach the front of the congregation. There, before the altar area, two towering wings, or transepts, extended from the central aisle to his left and right, forming the traditional cross shape of medieval church architecture.

And at that intersection, indifferent to the solemnity of the occasion, Carl Spencer stood facing him, grinning broadly, then stepping out into the aisle to greet him.

Trammel had met the man a few times in the past. Seeing him again underscored why he was so popular with the ladies. He cut a tall, athletic figure in his tailored charcoal suit. Sandy, gray-tinged hair and boyish, bland-handsome features made the 54-year-old Connecticut senator look warm and approachable. His infectious, hundred-watt grin displayed perfect teeth; his blue-gray eyes twinkled in the lights.

"Avery! So glad you accepted my invitation to join us," the senator said, a trifle too loudly, too cheerfully, and too ostentatiously.

The perfect politician, Trammel thought with contempt. Yet opinion surveys revealed most Americans saw him as "too slick" and "untrustworthy." The party's progressive base certainly held that view. Despite the hypocrisy of his own personal life, Ash at least could be relied upon in office to advance progressive ideals. By contrast, for Spencer, ideological pronouncements were merely manipulative tools for self-aggrandizement. The spoiled son of a wealthy Hartford insurance CEO, he loved attention from adoring crowds and ego strokes from compliant women. When not pursuing these directly, he was in the gym, working hard to maintain his chiseled physique, or attending parties where he could show off by performing classic rock riffs on his Fender Stratocaster.

"Thank you for the courtesy, Senator."

"Come on, now—it's 'Carl,' my friend," he chuckled, poking him playfully on the arm. Trammel felt his forced smile wilt; the politician's familiarity grated on him.

Spencer turned to introduce him to his party, which filled the second row. His invitation was not social, of course. No gathering in this city was ever actually social. With the death of his sole rival for the Democratic nomination, Spencer now hoped to inherit Trammel's formidable political clout and financial support. And because perception was power, their meeting here would communicate that implication to everyone present.

"My wife, Jill," the politician said, placing his hand on her shoulder. She remained seated, and Trammel leaned in to take her offered hand.

He knew all about Jill Dawson, of course. A former Miss Connecticut, now a morning-show anchor for a New York network affiliate, she had become Spencer's second trophy wife. Even marriage to a gorgeous TV celebrity failed to stop Spencer's womanizing. However, equally ambitious, she turned a blind eye to his wandering one, demanding only discretion as his political star ascended. As her part in the arrangement, the ambitious, aspiring First Lady contributed glamor, a son from her previous marriage, and a daughter of their own.

"How do you do, Mrs. Spencer—or shall I call you Ms. Dawson?" he asked, alluding to her television name.

"Mrs. Spencer is fine, Mr. Trammel," she replied with her own bright smile and a light squeeze of her hand. She clearly knew her role here. Trammel had seen her on television a year earlier, before her diagnosis of lung cancer. He could see now that her suit had been tailored to disguise the weight loss from her treatments, still evident in her slightly sunken cheeks. He wondered if her short brown hair was a wig. Even so, she remained remarkably attractive.

"You look wonderful," he said. "I trust that means you are feeling better?"

"Yes, thank you. My doctors believe I should have a full recovery."

"Excellent," he said, patting her hand. Trammel meant it. Her condition, and her husband's public fawning over her, had generated some of the only positives in his otherwise poor polling. But it also represented Spencer's greatest vulnerability: The man's political career would be finished should his infidelities during his wife's illness become public knowledge.

"Let me introduce you to some of my staff and colleagues," Spencer interjected. They exchanged the expected pleasantries. Then he took the aisle seat next to Spencer.

Trammel waited him out. After a moment, the politician leaned in, speaking softly.

"Such a shame, what happened to Ash. Sure, I wanted the nomination, Avery. And your support, of course. But not like this."

"I know exactly how you must feel."

Spencer nodded slowly, oblivious to the sarcasm. "So terrible, all this domestic terrorism," he went on. "None of us can feel safe anymore."

Trammel remembered the sight and smell of his own incinerated Gulfstream on the tarmac at Dulles.

"And that nutjob, Zak Boggs," Spencer went on. "My God, he's still out there somewhere." He lowered his voice further, barely above a whisper. "Avery... you don't think there's anything to what he claimed, do you? I know the FBI says there's no evidence of any association between Ash and Boggs. But you knew Ash as well as anybody. What do *you* think?"

Trammel had thought about that, a great deal. "Ash represented the progressive mainstream of the environmentalist movement, and he believed in reform politics. Boggs led the 'Deep Ecology,' ecoterrorist fringe. To him, Ash was a moral coward, a traitor to the cause. Which I believe was ample motivation for Boggs to assassinate him—then try to tar his reputation with the malicious slander that they had conspired together." He shook his head. "I find any association between the two to be preposterous."

Spencer turned away, sighing. "I just wondered. Because it's so hard to really know someone. To know what really motivates them, deep down, and what they may really be up to."

Trammel kept his face blank. "It certainly is."

He heard a noise and turned. To his right, Conn's family and relatives had just entered the south transept entrance. They were led by an usher who guided them into the first two reserved rows, directly across the aisle.

The usher seated Emmalee Conn, the senator's striking widow, on the aisle in the front row, a short distance away. She wore a tailored black jacket over a snug black dress. Trammel noticed strain in her eyes.

He felt Spencer's elbow nudge him.

"Even after what she's been through, she still looks hot, doesn't she?" he whispered. "Ash was one lucky man, huh?"

Trammel was taken aback. It was so inappropriate, in so many ways. He glanced at the senator: seated beside his gorgeous, accomplished, but ailing wife, yet with his eyes narrowed and fixed on the blonde across the aisle. He turned away before Spencer could notice his shock.

"She is a lovely woman," he replied, keeping his tone neutral.

"Wonder who'll get to her first, now that she's available?"

At that instant, Trammel realized all the hopes he had entertained in coming here were doomed. How could he have ever imagined trying to control this undisciplined, rutting adolescent?

Then, watching Emmalee tug at the hem of her skirt, he had a faint thought.

During the next eighty minutes, as a procession of Washington's political and social elites mounted the intricately carved stone pulpit to speak, Avery Trammel began to expand that idle thought into a plan.

4

At the end of the service, the ushers returned to dismiss the congregation, beginning with the family members. To the somber organ recessional of Handel's "Largo" from *Xerxes*, they filed out, led by Emmalee, heading back toward the south transept doors.

Trammel turned to Spencer.

"Senator, I do wish to chat with you, but I have a prior commitment. Please contact my office and I shall be glad to arrange an appointment."

Spencer looked disappointed, but forced a grin. "I look forward to that opportunity, Avery. Thanks once again for joining us."

Trammel said his farewells to the others. When the usher dismissed his row, he headed after the departing family. He crossed in front of the altar area and passed beneath the tall arches supporting the south balcony, backlit by majestic stained-glass windows. He had to jostle his way through congregants mingling at the doorway.

Emmalee was standing outside a black limousine parked at the bottom of the steps. She was surrounded by a small group hugging her and offering their sympathies.

He hastened down and approached, waiting patiently until she finished with the last of those around her. Then he stepped in.

"Mrs. Conn, I am Avery Trammel. Your late husband introduced us early this month, at the social you hosted in your home."

He saw the look of recognition. "Oh, yes. Of course I remember you, Mr. Trammel." Her face looked drawn and pale, her eyes clouded with a faraway look. "Was that this month? It seems like it was years ago."

"I cannot begin to know how you must feel. I am so terribly sorry. Please accept my most profound condolences. Your husband was a long-time friend and colleague. I shall miss him terribly."

"Thank you, Mr. Trammel. He—"

"Please—Avery."

The faintest of smiles. "Thank you, Avery. Ash spoke of you often. He was . . . we were both grateful to you for your generous support."

He took her hand, held her eyes, and lowered his voice.

"I wish to speak to you about that, Mrs. Conn. I can only imagine the enormous challenges that this tragedy has left you to face. And if possible, I would like to offer you my assistance."

She looked startled; her eyes came back to the present.

He looked around, concerned about the people hovering nearby. He spotted the entrance into the Bishop's Garden, just across the driveway.

"I realize you are preoccupied with your guests. But if I could have just a moment's word with you, privately?" He pointed. "Let us go over there."

She told her driver and a couple of waiting friends that she would be right back, then allowed him to draw her along by the hand.

The thick wooden doors in the stone wall of the garden stood open. They stepped through the arched entranceway onto the flagstone pathway. He led her a few yards inside, out of earshot of anyone lurking nearby. At this time of year, the boxwood trees stood barren, the fountains were idle, and a distant stone gazebo looked empty and forlorn. Still, there was a somber beauty here. Shielded by its stone walls, the garden was a private, peaceful sanctuary amid the turmoil of the city.

"Please let me be frank, Mrs. Conn. I—"

"Emmalee." Another tentative smile.

He answered with one his own. "Very well, Emmalee. As you may know, I shared several investment interests with your husband. In his last days, Ash and I discussed the difficult financial position in which he found himself because of recent events."

"You mean our CarboNot and Capital Resources stock. Yes. It's all worthless. We lost it all. And the explosion badly damaged our house, too." She shuddered slightly; the faraway look returned. "So I can't live there. And I just found out that Ash had borrowed a lot of equity from the house and poured it into the stock purchases . . . I don't know if his pension will even begin to cover what we owe."

This was better than he had dreamed.

"How terrible for you," he said. "Where are you living now?"

"I'm . . . staying with a friend."

He made a face. "Well, that is simply unacceptable." He looked away briefly, acting as if he were pondering the situation. Then he faced her again.

"Emmalee, I feel the weight of personal responsibility for your plight. No—I mean that. You see, it was I who encouraged your husband to participate in these investments. Had I not done that, you would not be facing your current difficulties. I would like to discuss with you how I might help you, going forward. As a first step, please allow me to arrange for you to stay at the Watergate. My wife and I—"

"Oh!" The shock in her face was almost comic. "But I couldn't accept—"

He waved his hand dismissively. "No, consider it done. My wife Julia and I maintain an apartment there, and it would be no trouble at all for me to obtain a residence for you, too. As I said, under the circumstances, your current problems are largely my responsibility. Besides, I am sure you and Julia will get along splendidly."

"Julia? . . . oh! You mean Julia Haight? That's right—you're married to *her*."

It amused him, the stunned look on her face. "Yes, *that* Julia. Once you are settled in, we shall have you over for dinner. Perhaps take in some shows. Anything to help you through this difficult period."

He watched her shudder. Then her eyes filled with tears.

"I . . . I don't know how . . ."

He waved his hand again. "Please. Think nothing of it. I am just relieved that I am in a position to help."

He reached into his overcoat and drew out a small gold case, from which he retrieved his business card.

"Here is my number. Please call my secretary at the beginning of the week. I should like to meet with you very soon in order to make all the arrangements. And perhaps to chat a bit about your future."

She was crying openly now. "Avery. I just can't . . . I don't know what to say. I've been so scared . . ."

He opened his arms wide and she fell shaking into his embrace. He inhaled her perfume. Felt strands of her blonde hair tickle his cheek. Felt the woman's full curves pressed tightly against him.

Felt himself stirring with anticipation.

He left her at her limo with a final hug, then walked around the cathedral to where his own stood idling. Lucas was waiting inside when the driver let him in.

"So how did things go with Spencer?"

As close as they were, some things not even Lucas Carver could ever be told.

"Better than I had dared hope."

"Really? You really think we can recruit him? Control him?"

Trammel pressed once again into the smooth, warm leather, raised his foot rest, then his waiting glass of whiskey.

"I have already taken the first step."

EIGHT

Hunter stepped out of the shower, wrapping the towel around his waist. Then moved before the bathroom mirror.

The scratches—three angry red streaks—started above his left eyebrow, then raked down across his cheekbone.

He tried to think of some plausible explanation other than the obvious one. And came up empty.

They looked exactly like what they were.

"*Mrrrrooowww.*"

The cat sat at his feet, her mottled black-and-white face turned up toward him. She seemed to be scowling, too.

"I know. They've scabbed over. I couldn't hide them with makeup."

"*Rowwwrrr?*"

"Not that I would try. No, Luna, I'm not going to spin her some fairy tale. She'd never buy it." He traced the deepest scratch with his forefinger, feeling the raised welt of the track. "Anyway, it doesn't matter if she'd buy it. I wouldn't do that. I promised her 'No more lies.' Even though she won't like the truth one bit."

The cat got up and began stropping back and forth across his bare calf.

"Glad you admire my impending act of martyrdom."

He sighed, peeled off the towel and started drying his hair.

2

She pulled her Toyota into his driveway and rolled up to the garage. She turned off the engine. Then felt herself smile as she picked up her overnight bag from the passenger-side floor. Remembering the first time she'd brought it with her.

Their first time . . .

That amazing weekend tryst in the Shenandoah Valley. The wineries. The incredible dinner at the inn's restaurant.

Then the charming little cottage with the big stone fireplace.

The canopy bed. That endless first night.

The jetted tub . . .

An image flashed in memory of how he lay on his back beneath her, and raised her with his thighs from the hot churning water, revealing her body in the mirrored ceiling above them, golden and naked in the candlelight . . .

She listened to the faint shrill cry of a seagull over the marsh behind his home.

So much had happened since that day, so long ago . . .

Then, startled, she realized that it had been only last September. September 20th . . . and today was—what?—March 21st.

Six months? It couldn't be possible.

Then other images from the intervening weeks began to rise in her consciousness. She unsnapped her seatbelt and left the car quickly, then went around to the passenger side.

"Okay, Cyrano, we're here now."

With her free hand, she picked up the pet carrier from the seat. The pup began squeaking eagerly. She bumped the door shut with her hip, then hurried up the short flight of brick steps to the front door.

She held in anticipation the memory of his face—strong, craggy, with intense hazel-green eyes. She had her keys in hand and was reaching for the knob when the door opened before her.

He stood there, waiting for her. Looking serious.

She saw his face and gasped.

"Dylan! What happened?"

"Shhh," he whispered. "Remember—out here, it's 'Vic.' Come on in."

He held the door wide as she swept past him, then closed it behind her. He turned to face her as she stood in the foyer. He made no effort to approach her.

"Your face," she said, taking in what looked like some animal's claw marks.

"I'll explain. First, let me take care of Cyrano outside, and I'll leave him on the porch. Just drop your bag right there, and go on into the den. I've poured some wine for you there."

When he returned, she was sipping Chardonnay in her favorite chair, a leather recliner near the blazing fireplace. He sat before her on its ottoman.

"I had to take care of a bit of unfinished business yesterday, Annie," he began. "Up in Baltimore. It's all over the news today."

She set the glass down on the side table carefully, because her hand was shaking. She was remembering the news radio story she'd heard only a few minutes earlier, while crossing the Bay Bridge.

"That was you?"

He nodded. He held her gaze openly, calmly, not looking away. Without the slightest bit of remorse.

"A few days ago, you heard me tell Bronowski I had a loose end to take care of. You remember the people at the Vigilance for Victims meeting in Susie's home last fall. Kate Higgins, George Banacek, Susie herself—at the time, the killers of their family members were all out on the streets. I saw how broken they were, how those monsters had wrecked their lives. So right then and there, I made a silent promise to them: to give them the justice the legal system didn't.

"Morgan and Lila Jackson were at that meeting, too. And the other night at the banquet, I could tell they were upset about something, so I spoke with them afterward. They told me about the boss of a drug gang—a piece of crap named Reginald Dixon. He's the animal who raped and killed their young daughter, Loretta. The reason they were upset was because on Friday, Dixon was released from prison on a technicality—a screw-up by the prosecutors."

He paused, as if to let it sink in. His eyes were green ice.

"Dixon was the last loose end," he said simply.

Then stopped talking. He waited for her.

She sat numb for a moment. "I see," she said finally, hearing the tightness in her voice. After another moment she added: "The news story said the cops thought it was a war between rival drug gangs. They said it was a bloodbath. A couple dead, one critical, some others beaten up." She stared at his motionless face. "But all of that . . . it was only you."

He gestured toward his scratched face. "That's how this happened."

She looked away, out the window. She could make out ducks or geese, she wasn't sure which, floating in the marsh. They looked adrift. Indecisive.

"I guess I had dared to fantasize for a few weeks that—after Boggs and Conn—you were done with this vigilante stuff."

"Annie, I meant it when I said Dixon was a last loose end. The last remaining killer involved with the folks at that Vigilance for Victims meeting. The people I'd made my promise to."

He stopped, forcing her to turn back and look at him. So that she could see his eyes, and what was in them.

"I kept my promise. So yes, Annie—I'm done." He smiled bleakly. "The vigilante is hereby officially retired."

She shook her head slowly. "Until you're provoked the next time. Until some new victim comes along needing an avenger. You're what Grant said you are, Dylan. A 'sheepdog.' It's in your DNA."

"Grant's wrong. I want a normal life. A future. A future with you, Annie. I want you to believe that."

"And I do want to believe that, Dylan. Just as I know *you* really want to. But wanting to believe it . . ."

". . . is not the same as really believing it. I know." He looked away, for the first time. When he spoke again, his voice was low. "I'm really not being fair to you. After all I put you through, I begged you to take my ring back. But a ring is a promise, too—a promise of a normal life.

And I've given you no reason to believe that promise." He faced her again. "That was wrong of me. I shouldn't have—"

She raised her hand. "Stop. Don't. Don't you *dare* rob me of your amazing proposal." She flashed the engagement ring. Forced a smile. "See? It's still here. And it's staying here." She chuckled. "Detective Cronin warned me you carry more baggage than Amtrak. But I accepted you, baggage and all. And I still do."

His eyes were wide.

"Annie Woods . . . I don't deserve you."

She rose from the chair.

"You don't," she said, extending her hand toward him. "But why don't we go upstairs and you can try to make it up to me."

3

"Mrrrrruugh . . . mrrrrrOWWWW!"

"Dammit, Luna, it's Sunday morning."

"Rowwwwww . . . mrrrahhhh . . ."

He opened an eye.

The cat sat on the bench at the foot of the bed, peering at him. The black buccaneer patch around one eye suggested she was winking at him. She held a fabric toy mouse in her teeth, its tail hanging from one side of her mouth, a long attached string dangling from the other.

"So, you want to play, huh?"

Annie stirred beneath the comforter beside him. "Not now," she murmured.

"Not you. The cat."

"Mmmm. What time is it?"

"Too early for you to get up. Stay here for a while. I'll take Cyrano for a walk and have coffee waiting when you come down."

He slid out from beneath the comforter and put on his bathrobe. Passing the cat, he grabbed and tugged the end of the string attached to the toy. It popped out of her mouth, and he dragged it along the floor behind him. Luna scampered after him, chasing the elusive rodent downstairs.

He had taken care of the pup, Luna was noisily munching her crunchies, and he was scanning the Sunday *Inquirer* and sipping coffee when his cell chirped on the table. He frowned; this early on a Sunday, it couldn't be good news from one of the few people who had this number.

"Yes, Wonk?"

"Please forgive my intrusion, Dylan. I do hope I am not awakening you."

"No, I'm up and having my coffee. You sound upset."

"I am. I need to see you, as soon as possible."

"Are you all right?"

"Yes, *I* am fine." He stopped.

"Can you tell me what this is about?"

"No. I do not wish to use the phone. Could you perhaps visit me?"

It had to be serious; Wonk didn't like visitors.

"I'm not nearby, Wonk. And Annie and I have plans today."

"Dylan, it is extremely important . . . *Please?*"

"All right. But would early evening—say, about six—be too late?"

"No. No, that will be fine. Thank you. I shall see you then."

With that, Wonk abruptly ended the call.

4

"This damned hunch of yours better pan out, Ed," Detective Paul Erskine said, pressing the elevator button for the fifth floor. "I hate coming in on Sundays. I had plans for an afternoon of beer and basketball."

Cronin gave his portly partner a slow once-over. "You playing forward or guard these days, Paul?"

"Funny man," Erskine said as the elevator door opened.

They were greeted in a small lobby area by a graying, bespectacled black man in a tan suit.

"Kevin Yost," he said, offering his hand. His eyes were bloodshot, his tie askew, and he hadn't shaved for a day or two. "I spoke to one of you on the phone this morning."

"That was me. Detective Sergeant Ed Cronin. And my partner, Detective Paul Erskine."

Above the open entranceway to a nearby office the word HOMICIDE stood out in garish black lettering, and an American flag stood sentry to one side. Yost brought them inside.

The Baltimore P.D. Homicide Unit worked out of a large room with low tile ceilings, partitioned into cubicles. Like Yost, many of the detectives working phones and computer screens were older African-American males. Uniform jackets, suit coats, ties, and umbrellas hung from racks on partition exteriors. Interior cubicle walls bore the usual profusion of thumbtacked notes, business cards, newspaper clippings, and suspended shelves displaying framed awards and family photos. Case binders and paperwork smothered the tops of desks, lockers, and file cabinets. The occasional potted plant affirmed some homicide investigator's stubborn commitment to life.

"We appreciate you letting us in on this one, Sergeant," Cronin said as Yost guided them through the maze. The detective halted beneath a large whiteboard on one of the walls, then turned to face them. With a weary chuckle he hooked a thumb at the board.

"See that?"

About fifteen feet wide, it displayed, in eight columns, thirty or more homicide victim names each. The names were in red or black letters, the overwhelming majority red. Topping each column, a card listed five or six detectives in the squad assigned to those cases.

"Red are open cases, black closed." Yost snorted. "As you can see, we ain't keeping up. I caught the assignment on the Dixon hit when it went down Friday afternoon. You know, it just doesn't smell like your normal gang hit. You want it, you can have it."

He led them to a cubicle where two other detectives hovered over a computer screen. Yost introduced the pair as Sean Moynihan and Barton McBride. In his mid-fifties, Moynihan looked like an old-fashioned Hollywood detective: white hair, handlebar mustache, charcoal suit topped by a dapper fedora. By contrast, McBride, in his forties, looked like a retired linebacker: a beefy black male with a shaved head, in a black pin-striped suit. His BPD credentials hung from his neck.

"Detectives Cronin and Erskine are with the Vigilante Task Force. They're checking to see if the Lawn Boyz hit is related."

"What makes you suspect that?" Moynihan asked.

Erskine snorted and nodded at Cronin. "His hunch."

Cronin shot him a look. "It's because your gang leader, Dixon, was in for raping and murdering a young girl down our way. And now he gets whacked the minute he's freed. That roughly fits the pattern of our vigilantes. They go after killers, especially for sex crimes, who get probation or early releases."

"Well, we'll share what we got, and you decide," Yost said.

McBride took over to explain in detail how they thought the hit had gone down. Then he pointed toward the computer.

"We're just going over the surveillance footage from outside the check-cashing store at the plaza. The gang used the gas station there as their H.Q., so they kept all the surveillance cameras off. But the owner of the check joint, he secretly kept his running, 'cause of the kind of clientele he gets." He turned to the screen. "Let me show you the clip. It's grainy, but here you see this Ford Focus pull in and park at the far end of the lot, right near the street. Notice he backs in. Driver stays inside, fiddling with what looks like a map... Now he's doing something else, we can't tell what. It goes on like this for about ten minutes. Here, let me fast-forward... Okay—there. Now you see him get out and cut across the lot, left to right."

Cronin leaned in close. The guy wore a baseball cap, dark glasses, jeans, boots, gloves. A brown jacket, maybe leather. Looked like he had blond hair and a goatee. He strode purposefully—even boldly—out of camera range, to the right.

"Let me run it again. This time I'll slow it down."

"What's that in his hands? A cup?" Erskine asked.

"Uh huh. Big paper soda cup. Makes him look normal and harmless, huh?"

"Except he's wrapped up like a mummy. You can't make out any details of his appearance."

"That's where our witnesses come in," Yost said. "Turns out this hitter wasn't blond after all. Two of them say it was a disguise. It came off for a minute or so during a tussle he had with one of them. The shooter lost his hat, and the blond hair was a wig that fell off, too. They saw he had dark hair."

A tingle crawled across the back of Cronin's neck. "Any details?"

"Dixon's girlfriend was pretty hysterical, but she saw him fairly close. She said dark, curly hair."

Cronin worked to keep his face expressionless. "Anything else? They notice his face, eyes?"

"He lost his shades for a few seconds, too," said Moynihan, "but the guy fighting him couldn't be sure about eye color or other details. He got a concussion during the fight and can't remember squat."

Feeling Erskine's eyes on him, Cronin kept his glued to the screen. "Could they identify the perp if they saw him again? Maybe in a photo lineup?"

"We asked," McBride said. "They aren't sure. But I doubt it. It happened real fast, and they were all scared shitless, ducking down or running away. Here, let me fast-forward some more, to where he comes back to the car . . . Okay, here we are. Now he's coming back, this time from the left. What he did was circle around behind the building and come out over on this other side. You see him from the rear now. Unfortunately, he's got the wig and hat back on."

Cronin carefully watched the man's stride, brisk and steady. He tried to connect it to the man he knew. But it was impossible to tell. The guy got back into the Ford, shoved the map off the dash, and immediately rolled out into the traffic. In seconds he was gone.

"What do you have for physical evidence?"

"Besides shell casings from a nine and the slugs in the bodies, we found the cup inside the store on the floor," Yost said. "But it was empty, dry as a bone. No prints. The lab is checking for DNA, but it doesn't look like he used it to drink anything."

"Just for camouflage, then?" Erskine asked.

"Maybe," McBride said. "But Sean has another idea about that."

Moynihan stepped in. "You notice in the tape how he carried the cup in both hands, like it was heavy? He probably wouldn't do that if the cup was empty, right? Well, turns out our shooter used a stun grenade to force entry into the interior office where Dixon was. Just like he was SWAT or something. I think maybe he used the cup to hide and transport the grenade."

Erskine whistled. "Ed, you were speculating last year that these vigilantes could be ex-cops, maybe SWAT or military."

Cronin could only nod.

"Well, whoever this one is, he's a pro, all right," Yost said. "Does a one-man hit on a gang headquarters filled with armed men. Uses a stun grenade. Pops three with a handgun. Takes down three more, hand-to-hand. Who the hell would have the balls to do that, let alone the skills?"

"Plus, he leaves very little evidence," McBride added. "He torched the Ford in a commuter lot a couple miles away. Incendiary device. The teams are working on all that. No security cams there, though, so we don't know how he got away—whether in a waiting car, or somebody picking him up. Cold plates on the Focus, and the VIN came back for a used car bought two years ago, under a fake ID."

The tingling now went the rest of the way down Cronin's spine.

"You have a name for that fake ID?"

Moynihan pawed through some papers. Found what he was looking for, squinted, then picked up and put on half-moon spectacles from his desk.

"Let me see . . . Okay, here you go. Name given to the dealer was 'Edmond Dantes.'"

Moynihan peered over the top of the spectacles, first at Cronin, then Erskine.

"What? That name mean something to you guys?"

5

After a half hour going over the M.E.'s reports and the witness statements, Cronin and Erskine stepped into a nearby empty cubicle and waited while Yost took care of some business with the others.

"Well. What do you know? 'Edmond Dantes.' You were right, Ed. This *was* our vigilantes."

Cronin nodded.

"You know, I've been thinking," Erskine went on. "We keep assuming this is a team doing all this shit. But here you have just one guy taking out an entire gang. And as I think back, we've never had a single hit where we know for a fact more than one guy was involved."

Cronin remained silent. He was reading a plaque hanging on the cubicle wall.

"Maybe we have this figured all wrong, Ed. I know this sounds crazy; but do you think this could possibly be just one guy?"

The plaque was "The Homicide Investigator's Creed."

No greater honor will ever be bestowed on an officer or a more profound duty imposed on him than when he is entrusted with the investigation of the death of a human being.
It is his duty to find the facts, regardless of color or creed, without prejudice, and to let no power on earth deter him from presenting these facts to the court, without regard for personality.

"Just one lone vigilante? . . . What do you think, Ed?"

NINE

Hunter left the Metro escalator at Dupont Circle and stopped at the doughnut shop. He had them fill a box with a dozen assorted, including four glazed piping hot from their oven. Then he proceeded the short distance down 19th Street to the office building where, by special arrangement with a certain intel agency, their prize contract researcher—and his—maintained an eighth-floor apartment.

When he reached the apartment door, he heard a commotion inside. Worried, he rang the bell—then, after a moment when there was nothing but more noise, he banged the door with his fist.

"Wonk! Are you okay in there?"

He heard slow, rhythmic creaking of the floorboards, then the sound of multiple locks being disengaged. The door swung open, revealing the human pyramid that was Frederick Diffendorfer.

Wonk's body was the approximate size and contour of a commercial blimp, stood on end. His stained, short-sleeve shirt bulged like a wind-filled sail, draping over enormous trousers that looked like twin grain silos. He had no discernible neck; instead, about an acre of flesh rose in three folded layers from his chest, the last serving as his chin. His tea-colored hair matched his eyes, partly obscured by thick, black-framed eyeglasses. One temple of the frame clung precariously to the rest by white adhesive tape.

The eyes exuded panic.

"Oh, Dylan! I am so relieved that you have arrived!"

"For God's sake, what's happened?"

Wonk seized Hunter's wrist with damp, sausage-like fingers.

"Iggy will not come out of the closet!" he whined in his high-pitched voice.

Hunter stared at him, uncomprehending.

"Wonk, forgive me . . . but is that supposed to be some kind of metaphor?"

The researcher blinked. "Dylan! I am not jesting. This is *serious*. I am referring to Iggy—my pet iguana!"

"Your . . . *what?*"

"My iguana! Iggy wandered into my electronics storage closet and is wreaking *havoc!* I can neither reach him nor coax him out. Would you please assist me?"

"Wonk, did you have me rush all the way over here just to rescue—"

"No! That is about an entirely different matter, which has nothing to do with Iggy."

He followed Wonk inside his immaculate, upscale living room, decorated with classical art prints and sculptures. They proceeded past the pristine kitchen, where Dylan left the doughnuts on the table, and went on down a hallway. The morbidly obese man rocked from side to side with each step, as if on the pitching deck of a ship.

At the end of the corridor, they came to a closed metal door with an electronic lock above the knob. Wonk drew a card from his pocket, swiped it over the lock, then—shielding it from view with his vast bulk—keyed in a series of numbers.

"Nice. So they set you up to work remotely in your own SCIF office. I'm impressed, Wonk."

"In allowing you in here, I am grossly violating procedures for a Secure Compartmentalized Facility. However, I am too embarrassed to contact the . . . relevant agency for assistance. Iggy slipped into the office when I opened the door to get a snack." Wonk considered him for a moment. "I have come to trust you, Dylan. Still, I must insist on your complete discretion about what you see while inside."

"Of course."

The researcher pushed open the door.

They entered a surprisingly spacious, windowless office, lit solely by overhead fluorescent lighting. In its center a large desk and adjoining side table held three desktop computers with oversized monitors, plus a printer, a communications jammer, and a few other mysterious devices. Behind it, a long, separate table ran almost the length of the room, bearing an array of sophisticated electronic equipment. One wall was crammed with black, four-drawer filing cabinets. Eight flatscreen television monitors hung from another, two airing news channels, the rest displaying the kind of images he suspected were being securely transmitted here from intelligence agencies.

Wonk noticed. "I must request that you avert your eyes from what is on those screens."

"Roger that. So, where's this lizard of yours?"

They went to a large walk-in closet with stacked racks and shelves of state-of-the-art electronics. But some items were strewn about, and a few lay broken on the floor. Wonk was too huge to maneuver easily in there. He leaned inside and looked around, then up.

"Oh, there you are, you bad boy!"

Iggy perched defiantly on the top rack. He looked like a miniature version of a 1950s science-fiction monster. At least two feet long, he was bright green, with a toad-like face and a black-banded tail. A row of spikes ran down the length of his back; a flap of skin dangled from his neck; and he gripped the metal rack with what looked like sharp claws.

"I had a friend who had an encounter with a 'pet' iguana in Mexico," Hunter said. "It took twenty stitches to close up his arm."

"I assure you that Iggy is completely harmless."

"Maybe. But how about you fetch me a nice thick towel?"

2

It took ten minutes to capture the scrambling animal and return it to its cage in the bedroom. Hunter was sweating from the exertion and downing a second can of cold Pepsi as they got settled in the living room.

"I cannot thank you enough," Wonk began as he slowly lowered himself into his oversized club chair.

Hunter waved it off. "You're welcome. Now, what's the real reason you wanted to meet with me?"

The man took a deep breath and let it out. He took off his glasses and began to polish them with the bottom of his shirt.

"It is about my dear friend Arnold Wasserman. Like you, he is an investigative journalist. I was conversing with him by phone on Wednesday evening. He was excited about his latest project. So much so that he cancelled our regularly scheduled chess match at the Jewish Community Center. Arnold informed me that he had discovered something of enormous importance concerning political money-laundering through the Currents Foundation."

"Currents? Why does that ring a bell?"

"It was mentioned in passing in the background material we went over weeks ago—the research I compiled about the various CarboNot investors. It is part of—"

"I remember, now. Isn't that part of the charity network Avery Trammel is involved with?"

"Precisely. Anyway, Arnold said"—he closed his eyes and leaned back, his face tilted toward the ceiling—"'You will not *believe* whose money is being laundered through the Currents Foundation—and where it is winding up.' And then he added, 'This one is a bombshell. It has major implications for the presidential campaign. I think it is going to blow the whole election race sky-high!'"

He stopped, opened his eyes, looked at Hunter.

"That is exactly what he said. And then—" He stopped. Swallowed hard. Looked away.

"What, Wonk?" Hunter asked gently.

"He said somebody was at the door, and that he would call me right back. He ended the call . . . But he never called me back, Dylan. He . . ." His eyes started to fill with tears.

"What's the matter?"

Wonk pulled some tissues from a box on the lamp table beside his chair.

"When I did not hear from him, I assumed that some friend must have come by, and that he became distracted. But he never phoned back that night. Nor the next day. I began to call, but no one answered. Not until last night. Only it was not Arnold. It was someone who identified himself as a police officer. The police were at his apartment."

His voice cracked.

"Dylan, he is dead! His body was discovered drowned in his bathtub. It is in the papers this morning."

"Oh, Wonk! I'm so sorry."

He nodded, weeping openly now. "The police statement says it appears to be accidental. That he fell in his bathtub while bathing, hit his head, and drowned."

"Really? That seems pretty far-fetched."

"That is what I think, too," he said, dabbing his eyes and nose.

Hunter got up from the sofa, went over to the man and put his hand on his shoulder. Squeezed. "I can see you were very close friends. This has to be an incredible shock."

He nodded, tears flowing over his round, pink cheeks.

"Something is not right about this, Dylan. Not just *how* he died, but *when* he died. The news accounts report that the coroner places the time of death as Wednesday evening. That would be not long after our phone conversation." He hesitated. "And not long after he went to answer the door."

Hunter's roaming eyes rested on a gold-framed print of Vermeer's *The Geographer*, a personal favorite. A scholar, in rapt thought, studying a globe, charts, and maps. Searching for clues about the world. Perhaps experiencing a flash of revelation.

"He begged off on our chess appointment because of the story he was working on. He gave me the distinct impression that he planned to work on it for the rest of the night. But he also was eager to continue to talk to me about it. Perhaps to brainstorm. So why would he end the call to answer the door, promising to return my call immediately—and then go take a bath, instead? Or why would he take a bath instead of continuing his work?"

"And now he's dead," Hunter said quietly.

"Dylan . . . I do not like this."

"I don't like it either, Wonk."

"I wanted your confirmation that I am not just imagining things, before I go to the police and tell them what I know."

"No. Don't do that." Hunter thought rapidly. "Don't talk to the police or anyone else. At least, not yet. From what you say, Arnold believed he had a huge, high-stakes political story. One that might blow the election sky-high, he said. If that's true, then some people would have a strong motive to stop him before he could go public. And if they are that desperate . . ."

He paused to let the implication sink in. Felt Wonk shudder.

"Here's what I think you should do, instead. Find out whatever you can about the Currents Foundation. But be cautious about it. Don't call or email anyone there, or ask them direct questions. Don't let anyone know you're looking into it. Keep a low profile, and don't leave any tracks back to you."

He gave the shoulder another squeeze.

"Meanwhile, I'll poke around on my end, too. I have an assignment for Bronowski—ironically, it's election-related, too. But I'll carve out time for this."

"He *was* a dear friend, Dylan." Wonk looked up at him. "But so are you."

TEN

Hunter left Interstate 66 in Manassas. It was almost another mile to the turnoff for the Helm International Resort. Half a mile beyond were the traffic booths.

A chartered bus sat on this side of the barriers, and next to it a knot of about twenty people stood waving signs. Four Virginia State Police troopers stood between the protesters and the traffic backed up at the booths. The booth farthest right and nearest the demonstrators bore a sign: "Official Business and Employees Only."

He angled his Forester toward that lane, drifted up to the booth, and lowered his window. From here he could read the banner on the side of their bus: *The Caring and Sharing Alliance.*

A guy with a bullhorn led them in a sing-song chant:

"Cage the Wolf! Cage the Wolf!"

"Hello, sir," the young female attendant greeted him. "Sorry about the noise. May I help you?"

"Dylan Hunter, with the *Capitol Inquirer.* I have a nine o'clock appointment with Mr. Helm."

"Yes, sir," she said, double-checking her clipboard. "I was told to expect you."

She instructed him where to proceed and park, but asked him to first move ahead and stop his car for inspection. Four uniformed Secret Service officers with a dog waited beside a black SUV. One watched him carefully while a second approached to check his ID again against his own list of authorized names. A third led the explosives-detecting canine around his car, and the fourth made the circuit in the opposite direction, inspecting the vehicle's undercarriage with a large mirror on an extended handle.

They waved him through and he continued into the resort. The grounds were expansive and lush, filled with trees, flowers, and ponds. He drove past part of its renowned 36-hole golf course, then turned down an oak-lined boulevard toward pillared, classical-looking buildings on a distant rise. More signs directed him into an underground garage. He descended three levels and parked. At the elevator, two more Secret Service officers sent him through a body scanner before phoning in his arrival.

Hunter emerged onto the top floor of the resort's headquarters, whose exterior—he discovered later—blended in with the ancient Roman architectural features of the surrounding structures. The woman at the front desk directed him down a hallway. He went through another Secret Service checkpoint outside the office of the company's president and entered the waiting room. There the boss's secretary announced his presence.

A moment later, Roger Helm, president and CEO of Helm International Resorts—and Independent candidate for President of the United States—emerged from his office.

2

Helm was a tall, square-jawed, broad-shouldered man of fifty-nine. His thick hair, combed to the side and almost white, retained only hints of blond. His eyes, deep-set and intensely blue, exuded an alert intelligence.

They exchanged greetings, smiles, and a firm handshake. Helm led him into a large, surprisingly spartan office that offered few clues about the private man. But two others stood waiting: one large, red-haired, and ruddy-faced; the other dark, slender, and dressed nattily. Helm led him first to the big man.

"Mr. Hunter, I'd like you to meet Emmett Ragan. Emmett, this is

Dylan Hunter from the *Inquirer.*" While they shook hands, Helm added, "Emmett is founder and president of Ragan Analytics—the company providing data management and analysis for my campaign. He's also a long-time friend, and one of my earliest and most generous backers."

Helm introduced the other man as Stanton Ott, his attorney. They sat on a small sofa and club chairs around a low table bearing a beverage service and fruit.

"My staff tells me you're interested in the politically inspired attacks on my campaign contributors," Helm began.

"That's right," Hunter said, pouring himself a cup of coffee. "My editor and I think it's an important story, possibly with broader implications."

Helm's eyes narrowed. "If you do, then you're pretty much alone among the media. But from what I've read of and about you, Mr. Hunter, you enjoy being a maverick."

"Being a maverick is just a consequence of what I do—not the objective."

"What's your objective?"

He took a sip before answering. "Old-fashioned journalism. I enjoy digging up and reporting important facts. Especially important *concealed* facts. That makes me a maverick only because too many in the media engage in selective concealing."

"What do you mean?" Ott prompted.

"A lot of Beltway reporters have political or ideological axes to grind. Rather than report the facts, they spin slanted narratives about the facts. They turn the daily news into morality plays, and cast them with their own sets of heroes, villains, and victims."

Helm nodded. "I've been on the receiving end of such 'narratives,' as you call them, for most of my career. But now they've targeted my supporters, too. Like Emmett here."

"Tell me about that, Mr. Ragan," Hunter said, taking out a pen and notepad.

The big man set his cup on the table.

"I've been supporting my old pal here"—he hooked a thumb at Helm—"months before he decided to run. Because I believe in him, and in what he stands for. My company did the initial polling and demographic analysis that persuaded Roger he had a real shot at the White House."

"Otherwise, I wouldn't have bothered to run," Helm interjected.

"Then, a month ago, this group, the 'Caring and Sharing Alliance,' held a news conference and released a report about 'Roger Helms's Billionaire Bosom Buddies.' My name was the first on their list."

"I saw some of that group outside the gate just a few minutes ago," Hunter said.

"That's when the media also began to refer to Roger as 'the Wolf of Washington,'" said Ott, the attorney. "And all at the same time—as if it was centrally coordinated. Of course, the nickname is a smear. Roger's a political novice who's never spent time in Washington."

Hunter glanced at Ragan. "I gather that news conference was just the beginning of the harassment you've experienced."

"To say the least. President Glover said at a news conference he hoped Congress would finally get serious about 'the corrupting influence of corporate money in politics.' That same afternoon, right on cue, a senator and congressman from his party announced hearings about it, and demanded the IRS and Justice Department investigate possible 'violations' of campaign finance laws by me, my company, and others who contributed substantially to Roger."

Helm said, "That's also when the demonstrators began showing up here, and outside Emmett's offices. And at the businesses of others on that 'Bosom Buddies' list."

"And that's not all," Ragan added. "Last week, I got this in the mail." He reached a big hand into his jacket, pulled out a folded paper, and handed it to Hunter.

It was a certified letter from the IRS—notification of an audit.

"Emmett is not the only one to receive one of those," Ott said. He drew a similar letter from his briefcase and slid it across the coffee table toward Hunter. "So has Roger. So, in fact, have all the contributors named on that 'Bosom Buddies' list. All within days of each other."

Hunter nodded slowly. It seemed like a replay of the organized campaign against businessmen and property owners in northwestern Pennsylvania.

"As Mr. Ragan said—right on cue."

"That certainly appears to be the case, Mr. Hunter," Ott said. "Somehow, it is all being coordinated."

"Any idea who's doing the coordinating?"

"One name keeps coming up. He seems to be linked to a lot of this," Ott said. "Lucas Carver. He runs a—"

"I know who he is," Hunter interrupted, recalling a file Wonk had compiled for him. "I've seen recent examples of his handiwork."

"But we don't really know for certain who is behind this," Helm added. "We were hoping you might look into that."

"Of course I'll look into it."

3

The meeting broke up a few minutes later, but Helm asked Hunter to stay behind after the others left. He poured them both another round of coffee, then sat back and appraised Hunter with those narrowed, intense blue eyes.

"How much do you know—or think you know—about me, Mr. Hunter?"

"You want me to recite your bio from memory?"

A little smile played on Helm's lips. "I'm curious to see if you've done your homework."

Hunter shrugged.

"You're the son of an Indiana district attorney. But you were bitten by the entrepreneurial bug in high school. You worked summer jobs in a real estate office, putting money aside to invest in property. You 'flipped' your third fixer-upper house by the time you entered the University of Chicago, where you studied economics and business administration. But besides being financially ambitious, you've also always been intellectually curious, too. You told one interviewer you were a voracious reader, and that you studied classical economists while continuing to build your property portfolio."

"You *have* done your homework. Please continue."

"After graduation, you married a girl from this area—"

"Helen."

"And you relocated your business here. And you became hugely successful. Your real-estate business grew almost exponentially, year after year. Ten years ago, people urged you to share your success secrets and business philosophy. That's when you wrote *The Win-Win Way*. Which became a *New York Times* bestseller."

Helm smiled. "Readers have been very kind to me."

"Anyway, somewhere along the way, you came up with this idea of creating a nationwide chain of internationally themed resorts. You started here, putting your flagship property within easy reach of Washington. But about that time, you started to get politically outspoken, too."

Helm nodded. "I was angry about all the regulatory burdens that slowed my company's progress. And the taxes that drained our expansion capital."

"Most political observers say the turning point for you, politically speaking, was when you attended that televised White House business roundtable three years ago. President Glover gave this speech about his policies, and when they opened it for Q&A, you challenged him. You had him trapped there, with all the TV cameras running. He couldn't ignore you, or cut you off, or leave without looking like a coward. You made him look like a fool."

"That wasn't much of a challenge. I had the assistance of the fools who taught him in college."

"Regardless, you embarrassed the sitting President of the United States, right in his own home. And that's when people started pressuring you to run for the presidency yourself. There was that cover story about you in *Newsweek:* 'The New Reagan?' But you refused all the overtures from the Republican Party."

"Both parties have contributed to our current mess. I told them thanks—but no thanks."

"So what happened to prompt you to run as an Independent?"

"You've got all the resumé details right, Mr. Hunter. But you haven't mentioned the most important thing about me."

"Which is?"

"My *why*."

"So tell me."

Helm's voice grew firm.

"I don't like what's happening to our country, Mr. Hunter. It frightens me. People are rejecting the essence of what made our nation great."

"Which is?"

"Hard work and peaceful trade. You know, a lot of people—especially the politicians, the press, and the professors—have never really *created* a damned thing of any use to anyone. They truly don't understand what it takes to produce something—and how to deal with people as traders, not takers."

"So they label a successful man like you 'The Wolf.'"

"I know. It's so frustrating, and so false. A wolf is a predator. But I don't prey on anyone. That's not how I make money. I make money by creating experiences that help millions of people enjoy themselves—and they pay me for doing that for them. It's 'win/win'."

Helm stood. "Here, let me show you what I mean."

He led Hunter to his broad office window. Below them spread a remarkable sight.

It was as if ancient Rome had been re-created here, in the Virginia countryside. Directly across a wide plaza, modeled after the famous Piazza Navona, stood an exact reproduction of the Pantheon. In the center of the plaza stood a to-scale copy of its iconic Fontana dei Quattro Fiumi—"Fountain of the Four Rivers." At the far end was a precise replica of the famous Trevi Fountain, against the backdrop of a classical structure.

Hunter had read about this, but seeing it up close was breathtaking.

"This is unbelievable," he said. "I've been to Rome several times. You've captured these iconic tourist spots perfectly."

"Thank you. That was my aim." Helm chuckled. "And it was all created from scratch. The only people I stole any of this from were the long-dead sculptors and architects of ancient Rome. The Pantheon, and the building over there behind the Trevi Fountain—those actually are the hotels for this part of the Helm Capitol International Resort. We've kept the architectural features of their public areas as authentic as possible, though the guest rooms have every modern convenience. You can't see it from here, but off to the right we have reproduced the Spanish Steps rising from the *piazza*. Our resort guests love to linger out there in the evenings, just as they do at the real one in Italy. At night, we set up vendor booths and shopcarts in the plaza. They're operated by Italian nationals and immigrants, and sell authentic goods from Italy."

They returned to their chairs.

"It's the same with the other geographical locales in this resort," Helm continued, "just as it is in the other resorts around the country. This locale is Italy. If you take our Venetian gondola ride along the canal starting on the other side of the Pantheon, it brings you past Tuscany vineyards, then through French vineyards, and into France. We've reproduced the Place de la Concorde as its central plaza. The Arc de Triomphe towers over one end—with a French restaurant inside the top—and on the other end is a copy of the Palais Garnier, transformed into the main hotel. We've reconstructed a few blocks of Paris's 'Left Bank' shops and cafes, and the Moulin Rouge to serve as the entertainment venue. And so it goes with our other 'nations' here: Holland, Japan, India, Argentina. Each built around famous, meticulously reproduced sites in the actual countries. Each with its own authentic cuisine, shopping, and entertainment. Each run by private entrepreneurs from those nations."

"As I say, it's incredible. Where did you get this idea?"

He smiled. "I come from the Midwest, about as far away from global culture as you can get. Once I became successful, I was able to travel the world. But I realized many people back home, like my parents, might never have such opportunities.

"So one day, looking at a map of America, I had this idea: Instead of transporting Americans to distant places, why not bring distant places to Americans? What if I could build, not your usual amusement parks, but a series of resorts—each offering five or six small-scale samples of different nations that most people would love to visit? And what if I could site those resorts across the country, so that at least one of them would be within a day's drive, at most? Then millions of Americans could take short 'foreign' vacations—even weekend or day trips—at a fraction of the cost, time commitment, and travel hassles of the real thing."

"It's a brilliant concept, Mr. Helm."

"Thanks. Our thirty-year plan is to place a Helm International Resort in an almost perfect geographic dispersal throughout the country, so that everyone can be within a day's drive of a resort."

"So, here you are, a wildly successful entrepreneur. You could just continue doing this, making money, enjoying your life. What made you decide to run for president?"

Helm raised his eyes to the window. He didn't speak immediately; he looked as if he had thought about this question a lot, and found it painful to contemplate.

"It's what I was saying. I couldn't stand it anymore," he said softly. "The thought of how America—the country that has given me so much—was being ripped apart by conflict. The fact that the candidates of both parties were just representatives of different warring tribes. That the candidates' only personal goal is power over other people, and that they seek it by inciting group against group, race against race, class against class. That they and their followers view life as takers—not traders."

His eyes were fixed, now, as if seeing the whole continent beyond his window.

"This is not for quotation, Mr. Hunter. Because I know how cynical people are, I know it wouldn't be believed, and I know it would only be mocked. But you see . . . I love my country. And I'm scared for its future. We have to stop this tribal warfare. I got into this race, not because I wanted power—God knows, unlike my rivals, the *last* thing I want is power over others. I never aspired to be a politician, let alone president. I have plenty of other things I could do, and that I'd prefer to be doing.

"I got in the race only because I felt I *had* to. Because nobody else seemed willing to do what had to be done. Because I thought I might be able to make a difference."

He blinked, as if returning to the room. Then looked at Hunter and spread his hands.

"Does that make sense? Do you know what I mean?"

Dylan Hunter stared back at him.

"I know exactly what you mean."

4

He left the office a few minutes later and made his way back to the garage. Before starting his car, he inserted the battery back in his phone and powered it on to check for text messages.

There was only one, from Danika at the office.

> *Call from Sgt. Cronin Arlington PD. Says urgent to meet here today. Noon?*

Hunter had half-expected this. Cronin was smart. He texted back an "OK."

Then started the car.

Then, backing out of the parking space, caught sight of his face in the rearview mirror.

Then noticed the scratch marks, still livid.

Then cursed.

He drove slowly out of the garage, back toward the traffic booths, thinking.

Passing the exit booths, he saw the bus and the demonstrators again. And had an idea.

He proceeded to a turnaround spot, then returned toward the entrance booths. He rolled to a stop near the bus. The demonstrators stopped chanting and eyed him suspiciously. A state trooper immediately trotted over as he rolled down the window.

"Sir, you can't park here."

He flashed his press credentials.

"I'm from the *Inquirer*. I'm here to interview the protesters."

The young trooper went over to confer with the officer who was no doubt his supervisor. The latter waved him an okay.

Hunter got out and walked toward the line of protesters.

"Hi. I'm Dylan Hunter from the *Inquirer*," he said to the guy with the bullhorn, obviously their leader. "We're doing a story about your protest. Wondered if I could ask you a few questions?"

"*That* fascist rag?" the guy replied. He was tall and wiry, with tendrils of lank, dark hair hanging in his eyes.

Hunter lowered his voice so that the nearby cops couldn't hear him.

"You calling me a fascist, you pathetic jerk?"

The guy blinked. A couple of women next to him gasped.

"Yeah, you miserable communist creep," Hunter went on. "Somebody oughta slap your ugly face." He turned to those nearby, raising his voice a bit. "And the rest of you anti-American losers, you need an ass-kicking, too."

That did it. The leader dropped the bullhorn and rushed him. Hunter seized his shoulders and maneuvered them both into the middle of the roiling gang.

He didn't bother to defend himself. He let them swing at him, grab his sports coat. He endured a few tolerable, amateur blows to his face, then yanked the leader to the ground as the cops rushed in to break it up. He held onto the guy, taking a few more punches as well as a few kicks from those standing over them.

When the cops finally separated them, Hunter tasted blood trickling from his nose. Felt stinging on his left cheek, some throbbing on his thigh. Checking, he saw his jacket was a dusty mess with a torn pocket. One knee of his trousers had grass stains, and his shoes were scuffed.

The cops put the group's leader in handcuffs while his gang screamed and cursed. The young trooper came back to him.

"You okay, sir? We can call an ambulance."

"No, I'm fine. Just a few scratches, nothing serious."

"We saw the whole thing. We've arrested the one who attacked you, and we'll get his name so that you can file—"

"No, I won't be filing charges. Really, it was my own damned fault. I provoked the guy. My editor will *kill* me if he finds out, and if this blows up with me becoming part of the story. Please, let him go."

"But, we witnessed—"

"Honestly, I said some things that provoked him. I'm sure the rest of them will confirm that. It was very unprofessional of me. Frankly, officer, I'm embarrassed about it. You'll be doing me a great favor just by dropping the whole thing. Would you do that for me, sir?"

The trooper went back to consult with his supervisor again. He saw the older cop look his way, shake his head in resignation, then say something to the one gripping the handcuffed guy. The officer removed the cuffs, and the leader returned to his group, glaring at him.

Hunter smiled and bowed grandly toward him. Then, as the crescendo of curses rose again, turned his back on them and headed toward his car.

Inside, he rechecked his face in the rearview mirror.

And grinned.

ELEVEN

When Emmalee Conn entered the sleek, modern lobby of the Four Seasons Hotel in Georgetown, she experienced another jarring, painful instant of nostalgia.

It was such a familiar venue. Ash had often met here with other senators and lobbyists for power lunches, private dinners, and public receptions. Sometimes he invited her along to charm them—"grease the wheels," as he liked to say. More than once the "charming" had gone beyond mere eye contact and promissory smiles over cocktails. Far beyond.

With Ash's eager encouragement, of course. He and she had enjoyed an "open" arrangement from the outset of their marriage. At night, in their big four-poster, they found it intensely erotic to share the most graphic details of their trysts and conquests. The "sharing" became more adventurous, and literal, whenever they traveled—which was a lot, because of Ash's seat on the Senate Foreign Relations Committee. They often joked about the committee name. Because once outside the country, they could relax in anonymity and safely enjoy the thrill of the hunt for a willing partner of either sex—sometimes a couple.

She checked her diamond-studded watch again; 11:20 a.m. Probably a mistake to show up early for the appointment with Avery Trammel. It would look anxious.

Well, damn it, she *was* anxious. And he already knew that.

But she had a feeling that he was anxious, too. No, not anxious—eager. She remembered how he held her in that garden outside the cathedral. How he pressed himself against her.

Okay, maybe she didn't know much about politics and all the boring policy stuff that so many people in this town obsessed about. But she knew men. She'd known since her early teens how much sexual power she had over guys. She'd polished her skills back during those scary days in her early twenties, when she'd been a struggling dancer in a Vegas musical revue.

That's where Ash, then a young congressman, had spotted her. He was in town on a speaking engagement at some convention. After the show, he'd come backstage for an introduction that the stage manager couldn't turn down. Then he treated her to a late dinner and lots of drinks. A single crazy night in his hotel room, and he'd become obsessed with her. He told her how he hated constantly having to put on a goody-goody front for the voters—how she made him feel wild and liberated from all the political phoniness—how, with her, he could be *himself*.

With Ashton Conn, she finally realized and relished the fact that her sexual power could master even powerful men. That power became intoxicating this past year, as she began to entertain the once-impossible fantasy of becoming *First Lady*. The tabloids and women's magazines were calling her "Washington's Cinderella girl."

But now, her entire Cinderella life and future was shattered. She'd spent the days since Ash's death at a former boyfriend's house, lost in a stupor of alcohol and pills. But they'd been fighting a lot, so that arrangement wouldn't last much longer, either. She knew she had to do something.

And so she was here.

Avery Trammel was one of the most important men in the country. A billionaire, and such a potent political force that she'd even seen Ash behave meekly around him. And at her worst moment, he'd come to her, like some fairy-tale rescuer. Offering to help her, to get her a place at the Watergate, no less.

She knew such offers didn't come without strings attached. She thought of his strong face and trim body, his power and money.

Well, maybe she'd like his kind of strings.

Maybe her Cinderella story wasn't over.

She crossed the lobby and found her way to a ladies' restroom. She stood before a mirror and removed her sunglasses to check her appearance.

Not great. But not terrible. Makeup around her eyes mostly hid the recent dark circles and crow's feet. Her lipstick, crimson and wet-glossy, looked fine. Her hair—she'd spent a bundle she could no longer afford at the hairdresser's yesterday, to give her lush blonde hair the kind of deliberately mussed, wild, just-got-out-of-the-sheets look she knew most men found sexy. Diamond pendant earrings, glittering under the lights.

The short red cloth coat, tailored to fit her curves, matched her lipstick well. She unbuttoned and opened it, then let it slide a bit from her shoulders. It revealed an even-shorter, sleeveless black cocktail dress with scarlet trim. Completely wrong for this time of the day. But just right for the occasion: for grabbing a man's attention. Her bare shoulders and arms looked tanned and tight and polished. She still had her long, trim dancer's legs. Her breasts quivered slightly beneath the thin fabric of the dress. He would notice that she wasn't wearing a bra. He would wonder about her panties. The thought brought a smile to her glistening lips.

She checked her watch again: 11:32 now. She buttoned up the coat. Then looked back into the mirror. Into her eyes.

Saw and felt her old confidence returning.

She decided she would give it another five minutes. Make him wait . . . just a bit.

"You can do this," she said defiantly to the face in the mirror.

2

Avery Trammel sat in a partitioned booth of the Bourbon Steak dining room, drumming his fingers on the tabletop. He checked his Rolex, surprised and irritated to see it was now nearly 11:40. He had specifically told the woman 11:30. He figured she was so desperate she would arrive at 11:15.

Avery Trammel did not like to be kept waiting, by anyone.

He heard voices in the direction of the entrance, then saw the hostess approaching with Emmalee Conn following.

He slid from the brown leather seat to his feet, then forced a smile. The smile became genuine as she neared, and he got a good look at her legs.

"Forgive me for being late," she said, smiling brightly. "You know how the cabs are."

He bent over her extended hand, caught a whiff of light floral perfume.

"It is quite all right, Mrs. Conn." He motioned toward the windows. "I was just appreciating the view of Rock Creek."

He helped her out of her coat, astonished—but pleased—by the little cocktail dress she wore. He brushed her bare shoulder with the back of his hand as he asked the hostess to take it to the coatroom. Then he seated her, noticing the hem of her skirt riding up her thighs. He returned to his side of the table, smiled, and studied her face.

"I must say, you are looking much better than . . . than you did on Saturday."

She smiled back at him. "Thank you, Mr. Trammel. I—"

"Please—Avery."

"Of course. And it's Emmalee." Another dazzling smile. "It's been hard, but I'm slowly returning to the land of the living."

"I see that. One must not surrender to circumstance."

She nodded. Held his eyes. "Thank you so much for your kindness at the funeral."

"I meant every word I said." He reached into his jacket pocket, removed an envelope, and slid it across the table toward her. "Before we enjoy our lunch, I want you to know that this morning I secured an apartment for you at the Watergate. You will find the paperwork and your keycards in there."

Her eyes widened and lips parted. "Oh, Avery! You didn't!"

"I did."

She blinked rapidly, staring at the envelope. "I didn't dare believe . . ."

He reached across the table, put his hand on hers.

"I mean what I say."

She looked up at him. Held his eyes again.

"I don't know how I'll ever be able to thank you."

He stared back, unsmiling now, rubbing the back of her hand gently with his thumb, letting her words hang unanswered for nearly half a minute. Finally, he turned away, searching the restaurant.

"Perhaps we should order some wine before lunch."

3

"Hell-o, Mr. Hun— *Holy crap! What happened?*"

Danika Cheyenne Brown shot to her feet, then charged out from behind her desk.

Hunter paused in the lobby entrance of Crown Office Suites, the "virtual office" he used for public contacts and as a mail drop. Before he could utter a word, the gorgeous African-American receptionist rushed to him, hands fluttering helplessly, words a tumbling torrent.

"Were you in some kinda accident? Y'all need a doctor? I can call—"

"No, no, it's okay! I'm fine, Danika. Take it easy! I just had a close encounter with some uncooperative interview subjects."

"Y'all got in a fight? Oh my God, y'all look *awful!*"

"But as always, *you* look fantastic, Danika. It happened earlier this morning, but I didn't have time to go home and clean up before my appointment with Detective Cronin. Has he arrived yet?"

"Yes, sir. He be— He's down in 117."

He laughed. "You know, when you're flustered, *y'all* start to sound like the folks back in your old 'hood."

Her mouth worked a few seconds, then she burst out laughing.

"You mean, I forget everything I learned in school from The Man."

"It doesn't matter. Whatever comes from those lovely lips is music to my ears."

If her skin weren't dark, he was certain he would have seen her blush. She dimpled up and grinned.

"Well, aren't you the sweet talker. I bet your pretty girlfriend hangs on every word."

"Ha. If only women would pay attention to what I say . . . Well, I'd better join the detective before he thinks I've stood him up. By the way, you didn't flirt with him when he arrived, did you?"

More dimples.

"You know, Danika, Melvin would be very upset to know you've got the hots for a handsome white cop."

An added giggle. "Y'all git on back there and mind your business."

"And y'all have a nice day."

4

Hunter found the door to 117 open.

As on a previous visit, Detective Ed Cronin stood at the window, back to Hunter, looking down toward the traffic and pedestrians on Connecticut Avenue. His short-cropped, balding scalp gleamed in the noon sunshine.

"Excuse me, officer, but may I borrow some ibuprofen?"

Cronin turned. His expression morphed from cold and hard to shocked and concerned in an instant.

"Holy crap! What happened to you?"

"Those were Danika's exact words, too."

Cronin approached. "You look like you've been in a brawl."

"Your formidable powers of detection never fail to impress me. I was out in Manassas this morning at the Helm Resort, to interview the boss—"

"Roger Helm?"

"Your Sherlockian skills of deduction haven't failed you, either. Anyway, I had a mix-up with a group of protesters. Well, actually, with one of them."

"*One* guy did this?" Cronin was searching his face carefully.

Hunter spread his hands. "Yeah. One guy. It was humiliating."

"And you let him?"

"Who do you think I am? Jason Statham?"

"Hunter, you killed Adrian Wolfe, an MMA champ, in a knife fight." The hardness was back in Cronin's face and voice.

"I told you, Ed, that was sheer dumb luck. He almost killed me. Remember? Hey, mind if we sit down? My leg still hurts."

They pulled a couple of office swivel chairs to face each other.

"So, to what do I owe the dubious honor of your visit this time?"

"Where were you Friday, mid-to-late afternoon?" A small notebook and pen had materialized in Cronin's hands.

"Ah. You're here detecting, not socializing." Hunter leaned back in the chair, looked at the ceiling. "Let me see. Friday . . . I was in Bethesda, at my apartment. I got up early, around five-thirty, worked out downstairs. Then made breakfast. Then worked on the research notes for my next *Inquirer* story. I got hungry again early, so around eleven I ordered in some Chinese. They promise delivery in less than a half hour. So, maybe around eleven-twenty."

"What restaurant?"

"Hey, what's with the inquisition?"

"I asked you a question."

Hunter sighed and told him. "Look, what's this all about?"

"You have any proof—a receipt, or the name of the delivery person?"

Hunter blinked at him. "Hell if I know. I suppose you can ask the restaurant for name of the delivery guy. And who keeps takeout receipts?" He frowned. "Wait a minute." He reached into his jacket, pulled out his wallet. "I paid the guy at the door, so maybe . . . yes. Here it is. I stuck it in here, with my change." He dug out a folded receipt, looked at it, and passed it over. "There you go. Time of order, 11:02. Delivery, 11:25."

"What about later in the afternoon? Can you account for your time?"

"About noon I went down to pick up the mail from my lobby box. I remember, because I chatted for a couple of minutes with the guard at the front desk. His name is Darius, if that helps. I asked him if he wanted any of my leftover Chinese, and he said no. I remember he asked if I was heading out to investigate some new story. I told him no, I was staying in to write up my next piece. Which I did: It ran on Sunday. I didn't go out till the evening, six or so. The swing-shift guard, Earl, saw me leave."

"You make any afternoon calls? Send out any emails? Anything with a time stamp on it?"

"I don't think so. I turn off my phone and browser to protect my writing time from interruptions. Cronin, what's going on? You find another stiff or something?"

"You know Morgan and Lila Jackson?"

"Sure," he smiled. "They're great people. I saw them just last week, at a Vigilance for Victims banquet." He stopped. "Wait, are they all right? Are you here—"

"Settle down. They're fine. You know about their case?"

"Of course. Their daughter was raped and murdered by some drug gang leader. In fact, they mentioned it again the other night, because they'd just heard that the killer is supposed to be getting an early release sometime soon. They asked if I would write something about it, create some publicity that might prevent it. I told them I'd check into it. Why?"

Cronin did his hard-stare thing. "You're telling me you don't know."

"Know what?"

"That Dixon was released on Friday."

"Damn it. So it's too late to do anything, then." He looked out the window. "Soon as you leave, I'll have to call them. Poor Lila. She was beside herself. I don't know how she'll—"

"And he got whacked the same afternoon."

Hunter whipped his head around. "What?"

Cronin didn't say anything. His eyes were riveted on Hunter's face.

"Oh, so *that's* why you're here. For God's sake, Ed, will you climb down off your hobby horse?"

"Seems you have no eyewitnesses or other confirmation to actually place you in your apartment at the time of the hit."

"Maybe because I'm not in the habit of arranging alibis for my writing sessions at home."

"I came here to see if you're willing to come down and participate in a lineup."

"What?"

Cronin gestured toward Hunter's face. "But with you looking all puffy like this, I don't think any witness IDs would be worth crap."

Hunter leaned in. "You mean someone *finally* got a good look at one of these vigilantes? That's a big break . . . Look, Ed, I know we have a history. But still, if you have anything to share, I'd be grateful if you'd feed it to me first, before the *Post* or somebody else gets—"

"You're really some piece of work, Hunter. Or whatever the hell your real name is. You're a really good liar. Some days, even *I* almost believe you have nothing to do with these killings."

"Gee, could that possibly be because I don't?"

"Bullshit."

"If you'd stop wasting your time on me, maybe you'd catch these guys."

"*Guy.* Singular."

That caught him unexpectedly. He sat back. "There's just *one* vigilante?"

"That's what me and my partner, Detective Erskine, think."

"But . . . but how could that be possible? I thought—"

"The latest hit. Just one guy. Just a handgun. Middle of the afternoon. He waltzes into Dixon's gang headquarters up in Baltimore. Single-handedly has a shoot-out with a whole bunch of them. Leaves Dixon and another gangster dead, puts another in the ICU with a slug in his gut. Goes hand-to-hand with three more and sends them to the E.R. Then walks out, nice as you please, and calmly drives away."

Cronin paused, staring at him, unblinking. "Just. One. Guy."

"That's . . . unbelievable. You really think—"

"You know what I think."

"For God's sake, Cronin! Look at me. I can't even defend myself against one skinny protester."

"And about that, I'm thinking: 'How convenient.'"

"'Convenient'? What do . . . Wait. Are you implying I *let* myself get beat up?" Hunter let his mouth hang open in disbelief. "Why in hell would I do something that stupid? It makes no sense."

"Oh, I don't know. It would make perfect sense, if you were trying to convince us you couldn't fight to save your soul. Which I and Adrian Wolfe found out you can. And maybe also hide signs of any injuries you received during the hit on Friday. See, you—okay, okay, the shooter—got into a fight with one of the gang. Turns out the shooter wore a blond wig and fake beard that came off during the fight. Turns out we have witnesses saying he had dark hair." He gestured toward Hunter's head. "One says, 'dark curly hair.'"

"So *that's* why you're here. And that's all you've got?"

Cronin stood. His smile stayed out of his eyes.

"Who says that's all we've got?"

5

Hunter remained in his chair for a moment after Cronin left.

He had to hand it to the guy. He was good. And relentless.

A lot like himself.

In another world, they'd be good friends. Maybe be working together, on the same team. He'd had buddies like that out in the field. Guys you could always trust to watch your six. Like the SOG operator who saved his butt when that warehouse bomb went off in Kandahar . . .

He stood. Cronin would be watching him closely again, because now he smelled blood in the water. So it would take some new trick to throw him off the scent. Meanwhile, he'd have to lie low.

He left the room and walked down the hall to the reception area. Danika stood at a file cabinet, her back to him.

"So, did you give him your phone number on his way out?" he teased.

She spun around. "Oh, you! Now you stop that!"

"I know it's hard, Danika, but you have to be a good girl. Remember, Detective Cronin is a married man. Remember, Melvin is your little

Tyrone's daddy. You *do* remember Melvin, don't you?"

"Yeah, yeah. I remember."

"Such enthusiasm."

"Oh—you got a call while you were talking to him."

She glided like a runway model to her desk, her spiky heels *clip-clopping* across the marble, then swooped into her chair and swiveled to her message pad.

"Yes, here . . . A Mr. Lasher called to say hello."

He searched his memory. "He said Lasher? I don't think I know anyone by that name."

"He said you may not recall him. He told me to remind you that he's the gentleman who met you over a year ago, out in Linden, Virginia. He said he also ran into you outside the EPA some months ago, and then again not long ago outside the Starbuck's at Connecticut and K."

Hunter worked at controlling his breathing and facial muscles.

"Of course. How could I forget . . . Did Mr. Lasher say anything else?"

"Just that he's been enjoying getting to know you and wants to meet you again, very soon."

She swung around, extending the pink note.

"He left his phone number."

TWELVE

Before leaving the office suite, Hunter ducked into the men's restroom. He washed his hands slowly, mechanically, trying to puzzle it out.

He recalled this "Lasher" from the previous encounters. The first time was almost exactly one year ago, on that road near the CIA safe house in Linden. The guy had been in camo, carrying a rifle and handgun. Later, Garrett, Annie, and he concluded Lasher had to be a sniper dispatched to silence the CIA mole, Muller—except Hunter beat him to it. So he had to be working for the Russians.

Then, six weeks ago, he'd spotted Lasher shadowing him outside the EPA. And again, only a week ago, Lasher had somehow tracked him right here.

After what he had done to the Russians in Afghanistan, they'd tried to kill him and almost succeeded. He'd always worried they might try again, if they could find him—which was why he vanished and changed his identity.

Well, now they'd found him again. And put a professional assassin on his tail. Somehow they had cracked his cover and knew he maintained an office here. Somebody at the *Inquirer* probably blabbed.

But what else did they know? If they knew about his Bethesda apartment or Maryland house, or Annie's house, and their goal was to take him out, Lasher probably could have done that already. So maybe his journalism cover, and this office, were all they knew about his life.

Still . . . something was off.

He'd only seen one guy tailing him, Lasher. Not a surveillance team.

Why wouldn't the Russians deploy a full team?

Something else was nagging at him.

He stood still, hands dripping over the sink, staring blankly into the mirror, trying to wrap his head around it. He went through each of the encounters, step by step, trying to put his finger on any anomalies.

Then it hit him.

The meeting at the EPA, six weeks ago . . .

That morning, he'd taken the Metro directly from his apartment to the meeting at Nature Legal Advocacy. He was sure nobody had been following him then. He *knew* he was clean when he visited, then left the environmental group's offices on 15th Street. After that, he'd grabbed lunch at a restaurant near McPherson Square, to go over his notes in prep for the EPA encounter. Then he took the Metro again to the Federal Triangle stop, right outside EPA headquarters. It was only then and there, just as he arrived for his two p.m. meeting with the administrator, that he picked up the tail.

Lasher had gotten there ahead of him. Waiting for him.

How did he know where Hunter would be, ahead of time . . . unless somebody told him?

He knew that after his testy morning meeting at Nature Legal Advocacy, its president, Gavin Lockwood, had called EPA administrator Jonathan Weaver to warn him what to expect before Hunter arrived for their afternoon meeting. Either of them could have told Lasher. But they were only two players in the extensive political network he had uncovered. After meeting with Lockwood, word would have spread quickly throughout that network that Hunter was investigating them.

Anyone in that network could have tipped off Lasher.

So didn't that mean one of them was working with the Russians?

He thought of the message Lasher just left him. If he *is* a Russian assassin, and targeting him, why would he be taunting him and asking for a meeting? In effect *warning* him in advance? That made no sense. Just as it made no sense that Lasher appeared to be operating alone.

Then he understood.

A contractor.

That made more sense. Not a Russian national, but a deniable operator hired by the Russians to hit Muller. And now hired to go after *him*.

But much of the rest still didn't make sense.

After a moment, he had to give it up. He needed more information. And there was only one way to get it.

2

He pulled out the message slip, his latest burner, and a fresh battery. He tapped in the number.

The phone rang for about twenty seconds before it was answered.

"You're interrupting my lunch, Mr. Hunter." A mocking tone. A hint of a Southern drawl.

Hunter spoke in Russian. *"Yesli poyedish vnizu v fud-korte, vstrechimsya seychas."* "If you're eating downstairs in the food court, we could meet right now."

"What?"

Again in Russian: "Are you afraid to meet me right now, tough guy? Or can't you speak Russian?"

"Stop playing games, asshole." The cockiness was gone. "Speak English."

Not a Russian, then. Definitely an American contractor.

"Your cover is blown, and you know it," Lasher went on. "And you know *I* know it. I could expose you any time I want."

Hunter reverted to English. "So, you want money?"

Lasher hesitated. Which meant he had to think about how to respond. Which meant it *wasn't* about money.

"That depends," he replied.

"On what?"

"On you meeting me today."

"Why do you want to meet me?"

"Look, pal, you're not calling the shots here! *I* am. You don't really have a choice, now, do you? So, you're going to do exactly what I say."

Hunter gave it a few seconds. *Let him think he's got me.*

"All right. I'll meet you. But I know enough about you, Mr. Lasher, to set some ground rules. It's going to be in a nice, safe, public place. And not today. Tomorrow."

"Just a damned—"

"I'll call you on this number tomorrow morning at nine," Hunter said. Then he broke the connection before Lasher could say another word.

He immediately shut down his burner. Removed the battery and SIM card. Wrapped the phone in a damp paper towel after wiping it down. Dumped it in the bathroom trash receptacle.

Moving quietly and cautiously, he took the stairs all the way down from the tenth floor into the basement garage. He moved warily from the stairwell to the nearby spot he'd reserved for one of his three vehicles—the BMW 7 Series High Security sedan. He entered the armored vehicle quickly. Locked the doors. Sat in silence for a moment.

First, Cronin.

Now, Lasher . . .

3

At 0855 the next morning, Lasher put the battery and SIM card back into his burner and powered it up.

At 0900, a text message came through.

He read it and swore.

At 1130 hours, as instructed, he was standing at the curb outside the L'Enfant Plaza Metro entrance near 17th and C Street, with a copy of the *Inquirer* in his left hand. A new text *pinged* through, telling him to look for a silver Honda Civic. It pulled up within two minutes. The guy rolled down the passenger window.

"Are you Mr. Lasher who ordered the Uber?"

"I guess so," Lasher snapped, getting in the back and tossing the newspaper onto the seat. He fastened his seat belt as the driver pulled out into the mid-day traffic. "So where you taking me?"

The college-aged kid met his eyes in the rearview mirror, looking surprised.

"You don't know?"

"I asked, didn't I?"

"Sorry. The message said I'm taking you to the Gaylord Hotel. At the National Harbor."

Lasher shut his eyes and swore some more.

This was not going at all as he had anticipated.

Fifteen minutes later, they were in the sprawling National Harbor complex bordering the Potomac River south of the city. The driver wound his way along Waterfront Street, past shops and eateries, then into the entrance of the Gaylord National Resort & Convention Center. He pulled under the broad, six-lane porte-cochère, stopped, then turned to him, gesturing with his phone.

"The gentleman meeting you just contacted us. He asked you to text him when you arrive."

Lasher glared at him and got out, taking care to tug his leather jacket down over the Glock 17 in the waistband holster at his back. He stomped across the other parking lanes, ignoring the greetings of the valets, and marched into the hotel lobby. There he paused to text Hunter: *"Well???"*

The reply came a few seconds later. More instructions. Steaming, Lasher stormed across the spacious, modern lobby and turned right.

He found himself in a cavernous atrium of jaw-dropping dimensions. Fifteen or twenty stories of hotel rooms rose behind him and on either side, their balconies overlooking the atrium. Directly ahead, a massive glass wall, presenting a grand view of the Potomac, soared skyward to meet the enormous glass ceiling that arched high overhead.

The bar lounge where he stood served a few customers seated on upholstered yellow chairs and brown sofas around glass tables. The lounge occupied a broad balcony overlooking what appeared to be a miniature indoor village one floor below. In its middle sat two small, quaint brick structures made to appear like two-story houses with chimneys. Surrounding them were trees, flowers, and brick walkways lit by old-fashioned street lamps. Just beyond, a fountain sprayed gaily, attracting tourists and noisy kids.

He rode a side escalator down to that lower level. Directly under the upstairs lounge he found the National Pastime Sports Bar & Grill. It offered outside seating at small cafe-style tables. A customer at an isolated table wore mirrored sunglasses, denim jacket, jeans—and was eating a salad. The man looked up as he approached, put down his fork, and smiled.

"Buy you lunch, Mr. Lasher?"

4

It was the first time Hunter had seen Lasher up close. Big guy, about six-three. Thick shoulders, narrow waist. Clearly a gym rat. The battered knuckles of a boxer or martial artist.

Lasher looked down at him and sneered. "What happened to your face?"

"You should see the other guys." He motioned to the chair opposite him.

The man dragged the chair around so that his back would be to the glass wall of the restaurant. As he settled into the seat, for just an instant the reflecting glass revealed a tell-tale bulge beneath the lower back of his jacket.

"Seriously, order whatever you want. This may be the last time I'll be nice to you." He gestured with his fork toward his salad. "Their salmon Caesar is good."

"I'm not hungry." Lasher didn't smile. His eyes were the color of a winter sky, pale and cold and dead.

"Then at least let me buy you a beer. A salute to a worthy adversary."

He saw a faint spark in Lasher's eyes. *So, flattery works. Good to know.*

"All right. Sure." Lasher motioned to a nearby server who took his order for a Guinness. Hunter asked her for a refill on his coffee and ordered a sandwich to go. They watched her retreat back inside the restaurant.

"You're not what you pretend to be," Lasher began.

"And you're not what you think you are."

Hunter saw the flash of anger. The guy had thin skin. So if he was going to learn anything from him, he couldn't remain adversarial.

"But hey, let's play nice," he transitioned, offering a smile. "I'm sure you're as curious about me as I am about you."

"I know a lot already. I know 'Dylan Hunter' is a fake name. I know you killed a guy, hand-to-hand, last Christmas—it was in the papers. But I also know you were the shooter at Linden last year who took out that *traitor*, Muller."

The way he stressed *traitor* was interesting.

"What's 'Linden'? Who's 'Muller'? And what do you mean, I 'took him out'?"

"Oh, give me a break! I have eyes. I was there and saw you out on the road after you nailed him with that cannon you were toting—looked like a Barrett .50." He smirked. "Besides, if you really didn't know what I was talking about, you would've ignored my message and you wouldn't be here. So let's not fool around."

Ingrained CIA training taught Hunter never to blow his cover by admitting anything. But denial now seemed pointless. He needed to learn who hired Lasher and why—and he wouldn't learn anything if he didn't swap a bit of info with the guy.

"All right. Sure, that was me."

"So you're a trained sniper. Like me."

"Probably not much like you."

Lasher's jaw tightened. "You think you're hot shit. If I'd had that Barrett .50, I'd have nailed Muller myself, and we wouldn't be having this conversation . . . So, who were you working for?"

"Actually, it was a Barrett M99 in .416. And maybe I wasn't working for anyone."

"You mean—what? That you shot him for no reason?"

"Of course I had a reason. A personal reason."

Lasher nodded slowly. "I wondered about that. About who would have sent you. I couldn't figure it out."

"But in your case, it wasn't personal at all. You were hired for a contract hit."

Lasher shrugged. "Oh, it was a bit personal, I suppose. I hate traitors." He smirked again. "But you're right. In that case, money was the bigger motivator."

"And the Russians certainly have plenty of that." He watched Lasher's eyes closely as he said it.

Just an instant of puzzlement before he caught himself. "*Oh*, yeah. The Russians do have plenty of that."

A lie.

So, it wasn't the Russians?

The server returned with the beer, coffee, and a bag containing his sandwich. He opened the bag and checked it while Lasher took a long draught, draining nearly half the glass.

Hunter decided to play along with the lie.

"If the Russians hired you," he ventured, spearing a chunk of salmon, "you must have established quite a rep."

"You better believe it. Anybody needs a shooter, they call for me. And I get top dollar."

"Where did you train? Quantico? Lejeune?"

Lasher snorted. "Jarheads." He took another sip.

"Benning, then."

He looked off into space and shrugged.

So—Army sniper school.

"You see any action while in uniform?"

A scowl. "Sure. But that was a long time ago. I'm my own boss, now."

The scowl was interesting.

Hunter nodded. "I get that. But what I don't get is why the Russians are sending you after *me*."

Surprised, Lasher turned back to him and laughed. "What makes you think *they* sent me?"

"Who else?" Hunter scooped up his last piece of salmon.

Lasher stopped smiling. It was obvious that he was weighing his next words carefully.

"You've made lots of enemies. Any one of them might have a motive."

"I suppose. But most don't have the money to hire a contractor. And you said you get top dollar."

"You're assuming a lot. What makes you think somebody hired me to whack you? You had it right earlier, on the phone. You're afraid I'll expose you. You came here to pay me and make that threat go away."

"So this is nothing but a shakedown, then. And you're here to arrange the payoff."

"That's right." Lasher smirked. It seemed to be his favorite facial expression. He drained the last of his beer.

Hunter put down his fork, wiped his mouth with his napkin, and sat back.

"Bullshit."

Lasher's pale blue eyes hardened again.

"What do you mean, 'bullshit'?"

"For one thing, you were waiting for me that day when I visited the EPA. Somebody tipped you in advance that I'd be going there. You were working for that someone."

Lasher didn't respond.

"Then you located the office on Connecticut where I hang my hat. If you only had blackmail on your mind, you wouldn't have wasted what must have been days or weeks staking it out, waiting for me to show up. You would have left me a message to arrange this meeting much sooner."

Lasher remained silent.

"Another thing. Reporters aren't rich. We're lousy blackmail targets. High risk for low reward—certainly not the kind of a payday you're used to. Besides, blackmail isn't your gig. You're a killer, Mr. Lasher. A hired gun. But you couldn't take me out at my office, not with cameras and hundreds of people around. And if you knew where I lived, you'd have already taken a run at me there. So your only play was to get me to expose myself. Get me to meet you."

Holding Lasher's eyes, Hunter took the food bag from the table and placed it on the floor next to his chair. Then leaned in to speak quietly, keeping his left hand under the table.

"Except I insisted on meeting here, in a public place. Now you hope to tail me from here to some isolated spot where you can do the job"—he gestured overhead—"away from surveillance cameras." His eyes drifted down Lasher's body. "Why, you're even packing a pistol for the occasion." He grinned. "Of course, so am I."

Lasher's eyes widened a little at that. "You're bluffing."

Hunter held the grin. "You didn't think a pro like me would meet you unarmed, did you? I've got a Sig P228 under the napkin on my lap, aimed right at your gut."

He could tell Lasher believed him. He went on.

"So. Somebody's hired you to take me out. Probably somebody among the rich and powerful I pissed off recently. Have I got it all about right, Mr. Lasher?"

Lasher leaned in, too. Their faces were just a foot apart, now.

"You really do think you're hot shit," he said softly, eyes boring into Hunter's. "But you're not as smart as you think. You got a few things wrong. Yeah, I'm being paid to follow you. But nobody's paying me to *kill* you."

Hunter shook his head. "It's obvious you aim to kill me."

Lasher's jaw muscle was working. It was obvious he was struggling not to say too much. But he couldn't help himself.

"You weren't listening. I said: Nobody's *paying* me to do that. You say you shot Muller because it was personal. Well, when you took him out, it became personal for *me*." Lasher's balled-up right fist rested on the table, the gnarled knuckles bone-white. "I was paid quite a lot to shoot Muller. Only two people know I didn't. Me . . . and you."

"So, you're worried I'll rat you out," Hunter said. Then, seeing the hatred in Lasher's eyes, he understood. "No, wait—it's not that at all. It's really because I finished a mission that you *failed*. You can't stand that, can you?"

"Shut up!" Lasher growled, teeth bared.

"Sure, that's it. Lasher, the famous international assassin. They gave you a big assignment with a big payday—but I beat you to it . . . That must gall you, huh?"

"I said shut up!"

"And it must have *really* pissed you off that I was able to lose you while you were tailing me—not just once, but twice."

Lasher swore and looked poised to rise.

"Now, now, Mr. Lasher. Remember the Sig in my lap. And all the surveillance cameras watching us. I don't think it would benefit either of us to bring EMTs and cops into this."

"I'm gonna nail your ass, you son of a bitch."

"Better men than you have tried. Of course, in your case, that's not a high bar to hurdle."

Lasher sucked in a deep breath, fighting to regain control.

"You're so tough, why don't you prove it? Why don't we go somewhere private? No guns—just bare-handed. Only one of us walks away, and he gets to keep the rest of his life, and all his secrets. So how about it? You have the balls to fight me—winner takes all?"

Staying close and keeping eye contact, Hunter pretended to be thinking it over while his left hand, unseen, slipped the Sig from his lap into a deep pocket inside his jacket. At the same time, he casually moved his right hand near Lasher's empty beer glass. He sighed, shook his head.

"I'll take a rain check."

Then, gripping the edge of the table with his left, he rose suddenly while simultaneously grabbing the beer glass with his right. The entire table, including his hot cup of coffee, tipped over and spilled onto Lasher's lap. The killer jerked backward instinctively, while Hunter reached down and dropped the beer glass into the open food bag.

"Shit!" Lasher yelped and shot to his feet, sending his own chair tumbling. Plates, water glasses, and the coffee cup shattered noisily on the brick floor.

"I'm sorry! I'm so sorry!" Hunter shouted. Everyone nearby turned, and the server rushed over to them.

"Goddamn you!" Lasher yelled, grabbing a napkin from the floor to wipe the coffee and water splashed over his shirt, jacket, and jeans.

"It's my fault," Hunter said to the server. He pulled out his wallet and peeled off a hundred-dollar bill plus a fifty. "Here, miss—this should cover the meal plus the damages, and the fifty is for your extra trouble."

"Oh, you don't—"

"No, please take it. Is there a men's room nearby where my friend can tidy up?"

"Of course. Right inside. Here, sir, I'll show you."

Lasher glared at him. "No, I'm fine. It's okay."

Hunter said, "I'll go fetch a towel and broom to clean up my mess."

"Sir, you don't have to do that. It's our job."

"I insist. I'll see the bartender and be right back."

Before Lasher could move, he grabbed his bag from the floor and darted inside. He headed first toward the bar, then veered away into a run. It was a big place he'd scouted in advance. He ducked out another exit, then walked quickly to the elevator. Through the glass walls of the rising cage he could see the entire atrium. No sign of Lasher. He'd be searching inside the bar.

He got off on the tenth floor, proceeded down the hall, and took out a keycard. Then entered the room he had booked the previous day.

Moving to the closet, he changed into an expensive suit, tie, and wingtip shoes. He dumped his denims, boots, shades, plus the bag with the beer glass into a roll-aboard overnight bag.

In the bathroom, he put on a latex facial disguise, with a blond wig and mustache. He obscured the still-visible wounds with some flesh-toned makeup. Donned a pair of eyeglasses. Checked his handiwork in the full-length mirror.

He called down to the valet station and asked them to bring his car around. Then phoned the front desk and told the receptionist that, due to a change of plans, he'd be checking out immediately.

"I hope you enjoyed your stay with us, Mr. Grayson," she said.

"I did indeed."

Hunter rode the elevator to the first floor and rolled his overnight bag toward the main entrance.

Lasher stood in the middle of the lobby, turning slowly. Scanning for a dark-haired guy in denim.

Hunter didn't look at him. Thinking "I am a wealthy financial planner," he strode confidently right past him, barely twenty feet away. Outside, he handed his claim check and a generous tip to the valet.

Then he entered his waiting BMW and drove off, without a backward glance.

THIRTEEN

When Emmalee opened the door, she was surprised to see Avery Trammel standing alone in the hallway. He wore casual-but-expensive clothes: black shirt, slacks, and loafers. He gripped a bottle of champagne by its neck.

"I regret that Julia cannot join us this evening," he said. "When I called to arrange this little house-warming party, I did not realize she would have a schedule conflict. She will be out tonight until quite late." He smiled at her, pointedly. "I hope you are not disappointed."

Despite his age, he looked dashing. Slim. Self-assured. Cocky.

"No, not at all . . . I mean, I'm sorry she can't join us, of course." She smiled at him slowly. "Perhaps another time."

"Of course."

She let him in. "Forgive the mess. I'm still unpacking. At least I have my furniture in place. Thank you for the bubbly. Why don't you put it over on the counter?"

"Certainly . . . Does the apartment suit you? If not—"

"Oh, no! I love it!"

She strolled over to the floor-to-ceiling glass doors leading to the balcony. She felt his eyes on her as she moved, glad she'd decided on a short red skirt and matching heels instead of slacks. The dusk sky held a faint, glowing memory of the day. Below, the Friday evening traffic hugged the curves of the Potomac, and the lights of the city sparkled all the way to the horizon.

"What a gorgeous view."

"It certainly is," he said behind her, a slight stress in his voice.

She smiled to herself and remained silent, letting the tension mount.

"Perhaps I should open the bottle now," he said.

"Perhaps you should," she said, without turning.

In a moment she heard the pop, the clink of glass-on-glass as he poured.

"Where would you like it, Emmalee?"

"Why don't you bring it over here, Avery?" she answered, still not turning.

She heard his footsteps behind her.

So, this is how it's going to be . . .

2

Café Normandie looked out upon Main Street, just a few blocks up from the Annapolis city dock. It was a local favorite for its Old World ambiance, superb French cuisine, and excellent wine list. To get good seating on a Friday evening, Hunter had to make the reservation well in advance.

They faced each other across a table of gray marble, in a booth of dark oak. Above the matching wainscoting, rough plaster walls rose to a ceiling of exposed oak beams. Though the walk from the parking spot had been chilly, they now enjoyed the warmth of the glassed-in fireplace, which stood on a stone base in the middle of the dining room.

He looked up from the menu to catch Annie staring at his face, shaking her head.

"What?"

"I'm sure glad you warned me in advance about how you got those scratches and bruises. Otherwise, I would have thought . . ." She let the thought trail off.

"That I had broken my promise," he finished. "That I'd gone after another target."

She nodded.

"I told you: The Vigilante has retired."

She shrugged. With her, even a simple movement like that was so graceful that he found it erotic. Like himself, she was dressed casually: a tailored jacket of chestnut suede over a white blouse and snug brown slacks. Strands of her deep auburn hair glowed red in the soft light of the wall sconce.

"But while I may look awful, you are a vision, Annie Woods."

Her gray cat's eyes sparkled. "Thank you. I just hope this fight doesn't leave you with any more scars."

"Aw, you *love* my scars. Maybe I'll add an eye patch, and you can pretend I'm a pirate. *Arrrrrgh.*"

She laughed.

"Dylan . . . do you think Cyrano will be okay out on the sun porch till we get back?"

"Oh, sure. Nothing valuable out there for him to chew on. And that lets Luna have the run of the house."

She nodded. But still looked pensive.

"You look far away," he said.

She gave her head a little shake. "Sorry. Just bringing work thoughts to dinner with me."

"So how's it going?"

"Grant seems more worried by the day. Over the reorganization"—she lowered her voice and leaned in—"and over the mole. He's been brooding and not talking much."

"Maybe we can invite him for dinner again next week. I could try to draw him out."

"We could. You're good at that, Dylan."

"I'm just sorry we can't spend all day together tomorrow," he said. "But I have to attend that funeral for Wonk's friend. I'll be back by mid-afternoon, though."

"That's okay. I brought a good thriller to read . . . It's so nice to have an evening's break like this. It takes my mind off the investigation. I'll have to stay at my place and work overtime all next week."

"Then let's enjoy tonight." He gestured toward the menu. "Have you decided?"

"Well, I'm in a French restaurant; they're playing French-café accordion music over the sound system; and I'm sipping French Chardonnay. Should I go rogue and order a burger and fries?"

"*French* fries? *Peut-être.* But I think they stopped serving burgers at lunch."

"Well, then, I'll just have to suck it up and settle for the Scallops Provençale."

"Excellent choice, *mademoiselle*. May I suggest we start with the Baked Brie?"

"Mais oui, monsieur . . . Et pour vous?"

"I'm in the mood for their Angus Steak with Bordelaise Sauce."

He motioned to their waitress and she came to take their order.

Then he raised his glass of Château Greysac.

"To the love of my life," he said softly.

She raised her glass to touch his.

"To my man."

They drank, holding each other's eyes.

After a moment, she said, "You know . . . we haven't discussed our plans lately."

"No. I guess we haven't," he said, swirling and studying the wine in his glass.

"Such as, when and where we'll have the wedding. What kind of honeymoon we want." She looked down for an instant, then back up at him. "And about maybe having a family."

He felt his heart beat faster. "Yes. We need to set aside some time to do that."

"What about now?"

He nodded slowly, but remained silent.

"What's wrong?" she asked, looking at him closely.

He forced a smile. "Not a thing. I'm fine."

"No, something *is* bothering you. Every time I bring up the wedding, you get distant."

"I'm sorry. I've been a bit preoccupied with something."

"Something? What?"

He took a deep breath.

"I'm being tailed by somebody. For the past several weeks."

Her eyes widened. "Who?"

"It's the guy from the Linden safe house. The other shooter."

"What?" She almost dropped her wine glass.

"Shhhh! Take it easy. It's okay. I—"

"What do you *mean*, 'okay'? Why didn't you tell me this?"

"Because of how you're reacting right now. I didn't want to scare you."

"*Shouldn't* I be scared?"

He shrugged. "Maybe. I don't know. But after what I've already put you through—first with Adrian Wulfe, then with Boggs . . ." He stopped. "I just need to make sure you're safe, until I can deal with this."

"'Deal with this.' You mean deal with *him*. Like you always do."

"Annie, please. That's not what I meant, at all. Let me explain. You see, he saw me out there that day. And I think he must have recognized my face, maybe on TV or in the *Inquirer*. Once he knew who I was, he found out about my office downtown and tracked me there. Probably through the newspaper. So, I confronted him the other day. In a public place, where it was perfectly safe. I needed to know who he was, who he is working for, how much he knows about me . . . and if he knows about *us*."

"And?"

"And he doesn't. He doesn't know anything about my past, or where I live, and I'm certain he doesn't know about us. Now, we have to find out who *he* is."

"Just how are we supposed to do that?"

"During our meeting, I managed to get his fingerprints. They're on a beer glass. And probably his DNA, too, because he drank from it. I have it back at the house. Since this guy knew about the Linden safe house, Grant will definitely want to find out who he is. And when that happens, I'm sure the Agency, or the FBI, will be able to deal with him, and leave us out of it."

"That's your plan?"

"That's my plan. I mean it. And you can help." He reached across and put his hand on hers. "Do you think you could ask Grant to run his prints and let me know what he finds out?"

She stared at him a moment. Swallowed hard.

"All right."

"Until then . . . remember. This guy doesn't know about us. About you. And we need to keep it that way. So for the time being"—he hesitated, then plunged ahead—"we can't tell your dad about us, or go public about our engagement.

Something died in her eyes.

"Annie, really, it'll be only a brief postponement of the announcement, until they find out who this guy is, who hired him and why—and arrest them."

"Sure," she said dully. "Just like you 'briefly postponed' the announcement last month—because that Damon Sloan guy sent thugs after you. And when Boggs planted the bomb in our cabin."

His mind flashed back to the sight of the booby-trapped bomb above the door of their cabin in the Allegheny Forest. The bomb that had almost killed her, right before his eyes . . .

"Annie . . ." he began, then stopped.

She raised her eyes to him; they were the color of an overcast sky.

"It will always be like this. Won't it."

It wasn't a question.

"Of course not," he said, squeezing her hand and grinning. "You know how much I want to marry you. Don't you remember my extravagant Valentine's Day proposal?"

It evoked barely a flicker of a smile. "I remember."

"Well, then. It's only a matter of time."

She shook her head slowly.

"I wish I could believe that, Dylan."

3

"Hey, Betsy! . . . Here, Betsy! . . . Come on, girl!"

Bob Jenkins clapped his hands and whistled, wondering where the hell his young Lab Retriever had run off to. It was her first spring off the leash out here in the woods, and he needed to get her trained before this year's small-game season. He heard a couple of distant barks, so he trudged down off Forest Service Road 209, right where it crossed the little bridge over Otter Creek.

Bob had lived in the Allegheny National Forest over twenty years, moving from northeast Ohio over here to Pennsylvania after his wife, Ginger, died of the breast cancer. He needed peace after that ordeal. And he found it in the Allegheny. He'd always liked the woods and hunting. Plenty of small game, and lots of deer and bear out here.

He'd bought himself a fixer-upper for a good price about a mile away, but decided to hike down here today because this stretch of woods was so isolated. Betsy could run loose without crapping up any neighbor's yard. He saw her footprints in the mud, so he followed them along the creek bank, keeping up his calling and whistling. But no barks, now. She must've gotten into something interesting. Long as she didn't tangle with some bear. They were out of hibernation, now, some with cubs. Which is why he carried his Mossberg loaded.

He heard a *yip* just up ahead, over a little rise. He whistled again, but she wouldn't come. He headed toward the sound, following ruts from somebody's ATV through the weeds. He saw a big old lone maple sticking up from the weeds and bushes. Getting closer, he caught sight of her yellow coat moving around underneath it. He stomped over, kicking rocks and trying to loosen the mud from the soles of his boots.

Betsy had her nose down and her tail was wagging furiously. He saw what looked like a heap of rags at the base of the tree trunk.

"What you got there? Come here, you bad girl!"

The dog turned around and loped toward him, dragging what looked like a branch in its jaws. She ran right up to him. He leaned down to see what she was carrying.

Something fell in the pit of his stomach. He almost dropped the shotgun.

Betsy's jaws held a long, skinny bone.

The bone ended in the skeletal fingers of a human hand.

PART II

FOURTEEN

"Thank you so much for attending, Dylan."

Wonk looked up at Hunter, reddened eyes visible through his dirty lenses. A smudge of cream cheese glistened at the corner of his mouth.

Just before the end of Arnold Wasserman's service in the local Jewish funeral home, Wonk had left the chapel to embark upon the arduous thirty-yard expedition to its social hall, where the lunch reception was prepared. Before any other guests arrived, he already had made multiple pilgrimages to the food and dessert tables. Wonk could not risk a mere steel folding chair at one of the guest tables. Instead—accompanied by three paper plates piled perilously with slabs of cold cuts, mounds of potato and macaroni salad, a heap of cream-cheese-smeared bagels, fat wedges of Key lime pie, and thick blocks of chocolate cake—he occupied the entirety of a sofa on the periphery of the room.

"I'm honored you invited me, Wonk." Hunter pulled over a folding chair and sat facing him. "How are you holding up, my friend?"

A ripple, meant to be a shrug, flowed across the shoulders of his navy-blue sports jacket, which was the approximate size and configuration of a tribal teepee.

"It has been difficult. I cannot believe that Arnold is gone." His tongue discovered and snared the smear of cream cheese. He smacked his lips as he swallowed.

Hunter decided right then to give lunch a pass. "At emotional times like these," he said, "I find it's best to keep busy."

"I entirely agree. I have done just that. I believe that the best way to honor Arnold's memory is to continue his investigation. As you suggested, I have begun by concentrating on the Currents Foundation."

"Have you learned anything interesting?"

"It was founded a decade ago with ten million dollars in seed money from The Avery Trammel Foundation. It was registered under the federal tax code as a 501(c)(3) charitable foundation. Since then, it has served as a conduit for donations from many sources, both domestic and foreign, into a host of other foundations, organizations, and activities. I have been creating spreadsheets to track the flow of funds, relying heavily, though not exclusively, on the 990 federal reporting forms."

He paused to lick a wad of chocolate frosting from a plump thumb, then savor it before proceeding.

"Because most recipients of Currents Foundation grants are far-left activist organizations, their donors often do not wish that their identities become known. Thus they give what are known as 'donor advised' contributions to the Foundation. These allow them to maintain the appearance of a direct donation to the Currents Foundation itself. However, the Foundation then passes along their contributions to the beneficiaries they specify, without leaving any direct paper trail back to the sources."

"So the Currents Foundation is a political money-laundering operation," Hunter said.

"In fact, you may recall that Arnold himself used that very word, 'laundered,' to describe the deceptive flow of funds.

"I thought it was illegal for tax-exempt foundations and nonprofits to engage in political activities."

"Yes. But various circumventions are commonly employed. In this case, to create further layers of distance and deniability between itself and its recipients, the Currents Foundation established a subsidiary nonprofit organization, the Currents Center. The Center serves as an incubator and funding source for many groups that *do* engage directly in lobbying and political activities, and offers organizational guidance."

Wonk pushed aside his second empty plate and began to eye the third longingly. Hunter interceded quickly with a question.

"Wonk, do you have any idea to whom Arnold was referring when he said, 'You won't believe whose money is being laundered through the Currents Foundation—and where it is winding up'?"

"Not yet. This is proving to be an enormous financial spider web, Dylan. It will take me weeks to untangle all of the ways in which money contributed to the Currents Foundation has been redirected, and to whom. Also, we must remember that 'money is fungible.' Thus, a donation given legally, ostensibly for a non-political purpose, can free up resources that could be diverted to a political purpose."

Hunter clapped him on the knee. "I hope you can make quick progress, my friend. I don't want to give these people a lot of time to cover their tracks."

"There is only so much that I can accomplish in limited time, working alone. However, Arnold's colleagues at CAP are here."

"Remind me: CAP is . . ."

"The Center for Advocacy Profiles. They investigate and report on political advocacy groups. Perhaps we can secure their assistance." His eyes searched the room. "Oh, I see them over there"—he pointed with his plastic fork—"at that table, in the rear."

"All right. I'll see what they may know. I'll be back shortly."

2

Hunter headed to the back of the room. Several small tables had been pushed end-to-end there, to accommodate the roughly dozen staff members of the Center for Advocacy Profiles.

He easily identified the boss. A large man of about sixty, wearing an expensive suit, stood at one end, intercepting and shaking hands with those arriving at nearby tables. Hunter went over and waited his turn. The man turned to him, stuck out his hand, and flashed a broad smile.

"Hello. Dennis Hatcher, president of the Center for Advocacy Profiles. And you are . . . ?"

"Dylan Hunter. I'm an independent journalist, but I write mainly—"

"Oh! *Of course* I know who you are, Mr. Hunter!" Hatcher pumped his hand even more enthusiastically. "It's a pleasure to finally meet you. I've been reading your *Inquirer* articles for a long time. Great stuff! Great stuff!"

"Thank you. And I've been hearing fine things about your organization from my research associate, Frederick Diffendorfer. He said I should meet you and your staff."

"Freddie! Of course. He used to freelance pieces to us. Fabulous researcher, fabulous."

Hunter found Hatcher's overly effusive manner annoying. Washington nonprofits, good and bad alike, usually hired as their presidents glad-handing political types whose major talent and obsession was fundraising. From the cut and quality of his suit, Hatcher was good at his job.

He turned to introduce Hunter to the other staff members. They fit the mold for denizens of D.C. nonprofits: mostly young, casually dressed, exuding idealism and nerdy intelligence. He filed away their names and faces as each greeted him in turn.

"Why don't you join us?" Hatcher said. He grabbed an unoccupied folding chair from a half-filled table nearby and slid it in next to his.

"Only for a few moments," Hunter said, taking the seat. "I left Frederick alone over there. Mr. Wasserman's death has hit him pretty hard. They were good friends."

"We all loved Arnie," said Mark Deaver. A soft-spoken, gentle-looking man in his early fifties, Deaver was CAP's vice-president and research director. "It's hard to believe he's gone."

Hunter nodded. "It's clear from what everyone said at the service that he was a special person."

"You didn't know him, then?" Hatcher asked.

"I didn't have the pleasure. Frederick invited me here, as his guest." He turned to Deaver. "It turns out Arnold, Frederick, and I were independently investigating an overlapping area of interest: the Currents Foundation."

"Ah," Deaver said. "The Hive."

To Hunter's questioning expression, Deaver chuckled and gestured toward a dark-haired, bespectacled young researcher. "It's the nickname Tony gave it. Tell him, Tony."

Tony Ferino cleared his throat and smiled nervously.

"Yeah. So, you know how bees behave. Like when you see them out in a field, they each seem to be completely isolated and disorganized? They fly around all over the place, erratically. It looks completely random, like nothing but their independent whims guide them. But then they fly back to their beehive. And what do you find there? It's this perfectly designed, well-organized honeycomb, crawling with workers and drones. All tightly controlled and regimented. Each of them has a job. An assignment. All directed toward a single guiding purpose."

He paused to flick an awkward grin toward Deaver, who nodded encouragement.

"So, that's the Currents Foundation," he continued. "It's become, like, the central hive for hundreds of groups and thousands of individuals on the far, far left. All those workers and drones may seem to be going off in their own separate directions and working on their own separate projects. But then you check their 990 federal tax records, and you find they're getting grant money and assistance from Currents. Not always directly. Maybe only indirectly, through intermediaries. But it's all guided and coordinated."

"By whom?" Hunter asked. "Who's the queen bee?"

Deaver chuckled. "You mean king bee. Avery Trammel—you know, the billionaire investor and philanthropist."

Hunter kept his face blank. "People on the political right portray him as some kind of Machiavellian mastermind controlling everything happening on the political left."

Several at the table simultaneously said, "Well, *yeah!*" and "He is!" Then everyone laughed.

"Everyone knows Trammel has his fingers in pretty much everything going on in progressive politics," Deaver added. "His money—and money he's obtained from other sources—has bought him de facto control of the movement. He doesn't actually run the Currents network directly, you see. After he set it up with seed money from his personal foundation, the Currents outfits appear to function more or less autonomously. However, Trammel sits on the board of the Currents Foundation and continues to donate to it significantly. He funds all the key groups and personnel, so he sets the agenda. And through his intermediaries in 'The Hive,' he has a lot of influence on the media, too."

He recalled the man he had seen on the speakers' platform outside the EPA. Trammel had stood unmoving in the wind, hands clasped behind his back, eyes looking somewhere in the distance while his actress wife clung to his arm. He seemed aloof from it all, exuding a self-contained aura of power.

Hunter decided to play devil's advocate. "You're saying he's a capitalist who hates capitalism. How can that be?"

Hatcher, visibly chafing at being left out of the conversation, jumped in.

"That's a mystery. Not much is known about his early life. He says he came out of a painfully broken home, and he refuses to talk about it at all. But he was obviously brilliant and self-made. He went to business school here in the Sixties, I recall." Hatcher looked around for confirmation.

"George Washington University," Deaver added. "Their School of Government, Business, and International Affairs. He got there on scholarships and graduated *summa cum laude*. He was one of the student radicals of that period. He got arrested a few times during demonstrations and admits he was involved with some of the more violent Marxist groups. But later he said he'd been young and foolish, and that violence was no answer to social problems. Right out of school, he took jobs on Wall Street and soon became regarded as a financial prodigy. They say he had an uncanny knack for being able to anticipate what would happen next in foreign markets."

"That's a quite sudden turnabout," Hunter said. "From campus communist to Wall Street capitalist in just a few years. Yet from his current political activities, it doesn't seem he's changed his convictions all that much."

"Yeah. That's what Arnie thought," Tony said. "He chatted with me a few weeks ago, when he was just getting into his Currents investigation. He said he didn't think Trammel had really changed much since when he was a campus radical. Just his tactics."

"Interesting," Hunter said. "It's such a shame that Mr. Wasserman couldn't continue his work."

Deaver tilted his head to look down the table at Hunter. "You can be sure it won't stop with his death. We'll continue investigating the Currents network."

Hunter had to say it.

"Look. I have reason to believe—well, let's just say I think the circumstances Arnold's death are suspicious." His eyes roamed the table, stopping on each face. "In fact, I think it may have something to do with his investigation. I want to warn you folks to be extremely careful going forward."

"What?" Hatcher's mouth hung open. "You mean you don't think it was an accident? Are you saying—?"

Hunter raised a hand. "I'm saying some aspects of his supposed accident just don't add up. Arnold told Frederick he'd uncovered some serious things about Currents related to the election. Maybe they were so serious that they put him at risk. So until more facts come to light, I urge you to stop poking into 'the Hive,' as you call it. Stop stirring up the hornets—at least for the time being."

They all sat in silence for a moment, their eyes unblinking.

Tony cleared his throat. His eyes hardened.

"You're asking us to stop doing our jobs," he said, his voice suddenly firm.

"Yeah," said Heather Summers, editor of one of their newsletters. "Our job is to uncover and report the truth about these groups."

"I understand. And that's an admirable attitude. But I have to—"

"No 'buts,'" said Deaver, his own voice no longer soft. "We'd be betraying Arnie if we stopped now."

Hunter looked from face to face—mostly young, but all idealistic. Determined. He turned to the one he thought might be most malleable.

"Mr. Hatcher, I'm serious. If Frederick and I are right, there could be a considerable risk to your people."

Hatcher blinked. His own eyes moved around the table. "We've never faced anything quite like this," he said tentatively.

"Dennis," Deaver said to him quietly, "with the country coming apart the way it has been, it was only a matter of time until things came to this. We're here to give Americans the facts. We either do our work and fight back, or we might as well close our doors."

Murmurs of agreement circled the table.

Hatcher turned to Hunter.

"We appreciate your warning, Dylan. We'll proceed more carefully. But they're right. Our donors expect us to expose those trying to undermine our country. We can't allow them to silence us."

For all Hatcher's apparent character flaws, insincerity about his group's mission didn't appear to be one of them.

"Believe me, I understand and admire you for that," Hunter said. "Please, though—keep your investigation low-key. Try not to let them know you're looking into them until the day you publish your findings. After you've done that, you should be safe."

"That's moot at this point," Deaver said. "We've scheduled an appointment with the directors of the Currents network for this coming week. So they're going to know."

Hunter sighed. "Okay. Just be careful. Keep your eyes open, and notify the cops about anyone or anything strange that you notice. Meanwhile, Frederick and I are pursuing this, too. I'd like to get together with you in two or three weeks, so that we can perhaps compare notes."

"Absolutely!" Hatcher said, smiling again. "It's a relief to know that we're not the only ones out there looking into this."

"You're not. And maybe by then we'll know exactly what happened to Mr. Wasserman."

"So the police are investigating it as suspicious?" Deaver asked.

"I don't know," Hunter said. "But I am."

3

"No, Cyrano! You don't chew that!"

Just outside the front door of the house, Annie bent to extricate the leash from the puppy's jaws.

Hunter said, "Let's see how far we can walk before I have to pick him up and carry him."

"At this rate, we'll be lucky if he manages fifty feet," she said as Cyrano, tail beating the air like a flailing sword, paused at the bottom of the steps to sniff a dead leaf. "So, tell me about the service."

"It was well-attended. And moving. Wasserman was well-liked. Quite a few friends and family stood up to tell stories about him. So did his colleagues at the Center for Advocacy Profiles."

"Did Wonk speak?"

He shook his head. "Wonk's taking this pretty hard. Wasserman was one of his few close friends."

"You've said something seems off about his death. What's the evidence for that?"

"None that the police have found. At least, none they've mentioned publicly. But Wonk and I think the circumstances are disturbing."

"How so?"

Hunter explained in detail while they half-followed, half-tugged the bouncing, squirming pup down the driveway to the street.

"I agree that, in combination, all those circumstances do seem suspicious," she said. "Of course, we're trained to suspect everything and everyone."

"Everyone? Now, Annie—when have I ever given you cause to be suspicious of *me?*"

She rolled her eyes.

They followed the trotting little dog along the quiet residential street in the twilight. About a mile long, Connors Point was a narrow finger of land pointing out into the Chesapeake Bay. Well-maintained homes lined either side of Connors Point Road. Those on the right faced open water, while those on the left—the western side, where Hunter's house stood—abutted a marshy tidal pond. Hunter had chosen that side of the street because he loved the marsh's abundant variety of birds and wildlife. While Cyrano stopped to investigate a rock, he and Annie enjoyed a formation of geese silhouetted against the blood-red sunset, accompanied by the operatic twittering of a mockingbird.

"I'm sorry I got so upset with you last night," she said.

He wrapped an arm around her shoulders. "You had every right to."

"No. I know you're only trying to protect us."

"Well, I've been doing a lousy job of it this past year. I'm planning to operate a lot more carefully, now."

"Such as?"

"For one thing, in how I use my wheels. As you know, after I went off the grid as Matt Malone, I bought a lot of used vehicles, mostly in private sales, and registered each of them under one of my aliases. That was to give me plenty of options, in case I ever had to disappear again. I store them in long-term parking garages scattered all around the area, including Metro stops. That way, I can swap them out whenever I transition from one alias to another."

"Exactly how many cars do you own, anyway?"

"Cars, vans, trucks—I'm up to about a dozen, now. Last year I had to add quite a few for my, um, extracurricular activities."

"You mean running around shooting bad guys?"

"Well, yeah—if you insist on being crude about it. Anyway, since last Christmas I've gotten lazy and sloppy about which vehicle I drive under which alias. I've been pushing my luck that I don't have an accident or get stopped for a ticket. I have to be more consistent about who gets to drive which vehicle."

"'Who?' Do you mean—"

"I mean which alias. The names on the registrations, licenses, plates, and VIN numbers all have to match up. From now on, out here, Vic Rostand will have exclusive use of the CR-V, the Ford van, and the motorcycle. Up in the Allegheny Forest, Brad Flynn will be driving my latest acquisition, a Toyota pickup. Around D.C., Dylan will use either the Forester or the white van, which he keeps garaged in Bethesda.

That's also where Wayne Grayson parks the armored BMW beast. It's registered to him, so he gets exclusive driving privileges in it, except for emergencies."

"Damn. I love riding in Wayne's sexy Beemer."

"Stop pouting. How would it look for you to be seen gallivanting about town with a blond millionaire when you're supposed to be engaged to Dylan Hunter?"

"Well, until Dylan decides to *announce* our engagement, I'm free to fool around with any man I want."

"You shameless hussy . . . Anyway, if I ever have to use any of my other aliases, they'll drive the nondescript junkers I've parked elsewhere."

She slowly shook her head. "How do you manage to keep all this stuff straight?"

"How does an actor keep all his roles straight?"

"Don't you ever wake up wondering who you really are?"

"I used to." He squeezed her shoulders. "But not anymore. Up at the cabin, I made a New Year's resolution to become Dylan Hunter, for good. Brad, Wayne, Vic, and the other dudes—they're all just acting roles for Dylan, now."

"Still, I marvel at how you can switch from one character right into another, like flipping a switch."

"I *had* to get good at it, back when I was in Ops. If I hadn't, any slip-up could have gotten me killed." He grinned at her. "Knowing that was a strong motivator for me to rehearse a lot."

He felt the vibration of the phone in his hip pocket.

"Now what?" he sighed, fishing it out. It was a fresh burner, receiving calls through his usual series of spoofing websites and call-forwarding. He was surprised to see the name on the display.

"Hello?" he answered simply, not identifying himself, from an abundance of caution.

"Dylan? Is that you?" Dan Adair's unmistakable baritone conjured the image of his strong face, and the short-cropped, sandy-gray hair and beard.

"Dan! What a nice surprise. How are you, my friend? And Nan, and the family?"

"Doing great," the oil entrepreneur replied. "We all are. How's Annie?"

"Terrific. She's right here, waving hello to you. We're out walking our new puppy."

"A dog, huh . . . Well, that's ironic. That's why I'm calling . . . First, let me tell you that for security, I'm using a borrowed phone. Can you talk freely on this line?"

Hunter frowned. "We're good, Dan. What's up?"

"I just heard it on the local news. A guy walking his dog found a man's body out in the woods." He hesitated. "Out near Otter Creek."

He looked out over the marsh, at the grasses stirring in the breeze.

"You don't say."

"Apparently, the cops haven't identified the body yet. And they're tight-lipped about the manner of death, except they say it looks like it was under 'suspicious circumstances.'"

Hunter realized what must have been in his own face, because he saw its reflection in Annie's.

"I see," he said.

"I figured you'd want to know."

"You're right. Thanks for the head's-up."

"Dylan . . . You do know that whatever happens, you can trust us. All of us—including Will."

Hunter recalled Adair's duplicitous stepson—how he'd conspired with Zak Boggs and nearly gotten all of them killed. Before he could speak, Adair went on.

"When Boggs turned on him and was about to kill him, along with the rest of us—well, that changed him. He'd never been so scared in his life. Or more ashamed. And you were right: He *is* trying to make amends.

"I'm so glad for you, Dan."

"Well, I just wanted to let you know. I've got to run. Dinner's waiting."

"Thanks, Dan. I'm grateful. Say hi to Nan and the rest of the family."

Hunter ended the call. Pondered the news in silence as he removed the battery and the SIM card.

"Well?" Annie demanded.

He told her.

"You know what will happen when they ID the body," she said. "Cronin will hear about it. And he'll know."

"He won't *know* anything. And whatever he suspects, he won't be able to prove. There's no evidence I was even around that area at the time—because they won't be able to determine the exact date and time of death."

The puppy, tugging at the leash in her hand, began to whimper. She bent to pick him up. Held the little creature against her face, for mutual reassurance. Both looked up at Hunter. In the gathering gloom, the pup's eyes were wide and black and eager. Hers were narrow and gray and anxious.

"You say there's no evidence. But Dylan—how can you know for sure? I'm trained in crime scene investigations. There's always forensic evidence left behind. *Always.* Hair. Fingerprints. Footprints, blood spatters, fibers, DNA. You had to have left *something* behind that could lead them right back to . . ."

Her eyes widened and her voice trailed off.

"What?" he asked quietly.

She told him.

FIFTEEN

"I beg your pardon?" Trammel asked. He turned from the TV screen to face his wife.

Julia sat opposite him at the table in their breakfast nook. She wore a long green satin dressing gown and a concerned expression.

"I *said*: 'You seem distant the past few days.' Have I said or done something to upset you?"

He realized he had been thinking a lot about Emmalee lately. Especially after their Saturday night tryst.

"Oh. No. No, I have just been preoccupied lately. With work. I apologize if I have seemed a bit remote."

She nodded quietly. Then reached for the tall crystal glass and raised her Mimosa to her lips.

Thinking her mollified, he turned back to the screen, perched anachronistically atop the William IV rosewood chiffonier against the wall behind her. CNN was reporting the results of the latest ABC News/*Washington Post* presidential poll. Spencer was down fourteen points behind Helm, now. Ridiculous that an Independent political novice could be polling this well against the presumptive Democratic nominee. Even though it was six months until the election, he and the *Maestro* had a great deal of work to do if—

"It would be nice if we could share at least *one* meal without distractions."

He put down his fork and pushed away the plate bearing the remnants of his Eggs Benedict. Then pressed the mute button on the television remote.

"What is the problem, Julia?"

"It's just that we spend so little time together, Avery. When I'm not in L.A. trying to get work, you're off in New York or Geneva or God knows where, doing whatever it is that you do these days. So I was looking forward to spending Sunday together, for a change. But you got up so late yesterday morning, and then seemed so tired. And after a while, I could tell you'd forgotten. So I cancelled our matinee seating at the Center." To what must have been his blank look, she added: "The Juilliard Quartet. Remember? It was supposed to be your belated anniversary present to me."

He saw the hurt in her eyes, and silently cursed himself.

"Julia, dear, I am truly sorry. It was inexcusable for me to forget."

"Yes, it was!" She brushed away a strand of red hair straying into the green eyes. "What *is* it with you lately, Avery? This past month you've been so on edge, snapping at the house staff, giving me the cold shoulder. And yesterday—so lethargic, yawning all day. Are you depressed? Or is something wrong with your health? Is there something I don't know about?"

Holding her gaze steadily was an effort. He was not accustomed to feeling on the defensive. Usually she was compliant, easy to intimidate. He wondered if she suspected something.

"It has been a difficult month. As you know."

"I do. No, I really do. Your plane blown up; those lost investments; Ash Conn assassinated. I get it. A lousy month. But I've had a lousy *year*. Almost *two* years, now, and still no new roles. So stop feeling sorry for yourself. You said it yourself: the Gulfstream and stock losses barely make a dent in our assets, right? And yes, I know Ash was a friend; but he was never *that* close to you, was he?"

"No, he was not." He raised his napkin, monogrammed with their initials, and dabbed his lips. "You are right. Perhaps I have just been feeling sorry for myself."

She looked off, toward the bright, sweeping curve of the window. Below, out of view, Monday morning rush-hour traffic would be pouring into the city, bringing its daily transfusion of vitality and power.

For him, it was an unusually slow morning. His nine o'clock had cancelled; his first meeting, at the Russell Senate Office Building, was not scheduled until eleven. He glanced at his Rolex; that would be over two hours from now. So he could afford to give her the next half-hour. He had quite enough to occupy his mind without the further distraction of trouble from her.

His eyes drifted involuntarily back to the silent TV screen . . . and the image of a dark, bearded man he had seen televised many times in recent weeks. The words beneath the face shocked him. He grabbed the remote and clicked the volume back on.

> ". . . that the body of the suspected 'ecoterrorist' was identified through dental records. Those same police sources are not revealing anything about the exact cause of death, other than to say they are treating it as a homicide. This surprising development comes on the heels of the stabbing death of Boggs's close associate, Russell 'Rusty' Nash, just weeks ago in the same area. It raises questions . . ."

He heard the scraping of her chair.

Julia rose to her feet. The bright chandelier above her seemed to set her red hair ablaze. There was fire in her eyes, too. She threw her balled-up napkin onto the table, then stormed out, heading toward their bedroom suite.

2

"Two matters bring us here this morning," said CIA Director Mason Houk, taking his seat at the head of the massive table in the director's conference room. Behind rimless glasses, his gaze moved to Garrett's face. "And both of them concern you, Grant."

The seating positions of those at the table foreshadowed his message. Of the "front office" executives present, Garrett had been shunted into the chair farthest from D/CIA Houk. That he was probably in trouble was underscored by the smug half-smile from his chief adversary, CIA Deputy Director Wesley Burroughs. A short, intense, dark-haired man with a pugilist's face, the DD/CIA looked much younger than his fifty years. He occupied the first seat to Houk's right—always close enough to kiss the boss's ass, he thought. Perhaps the most telling harbinger, though, was that Garrett's immediate boss—Les Sisler, Director of Operations—chose to sit opposite him, rather than in his usual spot beside him. Garrett was curious to see a few others present who were positioned far lower in the Langley food chain. He wondered what their contribution to this special meeting was intended to be.

But mostly, Garrett wondered whether he'd still have his job by its end.

"The first issue is the reorganization," Houk continued. "As you all know, a panel of nine senior officers conducted the three-month study of the proposal. They polled four thousand employees and conducted fifteen focus groups." He nodded toward Garrett. "Because of its impact on Operations, you in particular, Grant, were encouraged to express yourself on the plan during the discussion phase. And you did. Long and loud." He ventured a smile.

"With all due respect, sir," Garrett replied coolly, "let's be frank. Everyone knows the plan was a done deal when you first announced it. The 'discussion phase,' as you call it, was really just an extended sales pitch to us. Because not a single concern or suggestion offered by critics like me altered the initial plan in the slightest. Oh wait—let me correct that: You did accept my suggestion to change our directorate name from National Clandestine Service back to 'Operations' again, and the Directorate of Intelligence to 'Analysis.' But that was about it."

In the dead silence that followed, Houk and Burroughs seemed to be competing in who could send him the coldest stare. Across the table, Sisler would not meet his glance; he was hunched over, swirling his water bottle.

"I assure you," Houk answered, his tone only a few degrees less frosty than his glare, "we took all criticisms and suggestions to heart. But at the end of the day, the panel concluded we urgently needed to knock down the walls separating the directorates. For years, the technical staff in Science & Technology, the analysts in Intelligence, and case officers in NCS have functioned in their own little silos, like rivals and sometimes even adversaries. That can't continue. Our national security requires cooperation across the directorates. We need to foster a single, overarching 'CIA intelligence officer' mind-set that transcends tribal loyalties to one's own directorate. That's why the panel endorsed the new 'mission center' concept. Going forward, we'll pool talent from each directorate into these mission-focused, fusion divisions, where they'll all learn to work together for the common good."

Houk removed his glasses and began to polish them on his pocket handkerchief. In his late fifties, the D/CIA's bland face was going to jowls and his once-brown hair to gray. A former two-term senator, then Secretary of State under a previous Democratic administration, Houk had been given this appointment seven years earlier by incoming president Gabe Glover. Glover made it clear that Houk's charge would be to "rein in the CIA's cowboy culture" and stop its "human rights abuses."

In particular, the Operations directorate was to be neutered. That wasn't the stated goal, of course; but it was the tacit aim of the reorganization: to transfer the Agency's geographical and topical-interest divisions—which used to operate under Garrett's purview—to the authority of the mission centers. Each of the eleven centers was to be run by some nerdy desk officer, not an experienced ops officer. The case officers and covert operatives Garrett supplied to the centers would no longer answer directly to him; instead, they'd be errand boys and girls for the nerds. And before launching or running any time-critical operation, he'd have to argue with, beg permission of, then take direction from more new layers of politicized, risk-averse bureaucrats. And with their operations now exposed to many more people across the Agency, covert operatives in the field also faced far higher risks that their covers would be blown, too.

"Now, Grant," Houk began again, forcing his voice to warm slightly,

"I understand why many case officers and Ops veterans like you aren't happy with the redrawn lines of authority. I'm sure it feels like a demotion."

"My feelings have nothing to do with it. It *is* a demotion, plain and simple."

"Well, you're right about one thing," Wesley Burroughs interrupted. "Your feelings do have *nothing* to do with any of this. The debate phase has concluded; the decision to move forward with the plan has been made. What we"—his hand swept around to include the rest of the table—"need, right now, is an explicit buy-in from everyone here on the seventh floor. And your pledge to make the reforms work."

Houk nodded. "That's right. Everyone else in the room is on board, Grant. So before we proceed, I need to know whether you're with us."

Garrett was tired. The job had become thankless: the hours interminable, the victories rare, the betrayals frequent. He had been tempted for several years to pack it in and retire. The reorganization portended a national security nightmare. Until now, only an inexplicable sense of duty had caused him to hesitate, to try to blunt its worst consequences.

Now, he had to decide whether he could endorse or participate any longer in their subversion of the organization to which he had given his life.

Garrett eased back into the black leather chair, its creaking the only noise in the soundproof room. His eyes paused first on the large plate of fat cookies in the center of the table; they reminded him he'd skipped breakfast. Then rose to the opposite wall, lined with photos of past CIA directors and the presidents they served, reminders of the many years he had worked here. Then slowly around the table, at each person in turn, noting whose eyes met his and whose scurried for cover.

Then to the figure of Mason Houk. The D/CIA sat motionless, waiting, arms crossed over his dark, somber suit. Behind him on the paneled wall, illuminated by a hidden spotlight, hung a large, two-tone metallic disk bearing the CIA emblem. Incongruously, it looked like a glowing halo floating above his head.

Finally, his gaze rested on Wesley Burroughs—who challenged him with an insolent smirk.

A moment ago, he had decided to tender his resignation . . . until he saw that smug half-smile.

Now, looking at the arrogant bastard, Garrett's teetering sense of duty was bolstered by a sudden, stubborn sense of defiance.

He knew that if it weren't for the dirt he'd compiled on Houk, and especially on Burroughs, they'd have fired him long ago. Even so, they were looking for any excuse—such as direct insubordination or provable law-breaking—to get rid of him.

Garrett decided not to hand them one. He still had one major unfinished task to perform.

He rocked forward. Placed his gnarled hands on the polished wood. Held Houk's eyes.

"All right. I'm in."

There were a few tentative smiles around the table, and a murmur of relief from Sisler. Not from Houk or Burroughs, though. The former simply nodded. The latter lost the smirk.

"Good," said Houk. "With that settled, we turn to the other matter. Wes has brought to my attention rumors from the Counterintelligence Center that you are continuing to raise the specter of a *second* Russian mole here."

Garrett scanned the faces. All registered shock or surprise.

Houk pressed on. "Do you have any evidence to support that suspicion?"

Garrett rocked back again. Crossed his own arms. Continued to scan the faces for subtle reactions.

"Whatever suspicions or evidence I may have, and about whom, are not topics I'll discuss in a room full of Agency employees."

For a few seconds, nobody reacted.

"That's outrageous!" Burroughs blurted. "I demand that you tell—"

Houk rested a hand on his shoulder. "No, Wes—he's probably right."

"But he's insinuating that we—*any* of us—may be guilty of treason!"

"It *is* outrageous," muttered Agnes Headley, boss of the Directorate of Analysis. "I would think anyone in this room should be deemed trustworthy."

Garrett shrugged. "We all thought Muller—in the Office of Security, no less—was trustworthy. But, alas."

Headley's mouth set in a thin grimace. They detested each other, and neither missed an opportunity to express it.

"Happily," she said, "we don't have to question the loyalty of anyone, Mr. Garrett. We have been reviewing NSA intercepts that prove you're wrong in your suspicions. At Wesley's request, I've invited Kurt Spitzer to join us here. For those unaware, he's chief of the Office of Russian and European Analysis. Kurt, go ahead and tell us about those intercepts."

Garrett knew Spitzer; in fact, he'd had to challenge the man's opinions on more than a few occasions. But the veteran analyst had a friend in court: He had been an old college chum of Burroughs at Yale. Both entered the Agency right after school, and over the years they had boosted each other up the organizational chart. Spitzer wore long hair, expensive suits, and, like his pal, a perpetually arrogant expression. He paused to sip from his water bottle; then, pointedly ignoring Garrett, directed his eyes and words toward Houk and Burroughs.

"Thank you, Agnes. These NSA intercepts"—Spitzer tapped a stack of papers on the desk before him—"are from the electronic communication link between the Russian embassy here and the SVR in Moscow," he said, referring to Russia's external spy agency. "As some of you know, NSA discovered and tapped into it last year and managed to decrypt the messages. The back-and-forth in these reveals how upset the Kremlin is about losing Muller. The SVR laments the loss of their, quote, 'last Langley asset,' unquote. They go on to wonder if their illegals can recruit a useful replacement. Which clearly indicates they *don't* have anyone else on their payroll here."

Garrett didn't argue. He didn't want to reveal his evidence or to seem uncooperative.

"That sounds reassuring," he said instead. "But are we sure this is not just disinformation?"

Spitzer shot him a look of disdain. "Moscow has no clue we've tapped communications with their embassy. It's been a gold mine of intel for us."

"Thanks, Kurt," said Houk. "Which brings us to my next point. With the reorganization, Operations no longer has responsibility for the Counterintelligence Center. I know you're used to exercising a lot of autonomy, Grant. But running your own CI investigations in-house was never okay. Now it's completely outside of your authority."

"The last thing we need," Burroughs added, "is another Angleton-style witch hunt."

Spitzer and Headley chuckled; others nodded. They all knew Burroughs was referring to the late CIA spyhunter James Angleton, who was passionately certain of the existence of a Soviet agent buried within Langley. His obsessive mole hunt caused paranoia that nearly paralyzed Agency operations for years.

"Exactly," Houk concluded. "So, as of this meeting, that sort of thing stops. If there's any mole-hunting to be done, it will be handled by the appropriate CI people." He looked around the table. "I wanted the executive staff here, just to make sure there are no further misunderstandings about the new chain of command." He swiveled his chair to face Garrett.

"So, Grant . . . do we still have any misunderstandings?"

Grant Garrett had outlasted countless adversaries during his thirty-five years with the Company. Surely he could outlast and out-maneuver these weenies, too. At least for a little longer. At least until he unearthed the mole he knew was still burrowed somewhere in the Agency.

But he'd have to find him, or her, while these front-office mandarins were watching his every move.

Garrett kept his face blank and his voice steady when he answered.

"None whatsoever."

SIXTEEN

Hunter yawned, for the third time in as many minutes. He had been up late, his attention switching back and forth between his notes about Arnold Wasserman's death, and those he had compiled about the well-coordinated political attacks on Roger Helm.

Too little sleep last night. And too little progress on either investigation.

Raising his big ceramic mug to his lips, he found it empty. He stretched, rose from his desk, and headed out of the office to the apartment's kitchen. Luna was there, hunched over her water dish, her tongue darting up and down like a little pink jackhammer. While he filled the coffeemaker's filter, he tried to tamp down his frustration over his lack of progress on either story.

After hours with the cops and the M.E. yesterday, he was more puzzled than ever about the Wasserman case. They had discovered no evidence of foul play; it looked like a freak accident. Meanwhile, he confirmed that the attacks on Helm were orchestrated by media manipulator Lucas Carver, through the "progressive" public relations outfit he ran, Vox Populi Communications. Hunter was intrigued that Vox Populi received a lot of money from the Currents Foundation, and that Avery Trammel sat on its board. But he'd still uncovered no criminal flows of money into the election campaign.

While the coffee brewed, he decided to check his messages. He used his latest burner to call through the spoofing site to his voicemail, where he found a call-back request from Morgan Jackson. He thumbed in the number and waited. The man answered in his resonant baritone.

"You've heard the news," Jackson began after they'd exchanged greetings.

"I assume you mean about Dixon's death. How are you and Lila feeling?"

"We cried together for about an hour, going through a photo album of our sweet Loretta. After that—well, a sense of relief, I suppose. A feeling of closure, just knowing we never have to concern ourselves with that monster, ever again."

Hunter watched the cat move to her food bowl. "That's good, Morgan. I hope you'll be able to get past this, now."

"That's why I called, Dylan. I wanted to thank you for that."

There was something in the man's tone.

"But I didn't do anything, Morgan. I *wanted* to write about—"

"Not that . . . I think you know what I mean."

He kept his own tone noncommittal. "I'm confused. What *do* you mean?"

For a few seconds, there was only the sound of Luna crunching her food pellets.

"Dylan, we had our monthly Vigilance for Victims meeting last night. I got talking afterward with George Banacek, Kate Higgins, and Susie Copeland. We're especially close, because the killers of our loved ones were all set free. Last fall, we were beside ourselves. We didn't know where to turn. Then you showed up at our meeting. And you said, 'Perhaps I can help.' Do you remember that?"

"I remember."

"I can see it like it was yesterday. We all turned and looked at you. You promised you'd write about our cases—and you did. And it made a huge difference. At a really dark time, you were like a sudden ray of light from heaven. An answer to our prayers. You know how grateful we are. The award ceremony didn't begin to express how much."

"And I can't tell you how much that honor means to me."

"But then, something else started happening, too." Jackson gathered a breath, then plunged ahead. "Those killers all started to die."

Hunter stood motionless in the middle of the kitchen, phone to his ear.

"Somebody started to kill them all, one by one, and left your news stories on their bodies. Everybody started talking about some mysterious group of 'vigilantes' bringing justice when the legal system failed. Pretty soon, a lot of killers were being executed—that's what we called it: 'executions'—and some of them didn't have anything to do with our little group. But it all started with people who were at that meeting: George and Kate and Susie." He paused. "And now, us. Dixon's been executed, too—only two days after Lila and I came to you for help."

"Morgan, I don't know what—"

"Hear me out, Dylan. You need to know the five of us talked about this—but just among ourselves. Months back, a few of us speculated that maybe you were secretly communicating with the vigilantes. But until Dixon was executed, none of us connected all the dots. Just one guy managed to do that. Then Susie reminded us how you were able to track down and kill Adrian Wulfe. So—"

"You've got this all wrong," Hunter interrupted. "I'm just a reporter. What you're suggesting—"

"Dylan, Dylan," Jackson said, chuckling, "take it easy. We're not looking for you to admit anything. In fact, please don't! We don't ever want to have to put our hands on the Bible in some court and swear to repeat whatever you told us."

"Morgan," he said, feeling helpless, "do you have any idea how dangerous your idle speculations could be to me?" *And to Annie*, he thought to himself.

"About that—son, you don't have a thing to worry about. Like I said, we've only talked among ourselves. We prayed about it, after the meeting, and pledged we'll never say a thing to anyone else. In fact, we'll never even say another word to *you* about this. But we agreed I should call and thank you, privately, for what you've done for us—and the risks you've taken to do it. We can never, ever repay you, Dylan . . . No, don't you dare say another word. Just *please*—be careful, okay?"

Then he was gone.

Hunter slowly lowered the phone to his side. As he gripped it tightly, he felt the gathering weight of blood in his hand. The pulse in his fingertips.

The cat straightened from her food dish, stretched languidly, and turned to face him.

"Mraaaowwwh?"

2

"I'm glad you could come, Grant." Hunter took Grant Garrett's overcoat and hung it on a nearby rack. "Annie's in the kitchen. She just put her mystery dish in the oven."

"Thanks for inviting me," his old boss replied in his distinctive gravelly voice. He closed the front door on a man from his security detail, posted outside. "After the lamb she cooked up for us six weeks ago, I wasn't about to refuse." He moved away from the door and lowered his voice. "Besides, we can meet here privately without raising eyebrows."

"Hi, Grant," Annie said, poking her head into the doorway. She wore a short green cocktail dress and an apron imprinted with wine bottle images. "Why don't we all go into the living room while dinner cooks?"

Once settled in with cocktails, Garrett reached into his briefcase and retrieved a file folder.

"All right, I had the FBI run the prints from the beer mug, and here's what came back."

He opened the folder and tossed a photograph on the coffee table between them.

"Ronald Patrick Larsen, age thirty-seven. Current whereabouts unknown."

"That's him, all right," Hunter said, nodding toward the photo. Annie picked it up and studied it while Garrett went on, consulting notes in the folder.

"From his military records and criminal history, there's an unusual amount of personal background info on him. Parents of Norwegian descent, from Rochester, Minnesota. His mother was a strict Lutheran, his father a hotel manager. Juvenile records indicate Larsen showed early signs of sociopathy—tormenting animals, setting fires, hurting other kids—the usual. He was sent for counseling. The shrinks said he envied and hated his older brother, who was an outstanding student, and often did nasty things to undermine him. Larsen was smart, too, but intellectually lazy and a thrill-seeker. He played hockey, took up martial arts, chased girls, and did attention-seeking daredevil stunts. By his mid-teens he was hanging out with troublemakers, stealing cars, picking fights, and generally raising hell."

"That does sound like your classic sociopath," Annie said, tossing the photo back on the table.

"His mother sermonized and spoiled him, while his father tried to keep him out of juvenile detention. Larsen managed to squeak through high school, but was kicked out of college during his freshman year for peeping in the girls dorm windows. Fed up, his father and a judge gave him an ultimatum: join the Army, or go to jail.

"Larsen never forgave his father for that. Still, for a while, he seemed to find his niche in the military. Through sheer physical talent and determination, he got some promotions, then was accepted into the Army Rangers. Early evaluations were positive: They said he had superior skills, was 'driven to succeed,' and was 'relentless' in pursuit of objectives. But on deployments, he was disliked by his fellow soldiers, who said he was manipulative and sadistic. He was also suspected of being involved in a smuggling ring. Near the end of his second tour, members of his platoon caught him sexually assaulting a girl outside a Baghdad bar, and they turned him in. But rather than court-martial him, Uncle Sam avoided an international scandal by paying off the girl's family and dishonorably discharging him."

"So they just washed their hands of him," Hunter said.

Garrett put the papers aside and looked up.

"Which only brought out the worst in him. Larsen told a girlfriend he felt betrayed by his Ranger team and the American government—that they had wrecked his life and deserved payback. When she later tried to end the relationship, he beat her to a pulp, screaming at her about her disloyalty. She was too terrified to press charges."

"Loyalty seems to be a sore spot," Hunter said. "Lasher told me killing Muller wasn't only about the money. He said, 'I hate traitors.'"

Garrett nodded, then shuffled through the papers again. "After that, he was a drifter for a year or so. There were arrests in several cities for disorderly conduct, public intoxication, and fights. Then, through an Army contact and apparently using a fake ID, he got hired as a security contractor in the Middle East, under the alias 'Ray Lasher.' Which didn't last long, either. He was reckless and trigger-happy and within four months, he shot some civilians during an operation. He disappeared in the wind. That's when he started doing murders for hire. He's been at it for over a decade."

"He boasted to me he was one of the top contract killers in the world."

Garrett shrugged. "Actually, Interpol wouldn't argue. Larsen, Lasher—whatever name you care to call him—is a skilled sniper. Being a sadist, he also enjoys up-close work—knives, bare-handed, it doesn't really matter. Though he's undisciplined in his personal life, he's a meticulous professional about his hits. He plans his ops and getaways carefully. The only reason we know about his hitman career is from some snitches and ex-employers who were caught. So far, at least fourteen assassinations have been attributed to him and a half-dozen more are suspected. The targets have included some minor political figures in Europe and Asia, and at least one corporate tycoon in Chicago."

Garrett stopped and looked at Hunter, hard and steady.

"This is one dangerous dude. You were lucky to confront him and walk away."

"I could say the same for him."

"Maybe. But what worries me is somebody with money has hired him to go after you."

"But not to assassinate me."

Hunter explained what Lasher told him about that.

"So maybe he's not working for Russia," Garrett said. "Still, whoever hired him has their own motives. Maybe to expose or discredit you, or to blackmail you into silence. And you have no idea who they might be?"

"Here's what I know for sure. Whatever client hired Lasher knew I'd be headed to the EPA that day. That person must be among the network of environmentalists and political people I was investigating. That person also knew how to hire a contract killer on extremely short notice—just a few hours."

"Or possibly had Lasher on retainer," Garrett suggested.

Annie said, "I just thought of another possibility. Maybe whoever hired him was, or is, *working* for the Russians—but Lasher doesn't know it."

It hit him. Hunter stood.

"What is it?" she asked.

"And what if..." he began slowly, as the idea took shape. "What if Moscow's cutout is an agent *inside* that environmentalist network I investigated?"

Garrett frowned. "What would he or she be doing there?"

"Here's a guess. Russia is a major oil and natural gas supplier to much of Europe. For a long time they've had a virtual stranglehold on the EU's energy. Competition from U.S. fracking now threatens that. They have strategic and economic reasons to want to stop our fracking. So, it makes sense they'd place an agent of influence inside that anti-fracking network, right?"

"It makes sense," Garrett agreed.

Hunter began to pace in front of the fireplace. "Well, what if they also used that same cutout or agent to hire Lasher last year, to silence Muller? And to hire him again now, to find out about me?"

"Now you're unspooling a long string of mere assumptions."

"Think about it, Grant. For big, sensitive jobs, the Russians would stick with just a few proven, reliable contractors. From what Lasher told me, his boss—my hypothetical cutout—and his Russian handlers still think Lasher *did* nail Muller. He would have to be their golden boy. So, wouldn't they pick him again if they want to go after me?"

"That means your cover is blown and the Russians are on to you!"

Annie said. She huddled forward, clutching her hands in her lap.

He shook his head. "If they knew or suspected I was Matt Malone—the CIA officer who caused them so much grief—they'd have sent Lasher to kill me, not just follow me. No, Annie, I think the Russians were simply provoked by my articles exposing the anti-fracking campaign. They'd want to discredit me. But killing a high-profile reporter outright would raise too many questions and be too risky."

"I still think you're leaning way out over your skis," Garrett said. "However, just for sake of argument: *If* someone in that network is an agent for Russia, could it have been Senator Conn? We know he was a ruthless bastard, not afraid to get blood on his hands, at least through Boggs."

"Possibly," Hunter said. "But I'm sure Conn went through many security clearance investigations for his positions on various Senate committees. Has anyone ever discovered any links between him and the Russians?"

"Not that I heard," Garrett said. "I'll ask the FBI to share whatever they might have."

"Speaking of Boggs," Annie said, her voice tight. "Tell him, Dylan."

She was getting more upset by the minute. It would be a long night.

3

"The cops just found and ID'd Boggs's body up in the Allegheny Forest," he began, reclaiming his chair. "I'm sure they know now that somebody killed him, and how."

"Oh, great," Garrett said, raising his hand to rub his eyes.

"Detective Cronin—you remember him—already suspects me for the vigilante killings. But I had pretty much convinced him and everyone else that it was Boggs who murdered Conn and did those acts of sabotage. They theorized Boggs had a falling-out with his partner, Rusty Nash, and killed him, too. Now, though, with both of them murdered, they'll be looking for other suspects. And Cronin knows

Boggs sent a bomb to the *Inquirer*, targeting me. So, he'll figure I had a motive to go after him."

Garrett set his drink down carefully on the coffee table.

"All right. This changes everything. Dylan, you've got at least three adversaries hunting you. Cronin wants to nail you for a bunch of murders. Whoever hired Lasher, probably the Russians, want to expose your real identity and discredit you. And a professional hit man wants to kill you. The odds are high that one of those parties will succeed. It's only a question of which one gets to you first."

"I'm not worried about the Russians, because I'm sure they don't know who I am. And Cronin has no solid evidence against me. But Lasher is another matter. As long as he's out there, Annie and I won't be safe."

He got up again. Walked to the picture window. Felt their eyes on his back.

"Not as long as he's out there," he repeated, staring into the darkness.

"What exactly are you saying?" she demanded.

He turned to her. "You know exactly what I'm saying."

"I told you this killing would never end!" She gave a sharp nod toward Garrett. "Grant was right. Killing is in your DNA."

"Easy, now," Garrett said quietly, also rising. He approached her. "Let's settle down, shall we? Talk this through. Dylan, do you mind sitting down?"

He took his chair again. Garrett settled into his own seat, looked at him, and sighed.

"Well, son, your timing couldn't be any better."

"What do you mean?"

"It's April Fool's Day."

"You're a riot, Grant."

"Seriously," Garrett continued. "You're being foolish. You don't know where this character is. And you're no cop. If they can't find him, how can you?"

"They can't find him if they're not even looking. Has he been formally charged with anything? Is there anything in that file indicating any active investigations or open warrants?"

Garrett shrugged.

"There we are, then. A professional killer is gunning for me, and nobody is doing a damned thing about him. I can't show up at my office anymore, because he knows where that is. Eventually, he could manipulate the staff there or at the newspaper and track me down. Or he'll spot me at some news conference or public event. Unless I do what you suggest: run away and try to hide. Tell me, Grant: Do I spend the rest of my life running and hiding and looking over my shoulder?" His eyes caught Annie's. "Do *we* spend the rest of our lives hiding, love? Or living apart?"

She looked down.

Garrett coughed, then cleared his throat.

"I'll leave it to you two to work things out about that. I only wish I could help. But I'm under close scrutiny myself right now."

"Annie told me you're at war with Burroughs and Houk. That they're trying to neuter Operations."

"They already have. We had it out on Monday. They tried to goad me into quitting, but I didn't take their bait. Now they're looking to take my scalp if I make the slightest mistake. Sorry, Annie, I wanted to mention something sooner, but I didn't dare try to communicate at H.Q."

4

Garrett spent the next ten minutes bringing them up to speed.

"What are you going to do about it, Grant?" Annie asked, her voice tense.

Garrett pressed back into the armchair, smoothing the dark gray silk tie over his light gray shirt. Hunter knew Annie's own future hung on the spymaster's answer.

"I confess, I did seriously consider retiring. But I've outlasted a lot of jerks over the past thirty years. I might be able to outlast these idiots, too, if we elect the right administration this year. Besides, I don't want my legacy to include unfinished business."

"And that would be . . ." Hunter prompted, anticipating the answer.

"We still have another mole somewhere. But Houk and Burroughs ordered me—publicly and bluntly—to halt all counterintel operations, including our mole hunt."

"Damn it, Grant!"

"I know, Annie. My sources say they've asked your old pal, Rick Groat, to keep an eye on me."

"You really are on thin ice, then," Hunter said. "But I heard a few years back that you had dirt on Burroughs and Houk, and they know it, which is your insurance policy."

Garrett raised his brows. "Oh you did, did you?" A slight smile flickered and died. "Well, whatever insurance policy I *may* have might help me only to a certain point. Catching me breaking laws would neutralize that advantage. They'd just let others, probably Groat and the FBI, run the investigation, and I couldn't do a thing to stop them. So we're at a stalemate." He coughed. "And meanwhile, since I'm under direct orders and being watched, I can't risk doing what needs to be done to find and stop that mole."

"So now we're supposed to just sit on our hands?"

Garrett looked straight at her.

"I said *I* am under direct orders not to do anything. Who said anything about 'we'?"

She stared back at him. Then slowly smiled.

Hunter decided to take advantage of her brightened mood. He stood again.

"Love, don't you think your mystery dish is about done yet?"

SEVENTEEN

Something was moving around his feet.

Hunter's eyes snapped open. He found himself spooned around Annie's naked body. He raised his head and saw Luna marching up the comforter covering them. She paused to eye him, disapprovingly.

"Mrraooww."

"Shhh!" he warned as Annie shifted against him.

Defiant, Luna resumed her trek up the hills and valleys of the thick blanket, heading toward Annie's face. Purring now, the cat sniffed her hair. Then her pink tongue licked a strand. Then she sat and nestled up against the covered mound of Annie's body. Then, content, shut her eyes, still purring.

Hunter checked the clock on the night stand. Almost nine a.m. But they hadn't actually fallen to sleep till almost three. Someone had once told him that nothing was quite as good as "make-up sex" after a fight. He smiled to himself, remembering.

His lips grazed her smooth bare shoulder, and she squirmed just a little and murmured something. It was hard now to pull himself away from her warmth, the scent of her skin; but he had things to do. He'd let her sleep in. Grant had told her last night to take the day off so they could spend time together, working things out.

He slipped out of bed carefully so as not to disturb her, pulled on his bathrobe from its hook on the door, and went downstairs. As he entered the kitchen, Cyrano roused from his own slumber and made his little *yipping* noises at his approach. Hunter let him out into the back yard;

they'd had contractors come in during the past weekend to fence it in, allowing the pup the full run of the area.

Hunter was pouring his second mug of coffee when his burner chirped the distinctive ring tone he'd set for Wonk. He moved to the kitchen table and picked it up.

"You're calling bright and early. Does Iggy need to be rescued again?"

"No, Dylan, Iggy is just fine. I do have intriguing news to report, however."

"I'm all ears."

"Arnold's mother permitted me to look at his office files, cell phone, and computer yesterday. And I found nothing."

"What do you mean, 'nothing'?"

"I mean exactly that. There was not a single file or note in his office or on his computer pertaining to what he had been working on. Obviously, he would have compiled detailed notes and many records and files. Yet I found not one mention of Currents, anywhere. I even checked his online backup service in case he kept his notes there, for security. But I found no records, no files, no emails, either sent or received. He and I often exchanged files on thumb drives. However, no thumb drives were present in his office, either. Most curiously, his cell phone—which he told me he reserved exclusively for his business calls—had almost no incoming or outgoing calls listed in its history during the past month."

"That *is* intriguing. Any chance the cops confiscated that stuff?"

"Mrs. Wasserman has the key to the apartment. She was present to meet a detective who returned to question her the next morning. He asked to look around Arnold's office and did so in her presence. She said he remained for less than thirty minutes, looking through his file drawers and his cell phone. She said it seemed superficial; he was chatting with her as he worked. When he left, he took nothing from the office with him."

Hunter swallowed some coffee. Something tugged at his memory.

"At the funeral, the CAP folks told me Arnold sent them a cryptic email message about Currents the night he died. Didn't you find that message in his 'sent email' folder?"

"No such message was archived. And before you ask, Dylan, I also checked his 'deleted files' folder. It was empty."

"Well, we *know* he sent that message. So if it wasn't there . . ." Hunter found himself carefully aligning the silverware on his place mat. "Wonk, you realize this supports our theory."

"I know." He heard the researcher draw a long, shaky breath. "Of course, nothing ever truly vanishes in the digital world. For example, records of his phone calls would exist with his service provider."

"True. Maybe when his next phone bill shows up, his mother will let us have a look."

"Perhaps. Meanwhile, I hope your efforts have been more fruitful, Dylan."

"They only add to the mystery. I spent much of Tuesday with the cops and the medical examiner. The official ruling is death from asphyxiation by accidental drowning. The facts at the scene give them no cause to suspect foul play. Arnold had a gash and bruise on his skull, consistent with having slipped and hit his head on the faucet and tub edge. They found traces of blood in the soapy water in his lungs, also consistent with drowning after a fall. But no other marks or injuries. No signs of a struggle, drugs, or chemicals in his bloodstream. Since their investigation is closed, a detective kindly walked me through the photos of the scene. They show the position of the body in relation to various items in the bathroom. All of it apparently supporting the accident theory."

"And yet we are presented with all these other anomalies."

"'Anomalies.' Nice word for facts the cops don't know about, and which contradict their official conclusion."

"But how does one explain the lack of evidence of a struggle? Arnold would not have meekly allowed himself to be drowned."

"Perhaps he opened the door to an armed intruder, was herded into the bathroom at gunpoint, forced to undress, then knocked unconscious and drowned. The rest could have been carefully staged. The killer or killers then could have gone methodically through his office, eliminating anything related to his Currents investigation."

"That seems extraordinarily complicated, hence unlikely. I believe in Occam's Razor."

Hunter knew, first-hand, how people trained in wetwork could disguise murders to look like mundane accidents. But that was knowledge he could not share.

"I know. But there's no other logical explanation for everything that's gone missing from his office. What you've just told me makes me more certain than ever that Arnold was killed in order to stop his investigation. Remember what Arnold hinted is at stake here."

"I do. So, what is your plan now?"

"For openers, I've been working on an initial article. It won't reveal all our suspicions or tie them to Arnold's death. I'll just stick to what we are learning about the Currents network. The article will hint that they may be improperly channeling money from anonymous donors into the presidential race."

"Is that not redundant? CAP already is working on the same topic."

"But they stick to examining financial records and compiling public information. I'm a reporter. I like to get in people's faces. I want to confront the Currents principals. Ask for documents, see their reactions to uncomfortable questions. Mainly, let them know somebody other than Arnold is still going after them."

"Why would you wish to do that? It might provoke them to react against you."

"Which is the idea. If that happens, it will confirm Arnie's death was no accident. I have to do more homework before I call them for some interviews, though."

"But if our hypothesis is correct, that would put you in danger!"

"Don't worry, Wonk. I can take care of myself."

Wonk fell silent for a moment.

"Dylan?"

"Yes?"

"Over the past year, I have gotten the distinct sense that there is much more to you than meets the eye."

Hunter knew from the tone that he had to be careful.

"Of course there is," he answered lightly. "All of us have untapped talents and abilities."

"That is not quite what I meant. I . . ." He stopped.

"What *do* you mean, my friend?"

"I hope you do not mind, but after all, I *am* a researcher. During the past months, I have utilized my resources—which are considerable, as you know—to try to learn more about you and your background."

Hunter laughed. "But you can't. I know."

"You . . . know?"

"Sure. I wondered if you'd ever ask."

Hunter spent the next five minutes repeating the same legend he'd once told Annie and Cronin: that he'd been a reporter in Ohio who publicly exposed an organized crime gang; that in retaliation the Mob put out a murder contract on him, still open; that for his own safety he had to go into the federal witness protection program and change his identity.

"So you see, 'Dylan Hunter,' my new identity, goes back only about three years. That's why you can't find out anything about my background. Which, for my personal safety, must remain secret."

"I see," Wonk said. "I must say, it is a most unusual method for a writer to acquire a 'pen name.'"

"What? Did you think I was some kind of secret agent, or something?"

"Honestly, Dylan, I did not know what to think. You do many mysterious things. I suspect—no, to be honest, I am almost certain—that some of your work involves illegal activities. You have asked me for specialized hacking software and surveillance equipment—the sort of things I develop and provide only to . . . well, *you* know."

"I do."

"And . . . how should I put this? Dylan, I am an exceptionally intelligent man. I am not blind to the fact that many subjects of your investigations over the past year have met with violent ends."

Not again . . .

Hunter asked, quietly: "Do you think I've had anything to do with that?"

Many seconds passed in eloquent silence. Finally, Wonk spoke.

"Here is what I do know, after working closely with you for two years. I know that those individuals who died were all terribly evil people who deserved what happened to them. And—whatever your involvement—I also know that you would never abuse my assistance to do anything that would harm innocent people, or harm our country."

"I'm glad you know that, Wonk."

"That said, I would be most grateful if your activities did not implicate me, in any way. I believe the term in the trade is 'blowback.'"

The trade . . .

"There will be no blowback against you. You can count on that, my friend."

He heard a sigh. "Your word is good enough for me . . . because . . ."

"Because what?"

"Because you are a good and decent man, Dylan Hunter . . . Well, I must run."

"Wonk?"

"Yes?"

"Thank you."

2

"I'm heading out."

Ed Cronin glanced up from his copy of the *Inquirer*. Ellen, his wife, had entered the den and was buttoning up her jacket as she approached.

"Heading where?"

"For a single-family showing here in Alexandria. It's less than five minutes away, near Fort Williams and Duke. A nice commission if they buy it, so wish me luck."

"You got your pepper spray?"

She raised her eyes heavenward, in exasperation, and patted her jacket pocket. "Always. Geez, Ed, this is a retired couple. Will you please stop worrying?"

"You don't see what I see every day."

"You tell me that at least ten times a week." She leaned down to plant a kiss on his cheek. Her wavy, light-brown hair tickled. "I'll be back before seven. Could you check on the kids' homework before then?"

"Sure. Not that I understand half of what St. Stephens is teaching them."

"Just don't argue with them again about what they're learning in social studies."

"You mean the liberal bullshit?"

"Oh, stop!"

He grinned and patted her ass as she turned away.

He checked his watch and saw it was just past six. He foraged around the sofa for the remote, then clicked on the screen.

> "... officially ruled a homicide. Boggs had been the subject of a nationwide manhunt for acts of ecoterrorism and the March 5th car-bomb death of Senator Ashton Conn at his suburban Virginia residence. A state police source tells Fox News that Boggs had been left bound to a tree in a remote part of Pennsylvania's Allegheny National Forest, under circumstances suggesting he may have been tortured before his death. An autopsy concluded that Boggs died several weeks ago, although it was impossible to determine whether that was before or after the murder of Senator Conn. The FBI, now in charge of the investigation, released a statement saying that they are trying to determine what, if any, link there is between the murder of Boggs and of his close associate, Russell 'Randy' Nash..."

Cronin watched only to the end of the segment, then shut off the TV.

He knew all that.

In fact, he knew more than the FBI or Pennsylvania cops did.

In fact, he had a suspect...

He pushed the newspaper off his lap and went to the kitchen to fetch a cold beer. He took a few deep swallows and stood there, back pressed against the cool surface of the fridge, eyes shut . . .

Since Monday morning, when he heard they'd found Boggs's body, he'd spent hours on the phone trying to get the details. In exchange for a promise to swap information, a state police detective filled him in on what they had, then transmitted to him the relevant paper.

Cronin hadn't bought the official version of events from the outset. Everyone assumed Boggs killed his pal, Rusty Nash, in some sort of falling-out. But if that were true, then you had to rethink whether Boggs really killed Senator Conn, too. Or could have. Because Nash was killed in the Allegheny Forest, hundreds of miles away, the night before Conn was blown up at his home here. So Boggs would have had to kill Nash there, then drive to D.C. to kill Conn the next night, *then* drive back to the Allegheny Forest, where he got himself murdered by some party or parties unknown.

And they were murdered in such gruesome ways: Nash stabbed multiple times; Boggs nailed to a tree, ritualistically; Conn blown to bits. Crimes of passion. Meaning: either by a person or persons close to them, or at least by someone who *really* hated them.

Who would have motive, methods, and opportunity to do shit like that? Someone in their gang? And why? Investigators had hauled in WildJustice members for questioning, but so far were drawing blanks.

Who else, then?

How about somebody who had been investigating that gang—and Boggs specifically? And also Conn. And also all those politically connected people who had their communications hacked and their property destroyed. Somebody hostile to them all—acting like a vigilante.

How about somebody already tied to our vigilante investigation? Somebody whose name and newspaper articles kept turning up at the crime scenes of *both* investigations.

How about somebody operating under an assumed name—a man without a past? Somebody with a girlfriend in the CIA and an Agency boss running interference for him. Somebody who could kill a giant MMA expert in hand-to-hand combat—also with a knife . . .

He pressed the cold beer can to his forehead.

Yeah, I have a suspect, all right.

But he had zero evidence Hunter was in the Allegheny Forest during the time frame when Boggs or Rusty were murdered there. Or that he was at any of the other crime scenes, for that matter.

Unless forensics could turn up some solid physical evidence at those scenes, he was dead in the water. He couldn't pull in the rest of the Task Force on the basis of mere hunches. Abrams would chew his ass for even bringing it up and wasting their time.

One piece of potential evidence was Boggs's recorded confession, sent on a thumb drive to the *Inquirer*. The paper had surrendered the original to the FBI, but of course kept a copy. And Cronin had requested and gotten his own copy from the editor, Bronowski. Cronin turned it over to a consultant who would subject the recording to a voice stress analysis. Maybe by tomorrow he'd know whether the confession had been coerced. If so, then that would help narrow down motive.

Because it would mean Boggs's killer wanted him not just to confess to his murders, but also to expose a presidential candidate as his partner.

And who would have *that* as his motive?

But for now, there was no point directly confronting Hunter again. He'd proved he was way too slick to show signs of guilt or trip himself up under interrogation. Besides, Cronin had no valid reason to call him in for further questioning, let alone arrest and charge him with anything. And why tip him off that he was now under suspicion for Boggs's murder?

No, he'd have to gather more evidence on his own. And hope the cops in Pennsylvania came up with something more from the crime scene.

He thought suddenly of Erskine. He felt conflicted about not bringing him in on this. Paul had been his partner for a long time, and not sharing stuff with him felt like disloyalty. It started when Abrams and that CIA spook told him to lay off Hunter, offering bullshit "national security" reasons. They ordered him not to say anything to Paul or anyone else about it, too.

At the time, Cronin pretended to go along. But it made him angry.

Nobody was going to tell him to bury an investigation. He continued to stay on Hunter. Still, he didn't want to get Paul in trouble, so he kept his investigation to himself.

That's what he told himself. But he sensed, deep down, that something else was stopping him from sharing his suspicions about Hunter with Paul. He couldn't quite put his finger on it.

Or maybe he didn't want to . . .

3

Avery Trammel stood inside his spacious clothes closet, selecting the tie he would wear to the banquet, when he heard his mobile phone chirp in the bedroom. He frowned; that particular ringtone was associated with a man who should not be calling him after normal business hours.

Half-dressed, he emerged to see Julia seated at the vanity, toying with her hair.

"Up or down?" she asked, raising her red hair in a pile atop her head. She was to receive a special award tonight for her charity work on behalf of undocumented immigrants.

"Give me a moment," he said, hurrying past her to grab the phone he had left on the bed.

"Wallace, I am afraid I cannot chat right now. We—"

"I'm so sorry, Mr. Trammel." The annoying, lisping voice had taken on a tone of whiny pleading. "I didn't want to bother you at home in the evening, but I didn't think this could wait."

Wallace Rouse was the president of the Currents Foundation, the funding conduit for much of Trammel's political activism.

"Let me be the judge of that. What is it?"

Rouse told him.

Trammel did not move as he listened. Nor did he speak.

"Mr. Trammel?"

He realized that Rouse had stopped talking and was waiting for a response.

"You were right to let me know about this promptly, Wallace. For the time being, do not communicate with them any further. Tell them to direct any future communications to our attorney."

He slowly lowered his hand and dropped the phone back on the bed.

"Well? Up or down?"

He turned to her. "What?"

"I need to know whether to wear my hair up or down tonight. Up, and I can wear the emerald earrings you gave me for my birthday. But those might be too ostentatious. Down, and I—"

"Julia," he said, approaching, "that call—there is a crisis I must attend to tonight. I am afraid that I shall not be able to accompany you to the banquet."

"What?" She leaped to her feet.

"I am truly sorry, but this—"

"You're *sorry?* You are actually going to make me attend the banquet *unescorted?"* Her pale-green slip began to tremble. "And I'm their *guest of honor!* Do you have any idea how that will *look?"*

"It simply cannot be helped. I must . . . arrange a meeting tonight to deal with this emergency immediately. I am likely to be out till quite late."

Her mouth gaped open and tears gathered in her eyes, glittering from the lights surrounding the mirror. She sank back onto the padded vanity seat.

"I can't believe this! I can't believe you would do this to me. You . . . you've been so *distant* lately—and now . . ." She began to cry. "And you say it all so cold and calm and matter-of-fact . . . like you really don't mean it. Like you really don't *care.* Avery, what in hell is *wrong* with you? What is happening to us?"

He took a step toward her, raising his hand—then dropped it, knowing it was useless. The woman would not be mollified, of course. He would just have to deal with her later.

"I am sorry," he repeated, then turned away.

Moments later, he was back in casual attire and headed toward his study. Two weeks ago, it had taken him twenty minutes to decide what to do about that writer, Wasserman. This time he had made up his mind before the call with Rouse ended.

He tapped in the keypad code to unlock the door, then entered and locked it behind him. He went straight to his desk and opened its hidden safe. He retrieved a flat device with an antenna and powered it on. A screen on its surface lit up, opening a virtual keyboard. He tapped rapidly with his thumbs for a couple of minutes, then a press of a button dispatched the encrypted message in a high-frequency burst.

Ten long minutes later, he received a reply on the same frequency. He read it, automatically decrypted, and grunted in relief. He keyed in his brief acknowledgment, then powered down and replaced the device back in the safe. He was preparing to close and lock it when, on impulse, he grabbed and pocketed the Sig-Sauer and a spare magazine.

Though he had worked with them for a long time, he knew that these people never could be fully trusted.

EIGHTEEN

The motel on New York Avenue in the Northeast section of Washington was a dump, frequented by the city's nocturnal predators and their prey. A man like Avery Trammel would never be caught dead in such a place. But for this meeting, secrecy was paramount, and he knew that the man who booked the room would have paid the night clerk handsomely, in cash, so that the security cameras would go dark for the next hour.

Trammel had taken the Metro from the Watergate to Union Station. There, in a restroom stall, he changed into shabbier clothes, a fake mustache, eyeglasses, and a broad-brimmed hat, which he had brought with him in a shopping bag. Then he caught a cab to deposit him here.

The night clerk—young, male, and African-American—sprawled in a chair behind the desk, wearing headphones attached to his phone. His eyes were closed, and he rocked and bobbed to a thumping beat Trammel could hear from the doorway when he entered. He had to shout to get the clerk's attention. At his request, the guy handed over the key to room 109 without a word, then shut his eyes and began bobbing again.

Trammel kept a hand in his windbreaker pocket as he crossed the parking lot, taking comfort from the feel of the loaded Sig-Sauer. Unlocking and entering the shabby ground-level room, he was assaulted by the mingled smells of cigarettes, urine, and bleach. He closed the door behind him, latched the security chain, turned on the lights, and glanced around.

He had endured places far worse during his childhood. He placed the bag bearing his change of clothes on the desk, and crumpled it shut to keep out any vermin. Covering his fingers with a tissue, he pulled shut the curtains, which hadn't been washed in years. He was glad to be first to arrive: He settled onto the cheap laminate chair, leaving his contact to brave the ancient gray-brown bedspread, if he dared. Then he checked his Rolex, which he had transferred from his wrist to his trousers pocket, to remain inconspicuous.

It was three minutes before eight p.m.

Right at eight he heard footsteps on the sidewalk outside. Three quick knocks were followed by two more, spaced out. Trammel got up, taking the pistol with him. He looked out through the door's security peephole, just to make sure. Then he dropped the gun into his windbreaker pocket, unlatched the chain, and opened the door.

2

The middle-aged man who entered had the sort of pleasant, darkly masculine, yet unremarkable features that never drew much attention. That served him well, because Leonid Dimitrievich Sokolov was Russia's most valuable spy in America.

He took in Trammel's disguise and laughed heartily.

"Am I in the wrong room? You *are* 'Allan Jones,' right?" he said, using the alias Trammel had been told to give the motel clerk.

Sokolov's accent was impeccable. He had been trained intensively to pass for an American native, and he had been living in the United States for two decades as an "illegal," under the alias of Leon Sokol. Trammel had once visited Sokolov at his modest home in Takoma Park. His pretty American wife and two boys had no idea that "Lenny" was a high-ranking officer in Russia's SVR.

His cover job was executive director of Brotherhood Without Borders, a nonprofit educational and lobbying organization ostensibly promoting "international cultural understanding and cooperation." In actuality, it was a Russian influence operation—a conduit for *dezinformatzya*, often coordinating with RT, the Russian state's international television network. The group maintained headquarters in the District and satellite offices in several European capitals, which gave Sokolov a plausible reason to travel frequently. On such trips he often hand-delivered to his SVR bosses troves of intelligence gathered by the spy ring he also handled. The ring had included James Muller at the CIA; it still included the second mole there, whose identity had never been revealed to Trammel.

And, of course, it included Avery Trammel himself.

Brotherhood Without Borders was funded largely by generous grants from the Currents Foundation—Russian money, laundered through the Trammel Foundation. The Currents connection allowed Sokolov to meet with Trammel regularly and publicly.

But this irregular meeting could not be public.

Keeping his right hand on the gun in his windbreaker, Trammel retreated back to the chair. The man across the room had killed before. One could never tell what orders he had been given.

"What? No handshake?" Sokolov laughed again and secured the door behind him. Then he turned, took in the room, and wrinkled his nose. "Oh. Well, never mind the handshake, old friend. I don't know what in here you might have touched."

"We could have met in some park, you know."

"What? You don't like our accommodations?"

"Be my guest," Trammel replied, nodding toward the bed.

Sokolov looked at the stained bedspread, then around the room for another chair. Finding none, began to pace. Trammel waited him out.

"All right, then, down to business. I can inform you that the Kremlin debated your plan for a long time. To be more accurate, they argued about it violently, for two days. And with good reason. The risks are enormous."

"I acknowledged the risks in my proposal."

"Frankly, most of the leadership thought it *too* risky. Many said the plan was insane. But Putin concluded that circumstances had turned critical—

desperate, in fact—and therefore, desperate measures were required."

"Which means what, exactly?" Trammel asked, gripping the arm of the chair.

Sokolov stopped pacing.

"It means he overruled them. Yes, my friend, your crazy operation has been green-lighted."

Trammel felt like dancing. Instead, he kept his expression sober and simply nodded. He knew he was safe and could relax, now; he released his grip on the gun in his jacket pocket.

"Naturally," Sokolov added, "Putin wishes it were otherwise. All of them are still howling about Ashton Conn's murder. Nobody can believe it. They had so much riding on his election."

"We all did," Trammel said.

Sokolov waved his hand dismissively. "Nobody gives a damn about your 'green energy' investments, Avery. We push those only to offer options to fracking, not to make you even richer. Okay, sure—it would have been nice if they *had* paid off for you. Maybe then we could have cut back on our subsidies of your lavish lifestyle. Every time I submit your requests for another infusion of cash, the Center screams at me."

"That 'lavish lifestyle' has been instrumental in maintaining my profile and influence here. I should think that, after all these years, they would realize that. I am one 'investment' that has paid Moscow handsome dividends, for a long time."

Sokolov came and stood over him. His eyes, usually soft and affable, narrowed. "True. But it may surprise you to learn that, in recent years, we had started to doubt your loyalties, my friend."

Trammel sat back and crossed his arms. "It may surprise *you* to learn that I had sensed as much, Leon. Even though I have never given you cause to doubt me."

A little smile curved the corners of Sokolov's mouth.

"Be that as it may, you proved your commitment last year, when you responded so quickly and effectively to our urgent request to deal with Muller."

"You made it abundantly clear what the stakes were."

"And thanks to you, our other asset is still in place at Langley." He bobbed his head, a salute. "For which we are eternally grateful."

"So. I passed the test, then."

Sokolov grinned. "With flying colors. Still, you must be more reasonable in your spending habits. Things are tight and getting tighter. With Conn's death and the fracking moratorium lifted, oil and natural gas prices have collapsed again. American fracking is taking a terrible toll on the Russian economy. It's killing our energy export market. If we don't do something about it, it's only a matter of time until liquified natural gas shipped from here will wean NATO countries like Germany from their dependency on Gazprom."

"You are merely reiterating the arguments I put forth in my proposal. What did they say, specifically, about the plan itself?"

Sokolov glanced again at the bed cover, reconsidering the risks. He resumed pacing.

"Beyond the fracking issue, they like the fact that your plan will undermine Americans' faith in their government and its ability to protect them. It will cause them to panic and stampede toward the candidate who seems most willing to go to extremes to protect them."

"Which is neither Waller nor Helm," Trammel said.

"In fact, that's what they found most ingenious about your plan, my friend. It exploits the public's lack of confidence in Waller, whom they believe is unprepared and unstable. And when it drives them to demand more security over liberty, that will turn Helms's passion for civil liberties into a major political liability."

"Precisely," Trammel said. "My media associates, such as Lucas Carver, will hang the 'weak on terrorism' label around his neck like an albatross."

"Which brings us to Spencer. He's the wild card. Are you absolutely sure you can co-opt him? You didn't specify how you plan to do that."

Trammel spent several moments explaining. Sokolov still looked uncertain.

"You understand that we'll give the operation a final 'go' only if all those things you promise *do* happen?"

"I understand. As for the operation itself, to insure security, it will be implemented through multiple layers of intermediaries—"

"'Cutouts.'"

Trammel chuckled. "You people and your theatrical spy jargon."

Sokolov raised his chin. "That 'spy jargon,' as you mock it, is an integral element of tradecraft," he shot back. "It serves us well, just as it served your own father well."

It felt like a slap in the face. Trammel shot to his feet.

"Did it, now?"

"Oh God, Avery. That was stupid of me." Sokolov's voice turned suddenly soft, mollifying. "I didn't mean to—"

"I told you *never* to mention my father."

"I'm truly sorry. I know how painful the subject must be, even after all these years. I cannot imagine what a nightmare it was for you as a child."

"No. You cannot."

He steadied his breathing and sat down. "Now, let us stick to the reason for this meeting, shall we?"

"Of course, of course. Let's discuss the logistics.

"Finally," said Avery Trammel.

3

After Sokolov left, Trammel called for a cab. While he waited, he wiped down every surface either of them had touched, including the door knob as he departed.

He had the cab drop him off back at Union Station. Carrying the shopping bag, he returned to the restroom. He got rid of the disguise and changed back into the clothing he had worn at the beginning of the evening. He rolled up the disguise and shabby clothes in the bag and stuffed it into the restroom's garbage can, beneath a heap of used paper towels. Then he retraced his path on the Metro back to the Watergate.

The residence was empty and quiet. Julia would return from the banquet angry and upset. The prospect irritated him. Much as he was tempted to spend the night downstairs with Emmalee, it would be imprudent and risk raising needless suspicions. He would have to stay here to endure Julia later.

Trammel went to his study, locked the door behind him, and returned the gun to the desk safe. He retrieved his satellite phone and punched in the code for Lasher. His call was returned quickly.

"Unfortunately, it appears that our concerns about the CAP organization were justified," he began.

"So, where does that leave things?" Lasher asked.

"They now have become loose ends."

He knew Lasher would understand.

"All right. How many are we talking about?"

"Thankfully, it is a small nonprofit. From what I learned from their website, only about a dozen people, including support staff."

"That's still a lot of loose ends."

"The numbers do not matter. I have made clear to you that a great deal is at stake. Much more than you could imagine. The information you brought me from the researcher's office—it cannot get out, under any circumstances. Is that understood?"

"I understand, sir. But that many people . . . it will be complicated. It'll require a lot of planning. And the involvement of others. I'll need a team. The logistics alone . . ."

"I have been giving the matter a great deal of thought. An associate and I have developed a general plan. I shall be able to supply you with the contacts and resources you will require. I do not believe you will have to be involved directly in the actual . . . events. In fact, it is best that you keep your distance from the operational side. I see your role as the planner and coordinator."

"These contacts of yours . . . are you sure we can trust them?"

He had to smile at that.

"We have worked together for decades."

NINETEEN

"Okay. Now try a three-shot group," she heard Dylan say.

Squinting through the amber lenses of her protective glasses, Annie settled the front sight of her .40 caliber Glock 27 onto the center of the hanging paper target, a man-shaped silhouette ten yards down the firing lane. She made sure her double-handed grip was right, thumbs pointed along the barrel toward the target. She moved her right forefinger from its position alongside the trigger guard and onto the trigger. Then she fired three shots, each about two seconds apart.

"Your shot grouping is good and tight," he said from his position behind her in the firing lane. "But pulled to the right of center, and low. I think you may be instinctively tightening your grip just as you fire. Keep your grip pressure nice and steady. Move only your trigger finger. Okay, try three more."

She did.

"There you go. All in the red. I officially pronounce the target dead."

She chuckled and placed the gun on the table, pointing down range, then turned to him. "Okay, cowboy. Top *that*."

He smiled. "Let's make a wager. If I win, I get to have sex with you later."

"And if I win?"

"Then you get to have sex with me."

"Gee, how perfectly fair."

They swapped positions and she took the small pair of binoculars from him. The acrid smell of gunpowder and the bursts of gunfire from the surrounding lanes filled the air.

Dylan adjusted his protective electronic ear muffs. Then, smiling back at her, he sent the suspended target out to twenty-five yards. He picked up his own gun from a basket on the table—a Sig-Sauer P228 in 9 mm. Maintaining an upright, fully forward-facing stance, he raised the pistol and immediately fired five times—so rapidly it almost sounded like an automatic weapon. She raised the binoculars.

A starburst perforated the red center of the target.

He placed the Sig back on the table, then turned to her, an eyebrow arched.

"How did I do?" he asked innocently.

"Show-off."

"Now, don't be a sore loser."

"That depends on how gentle you are tonight."

He gave her his lopsided grin and shrugged. "You know me."

"Some days, I'm not so sure."

Dylan made a habit of going to the indoor range in Upper Marlboro, Maryland, at least once a week. She had not accompanied him since last fall. But with Lasher somewhere out there, she knew she couldn't afford to be rusty.

They spent about forty-five minutes practicing, making everything second-nature, until she felt confident she could hit what she aimed at. For his part, Dylan focused on rapid, single-handed firing, switching hands.

2

They were outside in the light drizzle and heading to his Ford van in the lot when he heard the *ping* of a forwarded text message on his phone.

Inside the van, he paused to read the text.

"You're smiling," she prompted, dabbing her dark damp hair with a towel from the back.

"It's an invitation from Roger Helm's office. He's reserved two tickets for me at the CNN 'town hall' next weekend. It's not a formal debate, so it's limited to only the three leading candidates in the polls—him, Spencer, and Waller."

"Obviously, he likes you. You must have impressed him."

"I guess so. It's awfully nice of him. If I go, I may be the only member of the media there except for CNN folks. I could get a scoop or two." He thought about it for a moment. "And of course Lasher won't expect me to show up there, either. Even if he spots me on TV in the crowd, he couldn't get close with all the Secret Service. Or have time to get there and plan anything. So it's safe."

"Two tickets, huh?"

"Come on, Annie. It's out of the question. We can't be seen together in public."

"I know. But who says we have to sit together? I'd love to attend. One of those guys is going to be our next president. *Pretty please?*" She batted her eyes at him and stroked her hand up his thigh.

He laughed. "Well, I'll check with Helm's office on Monday and see if it's assigned seating. If not, I suppose we could sit apart. Pretend to be total strangers."

"If I'm by myself, maybe some handsome Secret Service agent will hit on me."

"I'm afraid they'll all be preoccupied."

She moved her hand higher. "You think so?"

"Okay. Maybe not *that* preoccupied." He leaned over and kissed her. Then sat back behind the wheel, staring ahead.

"Why aren't we moving?"

"I know how upset you have been about hiding our engagement and postponing our wedding."

"I still am. Dylan, I *hate* this."

"Me too. I've been thinking how unfair this is to you." He watched her face. "I think we should at least tell your father that we're engaged."

Her expression brightened. "You do?"

"I do. Because we *are* going to be married, sooner or later. Besides, like Susie, he'll notice your ring and ask questions. And he'll need time to process it. He has to hate my guts for what I did to him and his foundation."

She shook her head. "I've talked to him. He doesn't hate you, Dylan. He's not that kind of man. And after all, he knows you saved my life. He's just . . . very conflicted about that. It's hard for him to accept that the man who publicly humiliated him also rescued his daughter from a killer that his own foundation helped set free."

"Well, if we meet him—together—maybe we can help him get past it."

She lit up at that. "I'd love that. He's on the West Coast for the next couple of weeks on business. I'll see if we can set it up when he returns."

"Great." He started the car. "Now it's time to hurry home."

"Why the hurry?"

He flicked a glance at her.

"Remember? I won our wager."

3

Trammel rolled off her, gasping for breath. The tiles of the kitchen floor were cold and hard against his naked back. He remained still, eyes closed, waiting for his racing pulse to slow.

"What I like . . . about you . . . Emmalee . . . is your utter lack of . . . sexual inhibitions."

He heard her giggle beside him. He turned to face her.

She lay on her back, too, her own eyes closed, face flushed, blonde hair disheveled, heartbeat pulsing rapidly at her throat. Her full lips were touched by a slight smile and a dollop of whipped cream. His gaze traveled down over her bare breasts, rising and falling like sea swells.

After a moment he sat up. She looked at him now through half-closed lids, arms stretched to either side and tied at the wrists to the legs of two kitchen chairs. The discarded can of whipped cream lay on the floor nearby.

"So . . . are you going to leave me here all night?" She pouted and squirmed on the floor.

"Of course not, my dear. What would the maid think?" He leaned over to untie her.

She laughed. "Oh, I don't know. Maybe she'd *like* to find me here like this. She's kind of cute." Holding his eyes, her tongue slowly traced along her lower lip, finding the remnant of cream.

"So. You like girls, too?"

Another giggle. "What's not to like . . . What about you, dear? Ever tried a threesome?"

Trammel saw his opening.

"Once, years ago. I found the physics to be a trifle complicated. But I gather you have been . . . more adventurous."

"If you only knew." Untied, she sat up, rubbing her wrists.

He rose and held out his hand.

"Tell me."

The conversation continued during their shower, and afterward, as they lounged in bathrobes on the sofa in her living room, sipping wine. Lit only by the shimmering red glow from the fireplace, she regaled him with tales of her sexual escapades. His questions encouraged her to become increasingly graphic and explicit, confirming to him that she was an exhibitionist.

"Ash enjoyed watching you with other men, then."

"Oh God, yes. It turned him on like crazy."

"I can see why," he said, running his hand inside her bathrobe.

"Mmmm." Her eyes closed and her head fell back against his shoulder. He nibbled her ear while his hand kept moving.

"You men are all alike," she sighed. "You fantasize about seeing your woman have sex with other people."

"I confess, I *would* enjoy watching you with another man. But only if I could control the situation."

It got her attention, as he knew it would. Her eyes grew wide and bright.

"Really? You would do that?"

"I was just about to ask you the same thing."

She threw back her head and laughed. He kissed her exposed throat. Then he raised his eyes and smiled.

"In fact, I happen to know that a very important man is interested in you. And I suspect you would be interested in him, too."

"Who?"

He looked away. "On second thought, I had better not say. I could get him into serious trouble."

"Avery! *Who?*"

He hesitated a few seconds more, then sighed.

"All right, if you insist. Senator Carl Spencer."

Her mouth fell open. "No! Not really!"

"Yes, really. He told me he thinks you are 'hot.' I am quoting. And I know for a fact that he likes to play around. His wife knows that, but they seem to have an arrangement about it. Just as you and Ash did."

"Oh. My. God! *Carl Spencer?*"

"You are making me jealous, Emmalee," he chuckled.

"No, no—don't be silly. I could never get seriously involved with a married man running for president." She sounded as if she were trying to convince herself.

"Or remain seriously involved should he win."

She nodded. "Right."

"Still, for now, I might be able to arrange an adventure . . . If you would like that."

"Yeah . . . I *would* like that."

"Well, we shall have to act soon, before he wins the nomination and gets Secret Service protection. That will make access virtually impossible."

She continued to nod; her eyes seemed glazed in the firelight. He knew she was fantasizing about being in bed with a second candidate for president. Another empowering sexual trophy for her.

And another one for Carl Spencer.

He found himself smiling. *This will be too easy.*

4

The next morning, he phoned Spencer from his study, calling the private number he had been given.

"Are you alone?" he asked when the senator greeted him.

"Yes, Avery. Jill is out at some Sunday brunch with friends. What's up?"

"I have a personal favor to ask, Carl. It is about Emmalee Conn."

"Ash's widow?"

"Yes. I have spoken with her on several occasions since the memorial service. As you know, Ash's green-energy investments took a terrible hit this past month. That, in addition to his death, left Emmalee in rather desperate financial straits. Their home was damaged in the explosion, but in any case, she has no way to make the mortgage payments, let alone repairs. So I leased an apartment for her here at the Watergate."

"That's extraordinarily generous of you, Avery."

Trammel found his hand toying with the watch in his pocket. He pulled it out and set it on the desktop. Its scratched silver surface gleamed dully under the chandelier.

"I am happy I can afford such gestures. But that still leaves the poor woman without means. And terribly embarrassed by her situation. You know how it is in this town."

"Yeah. It's all about image."

As you know too well, Carl. "Indeed. So she is desperate to generate an independent income. I would hire her in an instant, but my local office is fully staffed. However, I thought of you. As you ramp up your campaign staff, you might have a place for a well-connected Washington woman with strong social and communication skills—perhaps in your press office, or doing event planning."

"I . . . well, sure, Avery. I'll be happy to look into the possibilities. It sounds like she could be a great fit."

"I have no doubt you will find uses for her considerable talents."

"Yeah. Absolutely. Tell her I'll be delighted to meet her."

I have no doubt. "Wonderful. Thank you so much, Carl. I also think hiring the widow of your former rival would do wonders for *your* image, too. A sort of posthumous benediction from Ash—a passing of the torch, as it were."

"I see your point . . . yes. Have her contact my office Monday morning to set up an appointment."

Trammel spun the old pocket watch with his forefinger. It hissed softly across the polished surface of the desk.

"About that. I mentioned how humiliated she feels about her situation. She confided to me that she would prefer no one know she has been reduced to desperate job-hunting. So, perhaps a private meeting with you would be best."

"Oh . . . of course. I understand. That *would* be better for us."

"Us." You are a pathetically obvious creature, Carl. "I own a small apartment on I Street near Union Station, which I maintain for discreet business meetings and out-of-town guests. As it is so close to the Capitol, perhaps it would be convenient for you to meet there?"

"That sounds perfect!"

It was all that Trammel could do to keep from bursting out laughing.

"I know how busy you are, Carl, but she told me her schedule is open this week. Is there any way—"

"Certainly, Avery! I'll be happy to make time. The sooner the better . . . because we're hiring right now. Let me go check my calendar."

Avery Trammel picked up the old watch. The hands beneath its cracked crystal face had stopped moving years ago, forever freezing the most decisive moment of his life.

It had taken him decades of obsessive planning and action to reach this point, when everything he had fantasized about since that fateful moment would at last come to fruition. He felt suddenly like the director of some monumental film—the defining work of his career. He had invested every waking moment of his lifetime diligently, tediously acquiring and assembling the countless complicated elements of the production, all in service of a script he himself had authored long ago.

Now, his final bit players were taking the stage. Soon, on his command of *action*, each would perform his assigned role in the masterpiece . . .

In his epic of revenge.

TWENTY

The contact supplied by Trammel lived in a two-story apartment building on a quiet, tree-lined cul-de-sac, just off Route 50 in the heart of Fairfax, Virginia. The families in the tidy, modest brick homes across the street had no idea that the big, bearded bear of a man they often spotted smoking on his second-floor balcony was an international terrorist known as "the Chechen."

Lasher sat across from him at the man's cheap kitchen table, nursing his second bottle of beer, while the Chechen guzzled down his fifth. The man's beard had the consistency of steel wool and, like his eyes, was the color of soot. Those eyes, glassy from the beer, were deep-set under thick brows, and his face glistened with a sheen of sweat. The pungent odor of sweat and beer brought Lasher back to his Ranger days over in the Sandbox.

Trammel had provided only the sketchiest information about the guy: Ali Shishani, age 34, born in Chechnya, combat experience with weapons and explosives. Trammel gave the impression he knew nothing more. Lasher didn't like it. Shishani was a cipher to him, and totally unvetted, as far as he was concerned. Yet this guy was supposed to provide a team and the material to do the job. So far, all he knew was that he looked like a thug with a drinking problem. He'd have to do his own vetting, now, and if he didn't get the right answers, he'd tell Trammel to go find somebody else to run the op.

"Ali, my friend," he said, forcing a grin, "how much were you told about this job?"

The Chechen burped loudly and set down the empty bottle amid the growing thicket on the tabletop.

"I am told this is big operation. Like nothing here since 9/11," he said in a thickly accented growl. "You give me plan; my job is assemble and run team, and handle supply and logistics."

Lasher decided to go fishing.

"This is a very high-risk operation, Ali. Can you trust your contact?"

"With my life. We work together long time."

"That's good to hear. But the people arranging this operation on my side want to be sure you're experienced enough to handle something this big."

Shishani rested a huge, hairy, scarred fist on the table, jostling aside a couple of bottles.

"Let me tell you something, pretty boy. I got much experience."

Lasher clenched his teeth over the insult. "Can you be more specific? They'd like to know something about your background."

Shishani glared at him, his head weaving a bit unsteadily. He was obviously weighing how much he should reveal. Lasher figured flattery might loosen his tongue.

"Look, Ali, it's not *me* who needs reassurance. It's the people who hired me. I can see for myself you've 'been there, done that.'"

A slow, yellow grin split the middle of the black beard, like a quarter moon in the night sky.

"Yeah. I 'been there, done that.' I 'done that' *lots*."

"I can only imagine, my friend. How the hell did you get involved in this sort of work, anyway? You must have started pretty young."

"Shit," he snorted. "I start when I'm still snot-nose kid." He looked at Lasher speculatively. "How much you know about Chechnya and Russia?"

"Not very much." Lasher actually knew quite a bit, but wanted to get the man to open up.

"Yeah. You Americans—so full of selves you don't learn shit about rest of world. Well, Chechnya and Russia fighting since 1917. Take all week to tell you about wars. But you want to know about me, not history. Okay. So

Chechnya is Muslim republic. My father strict Sunni. He rule my mother and sisters and me with iron fist. Real prick, you know?"

"My father was the same way," Lasher said, egging him on. "A total bastard."

"Then you understand. I hate him. But I have to pretend I'm good Muslim kid, or he beat hell out of me. So I swear, one day I get back at him."

He stopped, seeming hesitant to go on.

"I don't blame you, my friend. My father forced me to join the Army. I swore I'd get back at him, too."

"Yeah, but I do lot more than join army." Shishani stopped again.

Lasher leaned in, grinning. "Yeah? What *did* you do?" he asked in a low, conspiratorial voice.

Shishani leaned in, too. His breath stank of garlic and cigarettes and beer.

"I talk lots to Russian neighbor—older guy—about my shitty life. One day he tell me he knows someone who give me opportunity. Pretty soon, he introduce me to other Russian. This guy is officer in FSB," he said, referring to Russia's internal security agency, successor to the infamous KGB. "He offer me lots of money to spy against Chechen Muslims fighting Russia."

"That had to be exciting work for a kid in a Muslim family."

"Oh yeah. He warns me, 'very dangerous'—but you know how that sound to teenager. All big adventure."

The Chechen kept talking while he got up and fetched yet another beer from his refrigerator.

"They tell me, 'Ali, pretend to still be faithful Muslim.' They give me cover story about getting trucking job in Moscow, so I can take long trips there and train. Weapons, bombs, what you call 'tradecraft' stuff." He flopped heavily into his chair. "I bring good money back to my family, so my stupid father approves. Nobody suspects." He grinned lopsidedly and took another long pull on the fresh bottle.

"So that's how Ali Shishani became an officer in the FSB," Lasher said.

"No, not officer. Agent. Like hired contractor. I report to FSB 'handler.' He give me assignments: Spy and inform and do nasty shit when FSB need somebody 'deniable.'"

"Oh . . . Well, since you weren't an officer, I don't suppose you were lucky enough to get really important assignments," Lasher prompted.

Shishani roared with laughter. "Like hell! Plenty important stuff. First assignment was because I attend main mosque in Grozny. I find out names in Wahhabi terrorism cell there—five guys—before they go to Moscow and cause trouble. FSB let me guide SVR hit team to houses and take them out. They let me shoot one myself!"

Lasher raised his bottle in salute. "I'm impressed, Ali."

"Just the beginning. Next year—summer 1999—Muslim rebels invade Russian republic Dagestan, near Chechnya. FSB says to me, 'Come back to Moscow, Ali; we have even bigger job for you.'"

Another pull almost emptied the bottle. The Chechen was relaxed and unguarded, now, slurring his words.

"Ray, you know about 1999 Moscow apartment bombings?"

Lasher had heard of the terrorist incident, but shook his head.

"Look it up. Ever since 1989 Soviet Union breakup, Russia want to bring Chechen Republic back into new Russia Federation. But they need excuse for invasion. So, 1999, Boris Yeltsin is sick, unpopular president of Russia. Vladimir Putin is young, powerful head of FSB. Then Yeltsin makes Putin prime minister, and Putin picks stooge to replace him at FSB.

"Right after that, September, bombs blow up apartment buildings in Moscow and couple other Russian cities. Three hundred people die. Authorities blame Chechen separatists for terrorism." He raised and wagged his forefinger. "But that is just official lie. Chechen Muslims did not do this." He took a last pull, draining the bottle.

Lasher frowned. "How do you know that?"

Shishani lowered the bottle and raised his eyes. They gleamed with a smug sense of pride.

"Because I help FSB plant bombs."

Lasher stared at him. "You did?"

"You damn right!" the Chechen replied, his fat lips in a loose, stupified grin. "I do this with other 'deniable' guys. See, this is FSB 'provocation.' And it work so good, too. When authorities blame Chechens, much anger all over Russia. Putin on TV promises revenge against murderers and orders bombing of Grozny. He leads Russia into war against Chechnya and becomes national hero. Next April, he is elected president, very easy, and replaces sick Yeltsin."

"You're saying Putin was behind those bombings?"

"You better believe! Stupid FSB officers even get arrested by Ryazan city police planting another apartment bomb. Many mistakes like that, so investigators figure out who really plant bombs. But those lawyers and reporters are then big danger to Putin. So he orders security services to eliminate them. And they do. Shootings. Poison. Car accidents." Another loose-lipped grin of bared yellow teeth. "I help with some of those, too."

Lasher was quiet a moment, thinking it through.

"You are still working with FSB?"

The Chechen shook his head. "Nah. I am—how is the word?—'blown' by somebody in Grozny mosque. They figure out I spy on them. So things get real hot for me in Chechnya. I barely get out alive to Moscow. FSB says, 'Ali, you are not too good for us anymore with Muslims.' But my handler likes me. He says, 'Ali is loyal and has good skills.' So they send me to SVR . . . You know which is which, Ray? FSB is like your FBI: for internal security. SVR is like CIA: sends spies and illegals outside Russia."

"So you work for SVR now."

"Sort of. See, SVR want 'deniable' agents, too. They send me here across Mexico border. But I work direct for 'Dignity and Honor'—organization of ex-KGB, FSB, SVR officers. Retired badasses, you know? Some still on contract and do active measures, 'wet work' against Kremlin enemies, all that shit. But sometimes they hire me, too, because I am never employee for Russia government. Even more deniable—you see?"

"I do see," Lasher said, smiling. Shishani's story at last confirmed what he had long suspected: Trammel *was* working with the SVR. That explained everything. How Trammel had been linked up with Shishani. The Russian security guards at his estate. Why he had dispatched Lasher to silence Muller. And why investigators like Wasserman and the CAP people had to be stopped, too, before the Russian network was exposed.

"Which brings us to our own operation, Ali. With your background, I see now why they picked you to help us. Did your handler explain who and what we need?"

"Yeah." Shishani's head bobbed as if barely attached to his shoulders. "No problem."

"You can get all the necessary people and materials into Washington?"

The Chechen rested a massive, moist paw on the bare skin of Lasher's forearm.

"Ray, I say *no problem*. Not only drug cartels smuggle across Mexico border. We have tunnels there, too. SVR makes plans way ahead. Long time ago, they send in everything illegals here need for any future . . . what is word?"

"Contingencies?"

"Yeah. 'Contingencies.' So everything waits for us in warehouse near Dulles."

"That's terrific, my friend. But can you smuggle in a team, too, on this short notice? We're on a very tight timetable, you know."

"Not necessary to smuggle. They are here already, too. See, U.S.A. Muslims do not know about Ali back in Chechnya. So, I join mosque here years ago, easy. For SVR *contingencies*"—he winked—"I recruit cell: four guys who want real bad to make *jihad* against America."

He paused to grin and shake his head.

"Stupid Muslim kids. They think I am ISIS. And they think I plan to die *with* them!"

Ali Shishani tossed his head back and laughed.

Ray Lasher laughed, too.

TWENTY-ONE

"Hey, Ed."

Cronin looked up as Erskine stepped into his cubicle. "Hey, stranger," he answered. "Haven't seen you in, what? It must be a week, right?"

"Sorry I haven't been any help lately. Chief still has me chasing my tail on the Fisher homicide. Just checking in to see how the hunt is coming along."

"Can't say I've made much progress. No fresh leads."

Erskine spun around a swivel chair to face backward, then settled his ample bulk astride it, resting his big forearms on its back.

"Whoever this guy is—and I'm almost positive now it *is* only one guy—he's one real piece of work," he said. "He must think he's the reincarnation of the Lone Ranger."

Cronin smiled. "Or maybe Zorro. The Lone Ranger went after ordinary criminals. Zorro went after corrupt political leaders."

"Our boy does both."

"He does. But his aliases suggest it's the same motive. It's all about fighting what he thinks are political and legal injustices." Cronin visualized his prime suspect. "Maybe you could say he's a *philosophical* Zorro."

"Yeah, but he hasn't used a sword or carved a 'Z' in any bodies."

Cronin chuckled. "Not yet."

"Give him time . . . By the way—I've been thinking about that dead ecoterrorist. Boggs. You doing any follow-up on him?"

"Should I be? What's he got to do with us?"

Erskine raised a brow. "Well, we suspected a vigilante connection in the attacks on all those 'green' businesses and environmentalists last month—right?"

"We did. But the FBI pegged Boggs as good for those." Cronin broke eye contact to fiddle with a sheet of paper on his desk.

"I'm not so sure, Ed. Those attacks involved a hell of a lot of complicated planning and execution. Far as anybody can tell, Boggs was the only one with brains in his group. He would've had to be here in D.C. all the time to organize and run things. But the interrogations of his followers established a timeline that shows he was almost always with them, out there in the forest."

"I know. Still, the bombings have his m.o. all over them," Cronin said, not looking up. "The pipe bombs mailed to Senator Conn's house and CarboNot headquarters. The ones planted in the senator's car. Boggs's cell phone dropped outside the senator's house. And his recorded confession. For once, I agree with the feebs. It's pretty open and shut that he was behind everything."

Cronin didn't mention that the stress analysis of Boggs's voice on the recording indicated he'd made the confession under duress.

"I read through their reports," Erskine said. "Yeah, sure, it looks like Boggs planted the bombs. But a lot of the other stuff just doesn't fit his m.o."

"What do you mean?" Cronin asked casually.

"The bomb out at Dulles, the one that blew up that billionaire's plane. The bomber used a drone to deliver it. That's a method never before tied to Boggs. He always just planted or mailed his bombs. And the type of explosive—the chemicals, the impact trigger—doesn't match anything he's ever used before, either."

Cronin shrugged, but still didn't look up. "Okay, so he tried something new. He was a genius, right?"

"It's more than that. The arrangement of dummy businesses at that virtual-office place, and the phone call intercepts—that was really sophisticated. Sure, a lot of it was set up by phone. But some of it couldn't be. Like planting the bugs they found in those various offices. The descriptions of the guys—or guy—who installed them, all on the same day, don't match Boggs. Then they'd have to monitor those bugs. Then pull off that complicated scam with the stock market, rerouting the calls of all those investors so they'd lose a fortune." He rolled his eyes. "That's 'Mission: Impossible' stuff. I don't think Boggs could've done a lot of it. Especially not if he spent almost all his time in the forest."

Cronin ventured a glance.

"Paul, the feebs figure Boggs was the brains and planned everything, then sent people from his WildJustice gang to do a lot of the doggy work. So he didn't have to be in D.C. himself all the time. He could have run things remotely."

"I just can't wrap my head around it," Erskine replied. "Genius or not, I can't see him and his pack of losers pulling off all this shit from a remote camp in the Pennsylvania woods, a couple hundred miles away. Even the cell signals are spotty out there. Besides that, the detectives couldn't find anybody else in his group who knew about the bombs. Even his girlfriend was in the dark. She insists only that pal of his, Nash, was in on it with him. And they say Nash wasn't that bright. So Boggs couldn't have delegated him to do all the complicated stuff." He scowled. "It just doesn't add up."

"But all the hard evidence points to them, and nobody else. Plus, Boggs had a strong motive. He was really pissed off against those targets. He thought they were all traitors to the cause."

"He may not be the only one with a motive, Ed. Don't forget the messages left behind at the crime scenes. Same signature ritual as the ones left at the vigilante murders. Same revenge elements and staging."

"Okay, so Boggs reads the papers and decides to be a copycat."

"But there's the other thing. The feeb theory is Boggs killed Nash up there about a month ago. Well, if he killed his pal, then who killed *him*? And why?"

"What are you saying, Paul?" Cronin forced a chuckle. "You think the vigilante got them both? That's quite a stretch."

"I'm saying it looks like there's another player or players out there, involved with all of this. Right now, it's just a theory. Once I get this Fisher case off my plate, I may pursue that angle a bit while you run down other leads." He looked out across the office, to where three tired-looking detectives huddled with their coffee cups, arguing about something. "While I'm at it, I might take another look at Dylan Hunter."

"What? You think he's—" Cronin began quickly.

Erskine laughed. "No. Of course not. His alibis are solid. Still . . . I get the feeling he knows more about the vigilante killings than he lets on. He seems to get inside information before anyone else. I think the arrogant bastard's been holding back on us."

Cronin felt himself relax. "Don't worry about working that angle. I've got Hunter on my own radar." He lowered his eyes back to the paper on his desk. "And if he *is* involved, I want to be the one to nail him."

Seconds passed. Cronin noticed the silence and looked up. His partner's fleshy chin now rested on his thick arms, crossed atop the seat back. Erskine was eyeing him steadily.

"Something personal about him I should know, Ed?" he asked quietly.

Cronin looked back, just as steady. Nodded slowly.

"Yeah. I don't like being played."

Erskine grunted, satisfied by the answer.

But Cronin knew it was only part of the truth.

2

The upscale apartment building on I Street favored a politically connected clientele. The location was ideal: Union Station and the Capitol were within walking distance. The architectural features and amenities included exposed brick walls, polished wood floors, floor-to-ceiling windows; a rooftop deck, pool, and cabana; a well-appointed gym, yoga room, theatre, and billiards parlor; plus common areas for socializing and parties.

Above all, discretion was insured. A uniformed security officer sat behind the desk in the modern lobby, greeting, announcing, and buzzing in high-profile guests. Each day's pages of the visitor log were run through a shredder the following morning.

The security officer was a conscientious young man who had served in the Army, and he regarded his responsibility to protect the privacy of residents and their visitors as a matter of personal honor. He asked no questions and never revealed the comings and goings of the rich and powerful to anyone, not even his wife. This evening he had been left specific instructions from Mr. Trammel, owner of Penthouse 1401.

At 1924 hours, a cab pulled up outside the glass entranceway. The back door opened, and he was surprised to see that the man who emerged was the famous Senator Carl Spencer, who was running for president. The politician walked inside quickly.

The young officer was sufficiently educated in current events to know that he didn't like the man or his politics. But, as always, he kept his manner professional and courteous, and—from habit born of experience—didn't let on that he even recognized him. He rose from his seat and offered a bland smile as the man approached the desk.

"May I help you, sir?"

"Yes. I am . . . Mr. Spencer. I am a guest of Mr. Trammel." He kept his head down and his eyes darted about nervously.

"Yes, sir." The guard made an unnecessary show of consulting his guest list. "All right, I have Mr. Trammel's authorization right here, Mr. Spencer. He said you are to go right up and make yourself at home. There is food and wine in the kitchen . . . Here is your key card, sir. The elevator is in the corridor behind me, to the right. Take it to the fourteenth floor. The key will open 1401."

"Thank you." The senator reached into the pocket of his expensive, tailored overcoat and his hand emerged with a twenty-dollar bill. Holding the guard's eyes and looking serious, he extended the money. "Here you go, young man."

"I appreciate that, sir," he replied, waving his hand, "but we have rules against accepting gratuities."

"Oh." He shoved the bill back in his pocket, looking more uneasy. "I just hope . . ."

He stopped.

The guard suddenly figured it out. This stuff happened here a lot. He had to force himself to put the smile back on his lips and a cheery tone in his voice.

"It's quite all right, sir. Mr. Trammel left instructions that after his guests arrived, there were to be no further interruptions of the meeting. But please feel free to call down here if you need a cab or anything."

The politician looked suddenly relieved. He smiled, showing a set of perfect teeth.

"Thanks so much! I'll be sure to put in a good word about you with Mr. Trammel. And your name is . . . ?"

"Joe."

"Thanks again, Joe."

The politician headed off toward the elevator.

Joe sat back down, closed his eyes, and sighed. He had let the woman go up twenty minutes earlier. He knew Spencer was married and that his wife had cancer.

It made him sick.

He thought of his own wife. At 26 and from a small town, Deb had no idea what crap he saw and heard every day. It made you cynical about the country and its leaders.

He wondered suddenly how long it would take for him to be affected—no, *infected* by it all.

He made up his mind, right then.

After the baby came, he would get them all out of this goddamned town.

3

In the bathroom of 1401, Emmalee stared at herself in the mirror and made a few last-minute adjustments.

Avery had told her to wear the same sexy outfit she'd worn to their lunch meeting at the Four Seasons. The little black cocktail dress—braless beneath. The spiky black heels. The diamond earrings.

She leaned forward to peer more closely. Her eyes looked better: the dark circles were gone now that she'd been sleeping again. Her lips, crimson and glossy-wet-looking, curved into a wide smile.

She looked *hot*.

And felt excited. She'd found photos online of Carl Spencer at some beach, shirtless and in swim trunks, playing volleyball with kids half his age. He had the body of a lifeguard—all biceps and abs and lean thighs. She watched a YouTube video of him playing lead guitar on stage with some band at a fundraiser. The way he moved and prowled the stage, like some big cat . . .

It was surreal. It was barely a month since Ash died. That was shock enough. And it left her with *nothing*. Then too, it had dashed her dreams of living in the White House as First Lady.

She'd thought her life was over.

Then, just over two weeks ago, Avery swooped in, like a knight on a white horse. One week later, she's living at the *Watergate*—the mistress of one of the most powerful men in the world. She'd managed to seduce him away from one of the most famous and beautiful movie stars in the world.

And now this man—with sexual appetites as strong as hers, and as adventurous as Ash's—wants to *share her* with the stud senator who is Ash's successor to become president!

It was insane. *Impossible.*

Yet, here she was . . .

Her eyes in the mirror were narrow and her face felt warm. She had never had *this much* power over men.

You've underestimated yourself, Emmy girl.

The images of Carl Spencer and Avery Trammel appeared in her mind's eye, standing side by side.

If you play this just right, you can have your pick of either of them.

She wondered which one she would choose, if it came down to that. After all, you have to think ahead . . . Avery was considerably older, but incredibly rich and connected. She'd never have to worry about money or social position for the rest of her life. Spencer was younger, even sexier, and probably rich *enough*. But of course there was no guarantee that he'd be elected president. On TV they were saying he was way behind in the polls.

She chuckled to herself. *It's like I'm Jackie, trying to choose between Kennedy and Onassis.*

Maybe it would all come down to which one might be willing to ditch his current wife for her. It was more likely Avery would do that. Spencer couldn't—not as someone running for president. Even more unlikely that he would divorce her if he *became* president.

Then she remembered what she read: His wife had cancer. So maybe, if she—

She cut off the thought. It wasn't nice to think that way. It would be *terrible* if she died.

Of course, tragic things happen in life, all the time.

And *if* it did, and he was free . . . and *if* he became president . . .

The doorbell chimed, startling her.

She took a last look. Tugged the v-neck of the dress to gape a bit wider. Then walked out and down the hall, past the guest bedroom . . . where Avery told her he'd installed a hidden, closed-circuit TV system, ready to film whatever happened.

It was like being a porn star, with other eyes watching her.

The anticipation was driving her crazy.

4

Carl Spencer had decided not to use his own key. It felt weird to just barge in, and she might take it the wrong way. He had to play this just right. So instead he rang the doorbell to 1401. He heard the faint chime inside. A moment later, the sharp *clopping* of a woman's heels, approaching.

When the door opened, she stood there looking up at him, back-lit by a crystal chandelier. Blonde hair, mussy-wild. Warm brown eyes. Wide, generous mouth, curved like a red Cupid's bow.

But not wearing business attire. He was astonished to see she was tucked, barely, into a little black dress, with lots of boob showing. Like she had just come from a cocktail party.

"Senator! How good of you to meet me here . . . privately."

Her voice was low, a silky purr. She extended her hand.

Or maybe the party was yet to come . . .

"Well, of course, Mrs. Conn," he managed, wrapping her smooth, warm hand in both of his, offering a grin he hoped had a bit of flirt in it.

She continued to appraise him for a moment, giving his hands a little squeeze. The tension rose in the silence. Just when things were about to get awkward, she broke the contact.

"Please, come in." She spun on her heel, sending the short hem of the skirt swirling a few inches higher, then walked away from him into the living room. Walked like a model, one tanned, sculpted leg crossing in front of the other, giving her ass a nice little wiggle.

Spencer knew women. And over the years, he had heard plenty of juicy rumors about Emmalee Conn.

She's giving me a show.

He was no longer nervous. He was excited.

"Avery left out some Chardonnay and fruit in the kitchen," she called out. Then she stopped and turned only her head, cocked to the side. "Hungry?" she asked, arching a brow.

He stepped inside. Closed the door behind him. Flipped the latch to lock it.

"As a matter of fact," he answered, "I am."

Spencer followed the trailing scent of her perfume into the kitchen.

They brought the now-opened bottle, wine glasses, fruit bowl, and some plates to the coffee table in the living room. She settled on the sofa, grinned up at him, and patted a place beside her. He took off his suit jacket, tossed it onto a club chair, then stretched, giving *her* a bit of a show.

"You don't look like most of the men in this town," she said, eyeing him up and down. "Ash had trouble staying in shape."

He slid into place beside her. "I try to work out every day. And watch what I eat. It's hard. Everybody on the Hill wants to meet at restaurants." He smiled. "So many temptations in this town."

She tossed her head back and laughed. "That's for sure."

His eyes roamed her body openly, now confident that she enjoyed it. "Well, it's obvious *you* keep yourself in great shape."

"Thank you. That's sweet of you."

"Tennis?"

"And swimming. I also do dance workouts. Did you know I used to be a dancer before I met Ash?"

"Oh, right. He told me that once . . . Again, Mrs. Conn, I'm so sorry about that." He felt he had to go through the charade. "He and I were always friends, even though we were sometimes rivals."

She patted his knee. "It was so nice of you to attend his memorial service, senator. And please, call me Emmalee."

"Sure, Emmalee. And it's Carl . . . It was such a shock to everyone," he went on. "I hope you've been managing to cope."

"Well, you can't cry forever." A little ripple of a shrug. "You have to move on."

"Yes. That's the right attitude . . . Here, let me pour some wine."

He filled the glasses.

"To new friendships," he said, raising his.

"And new beginnings," she replied, touching hers to his.

They held each other's eyes as they sipped.

"Avery explained your situation, Emmalee. I want to assure you that I came here to help. And please, don't think it's charity. A woman like you could be a great asset to me . . . to my campaign," he added quickly. "I can think of several positions for you."

"What positions did you have in mind, Carl?" She kicked off her heels and sat back against a pillow, drawing one leg under her.

"I can see you planning and overseeing a lot of the campaign events. You've had a lot of experience with those."

"Yes. Plenty of experience."

"Of course," he added, picking up a slice of mango, "the position would be demanding. It would involve months of travel with me and my staff, flying on my plane from city to city. Living in hotel rooms." He popped the mango slice into his mouth. "But you'd be well compensated."

"Oh, I'm sure," she said. "It sounds perfect, really. After all, I'm used to traveling with a senator and living in hotel rooms, you know." Her smile vanished. Her eyes narrowed. "Thank you so much, Carl. If that's an offer, I'm eager to accept. I just hope I can give you good value. I'd want to give you everything I gave to Ash."

"I have no doubt you will," he said. He had a hard time keeping his hand steady as he took another sip.

"Is that mango any good, Carl?"

"Delicious."

She set her wine glass down on the lamp table beside her.

"I'm comfortable here. Could you fetch me a piece?"

"Sure." He put a few slices on a small plate and moved closer, offering it. "Here you go."

"I'm nice and relaxed now. First time in days." She smiled, keeping her eyes closed. "Mind popping one in my mouth?" She parted her lips slightly.

His heart was pounding now. He picked up a piece from the platter. Raised it to her mouth. Tapped it against her lips.

Her eyes opened. She looked into his as she took a small bite of the fruit. Juice dribbled over her lip, down her chin.

"Mmmmm," she said, eyes dead serious now, and holding his like a vice.

He reached out and brushed his forefinger across her chin and lips, wiping off the wetness.

Not breaking eye contact, she took his hand in both of hers.

"We don't want all that tasty juice to go to waste, do we?"

She wrapped her glistening red lips around his forefinger.

5

Senator Carl Spencer was whistling when, at 8 a.m. sharp, he entered the stately, vaulted lobby of the historic Hay-Adams Hotel.

Though he'd had only three hours of sleep—and only after he returned to his own residence—he felt more energized than he had in months. He couldn't stop thinking about her and the night they'd just spent together. He couldn't believe the kinky stuff she insisted upon—things he'd never tried before, nor ever imagined he'd enjoy. Now, in the bright light of day, the memories embarrassed him . . . even as he had to suppress the impulse to grin like an idiot.

He trotted up the short flight of lobby steps and turned left, into the elegant Lafayette Restaurant. The dining room's creamy white walls, gold-framed art, crown molding, and beaded crystal chandeliers reminded him of the Neoclassical rooms in the nearby White House.

He spotted Avery Trammel already seated at an isolated window table at the far end of the room. Spencer let someone take his coat and made his way through the tables filled with breakfast diners. Trammel had a cup of coffee in hand and was studying a folded copy of the *Post* on the table before him.

"Good morning, Avery," he said cheerily.

The billionaire glanced up, but did not smile, rise, or offer a handshake. "Have a seat, senator." His eyes dropped back to the newspaper.

Spencer caught something cool in the tone. He felt his smile waver as he pulled out an antique-style chair opposite the billionaire and sat. Spencer reached for the silver coffee service between them and gestured with the pot.

"Freshen your cup?"

"I'm fine." Trammel didn't raise his eyes.

His manner, so different from their previous phone conversation. *Something is definitely off.*

"I appreciate your text message inviting me here this morning," he offered, pouring his own cup and trying to generate a pleasant mood.

"I'm most grateful for your generous offer of 'hands-on' assistance to my campaign."

At that, Trammel looked up again. His hard, colorless eyes reminded Spencer of a bird of prey.

"Actually, senator, I am here to rescue your campaign."

It surprised him. He put down the coffee pot.

"Rescue? I don't understand."

Trammel kept unblinking eyes on him as he sipped his coffee. Then lowered the delicate china cup to its saucer with a faint *clink*. Then raised his napkin to dab at his lips.

"You are a dismal fourteen points behind Helm on Gallup. And the *Post*"—he tapped the newspaper with a manicured finger—"has you down fifteen points. That deficit is still not insurmountable at this stage of the campaign cycle. However, you are not positioning yourself to turn things around. As Lucas told you weeks ago, your campaign has no theme and no narrative. Perhaps that is because the campaign is an accurate projection of the candidate himself. You realize that the progressive base of the party believes you to be a vacuous opportunist, without convictions or message. Based on your performance to date, I am inclined to agree with them."

It shocked him. It had been years since anyone had dared to criticize him to his face, let alone insult him.

"Now, wait a minute, Avery. That is completely—"

"No, *you* wait a minute, senator." Trammel leaned in, resting his clasped hands on the tablecloth. He turned to the tall, curtained window beside them. "Look over there," he said, lowering his voice.

Spencer's gaze followed his—out across Lafayette Park and its eponymous statue of the heroic Revolutionary War general, to the White House beyond, gleaming under the bright morning sun.

"Do you recognize that building, Senator Spencer?"

"Are you joking? What in the world are—"

"Do you truly wish to reside there?"

Spencer stared at him. "Avery, what are you driving at?"

Trammel turned back to face him.

"Just this. I have invested a great deal in the outcome of this election. Much more than you could possibly appreciate or imagine. And I am *not* prepared to see this singular opportunity squandered, due to your own shortcomings. For that reason, it is necessary for me to intercede and impose some discipline and direction upon you and your campaign."

Spencer couldn't believe the bastard's sheer arrogance.

"What do you *mean*, 'intercede'? What in hell makes you think you can just march in and start issuing orders *to me?*"

"Only this."

Trammel opened up the folded copy of the *Post,* revealing a large brown envelope tucked inside. He pushed it across the table.

Spencer undid the clasp and opened the flap. He reached in and pulled out the contents, which spilled onto the pristine white tablecloth.

The 8 x 10 photos were blow-ups, in full color. Most were full-body shots of her with him, showing graphically and unmistakably what they were doing. And some were close-ups of their faces, showing exactly who was doing what.

He felt his stomach lurch. Hands shaking and eyes darting around, he scooped up the photos and jammed them back into the envelope.

"Avery!" he croaked. "How did—"

Then, as he looked into those cold raptor eyes, *he knew.*

"You . . . You and *her,"* he hissed. *"*God damn you! You two set me up!"

"If it makes you feel better," he said, "she has no idea about this. You can keep those copies as souvenirs of your tryst. Naturally, I have retained the original digital images. Oh, and when you have a moment, do check out the thumb drive at the bottom of the envelope. It contains extensive video clips of your antics. I must say, *Senator,* you were both quite . . . uninhibited. Still, even in our liberalized society, I believe most voters would deem much of your behavior distasteful, if not disgusting."

Spencer seized the glass of ice water near his place setting, sloshing some onto the tablecloth. He took several large gulps, then he fell back, gripping the arm of his chair and trying to tamp down dizzying waves of terror and nausea.

"Why . . . are you doing this?" he gasped.

"You know me, senator. I must have my reasons." He took another sip of coffee.

"This is blackmail! But . . . it *can't* be for money."

That evoked a cold chuckle. "Of course not. You should spare yourself the torture of trying to guess my motive. You never will."

"Then what exactly do you want of me?"

Once again, Avery Trammel carefully lowered the cup to its saucer. Once again, he delicately dabbed his lips with the napkin. Once again, he leaned in, this time with a smile that was almost imperceptible.

"Now, *that* is the correct question. And the answer is: From now on, senator, I want you to do exactly what I tell you to do."

TWENTY-TWO

"I love riding in the *nice* car for a change."

Annie ran her fingers across the plush leather interior of his BMW 7 Series High Security car. "And you even have my 'smooth jazz' station on for me."

"Nothing but the best for my girl," Hunter responded, backing out of her driveway.

"But I thought you were limiting the use of this Beemer to your 'Wayne Grayson' alias."

"This is a special occasion. A wealthy gentleman doesn't escort his lady to a presidential debate in a Subaru Forester. Or—perish the thought—in a Ford van." He didn't mention his real motive for selecting this automobile from his collection. The BMW's body was armored, its laminate windows could resist anything up to a high-powered rifle, and it was loaded with state-of-the-art sensors and protective technology. The custom gun case between the seats was an added plus, and tonight it held a couple of serious weapons.

"But using 'Wayne's' car is a breach of your security protocols," she said, frowning. Then, after a short pause, she added: "Oh."

"What do you mean, 'Oh'?"

"'Oh,' as in: 'Oh—I get it.'"

"Get what?"

She sighed. "Don't play dumb, Dylan. We're in this armored tank tonight because *he's* out there somewhere. So it *is* for security."

He didn't answer.

She remained quiet, too, as they emerged from her Falls Church neighborhood onto Route 66 and headed toward Washington. After a while, she said:

"You're worried about him. And mainly for my sake, right?"

"We both just have to be a bit more cautious, that's all . . . So, how's the mole hunt going?"

"You're changing the subject."

"Yes, I am. So, how's the mole hunt going?"

"Dylan, you're impossible."

"Yes, I am. So, how's the mole hunt going?"

She punched his arm lightly. "Okay, we'll change the subject . . . Ah, yes, the Great Mole Hunt. Grant and I are just starting to launch the plan we hashed out after our dinner a couple of weeks ago. We have to narrow down the vast list of potential suspects. So, we're leaving multiple hooks dangling in the water, baited with the sort of information that would interest any Russian spy. But in each case, the bait is different, and accessible only to a specific, limited group of potential suspects. So if one piece of bait is taken, then the people in that group go on our short list for closer investigation."

"How are you supposed to find out if and when somebody takes the bait?"

"That's what has taken so long to work out. First, we need to find out which directorate the mole works in. So this week, Grant will put in a different request to each one, trying to stir the pot."

"What do you mean? Give me a for-instance."

"For instance, on April 15th Grant will visit the Director of Science and Technology in person and ask him to assemble his top people for what he'll describe as an urgent, high-priority request. He'll tell the group they need to design and supply him, within the next twelve hours, a miniaturized communications device with burst-transmission capability. He'll say it will be left by one of our case officers in a dead drop outside of London, then picked up on the evening of April 17th for use by a newly recruited, highly placed Russian agent. Grant will give them the exact address of the supposed dead drop, so they can research the site and camouflage the item to blend in. Then he'll say, 'I can't stress how important and sensitive this is. What I've told you *must* stay inside this directorate.'"

"That should arouse curiosity."

"Exactly. Any mole in S&T will have his antenna up for anything this big. He or she will immediately notify the SVR, and they'll hustle a team out to the dead-drop site to wait and see who their traitor is. The only access into the area is an isolated country road. Grant will hide a small surveillance team near the site to see if the SVR shows up. If they do, then we'll know our mole is in S&T."

"Of course, there's no real Russian agent, and nobody will plant that device in the dead drop."

"True. But if the SVR *is* tipped off about the drop, it should drive them crazy with paranoia, wondering who their traitor could be and why the drop never took place. And it will be a nice bonus if our surveillance team also gets some photos of any SVR illegals they dispatch to the site."

"It's a clever plan. Tell Grant I'm impressed."

She turned to him with a smug smile. "Actually, I came up with that plan myself."

He grinned. "Now, I'm *really* impressed. But a bit scared, too. I had no idea you were so sneaky, Annie Woods."

"Just remember that, if you're ever tempted to cheat on me, Dylan Hunter. And you'd also better remember I'm pretty good with edged weapons."

"Ouch. Copy that."

She spent the next few minutes describing several other schemes to smoke out the mole.

"The thing that scares us most," she added as they crossed the Roosevelt Bridge into the city, "is the possibility that the mole is someone on the seventh floor. Grant worries it might even be one of the people who attended that confrontation meeting with him in the director's conference room."

"How can you determine that?"

"Grant plans to vet each of them, subtly, by dropping fake-but-juicy-sounding information on operations in progress in different locations. He'll instruct the relevant station chiefs and case officers to be on the lookout for any increased surveillance or tell-tale reactions from their Russian counterparts, and to notify him directly if they spot anything."

He nodded slowly, thinking it through. "I hate to say it, but it wouldn't surprise me if it's one of the top people. Somebody even higher on the totem pole than Grant."

"Well, if it is, we have to find him or her fast—before somebody figures out what we're up to and shuts us down. So while Grant works from the top ranks down, I'll be working from the bottom up, in each of the directorates. If I can narrow the hunt to one directorate, then I'll have to try to isolate a specific division. But he and I can't be seen communicating, so I'm pretty much on my own."

The traffic was light, so he ventured another look at her. She was staring out her passenger-side window, toward the glowing obelisk of the Washington Monument that pierced the dusk sky as they passed. The city's lights flickered on strands of her short chestnut hair. Beneath her open, light-brown cashmere coat she wore a white silk blouse and a long, dark-brown skirt. She looked petite, feminine, vulnerable. But the fragile appearance was deceptive. He knew her strength.

"I'm so proud of you, Annie."

She turned, raising a brow. "Thank you. What prompted *that*?"

"Damned if I know. Hmmm . . . could it be love?"

She looked away, but he noticed the little smile.

2

Hunter pulled into a C Street parking garage behind the Newseum, the site for the CNN-hosted town hall. To avoid being spotted together, he and Annie separated before they reached the elevators. They made their way independently to the first floor, through the heavy security, past the coat check and reserved ticket desks, and into the Annenberg Theater.

Hunter hated crowds, and his situational awareness was dialed up to the max. He decided to head up to the balcony on the right. He walked past a middle-aged Secret Service agent, feeling the man's eyes following him as he took the aisle seat in the back row. From this darkened spot Hunter could watch everyone else and the proceedings on the stage without being visible.

Then he settled in to wait out the hour before the program began. He liked Roger Helm, and he was curious to see how well he would perform tonight against his two main rivals in this sort of setting.

More importantly, he knew that the fate of the nation would rest on which of the three men about to take the stage would become America's next president.

At nine p.m., the CNN anchor delivered his opening monologue and introduced to the stage each of the candidates in turn. Senator Carl Spencer was the first to emerge from the wings, to the applause of his partisans among the 450 audience members. Spencer stood by his chair under the bright lights, boyishly handsome, grinning and nodding in appreciation. His gaze sought out his family in the first row.

Avery Trammel did not trust Carl Spencer to remain on message tonight. To make sure he did, Trammel had arranged conspicuous seating for himself and Julia in the second row, directly behind Spencer's wife and children. A pointed reminder of what was at stake.

When Spencer's eyes met his, Trammel gave a little smile and nodded. He saw Spencer's grin waver. Still watching the senator, Trammel leaned forward and said to Jill Spencer, "You must be so proud of your husband."

She tilted her head, smiled and nodded. "Oh, I am!" She turned back to face her husband, applauding vigorously.

For an instant, Spencer looked scared, but recovered immediately. He flashed the grin at full wattage again, pointed toward them and gave a slight wave, then took his seat. It had been but a momentary lapse, no doubt unnoticed by the millions watching at home. But that little wave told Trammel his message had been received and understood.

For the first time in weeks, he began to relax. It did not matter that the applause was louder when Roger Helm was introduced. Just as the latest polls did not matter.

None of this will matter in eight more days.

"What are you laughing at, Avery?"

Julia was looking at him strangely.

He patted her arm. "I am merely amused by the carnival of American politics."

The candidates sat side by side in the middle of the stage, with their CNN host to their right, facing them. Crew members maneuvered cameras around the stage and on the auditorium floor below, projecting their images onto the large screen hanging behind and above them, and into millions of homes around the country. The moderator announced that the forum would begin with three-minute opening statements from each candidate.

Hunter pulled out a notepad to record his impressions.

First up, as winner of the coin toss, was the front-running Republican candidate, Governor Tom "Stonewall" Waller. To the cheers of his boisterous fans, the beefy man leaped to his feet and trotted to center of the stage. His curly black hair, twinkling blue eyes, and jutting jaw filled the screen behind him.

"Okay. Thank you, everybody," he began. "So, let me tell you about my life and why it qualifies me to be your next president."

Waller spent the next three minutes swaggering back and forth across the stage, making grandiose gestures as he boasted about his rags-to-riches rise. It all began in Boone County, West Virginia, he declared, as the only son of a poor coal miner who died from black lung disease. But by hard work and sheer determination, he won a football scholarship to West Virginia University. There he caught the eye of NFL scouts, became a first-round draft pick, and soon, "the star fullback" for the Pittsburgh Steelers.

"That's where I earned the nickname 'Stonewall.' Because that's what my opponents thought they ran into." Waller mugged and flexed his bicep, like a bodybuilder; the audience roared with laughter and applause.

After his football career ended, Waller landed TV and film roles, then hit it big as an action-movie star. ("You've all seen my movies, right?" More laughter and applause.) As he entered his fifties, his celebrity and wealth allowed him to reinvent himself once again—this time as a politician. Three years ago he ran for the governorship of his home state as a Republican, on a populist platform— "and I won in a landslide," he crowed.

"I have succeeded spectacularly in everything I've ever done," he concluded. "It's because I am a winner—and I'll never accept anything less than winning. I started with nothing, and with lots of privileged and powerful people against me. But I beat them all. I know you folks want to be winners, too. But the privileged and powerful are holding *you* down. And you can't fight them all by yourselves. You need a champion—somebody tough enough to stand up to the Establishment big shots—somebody who will put those bastards in their place."

He brandished his fist as his voice rose.

"I want to be your champion! I want to beat these guys for you! Because when they lose, you'll win! And that's gonna happen this November, when you elect 'Stonewall' Waller to be your next president! Thank you, my friends!"

Raucous cheers followed him as he trotted back to his seat.

In the darkness of the balcony, Hunter shook his head.

"God help us," he muttered to himself.

Next up was Roger Helm. He rose to enthusiastic applause, took a single step forward, then stood still, waiting for the crowd noise to die down. When he spoke, it presented a deliberately low-key, dignified contrast to the bombastic Waller.

"Thank you. I am not here tonight to talk about myself or my personal success. If that interests anyone, you can look it up. Instead, I want to talk about a subject that *should* interest you as voters: my vision for America."

He paused again, and the audience fell completely silent. The stage lights made his gray-blond hair look almost white, and his chiseled face projected both strength and warmth.

"Unique among all nations in world history, America was founded on a 'live-and-let-live' social philosophy. It was to be a beacon of liberty for the world: a country that allowed and encouraged each of us to enjoy productive lives, in peace and freedom. A land where we would relate to each other voluntarily and cooperatively, but would otherwise mind our own business. Where we would interact with each other by trading—not by taking.

"That was the unique vision of our nation's Founders, institutionalized in our laws and in our free enterprise system. And that's the vision that enabled America to rise to unparalleled greatness. Our nation thrived because of our mutual respect for each other, as individuals—because we viewed each other not as threats and adversaries, but as partners in friendship and trade.

"America became the greatest nation on earth because our entire system was built on 'win/win' social and economic relationships. Not on predatory relationships, in which one person or group wins only by making some other person or group lose. That us-against-them outlook was the dominant worldview of humanity's tribal past. Back then, our primitive ancestors lived, not by producing wealth, but as nomadic scavengers. In such a world, the rules were: eat, or be eaten; kill, or be killed; my tribe survives only by beating your tribe. And this zero-sum, win/lose worldview filled mankind's history with horrifying acts of plunder and warfare and bloodshed.

"Even today—despite enjoying the enormous benefits of a modern society based on 'win/win' relationships—too many people have never gotten out of the jungle, at least not in their minds and values. Take my opponents, for example. They would divide us into warring economic classes of 'haves' and 'have-nots,' and into warring racial, ethnic, and nationality groups. But whether they divide us based on class or tribe, both accept the same relic of humanity's violent past: the belief that you can only succeed in life at someone else's expense. They seek to elevate themselves to the presidency by promoting such conflicts.

"If America is to continue to thrive—or even survive—we must cast off the curse of primitive, divisive tribalism, once and for all. I see a future for America based on trading, not taking—where each of us is a maker, not a taker. That was the vision of America's Founders, and it is my vision, too. It's that individualist vision that sets me apart from my tribalist opponents. It's the same vision that enabled me, a kid from America's heartland, to take nothing but an idea and build it into a dynamic, hugely successful enterprise.

"That vision has a name: the American Dream. And this is my promise to you: My commitment to restoring the American Dream will guide me every day, if you honor me by electing me to be your next president. Thank you."

Helm sat down to thunderous applause.

Hunter found himself clapping loudly, too.

Finally, it was Senator Carl Spencer's turn to rise. Hunter had seen him on television many times. Tonight he was surprised that the usually smooth, confident politician looked uncharacteristically nervous. On the big screen, the man's eyes seemed to be glancing a lot at some particular spot in the audience.

Spencer began with his usual rhetoric about "compassion and economic justice for all the forgotten people left behind in America." To Hunter, it was the tired, insincere platitudes of a rich career politician who had never known personal privation or struggle, but who postured incongruously as a man of the people.

But suddenly Spencer paused. He wet his lips with his tongue before continuing.

"Yet while my enduring commitment remains to economic justice for all, I come here tonight to raise a different concern.

"As a member of the Senate Foreign Relations Committee, I gain access to important intelligence sources. Because of their highly classified nature, I cannot be too specific about some of the reports I see. However, recently I received an alarming warning from a knowledgeable intelligence official about planned terrorist attacks on the homeland.

"Now, you have heard very little from my Republican and Independent opponents about the ongoing dangers of radical Islamist terrorism on American soil. Perhaps they've not given the issue much thought. But protecting the American people against such threats is the first responsibility of any president. And it certainly will be *my* top priority as your next president.

"We need to do far more to identify the would-be Islamist terrorists in our midst, and to neutralize them before they can wreak havoc upon us—as they have all over Europe. Whatever other issues are raised tonight, I plan to focus on this topic, and to return to it repeatedly in the coming days and weeks. We are rapidly approaching a dangerous moment. And I aim to sound the alarm, loudly and clearly—before it is too late, and before my warning tonight proves sadly prophetic. Thank you."

Spencer gave a brief, unsmiling nod, then retreated to his seat. The applause in his wake was tepid, and a buzz of voices rose around the theater. The CNN host had to call for silence before moving on to ask the candidates the first question submitted by an audience member.

"What in hell is he doing?" the woman seated in front of Hunter said to her male companion. "He sounds like a right-wing Republican tonight!"

The man shrugged. "He's way down in the polls. Maybe he thinks by moving right, he can siphon some votes away from Waller and Helm. They call it 'triangulation.'"

"Well, he's just lost his Democratic base!" She raised her eyes, as if looking to heaven. "Ashton Conn would *never* have betrayed us like this. He had *principles.*"

Dylan Hunter smiled in the darkness.

Downstairs in the second row, Avery Trammel smiled, too. He was hearing much the same in the angry and astonished whispers around him.

But Carl Spencer had done his job. He had stuck to the script he had been given.

Their eyes met again, and Trammel rewarded the senator with another smile and a nod.

Spencer reached for the water glass on the coffee table before them and drained half of it.

If only he did not look so nervous.

But in another week, Trammel knew, how he had looked tonight would be forgotten. He would be remembered only for his prophetic warning.

3

Trammel and Julia greeted Spencer and his family offstage afterward and reassured him that he had performed just fine. Then he led Julia through the crowd filtering out of the theater into the lobby. As always, people recognized the movie star, gaped in awe, and parted to let them pass.

Julia asked to stop at the ladies' restroom before they went out to his waiting limo. As they neared, he felt an unexpected shock at recognizing a familiar face. His steps slowed.

"I'll be just a minute," Julia said, walking on. When she reached the restroom door, she had to pause as a young woman emerged. The pair exchanged brief smiles.

The young woman was extraordinarily beautiful. And she walked right over to where Dylan Hunter stood waiting with her coat.

He saw that Hunter was looking at him, too.

There was no point in pretending. And maybe he could learn something of value. Trammel walked over while Hunter helped her into her coat.

"Mr. Hunter," he said with a slight nod. "Though we have not been formally introduced, I believe we encountered each other a few months ago, outside of the EPA headquarters. I am Avery Trammel."

"Of course I know you, Mr. Trammel," the reporter said, his voice equally devoid of emotion. "And yes, I remember seeing you there with your lovely wife. Although I fear my presence may have disrupted an otherwise celebratory occasion."

Trammel noticed that the young woman's smile vanished at the mention of his name. He turned to her.

"And if I may ask, who is this charming lady?"

"Just a friend," the woman replied, her voice and expression as cool as the man's.

"I am so glad for you, Mr. Hunter. We all need friends in troubled times like these."

"Perhaps the times would not be so troubled, except for the trouble-makers."

"And who might those trouble-makers be, Mr. Hunter?"

The question elicited an insolent grin.

"You'll just have to keep reading the *Inquirer*, Mr. Trammel."

Trammel felt anger rising. "I limit my local reading to the *Post*."

"A pity. They offer a completely different narrative of good guys versus bad guys. Perhaps you'd find my narrative more persuasive."

"I doubt it. I took grave exception to the fairy tale you invented about CarboNot Industries."

"Oh, that's right. You were an investor, weren't you?"

Trammel felt a hand on his arm.

"Darling, I'm ready to go," Julia said. "But please, don't let me interrupt your conversation."

"Not at all. I was just about—"

"Miss Haight," Hunter interrupted with a smile and a nod.

She extended her hand. "Please, it's Julia. And you are . . . ?"

"Dylan Hunter," he answered, taking her hand and bowing courteously.

Trammel noticed her puzzled look, as if she had heard his name and was trying to remember.

"The *Inquirer* reporter, dear," he prompted.

"Oh!" She withdrew her hand.

"My mother's name is Julia, too," the young woman interjected, with an empty smile.

"We should be going," Julia said, tugging at his arm.

"Yes. We should," Trammel replied. "I am sure our paths will cross again, Mr. Hunter." He nodded at them both, then turned away.

"I can't wait," the cocky bastard called out after him.

Locked inside his study around midnight, Trammel called Lasher and told him about the encounter.

"So he has a girlfriend, then."

"So it would seem."

"Tell me about her."

Trammel described the woman. "See if you can find out who she is."

"What do you want me to do with her when I find her?"

"Just report back to me. It eventually may be necessary to use her as leverage against him."

"You sure you don't want me to take any direct action now, sir?"

"I do not."

He paused. Remembered the insolent grin. Then added:

"Not yet."

TWENTY-THREE

"Thanks for seeing me, Mr. and Mrs. Jackson."

"You are most welcome, Detective Cronin," Lila Jackson said to him, as he took a seat in an armchair facing them on their sofa. "You sure I can't get you anything—coffee, tea, water?"

He waved if off with a smile. "No, I'm fine, really. I won't be taking up more than a few minutes of your time."

They sat in the living room of the Jacksons' two-story, well-maintained home on the northern part of 17th Street, just a few blocks from Rock Creek Park. Before arriving, Cronin had done a quick internet search that reminded him Morgan Jackson was a high-ranking administrator at Howard University, while his wife taught in their music program. Family photos, including a pretty young African-American girl—who had to be their murdered daughter, Loretta—filled the mantel over the stone fireplace. Above that hung a large Impressionist seascape. Against the facing wall stood a well-polished Steinway upright piano, with music books stacked on its bench.

"When you called us, you mentioned you're with the Alexandria Police Department," Morgan Jackson said. "So we're sort of puzzled about what investigation could involve us." He paused; his eyes narrowing. "Unless of course it somehow involves Dixon."

"As a matter of fact, it does. It's about how he was killed."

They exchanged a quick glance. "What do you mean, 'how'?" Morgan said. "We heard he died in a turf battle with some rival drug gang."

He watched them carefully for any reactions to his next words.

"Well, there are some inconsistencies about that theory. It doesn't seem that it was gang-related after all."

Lila shifted in her seat. Morgan spread his hands on his knees and said, "But wasn't he running a drug gang?"

"Oh, sure. But the more the Baltimore Police look into it, the less it seems to have been about drugs. That's why we got involved. I forgot to mention: I'm not here representing the Alexandria P.D. I'm investigating this in my role as a member of the Vigilante Task Force."

Sudden, simultaneous nervous looks. Another quick exchange of glances.

"I . . . don't understand," Morgan said.

"I'm sure you're familiar with the recent wave of vigilante shootings," Cronin continued, watching closely. "How murderers freed by the legal system have been targeted for assassination by someone. It's been all over the news for months."

Lila Jackson averted her eyes and plucked at her skirt, while his hands balled into fists on his thighs.

"Certainly," he said. "Who hasn't heard about that? So . . . are you saying you think that group of vigilantes might have killed Dixon?"

"A vigilante group, perhaps," he said casually. "Or maybe just a single individual."

She licked her lips. He cleared his throat and said, "Only one vigilante?"

"I know it's hard to believe," he went on. "But the attack on Dixon and his gang was done by a single man. And that's caused us on the task force to rethink things. We've gone back and checked the prior vigilante cases, and we can't find a single one where we know for sure that more than one guy was involved."

"That *is* unbelievable," Jackson said. "How could that be possible?"

Cronin shrugged. "Obviously, it's someone of considerable combat skill and experience. But because this case with Dixon affects you so personally, I felt I should stop by and tell you about this new focus in our investigation, just so you wouldn't have to hear rumors in the media."

She continued to look away and fidget with her skirt, remaining silent, while his smile looked forced.

"That's awfully nice of you, Detective, to be concerned with our feelings like that."

"Well, I just know how the press can be. You've had experience with the newspapers, I know. Like those stories the *Inquirer* reporter has been doing?" He looked upward, as if trying to remember. "What's that guy's name?"

Another quick glance passed between them.

"Oh, you mean Dylan Hunter," Jackson said.

Cronin smiled. "Yeah. That's the guy. You've been following his articles, then. I recall he wrote about a victims rights group you belong to."

Morgan Jackson's eyes narrowed. He suddenly seemed wary, as if guessing Cronin's real purpose.

"Yes, Detective. In fact, our group, Vigilance for Victims, honored him last month with an award at our annual banquet, for his work exposing the leniency in the legal system, and for publicizing our concerns."

Cronin knew that, but didn't let on.

"Oh, really? Then I gather you approve of what he's been writing."

Lila turned back to him. "We do. We all do. Dylan kept his promise to us about publicizing victim cases and issues."

"You've known him for a while, then?"

"Just since our monthly meeting last September," Morgan said. "He was invited by one of our members, Susie Copeland."

The name shocked him.

"So Susanne Copeland is a member of your group?" he said casually, masking his surprise.

"She is. We often hold our meetings in her home."

Cronin's head was spinning with the implications.

"I'm glad he's been loyal to you," he said, forcing another smile. "Most reporters aren't like that."

"No, they're not," Lila said, a trace of bitterness in her tone. "But Dylan's one in a million."

He noticed the familiarity of the first name.

"I understand how grateful you must be." He sighed. "But, I have to tell you that, for us cops, his articles have been a mixed blessing."

"What do you mean?" A defiant edge in her voice.

"For all the positive attention he's given to you folks, the publicity he's given to the criminals in his *Inquirer* articles seems to have made them targets of the vigilantes." He spread his hands. "Or vigilante, as the case may be."

"So it seems," Morgan Jackson said, looking at him steadily.

"I recall that he wrote about the case involving Mrs. Copeland and her late husband. Has he ever written about your case?"

They both shook their heads. "We asked him to, at the awards banquet," Lila offered. "And he wanted to. But he said there wasn't any time to do that before Dixon was released from prison."

So Hunter lied. He did *know when Dixon was set to be released...*

Lila Jackson seemed less guarded than her husband, so he turned to her.

"I see. Has he written about cases involving other members of your group, Mrs. Jackson?"

She opened her mouth to answer, but her husband interjected.

"Detective, we appreciate your stopping by to let us know about these new developments in Dixon's death," he said, rising from the sofa to his feet. "But Lila has a doctor's appointment"—he glanced at his watch—"at two, and I'm afraid we have to get ready for that, now."

He noticed Lila's puzzled frown as she looked up at her husband.

"Oh, I'm sorry if I am holding you up." Cronin stood, too. "Thanks so much for your time."

Morgan led him to the front door. Then turned and offered his hand, but no smile.

"I do thank you for keeping us in the loop about your investigation, Detective Cronin."

Cronin shook his hand. "Of course. We're after the same goal, Mr. Jackson."

"Which is?"

"Making sure that justice is done."

Jackson's grip tightened. He locked eyes with Cronin.

"We'll never get our daughter back, Detective. But we've got our justice, now—at least, the only justice we can hope for in this life."

The man's next words came slowly, deliberately.

"Far as we're concerned, everybody should forget about Dixon, now. And just move on. So that Lila and I can move on, too. This has been very hard on her. On both of us." He released Cronin's hand.

Cronin's eyes moved to Lila Jackson in the living room, staring at him, hands clasped in her lap. Behind her, the photos on the mantelpiece looked at him, too.

"I'm a father, too, Mr. Jackson. I can't begin to imagine what you've gone through. And I truly wish I *could* forget about Dixon. But I have a job to do. I still have to find out who killed him. And who's killing all those other criminals. And why. That's what the law and justice requires. I hope you understand that."

Jackson nodded solemnly. "I do. But . . ."

"But what?"

"But maybe we have a different idea about what constitutes justice."

2

Back in his office, Cronin went online to the Vigilance for Victims website. He found a chronological archive of summaries and photos from the group's monthly meetings and events. He scrolled back to the September entry.

The monthly meeting had taken place September 10th. In addition to a brief write-up, a group photo of the participants was posted, with their names listed beneath.

Dylan Hunter stood right in their midst.

And Annie Woods was standing to one side.

Well, well, well . . .

Other names beneath the photo rang all sorts of bells.

Cronin opened a desk drawer where he kept bulging files about the vigilante murders. It took a few minutes of rummaging before he dug out Hunter's newspaper articles from last year. He spent more minutes scanning them, searching for and jotting down names from the stories that matched those listed on the group's website.

And he glanced repeatedly at the wall of his cubicle, where he'd pinned photos of the criminals killed by the vigilante. When he saw links between them and victims in the stories and on the website, he jotted down their names, too.

Each match felt like a lock's tumblers clicking into place.

After about ten minutes of this, he picked up and stared at his scribbled list.

One guy in the meeting photo was George Banacek. He was the father of Tommy Banacek—who had been murdered by Orlando Navarro and Tomas Cardenas.

Over the next two months, both of them were shot dead by the vigilante, along with a gang pal, Manuel Maldonado.

A frail-looking elderly woman stood next to Hunter in the photo: Kate Higgins, mother of a kid named Michael Higgins. Michael had been killed by Conrad Williams.

Also shot dead by the vigilante.

Then there were the Jacksons—at that meeting and in the photo. Their daughter Loretta—raped and murdered by Reginald Dixon.

Dixon, too, had been taken out by the vigilante.

Finally, of course, Susanne Copeland, widow of Arthur Copeland. Victims of the brutal attack by Adrian Wulfe, "Jay-Jay" Valenti, and William Bracey.

Valenti and Bracey had been gunned down by the vigilante.

And Adrian Wulfe had been stabbed to death . . . by none other than Dylan Hunter.

Cronin tossed his pen and paper on his desk. Began to rock slowly in his chair.

So there it is.

He stared at the photo. At the image of Dylan Hunter. Surrounded by the victims he had avenged.

He no longer had the slightest doubt.

All he needed now was iron-clad proof.

3

Hunter thanked Morgan Jackson again, then ended his phone call.

Then sat in the stillness of the living room in his Bethesda apartment, stroking Luna.

The cat lounged beside him on the sofa, purring contentedly. Whenever his hand stopped moving, she nudged it with her head or paw to remind him of his proper priorities.

Hunter petted the cat absently, staring out the sliding glass door, past the balcony, into the roiling mass of dark clouds on the western horizon that had grown to obscure the afternoon sun.

It was time to face the uncomfortable truth.

His Dylan Hunter cover was blown.

Wonk knew his cover identity was fake, too. And suspected him of having some sort of spy agency connection.

So did the Jacksons. And George Banacek. And Kate Higgins. And Susie Copeland.

Lasher—and whoever he was working for—knew it was an alias. And knew, also, that he was some kind of operator with combat and sniping skills.

Meanwhile, Avery Trammel had spotted him with Annie. That adversary knew they were linked.

And Cronin had known all along that the Dylan Hunter name was an alias. What Morgan just reported confirmed that Cronin was now certain he was the vigilante, and was out to nail him.

The status quo had become untenable.

Cronin would get the task force to focus on him. They'd obtain court orders to allow electronic surveillance, and subpoenas to compel his friends to testify against him—or to face criminal penalties. Which, of course, he'd never allow them to do.

Meanwhile, Lasher and his unknown employer, or employers, would be hunting him relentlessly—either to kill him or to expose him to the media.

Even if, by some miracle, he managed to get past Cronin and Lasher, it was only a matter of time before one of the angry targets of his newspaper investigations, like Trammel, would hire a detective to dig into Dylan Hunter's background. Or some competing newspaper or reporter would do so. It was amazing that had not already happened. But when it did, they'd reach the same biographical dead ends that Annie, Wonk, Bronowski, and Cronin had hit. They'd find a ghost. A man with no parents, home town, or childhood. No educational or work history. No known address.

Which would arouse their curiosity even more. The attention, questions, investigations would become relentless. They would pester Bronowski and others at the *Inquirer*. They would look closer into his death fight with Adrian Wulfe, at the implausibility of a mere reporter overcoming a giant mixed martial arts fighter. They would try to follow him every time he surfaced in public. That pursuit might lead them to Annie, endangering her. And through her, it could lead them to the CIA . . .

He got up. Began to pace the room.

It was so incredibly stupid that he'd allowed all this to happen. In his anger against the injustices he encountered, he'd violated every rule of tradecraft. Instead of remaining hidden in undercover obscurity, he'd gone off on journalistic crusades, putting himself under the glare of the public spotlight.

And now, it was only a matter of time—days, weeks at most—that it all would come crashing down on him. At the least, he would face public exposure. Worse, he would be identified as the vigilante killer and arrested. Even worse, Lasher would find him—and then he'd be on the receiving end of a sniper round from out of nowhere.

Worst of all, Lasher might discover his connection to Wonk, or to

Annie, and target *them* in order to get to *him*.

If he didn't disappear once again into the wind, and soon, he would lose his freedom. Maybe his life. Maybe theirs.

He would certainly lose Annie, one way or the other. It was inevitable . . .

. . . unless he came up with some fresh brainstorm—some new deception that would throw everyone off his scent.

But right now, he had no good ideas. No ideas at all.

"Mrrraaaooow."

He stopped pacing and looked at the cat. She looked back at him inquisitively, impatiently.

Expecting him to do something.

He went back to the sofa, sat, and began scratching her head again. She closed her eyes and resumed her purring.

"Luna girl, you already gave Annie and me one of your nine lives, out there in the Allegheny Forest. Do you have any more you're willing to spare?"

She opened her eyes just a slit and glowered at him.

"Mrrraaaooow."

He sighed and sank back against the soft plush cushion.

"I was afraid you'd say that."

TWENTY-FOUR

Heading into the glare of the early morning sun, Hunter left Massachusetts Avenue at Dupont Circle, then prowled east on P Street, hoping to find a parking place for the BMW Security 7 sedan. The blond wig and fake mustache, the phony IDs in his wallet, and the other pocket litter identified him as the car's registered owner: financial services consultant Wayne Grayson.

Hunter preferred not to wander the city under a different alias. At least, not without a compelling reason. Too many things could go sideways. But facing even greater risks, he felt he had little choice. If Lasher ever tracked him to the Bethesda apartment, then he could be ambushed while leaving the building's garage in his Subaru Forester, or while walking to the nearby Metro station. In disguise and behind the deeply tinted glass of Wayne Grayson's BMW, however, he could come and go undetected. If the worst still happened, the armored auto—with its array of security features and armament—offered a lot of protection.

P Street was lined with budding trees, apartment buildings, old brick row houses, and cars that filled the available parking spots. Just before he reached 17th Street, he got lucky when a local resident pulled out of her overnight space. He grabbed the spot, lowered his driver's visor, then bent low to quickly remove the wig and mustache, which went into a waiting plastic bag. He opened the glove compartment to swap out wallets and pocket litter, locking away Wayne Grayson's and jamming their Dylan Hunter replacements into his sports jacket.

Inside of thirty seconds, he emerged from the car into the frosty morning air. He made a show of stretching, which allowed him to turn and check for tails. Then he set out on foot. He continued east past 17th, crossing the street to its north sidewalk. He passed a corner pharmacy, a Thai restaurant, and a playground before turning left onto 16th.

A massive, Gothic-style Methodist church occupied the corner, and a bus stop shelter stood nearby. A young blonde woman sat on its bench, leaning over a child in a stroller. The woman was dangling a doll in front of its occupant, a little girl wrapped in a thick pink outfit. Like the woman, both the child and her doll had thick golden curls. The girl was grabbing at the doll, and her mother was snatching it playfully just out of reach. Both were giggling.

Hunter slowed as he passed, then stopped and smiled.

"She's adorable. How old?"

The woman, who looked to be in her late twenties, glanced up and smiled back. She had bright blue eyes, a pert nose, and deep dimples.

"Thank you. Nineteen months."

"She your first?"

"We have a four-year-old, too. A boy." She looked down at her daughter, who had seized the doll now and was clutching it ferociously. "My husband just dropped him at pre-school before heading off to work. It's such a gorgeous morning, I decided Ally and I would take a little walk after breakfast. Isn't that right, Ally?"

"Go!" the toddler shrieked, frowning and wriggling. "Go!"

"Okay, okay—we'll go!" The young woman rose. "She loves riding around."

"Just wait till the day she asks for the car keys. Well, you two have a nice walk . . . Bye-bye, Ally."

"Bye!" came a high little voice. The doll gyrated wildly in her hand, as if she were waving it. Her mother rolled the stroller north, past the church.

Hunter squinted against the sun, looking across the street. The address he sought was somewhere amid the row of adjoining buildings. He was about to cross when he heard the rising growl of a truck engine.

A white rental box truck had just turned out of P Street and was approaching from his right. It slowed as it came abreast of him. The driver's window was down, and a dark-bearded man hunched low over the wheel. He appeared to be Hispanic, perhaps Middle Eastern.

The driver flashed a glance Hunter's way. His expression was intense, irritated. Despite the cool temperature and the open window, his forehead and nose seemed to glisten with sweat. In the passenger seat beside him, a second man faced away, toward the row of buildings across the street, as if looking for a delivery address. The van slowed almost to a complete stop. Then the passenger gestured to the driver, who abruptly gunned the engine. Gears ground, and the van picked up speed again.

Hunter stood on the curb, watching it proceed north on 16th, feeling a moment's uneasiness. Then he noticed that the Monday morning rush hour traffic had thinned in both directions. He seized the opportunity to trot across 16th. Following the building numbers a few doors farther, he found his destination, near where the truck had slowed.

Set back about thirty feet from the street, the red-brick building stood semi-hidden behind some trees and hedges. Old and narrow, it climbed in three stories of bay windows to a gabled fourth floor. Hunter strode down its sidewalk into an arched, covered entrance and pressed the doorbell. A young receptionist whom he recognized from Arnold Wasserman's funeral reception greeted him and let him in.

2

The first thing Hunter did when entering any unfamiliar building was to check for exits. He had already done a search-engine "street view" tour of the neighborhood the previous night. Now his eyes roamed the interior.

The foyer, wrapped in dark oak paneling, looked faintly Victorian. A wooden staircase to the right of the receptionist's cluttered desk rose to the upper floors; he assumed there would be a rear staircase, too. A narrow hallway cut through the first floor, from where he stood in the foyer straight back to a distant rear door marked with an exit sign.

"It'll be just a few more minutes till our nine-thirty staff meeting," said the receptionist, a wide-eyed brunette named Samantha. "Mr. Hatcher told me he invited you to sit in. Our conference room is right here."

She led him into a room just to the right of the building entrance. A dozen swivel chairs surrounded a thick old conference table in its center. At the far end, a bay window faced the Methodist church across the street. The wall to his right was filled with framed photos of a grinning Dennis Hatcher shaking hands with politicians and a former conservative president, as well as framed copies of the Constitution and Declaration of Independence. The one to his left presented a brick fireplace; its marble mantelpiece held what looked like awards and mementos.

He declined Samantha's offer of coffee. She retreated to her desk, and he took the nearest corner seat on the left side of the table. There, his back was to the fireplace, and he had clear views of the street beyond the window and the entrance to the room. He pulled out his notepad from his jacket and reviewed his notes while he waited.

Five minutes later he heard creaking footsteps on the stairs outside the room. The staff began to file in and exchanged smiles and handshakes with him. Mark Deaver, the vice-president, slid into the chair next to his and flopped a file folder on the table. Dennis Hatcher was last to arrive and took the sole high-backed chair at the head of the table, the window behind him.

"We're delighted you could join us today to discuss our progress, Mr. Hunter," he began. "Were you able to learn anything more from the police about . . . about Arnie?"

"Not much. They shared with me the physical evidence in his apartment that led them to conclude it was an accident. But Won—Frederick managed to chat with his mother and visit the apartment. He checked Arnold's computer, phone, and files, and noticed some things that the police seem to have missed."

"Such as?"

"Such as not a single paper or computer file about his Currents investigation. Such as no related calls listed in his cell phone history.

Such as emails gone missing, too—including the one you say he sent you on the night he died."

"But he *did* send it," Deaver said, opening his file folder. He riffled the stack of papers, pulled one out, slid it in front of Hunter. "See the header? He emailed this at 6:33 p.m. on March 18th."

Hunter scanned the terse message, then thumbed through his own notepad.

"Okay, here . . . Frederick has a record of his own phone call to Arnold that evening. He said the call began at 6:34. So, it looks like immediately after Arnold sent you this message, he took Frederick's call. And then he told him somebody was at the door and he'd call back." He paused. "He never did. It was the last time anyone heard from him."

Nobody spoke. Everyone's eyes looked down, or into the distance.

"What about you folks?" Hunter said, breaking the silence. "What did you find out when you interviewed the people at Currents?"

"We didn't," Hatcher said. "We called them a day or so after Arnie's funeral and left a message. When they called back, they said they wouldn't meet with us, and that any further inquiries should be directed to their attorney."

"Oh, really."

"Yes. Really."

The sound of a noisy truck engine rumbled in through the bay window behind Hatcher. Hunter caught movement in his peripheral vision.

A truck moved into view, left to right.

The same white rental truck . . .

Its pace was glacial. The passenger window was down, and a second dark bearded man in that seat stared directly at their building.

Suddenly, the truck lurched forward, into a vacant parking spot out front . . . then nose first, jumped right up onto the sidewalk.

Hunter bolted to his feet, knocking his chair backward.

"Everyone! Get out of the room! Now!"

The passenger door of the truck burst open and the occupant spilled out. He held an AK-47.

The CAP staff sat frozen, gaping at Hunter as if he'd gone mad. He grabbed the front of Deaver's shirt and tie, yanking him upward, pointing out the window.

"*Terrorists outside! Run! Go out the back exit! Get out now!*"

They all spun toward the window. Saw what he saw. The girl seated across from him screamed. He propelled Deaver toward the room entrance and then pointed at her.

"*Out the back door! Go, go, go!*"

She leaped to her feet and stumbled after Deaver.

It was bedlam. The rest all jumped up at once, piling into each other, tripping over the chairs, shoving each other toward the doorway.

Keeping eyes on the scene unfolding outside, Hunter seized chairs from the path of those on his side of the table and pushed them back against the wall, clearing a path.

Now the truck driver, a big burly guy also brandishing an AK-47, lumbered around the front of the truck to join his companion on the sidewalk.

"*Run! Out the back, and keep running!*" Hunter shouted above the din, shoving a young man past him, the last person on his side. Then he vaulted onto the table and jumped down on the other side, where three screaming people, including Hatcher, had tumbled among the chairs in a panicked heap. He seized each of them by jackets and shirts, lifted them to their feet, pushed them out the doorway.

Then glanced back out the window.

The two terrorists stood thirty feet away, rifles held across their bodies, staring toward the building's front door.

Hunter knew what would come next. He shoved the last young woman past him toward the doorway and was just about to dive beneath the table to avoid the inevitable burst of gunfire.

Then, unexpectedly, the pair turned away and started to jog north, up the sidewalk and out of sight.

He stared, bewildered, at the abandoned box truck up on sidewalk.

Then understood.

He raced out into the foyer, following the stragglers down the hallway. Hatcher, overweight, was lumbering and limping as the others pushed past him and out the wide-open exit door. Hunter caught up with him. There was no time to explain. He grabbed his shoulder, arresting his progress, and before the big man could know what was happening, Hunter crouched, wrapped his left arm beneath his thighs, and lifted him like a baby.

He burst outside and saw that they had emerged into a private parking lot for another church at the far end of the block. Some ahead of him continued to run, full tilt, while others were slowing.

"Keep running! They've got a bomb! Go, go!"

Hatcher whimpered and his arm wrapped so tightly around Hunter's neck that he felt he was being choked. Yet he was unaware of the man's weight, unaware of any pain, unaware of anything but the desperate need to put more distance between themselves and that truck.

Ten seconds more and he was charging through a section crowded with parked cars when a white flash lit the church before him and a sudden vibration rocked his feet and then an enormous ear-splitting thunderclap and a wall of air knocked him forward and they crashed to the pavement between two vehicles . . .

Hunter's ears were ringing from the blast and piercing car alarms were going off around him. He pushed Hatcher away and rolled himself against one of the car tires, closing his eyes and covering his head with his arms.

Debris rained down, big fragments of things, thumping onto the cars, smacking against the pavement around him, just missing him, the crashing noises almost drowned out by the ringing din in his ears—then came smaller pieces that hit like hailstones, some finding his back and scalp and arms—then a rolling fog of choking dust and the accompanying stench of acrid chemicals and smoke. When the debris stopped falling, he rolled out and sat up, squinting and coughing. He yanked off his sports jacket, then pulled off his shirt and tied it around his mouth and nose, trying to filter the smoke.

He looked around. Despite his girth, Hatcher had somehow squashed himself, face first, almost completely under the pickup truck next to him; his body shook violently. Hunter crawled over to him.

"Are you all right?" he yelled, trying to stifle his own coughing, and blinking to clear the tears from his eyes.

Hatcher remained huddled there, coughing and whimpering and shuddering. Hunter tried to pull him out to check him for injuries, but he wouldn't budge. At least he was alive.

He rose to his feet. Chunks of unrecognizable rubble were strewn all around him on the cars and pavement. The smoke and falling dust were leaving a chalky, choking coating on every surface. Strips of pink insulation and sheets of burnt paper fluttered down like confetti.

Then the breeze picked up and shifted, and mercifully the smoke began to clear from the parking lot. He unwrapped the shirt from around his face and put it back on. Then his jacket.

He looked back toward the CAP building. Or where it had been. The four-story structure had collapsed into a single-story mound of smoking, flaming ruins. The buildings on either side had been demolished, too: They were sheared off at their tops, yet their remains stood slightly taller. In the distance beyond them, and looming above them, he could see that the Methodist church across the street still stood. Its windows and a section of its front stone wall had been blown in, and its belfry tower had partly collapsed. But it still looked mostly intact.

Hunter realized that a lot of people had to have died in those buildings and on the street.

His numbed ears picked up the faint, rising sounds of distant sirens, and of much closer gunfire. The terrorists were probably hitting some other nearby target. He gritted his teeth in helpless fury. He would have gone after them—but he had no gun on him.

And he had others to worry about, right here.

Leaving Hatcher, he began to search for the other CAP staff members in the parking lot. He stepped gingerly around the broken bricks, pulverized glass, sharp shards of wood, and large mangled metal chunks that may have been part of the box truck. He felt little pain. Probing with his fingers as he walked, he was incredulous that he seemed to have no serious injuries—only the ringing in his ears, the familiar sticky warmth of a small cut on the back of his scalp, and what he knew would be some welts and bruises.

He found them scattered, crying, shaking, moaning with pain. Some had been hit by flying or falling debris. Tony Ferino, the young researcher, was sitting on the pavement, dazed, his back against the tire of a car. His eyeglasses lay smashed beside him, and he had a nasty gash on his forearm. Hunter tore the kid's shirt sleeve and made a quick tourniquet to stop the bleeding. He reassured him and moved to find the others. Samantha was lying unconscious, her head resting on Mark Deaver's balled-up suit jacket; he appeared to be largely unhurt and doing what he could to make her comfortable.

Heather Summers, the pretty young newsletter editor, was the farthest distant from the blast. She sat in the grass near the other church, shivering uncontrollably. She did not appear to be injured. But fearing that she would go into shock, Hunter sat next to her and draped his sports jacket over her. Wrapped his arm around her shoulders.

"It's okay, Heather. It's all over."

Her teeth were chattering.

"You're safe, now."

Tears gathered in her widened brown eyes. Began to trickle down her cheeks. Cut dark little paths through the chalky dust.

He felt her shudder. She turned her face up to his.

"You saved me," she whispered.

He gave her a light squeeze. "You'll be fine, Heather."

"You saved me . . . You saved me . . ."

TWENTY-FIVE

The flurry of gunfire had been quelled quickly, after police cars swarmed the area north of the bomb site. Plumes of white and black smoke still rose from the ruined buildings, hanging above the area like a shroud. A cacophony of sirens echoed over the neighborhood.

Now he was making his way around the chaos, heading for his car.

And thinking about what had happened . . .

Within the first few minutes, Hunter had called for ambulances. They began to arrive almost at once. He waited with the CAP staff, trying to comfort them until the last were taken away. He was relieved when Samantha regained consciousness before being placed on a stretcher. And though he couldn't know for sure, it appeared that none of them were in critical condition.

Then he let two EMTs wash the dust and dirt from his face, head, and hands. Let his scalp be treated and bandaged. Swallowed four ibuprofens with two bottles of water, to dull the pain the brief adrenalin rush had masked.

During the treatment, he spent the time thinking. Working through everything that had happened today. And before today.

When they were done, he refused medical transport, assuring them he was fine, but yes, of course he'd get checked out later tonight.

Then, once alone, he texted Annie on her special access phone, to let her know what had happened and reassure her he was all right. He also asked her to contact Garrett and tell him he needed a callback immediately . . .

Now he was taking a circuitous route around the blast site. He crossed 16th two blocks south, cut across a parking lot, then managed to find an alley that let him return to his car.

Hunter always kept fresh clothes in his vehicles, along with well-hidden IDs. He changed in the back seat, hung his press credentials around his neck, then headed back toward the bomb site.

He got barely fifty yards, only to the corner of 17th and P. A carbine-wielding anti-terrorism unit in combat kit and body armor stood guard outside the yellow police tape now spanning the intersection. Behind them, cops and city workers were erecting traffic barriers. In all directions, blinding blue and red strobes pulsed on the police cars, fire trucks, black SUVs, and sedans clogging the streets. His hearing was returning slowly—a mixed blessing, with all the sirens blaring.

Of course they refused to let him pass. He could only wait there, hoping to hear from Garrett.

He didn't have to wait long, maybe five minutes, when the burner vibrated in his pocket.

"Dylan, this better be important."

"Grant, I was *there* when it happened. Right at the bomb site. I saw them. The terrorists."

"What?"

"We have to talk. Now. Just us. There are things you need to hear, and you're the only person I can trust."

"Where are you?"

"17th and P. Outside the police lines."

"I'm just coming into the neighborhood. I'll have my team divert your way and we'll pick you up."

Two more minutes passed. A pair of black SUVs with strobes flaring and sirens blaring raced up 17th from the south. He stepped off the curb and waved. The lead car swept past and stopped, nose facing the barricades, while the tail car pulled up beside him. The rear door opened. Grant Garrett leaned out.

"Get in," he barked.

2

Garrett badged their way past the antiterrorism team and around the barriers. They raced down toward 16th, but had to slam to a stop in the middle of the block because of rubble littering the street. They got out, then walked the rest of the way in, surrounded by Garrett's four-man security team. They stepped gingerly around large pieces of masonry, stone, and twisted metal. A fragment from a roof had crushed the hood of a parked car. A veil of sour smoke drifted in the air. Garrett began to cough and had to cover his nose and mouth with his handkerchief.

When they reached the corner of 16th, they stopped in shock.

The devastation was as bad as anything Hunter had seen in the Middle East. The facade of the Methodist church caved inward. The bus stop shelter had been blown to bits: shattered pieces covered the base of the church wall, along with two mangled, blackened vehicles. Next to one of the cars, a group of first responders spread a tarp over what looked like a partial corpse on the ground.

But the main damage faced them across the street.

Men from two fire trucks hosed water onto the smoking heaps of rubble. The truck bomb had obliterated the CAP building and the two adjacent ones. A couple of partial brick walls still stood at the rear of the buildings, but the interiors and roofs had been blown inward, upward, and outward to either side. A red Toyota, which been parked behind the spot where the box truck had pulled in, was now in two squashed, widely separated pieces halfway down the block.

Hunter approached slowly, treading carefully around and over piles of unrecognizable debris, moving past cops and firemen and crime scene investigators and men in dark suits. He stepped to the edge of the smoking, stinking crater where the truck had been. Chunks of its chassis had been driven down into the crater, and the pavement had cracked and buckled all around it.

"Give us some space, guys," Garrett growled from behind his handkerchief. "We have to chat."

His security team spread out at his command, and he approached.

"Okay, then. So what in hell were *you* doing here?"

"Believe it or not, I was working on a story—visiting an investigative nonprofit, the Center for Advocacy Profiles. CAP. They're housed in this building." He stared at the mound before him. "Or what used to be this building."

"It's a miracle you got out alive. How did that happen?"

"I saw the two guys who left the truck bomb here. Middle Eastern appearance, dark hair and beards. They came out with AK-47s and ran off in that direction. I cleared the CAP people out the back just before the bomb went off."

Garrett squinted at the ruins. "If I'm not miscounting, this is the third time you've barely managed to avoid getting your ass blown up. First by the Russians in Kandahar. Then by those ecoterrorists this year. Now by Islamist terrorists."

"Grant, the reason I needed to talk to you is I don't think this is about Islamist terrorism."

"Hey, you two!"

A man in a crisp dark suit was hustling toward them. He had dark brown hair, a mustache, and a scowl. He stopped and stood with his hands on his hips.

"Who are you, and what are you doing here?"

Garrett and Hunter exchanged a quick glance. The CIA man pulled out his credentials and held them in front of the guy's face. The man blinked.

"Oh! Sorry, Mr. Garrett. I should have recognized you."

"I would have thought so, too, Mr. Groat. We've crossed paths several times in the C.I.C.," he said, referring to the CIA's Counterintelligence Center. "So let me ask: What are *you* doing here?"

"The Bureau is short-handed during the emergency. I've just been reassigned on TDY as Special Agent in Charge at this crime scene."

"So you're Rick Groat," Hunter said.

The agent turned to him, surprised. "Yes. How do you know me?"

Hunter remembered what Annie had told him about this jerk—how he'd almost blown Muller's arrest and gotten her shot. "Somebody mentioned your name to me. So, you're in charge of the FBI team here?"

"That's right," he said, trying to recapture his self-important look. "And you are . . . ?"

Garrett interrupted. "He's with me. Undercover. Let's keep it that way. The Agency has an interest here, too. We're checking the dead terrorist names the Bureau shared with us against our databases and the DNI's. My people already have leads on some international Islamist connections."

"Well, this is an active crime scene, Mr. Garrett. You understand that we can't have people wandering through here now, possibly contaminating evidence. I'm going to have to request—"

Garrett took a step forward. He had three inches on Groat, and a lot more presence.

"Listen carefully, sonny," he growled, not loud. "I have friends at the Bureau, way above your pay grade. You either get out of our faces, right now, or I make a phone call to the director, and you'll be spending the rest of the day sharpening pencils back in your office."

Groat blinked. "Oh, I didn't mean to insult you, Mr. Garrett! I only—"

"Go manage your crime scene, Mr. Groat. My associate and I were trying to figure out who did this when you interrupted us."

Groat opened and closed his mouth. Nodded curtly. Then stalked off.

3

"Groat," Hunter muttered, watching him go. "Good God. Annie told me about him."

"I could tell you more. The Bureau won't get anything useful out of this site for days, with that jerk running the show." Garrett coughed again into the handkerchief. "Damn, this stench is getting to me. Smells like ammonia."

"Ammonium nitrate. I also got a whiff of something that smells like isopropyl alcohol. That would be nitromethane. The ingredients in

ANNM. That's the main explosive McVeigh used in his Oklahoma City truck bomb."

"You were saying this is *not* Islamist terrorism. But you're wrong. You probably haven't heard: They hit three other sites around town, too. The Jewish community center right up the street. Two guys came in and shot up the place, killing and wounding a bunch of people. A patrolman nearby nailed one coming out, but the other is still on the loose."

"I heard the gunfire. No doubt the same pair from the truck here."

"Right. So about the same time, a third guy in a suicide vest blew himself up inside a Jewish deli in Georgetown. And a fourth shot tourists at the Holocaust Museum before the guards took him out. Early witnesses say they were all yelling *Allahu akbar*. And the Bureau just ran the drivers' licenses on two of the dead ones. Both are in the databases—well-known Islamists, self-radicalized over the internet. So, how can you say this is *not* Islamist terrorism?"

"Because it's more than that. Grant, this isn't what it seems to be on its face. Somebody went to a hell of a lot of trouble to make it look like Islamic terrorism. So that everyone would go running after false leads, distracted from what is *really* going on."

Garrett spread his hands in exasperation. "Dylan. Get real. These dudes *are* Islamic terrorists."

"Sure they are. But I'm positive they're only part of something else. Something much bigger."

"What in hell are you talking about?"

"You said the other attacks were with automatic weapons and a suicide vest, right?"

"Right. So?"

"So ask yourself: Why did they position their most devastating weapon, the truck bomb, *here*, and not at one of the other more obvious and more symbolic targets, like the Holocaust Museum or that Jewish center just up the street? And before you say, Maybe they meant to take out that church over there: Why did they park the truck on *this* side of the street? Does that make sense to you?"

Garrett looked around, taking in the blast area while Hunter went on.

"See, the front of the church is badly damaged, but it's still standing. The real devastation is over here. They stopped in front of *this* building—the very one I happened to be visiting—and even pulled right up onto the sidewalk, to get closer."

Garrett looked incredulous. "Wait a minute. Are you claiming it was *you* being targeted?"

"Of course not. First of all, they had no way of knowing in advance that I would be here. This scheme had to take weeks of planning, and I hadn't even decided to come here until last night, when I texted CAP's boss. Nobody outside of the organization could have known I'd be here. Besides, if someone wanted me dead, why would they devise this enormously complicated plot, when they could have just sent some shooters at me? No, Grant, every way I've looked at this, my presence here was just a bizarre coincidence." He paused. "But maybe only partly a coincidence."

"*Now* what are you talking about?"

Hunter took a couple of minutes to explain the suspicious death of Arnold Wasserman.

"So Wasserman reports he's uncovered money laundering into this year's presidential race," he said, summing up. "That same night, he dies. My researcher finds evidence it was murder, but the crime scene is meticulously staged to convince the cops and M.E. it was an accident. Then CAP, which Wasserman was freelancing for, picks up his investigation and starts following the same trails. Now, within weeks, *this* happens"—he nodded toward the smoking ruins—"but it's also staged, this time to look like Islamist terrorism."

Garrett raised a brow. "You're telling me this CAP group was the main target today . . ."

". . . and the positioning of the truck bomb proves it. All the other smaller-scale terrorism around town was just a smokescreen, to throw the investigation off track. I think the same parties that murdered Wasserman recruited these Islamists as cannon fodder, gave them resources and a list of targets they'd naturally choose anyway—except for this one. Islamists have no interest in targeting CAP. But clearly, it was the main target. Why? Because they and Wasserman were getting too close to exposing something big—something that could affect the election outcome."

Garrett snorted. "Dylan, that blast must have rattled your brain. You're talking like a whacked-out conspiracy theorist. Who the hell in American politics would do something this crazy and extreme?"

"Have you already forgotten that, just months ago, Senator Ashton Conn conspired with ecoterrorists to commit murder and terrorism, just to put himself in the Oval Office? Who would have believed *that*?"

Hunter kicked absently at a pile of debris at his feet.

"And that's what got me thinking," he went on. "Because this reminds me of the bombing by Boggs in Pennsylvania. The one that took out that scientist, Adam Silva, and almost killed his son. That was meant to look like something else, too. But it was part of a conspiracy that ran right back here, to Washington. Right back to a United States senator running for president. And he might have made it, if I hadn't stopped him. But the terrorism and killing hasn't stopped. The election is still in play, and people are still dying."

"Wait. Are you drawing a connection between *this* and all that ecoterrorism, too?"

"When cold, hard facts and logic eliminate all the conventional theories, then what are we left with? Conn was headed to the White House, and people who got in his way wound up as targets of terrorism and murder. Now, other candidates are running for the presidency, and people investigating the money trail are targets of terrorism and murder, too."

He kicked harder at the pile of junk, venting anger.

"I don't believe in coincidences, Grant. And if I'm right, think about what it means. It means very powerful people, deeply invested in the outcome of the election, are plotting a *coup* to take over the country."

"You're really serious! And completely nuts. But okay, I'll bite. *Which* very powerful people?"

"*Qui bono*? Ask yourself that: Who benefits? That's what I've been doing for the past hour."

"And?"

"I have some suspicions. But no solid evidence. Not yet."

Garrett lowered the handkerchief. His eyes watered, but his craggy features remained immobile.

"Well, I don't buy it. It's too wild. Oliver Stone crap."

Hunter gave the pile another hard kick. Something colorful, incongruous, dislodged and rolled out.

He stared, disbelieving.

Then shuddered.

Then stood motionless while life drained from his body.

"Hey." Garrett's voice, from some faraway place. "What is it?"

While he still could, he forced himself to bend, slowly.

Pick it up, carefully.

In his palm, the remnant of a child's doll.

Just the head.

With a long, thin metal shard impaling its cheek.

Somehow, the thick golden curls were still intact.

"No," he whispered.

"Dylan . . . What's the matter? Are you all right?"

"No!" he shouted.

His burning eyes sought Garrett's face. He held up the doll's head before him.

Garrett's face started to blur.

"No!" he screamed. *"No!"*

4

Garrett led him back across the street. Sat him on a blown-off truck tire. Knelt beside him.

Eyes closed, Hunter felt his old mentor's steady hand on his shoulder.

He felt nothing else except the doll's head, cradled in his own big hand.

"I saw them, Grant," he said, visualizing them. "I talked to them. A mother pushing her little girl in a stroller. An adorable little toddler . . . Her name was Ally."

He opened his eyes. "She was holding this doll."

"Jesus Christ . . ."

"They were right over there . . . So pretty. Both of them. Golden hair, just like this. So happy . . . So full of—" He stopped. "Her husband had just taken their five-year-old boy to pre-school . . ."

"Dylan, I'm so sorry."

". . . and they were just out for a walk after breakfast. Because it was such a nice day."

He could feel nothing, but a distant part of him saw that the hand holding the doll was trembling.

"They died . . . just because it was a nice day."

He felt the hand tighten on his shoulder.

"It's got to stop, Grant." He gestured with the doll's head, pointing the ugly metal shard at the ruins across the street. "This has got to end."

"And it will. Trust me, son, I'm going to put everyone and everything into—"

"No," he interrupted softly. "Not you." He pointed the spike again, toward Groat gesturing in the midst of the army of cops and investigators crawling over the rubble. "Not him. Not them. You can't do it. Not your way."

"Dylan, I—"

"Remember what you told me at the Jefferson Memorial that day? When I said these people think they're untouchable? You told me you didn't know what people like us could do about it anymore—not when the system got this corrupt. Because the people who did this—they run the show. They'll run the investigations. They'll make sure to protect themselves. They'll bury the truth. And good people like you won't be able to stop them. You'll want to, and you'll try. But you won't." He paused, then added: "Not your way."

He gently shrugged off Garrett's hand. Pulled himself to his feet.

"But they *are* going to be stopped."

Now he felt something. Felt it come alive, pushing out through all the deadness. Felt it rise through his body, surge through his arm, pour into the hand holding the doll . . .

Dylan Hunter brandished the doll before Garrett's ashen face. Shook it. The sun flashed off the metal spike.

"Enough!"

TWENTY-SIX

Garrett rose from his knees. Brushed off the dirt. Nodded.

"Okay. I know better than to try to talk sense to you when you're like this."

"Good. I'm not in the mood for lectures."

Garrett coughed again. "Goddamn it," he said, shaking his head, "my lungs can't take any more of this. There's nothing else we can learn here, anyway."

He motioned the security team to join them. They made their way back toward the SUVs.

"I just realized," Hunter said, "they've cordoned off this entire area by now. So how do I get my car out of here?"

"Where is it?"

"Just down this street. Past 17th."

"Okay. We'll escort you out of here."

They piled back into the Agency's SUVs, turned around on the deserted street, and headed back. Once again, Garrett badged them through the blockades. As they came up to Dylan's car, a beeping sound filled the back seat. Garrett dug out his phone.

"Talk to me . . . Oh, it's you again, Harry."

He listened. His eyes widened.

"Great. Tell them to hold the guy till I get there. Do *not* call in the FBI, do *not* tell anybody else you have him, and nobody talks to him. You okay with that?" He listened to the reply. "How long? . . . All right. I understand. Whatever time you can give me, Harry. Thanks. I owe you."

He turned to Hunter. "We just got lucky. That was the D.C. police chief. An old buddy; we swap favors. His cops just grabbed the missing terrorist from the Jewish center. They're in an apartment on Corcoran Street, near Dupont Circle. Just a couple minutes away."

Hunter seized his arm.

"Once Groat gets him, the guy will go all Miranda and clam up."

"That's why I told Harry what I did. We need to talk to him first—and fast, before the Bureau hears about it and gets there."

"You realize we'll have to *make* him talk."

Garrett raised a brow. "You know I can't do that."

"No, not you . . . Grant, you asked me months ago whether I would come in and work for you again. And I said no. All right—I'll do it. But just this once. And my way."

Garrett nodded, while rolling his eyes toward the two security men in the front seat. "I can't accept whatever you may be suggesting."

"I understand. It's your call, of course. So I'll just tag along. I'll follow you out of here in my car."

"Well, hurry. Harry can't give us more than a half hour, if that."

Hunter jumped out and ran to his BMW. He tossed the doll's head on the passenger seat. Lit up the car's own strobes. Did a fast K-turn in the empty street. He was burning rubber after them within twenty seconds. At 18th they turned a few short blocks north, to New Hampshire. Two quick rights, and a half-block east on Corcoran. Three patrol cars had pulled over next to a narrow, three-story row home with an open front door. Garrett's car arrived first and he was trotting up the stairs when Hunter arrived.

He flicked the hidden panel release for the storage compartment between the seats. Pulled out a sheathed combat knife; shoved it inside his boot. Then his favorite firearm—the Sig-Sauer P228, loaded, plus an extra 13-round magazine. He tucked the Sig, in its belt holster, behind his back and under his jacket; the mag went into his jacket pocket.

Leaving the strobe flashing, he locked up, then ran up the steps, past a plastic bag of spilled groceries.

2

An elderly woman huddled on a sofa in the front room to his left, softly crying. A young cop sat beside her, talking to her soothingly. Hunter followed the voices along the hallway, past a powder room, to a bedroom on the right. Garrett's team stood outside. He squeezed by them and entered.

He recognized the terrorist as the rental truck's passenger. Wearing a torn windbreaker and jeans, he lay face down on the bed, hands cuffed behind him. Another beefy young cop gripped the back of the guy's neck, holding his head down, and kept a knee against his lower back, preventing him from moving. A much older cop stood at the foot of the bed, bringing Garrett up to speed.

". . . dumps the AK-47 back there and walks here. Probably heading for the Dupont Metro station." He nodded at the cop on the bed. "Officer Jenkins is driving by, recognizes him from the APB, and pulls over. The guy goes rabbit, then spots the woman entering this apartment with her groceries. He shoves past her to get inside. Maybe he thinks he can run out the back, or something, but then—"

"You all did great, Sergeant," Garrett interrupted. "But we still have an active terrorism emergency. Others may be out there, about to strike. We have to talk to this guy *right now* and see what he knows."

"No problem. I just got a call about that. From Chief Landrum himself. He says, whatever you need, I am supposed—"

"Right now," Garrett continued, noticing Hunter enter, "we need to be alone with the suspect, since anything he says may impact national security. So I'd like you to clear the building for us. Keep everyone outside and away. That includes anyone else who shows up here—I don't care what agency, what titles they have. We need time with this guy. A lot of lives hang on what we learn in the next few minutes. Can I count on your cooperation, Sergeant Devers?"

The cop raised his chin. "Absolutely, sir. I'll get everyone out. Shall I leave Officer Jenkins here to keep the suspect under control?"

"No need for that," Hunter interjected. "We've got this, Sergeant."

"Sergeant," Garrett said, "stay here one more minute. Dylan, come with me."

He led Hunter into the hall and away from the others.

"Dylan. We need to have an understanding."

"What am I supposed to understand?"

"I know what you've just gone through. I know you're thinking about that mother and baby. But you need to keep your eyes on the prize. This character is our only link to the people behind this. He's just a bit player. Kill him, and you let his bosses get away. Is that what you want? Do you want to give them a pass? A chance to kill more babies?"

He saw the baby girl waving her doll . . .

"Dylan, look at me. I expect you to act like the pro I know you are. If you have to rough him up to get him to talk, do it. But I expect him to be alive and intact afterward. Do we have an understanding?"

Hunter felt himself climbing to his cold, high place. He nodded.

"We do."

They went back into the room.

"Thank you, Sergeant," Garrett said. "I'll be sure to let Chief Landrum know how well you and your officers performed."

The two cops left. Immediately, the terrorist tried to wriggle off the bed. Hunter stepped over, raised a boot, and stomped the back of his thigh. The guy howled, falling back onto the bed, face down.

Hunter turned to Garrett.

"Perhaps you ought to wait outside too, Grant."

"Perhaps I should."

He grabbed a pillow, stripped off the pillowcase, and tore off a piece.

"I want to call my lawyer," the guy on the bed moaned, his accented voice muffled against the bedcover.

"Dream on, asshole."

"You know you can't do this! I have rights. I—"

Hunter punched him solidly in the right kidney. The guy gasped.

"Sure you do. You have the right to remain silent. But only for another minute or two."

He balled up the piece of cloth, grabbed the back of the guy's hair, yanked his head off the bed, and jammed the cloth into his open mouth.

He knew that the combination of the punch and the gag would make it hard for him to breathe. That was the idea. He wanted him to know exactly what that felt like.

He also wanted to muffle any screams to come.

Hunter seized the handcuffs behind the guy's lower back and slowly raised his wrists, straining his joints.

A muffled, gagging scream . . .

"You know, if I tug just a wee bit harder on these cuffs, something is going to pop. I wonder which will go first? An elbow? Nah, I bet it's going to be a shoulder."

The guy's squirming began to slow. He couldn't afford to let him to pass out, so he lowered his arms again. Flipped him over onto his back. Straddled his stomach. Reached down to his boot and pulled out the knife.

The terrorist looked woozy, eyes unfocused; his face was red from lack of air. Hunter slapped him, hard, and pulled out the gag. The man coughed and sputtered, then gulped for air.

Hunter waved the blade in front of his eyes, letting it flash in the overhead light till those eyes came back into focus. And widened.

"Listen to me, very carefully. I know you think you are a big, brave, devout Muslim. I know you think you're going to defy the infidels. You think you won't talk and betray your pals. You think you can hold out.

"But you're wrong. I have dealt with other big, brave, devout Muslims before. In Pakistan and Afghanistan. They were just like you. They weren't going to tell me a thing. But you know—they did. They always did. Some of them held out on me. One guy even lasted, oh, ten minutes. But in the end, they always wished they hadn't tried, because of what I did to them. And because they ended up talking, anyway."

Hunter grabbed his beard, pulled down to open his mouth, and tapped the blade against his teeth.

"What a terrible waste," he continued. "To lose your eyes, your ears, then your balls—only to wind up screaming out all the answers to my questions, anyway. I hope you're smarter than that. You're still young enough to father children. But one way or the other, you *will* tell me everything I want to know, within the next five minutes. If you try to hold out—if you want to be as stupid as they were—well, here is exactly what happens next."

Hunter explained his six-step interrogation sequence. When he had finished, he leaned over, inches from the man's sweat-soaked face.

"Did you understand what I just said?" he whispered.

"Yes," the quivering terrorist replied, tears flowing over his cheeks.

"Do you *really* want any of those nasty things to happen to you?"

"No! Please! I'll tell you!"

"Well, that's good. That's very good."

He straightened. Then gently, carefully, he lay the knife blade flat along the man's left cheek, and held it so that its point was barely touching his lower eyelid.

"Okay, so here is my first question. Please—answer truthfully. And quickly."

He did.

3

Eight minutes later Hunter emerged from the apartment. Garrett stood like a tall gray pillar at the bottom of the steps, while the others waited next to their cars.

"Okay, he's back in your custody, Sergeant," Hunter called out to the older cop, then descended toward the CIA boss. He continued past, toward his car.

"Hey, wait a minute," Garrett called out, hustling to catch up.

"I don't have a minute."

"I need to know what condition you left him in," Garrett said, lowering his voice.

"Don't worry, he's fine. He'll have only a sore leg—you saw how that happened—and a bruised kidney. You know—typical injuries sustained while resisting arrest."

"But did you get what we need out of him?"

Hunter stopped at the door of the BMW and faced him. "Enough for now."

"That didn't take long. I'm surprised he didn't try to resist or hold back."

"Not after I told him what I'd do to his eyes and balls if he did."

Garrett snorted. "So the idiot really believed you meant it."

"The idiot could tell I really meant it."

Garrett raised a brow. "Wow."

"Look, Grant, I'd love to continue this delightful chat, but I have to follow up on what he told me."

"Which was?"

Hunter pulled out his notepad, thumbed it open, tore off a page.

"This. The name and address of the guy running their cell. Ali Shishani. Nickname is 'The Chechen.' Run that through the databases. The guy inside didn't know anyone but his other cell members. He said Shishani coordinated with all their outside contacts for money, weapons, and explosives. So he's our key to finding out who's behind all this. It's a long shot, Grant, but if he's still at his apartment, maybe I can get to him and squeeze him before the feds read him his rights and ship him off to vacation in Guantanamo."

"Don't you want backup?"

He tapped the roof of the car. "I have what I need in here. But why don't you give me"—he looked at his watch—"one hour. Till 1300. If you don't hear from me by then, take that as a bad sign and send in the Marines."

He reached to open the car door. Felt Garrett's hand on his shoulder.

"Try not to tempt fate again today," Garrett said.

"So far, fate hasn't been tempted. Tell Annie I'll call as soon as I can."

4

Ali Shishani was half-listening, half-watching the TV news coverage as he finished tossing the last items into his bug-out bag.

He paused occasionally to watch a few minutes of video from the bomb site, and to gloat at the carnage and chaos he had engineered. The scene reminded him of how the Moscow apartment building had looked back in 1999.

He had already run any incriminating papers through the shredder and carted the trash bags to a suburban dump two days before. And he had packed his SUV last night with suitcases and supplies for the long trek back to the Mexican border.

It pissed him off he had to leave America again. This country had so much more to offer than Russia. But he knew how investigations worked. Even though the cell members were all dead, it wouldn't take long before the American FBI would be crawling like cockroaches through their apartments looking for clues. It would take time, but it was certain they would eventually find overlooked—how do they say?—yes—"loose ends" that would lead them back to "the Chechen." A receipt from a gas station, a crumpled note in a wastepaper basket, video from a store's security camera, GPS coordinates from cell phone records. They would piece together these scraps, and the trail would lead them to Ali.

So of course he had to leave. But he would leave much richer than when he arrived. He smiled. Lasher would be here in a few minutes with the rest of his cash, and then he would be on his way.

And when he got back to Moscow, he would ask his contact in Dignity and Honor if next time they could send him to a nice place. Maybe Switzerland. He had never seen the Swiss Alps . . . Or maybe Amsterdam. Yes—even better. He wondered if they still had naked whores in store windows, right on the streets. Imagine, window-shopping for ass, just like for clothes! Yes, the real thing—so much better than stupid videos on the internet. And he would have the money to buy the best, too . . .

The doorbell chimed.

His heart leapt . . . then suddenly turned cold. What if something had gone wrong? What if it was the cops, not Lasher, at the door downstairs?

He shut off the TV so that he could hear in the silence. Hurrying to his shoulder bag, he withdrew the loaded Smith & Wesson .38 from its hiding place under a folded shirt. Then he went to the intercom near the door and pressed the button.

"Yes?"

"It's me, Ali."

Relieved, he pushed a second button. Heard the buzzer downstairs, then the door click shut, then footfalls on the creaking stairs. He unlocked his door and left it ajar. Realizing the gun was still in his hand, he jammed it into his belt.

Time to celebrate. He rounded the corner to the fridge, grabbed a couple of cold beers, brought the bottles to the kitchen table. They could spread out the cash here, and he would count it. Every last bill. There was something about the pretty boy he didn't trust. He was too—what? Smooth. No, *slick*. Yeah, like oil. He wouldn't put it past the prick to skim off some of the cash.

He heard approaching footsteps in the hall as he flopped into the chair. The butt of the gun jammed painfully into his ample gut and he grunted. *Idiot! You could shoot off your balls like that.* He yanked it out of his belt just as he heard the footsteps stop outside.

The apartment entrance was just around the wall of his small kitchen; he couldn't see the door directly. But a full-length mirror hung on the adjacent wall.

In the mirror, he saw the door ease open. Lasher stepped in.

Empty-handed.

Ali frowned, about to speak, when he noticed Lasher's right hand was not empty at all.

Animal instinct kicked in. Ali raised the revolver and steadied it in both hands, bracing his elbows on the table. Lasher took another tentative step, coming into view. His head was turned away, toward the bedroom.

"Freeze!" he shouted.

Lasher's head snapped around. His eyes flared wide. But the rest of his body, including the gun in his hand, remained frozen in place. Ali saw its barrel ended in a long silencer.

"Drop that!" Ali ordered. "Then put hands on head."

He did. Ali saw the hands wore white surgical gloves.

"Now, kick gun away. Over near TV."

Lasher obeyed.

Ali eased himself up from the chair. Stepped carefully out from behind the table, then toward the man. On the surface, he felt oddly calm, steady enough to keep his aim unwavering. But somewhere inside he felt the churning rage of betrayal. He saw the whole thing, instantly.

"So, let me guess, pretty boy. You want cause terror in Washington, then blame Muslims. You need somebody to recruit Muslims, so you pick Ali. All his Muslims die in suicide mission. But Ali still lives. So, rather than pay, you come here now to take care of"—he smiled bitterly as he recalled the words again—"loose end. That's all he is now, right? Loose end."

"You keep saying 'you.' But this isn't my show, Ali. I'm not calling the shots here."

"Yeah. You just hired help. So, who hired you?"

Lasher looked strangely calm. "I'm not at liberty to say. But that doesn't matter. You should be a lot more worried about who's paying for all this—and is paying the person who hired me."

Ali took two more steps toward Lasher, then carefully side-stepped in front of him, keeping a safe distance.

"You mean SVR?"

"Bingo! You know, I feel sorry for you, Ali. After what you told me about your career . . . all the things you did for them, all the risks you took. And now today. Here you take your biggest risk yet, and you pull off the biggest mission of your life for them—maybe change the course of history. And this is the thanks you get. Instead of sending you a medal and money, they send me." He paused, then slowly smiled. "Oh, I forgot. You aren't really working for the SVR. You're working for—

what do those retired KGB spooks call themselves?"

Ali licked his lips, tasting salty sweat. "Dignity and Honor."

Lasher laughed. "Now, that's rich, isn't it? Ali Shishani is betrayed . . . by Dignity and Honor."

Ali had to make an effort to suppress the rage, now. Because he knew what the killer was saying was true.

"Well, I am still alive, pretty boy. Not you, though."

"Firing that gun in here would be real stupid, Ali. You pull that trigger a few times, then run out of here, and your neighbors will have this place swarming with cops in minutes. Even if you get out of the neighborhood and past all the roadblocks, within an hour they'll know who you are and what your connection to the terrorists is. Your photo will be on every TV station and in every cop car in the country by suppertime. They'll be right behind you, Ali, and they'll hunt you down like a rabid dog. Is that what you want?"

Ali felt a pang of uncertainty. Then the obvious solution occurred to him.

"No, *you* the stupid one, pretty boy." He edged his way toward the TV and the silenced pistol on the floor.

Lasher saw what he was doing and frowned.

"No, wait. We can work something out, Ali. You were counting on a big payday, right? You'll need money, lots of money, to get out of the country and stay away from the SVR. Well, that's exactly what I got for this job. And for others. Lots and lots of money."

Ali thought about it, but continued to shuffle toward the suppressed pistol.

"Look, I have bank cards in my wallet. I can give you the PIN numbers. The accounts are loaded with all the cash you need. Several million. My wallet's right here, inside my jacket."

Ali snorted. "And I supposed to let hitman reach inside jacket?" He shook his head. "So let's see if you have another gun there. You very slow take off jacket. Just right hand."

Lasher's face was blank now. Keeping his white-gloved left hand on his head, he lowered his right arm, drew open his sports coat, then tugged and shrugged it off his right shoulder. But the right sleeve still clung to his arm. He began to shake his hand, and the sleeve began to slide free. He swept it around behind him . . .

. . . and his hand came back holding a long, thin knife that he raised and pointed at Ali.

It startled him, but just a second. Then he burst out laughing.

"You really something, pretty boy! What they say? 'Never bring knife to gun fight.' I fill you with holes before you get close, asshole. You stay right over there and drop that stupid thing."

Lasher didn't move. He remained four or five meters away, still pointing the knife directly toward him.

Ali knew Lasher was right about firing the noisy .38. He wouldn't unless he had to. Keeping his eyes and the gun barrel trained steadily on the assassin, he squatted slowly, groping the floor with his left hand for the killer's pistol. His hand found the suppressor. He picked it up and started to rise.

Lasher smirked and slightly raised the knife. Squinted down its length.

A loud *snap* and a blur and something smashed into Ali's face below his right eye, a spear of fire that burned deep into his skull and knocked him back onto the floor . . .

. . . then searing bolts of impossible spasming pain in his head . . . a face hovering above saying Don't Call Me Pretty Boy and pressing a cylinder between his eyes that exploded . . .

Lasher removed the suppressor and returned it and the pistol to the special pocket inside his jacket. It took a minute of forceful wiggling and tugging to retrieve the barely protruding blade of his ballistic knife from the Chechen's fat-covered cheekbone.

He rinsed it off in the sink, then found a bottle of bleach beneath the counter and used that to remove the last traces of blood and DNA from the blade and his surgical gloves. He reinserted the blade into the knife's cylindrical, spring-loaded handle, locking it into place. Then slid it back into the customized quick-release sheath on his right forearm.

Now for the staging.

Lasher picked up the revolver carefully in his gloved hands and placed it inside the suitcase, under some clothes. From his pocket, he pulled out a thick envelope holding eight thousand dollars in cash, dusted with some cocaine residue. He pressed it against Shishani's palm and shoved it underneath the clothes in the suitcase, too. He also took out a plastic sandwich bag containing a little cocaine and sprinkled the powder into the travel bag's zippered pockets. Finally, after pressing the Chechen's fingertips against them, he added a couple of folded maps, marked with circled spots near the Texas-Mexican border, and a route down into Mexico traced with yellow highlighter.

As a final, ingenious touch, Lasher placed a copy of the Koran inside the suitcase. Inside, the pages had been cut to create a hollowed-out rectangle. In that space was a small chemical kit to test for drug purity.

Detectives would take in all of this, and even when they discovered that Shishani attended a local mosque and had a foreign background, they would conclude that he was using Islam as a cover for drug trafficking. And that some deal had gone terribly wrong.

He retrieved everything he'd brought with him, and left.

It was twelve minutes after noon.

5

With strobes flashing on a black sedan bearing fake diplomatic plates, and a terrorism emergency underway, Hunter felt he could risk a high-speed race along Routes 66 and 50 from Dupont Circle to downtown Fairfax. He made the usual nineteen-mile, half-hour drive in only seventeen minutes.

When he pulled into the quiet side street, he killed the strobes and proceeded at a normal pace. Following the GPS, he turned into the cul-de-sac housing the apartment complex. He spotted the number on Shishani's building and drove on past, parking in the lot behind the next building.

He checked the Sig and his boot knife, added a small lockpick set to his pocket, and donned sunglasses to help against both the glare and the security cameras. To make himself look more innocuous, he fetched a clipboard and some papers from a briefcase behind his seat.

He set off nonchalantly along the sidewalk. Small signs for a local security-alarm company appeared next to several buildings; obviously they had the contract here. Whistling, he marched purposefully up to the front of Shishani's building, browsed for his name and apartment number on the intercom listing, and buzzed other residents, one at a time.

"*Yes?*"

"Eagle Security, ma'am. We're conducting our semi-annual inspection of our alarm system here. Could you buzz me in, please?"

The buzzer went off and he went in.

He took the stairs to the second floor. Clipboard in hand, he strolled casually down the hall to number 203. He looked around, drew the Sig, and held it flat beneath the clipboard. Then, standing to the side, he rapped on the door.

"Hello!" he called out. "Alarm inspector."

He heard nothing. He tried again. No response.

He placed the clipboard, with the gun underneath, on the floor. Opening the pick case, he selected the right ones and went to work on the lock. It took seven seconds. He pocketed the picks, retrieved the clipboard and gun, then, again standing to the side, eased open the door with his boot.

Dead silence.

He slipped inside, Sig at the ready. Softly closed and latched the door behind him.

Seconds later, he spotted the body on the floor next to the TV.

He glided through the apartment, clearing each room and closet before returning to the body. There he crouched.

He put his hand on Shishani's throat. Still warm.

He studied the bullet hole between the eyes. Saw the powder burns. Intrigued, he closely examined the hole in his cheek. Closing his eyes, he tried to imagine the sequence.

Next, he poked through the dead man's pockets and wallet. Finding nothing useful, he wiped down and replaced the wallet. Then he moved to the travel bag and checked it for paperwork, receipts, anything helpful. He opened the maps gingerly, then photographed the markings with his phone and replaced them. He found the envelope with the cash, and the revolver. Neither surprised him. But the traces of coke, plus the hollowed-out Koran and its hidden drug kit, did. It looked like the contractor was also involved in the drug business. He put it all back as he had found it.

Proceeding methodically but quickly through the apartment, he checked every drawer, closet, and cabinet, opening things with his handkerchief to avoid leaving prints or DNA, and being careful not to disturb anyone else's. Everything had been emptied out.

Returning to the kitchen, he suddenly felt bone-tired. And became aware of all the nagging little pains from where debris had pummeled his body.

He pulled out his burner, popped in the battery, and took a chair at the kitchen table. The two beer bottles there caught his attention. So did the sweat beads on them, and the small puddles surrounding them on the tabletop.

He tapped in the special direct number.

"You find him?" were Garrett's first words.

"Dead end. Literally. Someone took him out. Looks like it happened just before I got here. Also looks like he was packing to leave. The place is completely cleaned out, except for some food in the fridge. But two fresh beers are sitting here on the kitchen table, unopened, still cold."

"Like maybe he was expecting someone he knew."

"Or someone he *thought* he knew."

"So, what is your gut telling you?"

Hunter's eyes roved the room. Settled on the body.

"I ask myself, 'Why did we want to talk to this guy?'"

"Because he knew the other people involved."

"Exactly. I think he died for the same reason."

A long sigh, a short cough. "They didn't leave us with much, did they."

"That was the plan. This was a real pro hit. Which makes me more convinced than ever that I'm right about this. Maybe his background will tell us something. Or maybe the Bureau will find something when they pick through this place. But I'm not going to wait around for somebody else to get lucky and stumble into the people really behind this. Not when everyone's running around looking for more Muslims."

"What do you have in mind?"

Hunter looked over at the pool of blood congealing around Shishani's head.

"They've gone after everyone who's trying to find out about them, or who knows anything about them. Anyone who becomes a threat to them. So that's how I'm going to smoke them out. I'm going to become a serious threat to them, too."

"You mean make yourself their next target? What makes you think you won't wind up like the others?"

Hunter hauled himself to his feet. Felt the Sig pressing against his back.

"The others didn't know they were targets. And they didn't shoot back."

TWENTY-SEVEN

Vox Populi Communications occupied the entire top floor of a glass-walled office building on First Street, just three blocks from the Capitol and Union Station. The location allowed VPC's founder and CEO, Lucas Carver—as well as his considerable staff—ready access to the city's political movers and media shakers.

The building also offered exceptional security and privacy. Key card access to its entrances, private underground garage, and elevators—all monitored at the security desk—limited admission only to employees and VIP clients. That privacy would be imperative for the highly sensitive, closed-door meeting taking place this morning.

Avery Trammel strode into the organization's conference room first and selected the chair at the end of the conference table. That compelled the trio following him to take the chairs on either side of him. Carl Spencer sat to his immediate right. Lucas Carver took the seat opposite the senator. The newcomer, Sid Cunningham, settled in next to Carver. All wore grave, numbed expressions.

Despite his own much different mood, Trammel reminded himself that he had to be careful to mirror theirs. In the wake of the terrorist attacks, any reaction other than shock and outrage might provoke curiosity. Curiosity might provoke questions. And at this delicate moment, questions might be dangerous. He turned to his friend.

"Lucas, I wish to thank you for agreeing to host us on such short notice. Under these terrible circumstances, I felt it necessary that we meet immediately."

"Of course, Avery. What happened yesterday"—he looked down and shook his head—"is just unbelievable."

Spencer sighed heavily. "To think that anything so horrendous could happen right here in the nation's capital. Nobody is safe anywhere these days."

"It's like the morning after 9/11," Carver said. "Yesterday was another game-changer. We've awakened into a different world."

"Everything *has* changed," Trammel replied. "Yet, regardless of our shock over this tragedy, it is now our responsibility to respond swiftly and prudently." He looked at the newcomer. "Sidney, I do not envy you the task of taking the reins of the senator's campaign under such trying circumstances."

Sid Cunningham nodded slowly, not speaking. This morning was the first time Trammel had met him. An old colleague of Carver's, Cunningham was known as a wily, cold-blooded campaign consultant. Underscoring that reputation was his ferret-like appearance: short and slight, with a narrow blade of a nose, close-set gray eyes, and thin lips. Lucas had assured Trammel that the new, hand-picked campaign manager was a committed progressive and brilliant tactician, with an encyclopedic knowledge of the American political landscape.

Spencer broke the silence. "I don't envy Sid, either. After the beating I was taking in the polls before the debate, this terrorist attack screws up everything even more. People won't be talking about anything else for months."

"Actually, the event confirms the wisdom of your prophetic warning about radical Islamic terrorism," Trammel said. "The terrible, tragic irony is that your candidacy may actually benefit from this atrocity."

They all stared at him.

"I hadn't thought of that," Spencer said, his voice low.

"Of course not," Trammel said, patting his arm. "You are too decent a man to think about exploiting political advantages at a time like this."

Carver cleared his throat. "About the debate. I couldn't believe it when the senator said what he did. Frankly, Carl, I was appalled by the—well, abrupt right-wing shift in your foreign policy."

"Me, too," Cunningham added. "No sooner had I decided to accept your offer to take over the campaign, when you blindsided me—*all* of us—with that about-face. I told you that night I'd have to reconsider. I was afraid you'd lost the entire base, and I'd be jumping aboard a sinking ship."

Spencer's eyes darted to Trammel's before he spoke.

"That's why I asked you to hold off making a quick decision, Sid. I fully understood your position. But I hope you understood mine. After receiving a warning about a potential terrorist attack, it would have been irresponsible of me to keep it to myself. I had to follow my conscience, regardless of the political cost." He glanced over again; Trammel rewarded him with a smile and nod.

"Lucas," Trammel said, "you recall that after the debate, I asked you, too, to wait and see how Carl's stand would play out."

"Yes you did, Avery. And frankly, I'm stunned. How could you possibly have imagined that things might turn out like this?"

"Obviously, I could not. No one could. I simply had confidence that Carl knew what he was talking about. In addition—and at risk of sounding cynical—there is the matter of 'triangulation.' The polls showed that Carl was perceived as 'too weak on defense.' I felt Islamist terrorism was a safe issue, on which he could stake out a position to the right of both Waller and Helm, and thereby strengthen his image and broaden his appeal. So, that is exactly what I counseled him to do, when we discussed strategy before the debate."

"*You* are the one who encouraged him to do that?" Carver exclaimed.

Spencer chuckled. "He did. To be honest, Lucas, even *I* worried that it was terrible advice. But since the campaign was already on the ropes, I figured we had little to lose. So I went along with him—and just look at how things turned out! You're a fortune-teller, Avery."

Trammel could not resist a small smile as he waved it off. "No. Just older and perhaps a tad more experienced than the rest of you. History teaches that unpredictable foreign-policy events frequently become the most decisive factors in a presidential campaign." He cast his eyes down. "And who could have anticipated *this?*"

He glanced up. Saw that his answer seemed to satisfy them.

"Well, in any case, I'm relieved now that I didn't back out of the job right then," Cunningham said. "Because this *is* a game-changer. I think the senator is positioned to recast his image and rejuvenate the campaign."

Carver raised a hand. "But only if we play it very carefully. How we respond now, and over the coming days, could make or break this campaign."

"I've been worrying about that," Spencer said. "I sure don't want to say or do the wrong things."

"That's why we're here," Carver said. "As always, the key thing going forward is to control the narrative. I spoke to Avery about that last night. We agreed your best course at the moment is to hold a brief news conference today around noon, announcing a one-week suspension of your campaign, 'in honor of the many victims of this atrocity.' We want to announce that before the other campaigns get the same idea. It will show sensitivity and statesmanship."

Spencer looked at Trammel. "If you say so."

Carver continued. "We can anticipate some reporter at the presser will comment about how prescient you were to foresee the terrorist strike. It's *really important* for you to reply *humbly* about that, not taking any credit. Something like, 'I'm grieved that my intelligence source was correct in his warning, and that my greatest fears have been realized. I would give anything to have been wrong about this.'"

"I like it," Cunningham said. "Don't take credit for being right. Let the facts speak for themselves."

"And when reporters press you about the political ramifications of the attack, you need to show anger," Carver added. "You know: 'Come on, people! This is not a day to talk politics! This is a day for all Americans to come together, to pray, and to mourn our dead. Let's show a little decency and respect, okay?'"

Cunningham smiled, snapped his fingers, and pointed at Carver. "Perfect! Very statesman-like."

"You can bet the media will frame it that way," Carver went on.

"Especially Vox Populi's go-to media contacts. Carl, I want you to remain silent this week. Keep your word about 'no politicking.' Just attend funerals, lay wreaths, that sort of thing. Let us and your surrogates frame the messages about all this. We handle this right, I'll wager we see a ten-point jump in the polls by next week."

Trammel leaned forward, elbows on the desk, steepling his fingers.

"Carl, Lucas has unparalleled instincts about these things. We need to heed what he says. Sid, I know of your strategic abilities, too. However, as we reboot the campaign, we need to establish a clear division of labor. I believe your role should be to run everything on the organizational side. But I also think we all should defer to Lucas and his organization when it comes to shaping the campaign messaging and narrative. And, Carl, as candidate, your job should be to faithfully embody and articulate that narrative."

"What about you?" Cunningham asked pointedly.

"I see my first task as making certain that the campaign is amply funded. And my second responsibility will be to enlist the full support of the Currents network. Primarily, to go after the other two candidates."

"That's right," Lucas said. "You see, Vox Populi is basically in the storytelling business. We don't really focus on ideological arguments. Instead, we fight for progressive change by creating positive *narratives* about our clients and their causes, while circulating contrasting, negative narratives about their opponents. We spread stories of heroes, villains, and victims all over the media—"

"—with the help of sympathetic nonprofits in the Currents network," Trammel finished. "*Our* job is to lend support to Vox Populi's messaging, by providing the media with quotable experts, research studies, and armies of activists."

"Of course, all this is done completely independently," Carver added, winking. They all chuckled. He glanced at his watch.

"It's already nine-thirty. We don't have a lot of time to set up a noon press conference. I'll get my staff to put things in motion and spread the word. What the four of us should do now is refine his talking points. Oh, and later this afternoon, after the presser, we should hold a follow-up meeting back here to assess how things went and plot our strategy going forward." He frowned at the candidate. "Carl, that yellow tie is a little too cheery right after a major terrorist event. I'll have our television team get you something more subdued . . ."

Trammel fought to keep his own manner subdued. It was a struggle, considering the jubilation he was experiencing. It had been a nerve-wracking month leading up to yesterday. But the entire operation could not have proceeded more flawlessly. Now he could afford to sit back and allow the *Maestro* to step into the spotlight and handle the details.

Still . . . he, *Geppetto,* would remain unseen in the background, pulling all the strings.

He could barely contain himself. He knew he would need to celebrate tonight.

2

Julia was lying awake, staring at the ceiling, when faint noise somewhere in the apartment told her he was finally home.

She turned to the bedside clock. One thirty-five in the morning.

A few moments later, she heard the sound of the shower running in the guest bedroom down the hall.

She rolled over, facing away from his side of the bed, pretending to be asleep.

It was another fifteen minutes before she heard him tip-toe into the bedroom. She listened to the familiar sounds of him hanging his bathrobe on a nearby wall hook. Then felt the shifting of the mattress and rustling of the silk sheets as he cautiously slipped into the bed.

He remained distant from her, as he had for almost a month.

She smelled the heavy scent of mouthwash. Wondered what else on his breath it might be intended to mask.

Julia waited long minutes, not moving, until he stopped stirring, too—and until his breathing grew deep and steady.

It was almost three-thirty when, heart pounding, she dared to inch her way from beneath the covers. Then, one careful step at a time in the near-dark, she made her way across the room, and out into the hall.

She shivered, but not just from the cool air against her thin nightgown, or the cold marble beneath her bare feet. Small nightlights down the hallway allowed her to make her way to the laundry room. She entered, quietly closed the door behind her, and turned on the light.

The sports jacket and trousers he had worn this evening were zipped inside a hanging plastic bag, for the maid to take downstairs to the dry cleaners. She unzipped it and examined them, checking the pockets, then every inch of the fabric, but finding nothing other than wrinkles.

Then, taking a deep breath, she untied the cloth bag sitting on the laundry table. She pulled out his balled-up shirt, opened it, spread it out on the table.

And immediately noticed the red smear on the sleeve.

Then caught the unmistakable scent of perfume.

Julia began to tremble, then shake violently.

Her back pressed against the door, she slid slowly down to the floor, burying her face and her sobs in the stained shirt.

3

"Once again, you outdid yourself with the lamb shank, love," Hunter said, lowering his empty wine glass.

"Thank you. It's one thing I can do right in the kitchen."

"But not the only thing." He got up from his chair at her dinner table and took her hand. "Let's leave the tidying up for later. I need some time with my girl."

Annie rose and they moved, hand-in-hand, to the living room sofa. He sat first, then drew her into his lap.

"Now, tell me about your day."

"Don't you want to talk about—"

He shook his head. "No. I've thought about nothing else for the past two days. Tonight belongs to us."

"All right, Dylan." She gave him a light kiss. "I suppose you want a status report about the Great Mole Hunt, right?"

"Sure. Let's start there."

"The good news today is that in our march through the directorates, we've already ruled out DS&T, Support, and DDI. Digital Innovation was easy; it's new and hasn't been around long enough for our long-term mole. That narrows the possibilities to either Ops or Analysis. I'm waiting to see if one of about a half-dozen juicy bits of bait we dangled is nibbled by anyone in Ops."

"What kind of bait?"

"Different things. Like tantalizing but phony reports left in plain sight near a target's photocopier. Or circulating what looks like exactly the same memo to each Ops division, but subtly misspelling or changing just one or two key details. We've enlisted contacts at NSA to help. If they, or our own CI people, pick up from our Russian sources any one of those unique identifiers, we'll have a good idea where the leak is."

"Your idea again?"

She shook her head. "Grant's. I'm tracking other things. As with DS&T, we announce we're dispatching an officer or arranging a meet with an asset somewhere in the world. We circulate different memos about these to the relevant Ops divisions. Then, depending on where and how we see the Russians react, we'll know if the mole is in Ops, and, we hope, in which division. Of course, then we'll have to double-check to eliminate the possibility of coincidence. And after that, we'll try to narrow it down even more, office by office."

"It sounds incredibly tedious."

"It is. But Langley is loaded with thousands of people. Process of elimination is the only way to do these investigations."

"If you get no nibbles in Ops . . ."

". . . then we move on to Analysis."

"And all of its own divisions, offices, centers, projects, and God knows what else."

"I know," she sighed, resting her head against his shoulder. "This would be so much easier if we had a team helping us. But for obvious reasons, it's just Grant and me. And the clock is ticking. So it's running us ragged."

That gave him his opening.

"Look, I realize you've got to stay completely focused on this right now. And that's probably just as well, because I'm preoccupied for the time being, too."

"Preoccupied, how?"

"Annie, somebody is trying to screw with the presidential election, and they have to be stopped. But so far, they've killed everyone who gets too close to figuring out who they are. Nobody in government is even aware this is happening, or would believe me if I told them. So, it's up to me to prove it."

"How can you possibly do that?"

"As I explained to Grant, I'm about to become a royal pain in the ass to them. Make it known that I'm investigating them. That should smoke them out."

She pressed her palms against his chest, drawing back.

"You're deliberately making yourself a target for *them,* too? Even while Lasher is already hunting you?"

"I wish there were a better way, but this looks like the *only* way. So, yes—besides watching out for Lasher, I'll also be watching out for anyone they send after me."

He raised his hands to cup her face.

"And that's another reason why, after tonight, it's important that we keep our distance from each other for a while."

"You mean . . . not see each other *at all?*"

He nodded.

She pulled back from him. "So . . . just how long is 'a while'?"

"I'll start rattling their cages tomorrow. I don't think it will take long for them to respond."

"'Respond.' You mean, try to—"

"Annie, please remember a few things. Unlike the others they've targeted, I *know* I'm a target, so they won't catch me unawares. Or unprepared. As you know, I have the ability, resources, and motivation to respond." He grinned. "Frankly, I'd much rather be me than them."

She lowered her eyes and started to fidget with the engagement ring. "First you said we couldn't announce our engagement, because of Lasher. Now you decide we can't even *see* each other anymore."

"Not 'anymore.' Just temporarily. You know I'm right about this," he said softly.

"Dylan . . . why do I feel that something terrible is going to happen? That we're *never* going to—"

"Don't talk nonsense, love." He took her hand, raised it, and kissed the ring.

Then he kissed her lips.

"Since we won't be together for a little while," he said, looking into her gray cat's eyes, "we shouldn't let the evening go to waste—don't you think?"

She nodded. "Why don't we take Cyrano for a romantic moonlight walk first?"

"Yes. Why don't we?"

They lit scented candles in the darkened bedroom. Then, in the flickering light, they undressed each other, taking turns as they removed the other's garments, one at a time. They did not touch each other's bodies; instead, they held back, deliberately allowing the tension to build.

Moving behind her, he unfastened her lace bra, brushed it from her shoulders, and let it whisper to the carpet.

Then he stood motionless as she turned to face him. He watched the soft candlelight play over her lips, her neck, her naked shoulders, her breasts. She slowly unbuttoned his shirt, then pushed it from his shoulders and arms, to fall atop her blouse and bra. He heard the sudden intake of her breath.

"Oh!"

"It's nothing. Just some minor welts and bruises. From yesterday."

She looked up into his eyes. Hers narrowed.

"Let me make them all better."

She leaned forward at the waist, her breasts suspended like soft ivory teardrops. She pressed her lips against a spot on his chest. He felt their warmth, then her hot breath—then the slow, moist movement of her tongue against his skin.

He closed his eyes and drew a ragged breath. Began instinctively to raise his hands.

"Don't touch me," she ordered. "Stand still."

He did.

Eyes squeezed shut, he savored the grazing movement of her lips across his chest, pausing at each wound. He quivered under the hot flicks of her tongue—then, as it roamed on, at the air's sudden chill against his wet skin. He listened to the deep, rising sounds of his breathing . . . and hers. He inhaled the light scent of her perfume, and of her skin.

He felt the soft, full lips begin to descend, inexorably, down his belly.

Endured the touch of her fingers undoing his belt. Then their feather touch at his zipper.

Endured it all, until he could endure no more . . .

It was a night of storming passion, like those they had experienced when they first met. But this time there was an edge in their lovemaking—a spirit of defiant protest against the inescapable circumstances always threatening to drive them apart. That, and a sense of desperation and foreboding, made them both insatiable.

They did not speak. They would not sleep. And for hours, they could not stop.

Finally, sometime long after midnight, she lay in his arms, shivering and crying.

He held her gently.

Rocking her. Stroking her hair.

Staring into a dying candle across the room.

TWENTY-EIGHT

The Currents Center occupied the third floor of a modern office building on K Street. It was a cliché address for a political lobbying group, Hunter mused. But the appearance and manner of the two men sitting across the coffee table from him were clichés, too.

Short and bald, pug-nosed and wide-mouthed, Wallace Rouse looked as if a toad's face had been glued onto a pink egg. He had a nervous, ingratiating manner and when he introduced himself, he pronounced his name with a severe lisp. From his research, Hunter knew the man had inherited both his wealth and his vaguely liberal politics. But he seemed more of a social schmoozer than an ideologue. Perhaps solely because of his pedigree, this unimpressive creature had been elevated to be president of the Currents Foundation—the main funding source and New York parent organization of the D.C.-based Currents Center.

The Center's executive director, Paul Ratzenberger, couldn't have been more different. Sporting tweeds that color-matched his gray-brown hair and beard, he could have passed for an Ivy League professor. But the dark eyes behind his wire-rimmed glasses exuded wariness and cunning. Over three decades Ratzenberger had established a reputation as one of the left's most effective and ruthless organizers.

Hunter sipped the coffee he'd been offered and let his eyes rove around Ratzenberger's plush office before replying to his question.

"Specifically, I asked to see you gentlemen because I'm working on a series about 'money in politics.' But it's a different take on the topic, which usually focuses on campaign contributions from big corporate interests. My attention is on the flow of foundation and nonprofit money into politics. And my research raised some questions about your respective organizations that I hoped you would be able to clear up."

Rouse blinked and smiled. "Of course, Mr. Hunter. We strive for transparency. We'll be happy to help, if we can."

Ratzenberger sat back, folding his arms across his chest. "What questions?"

Hunter pulled out his notepad and thumbed through a few scribbled pages.

"First, to you, Mr. Rouse. This past year, federal reporting forms described the purpose of five large grants from the Trammel Foundation to your Currents Foundation as being for 'energy awareness advocacy.' I wonder if you could explain what that means?"

"Why, it means exactly what it sounds like," he replied, smiling too effusively. "The grants are for educational purposes: to make the public aware of the full human and economic costs of carbon-based fuel sources, and to advocate for renewable energy alternatives."

"Options," Hunter said.

"What?"

"'Options,' not 'alternatives.' Everyone gets that wrong. 'Options' are multiple; but there is only one 'alternative.'" He smiled. "Anyway, as far as I can tell, most of the advocacy you're funding directly with that grant money seems to go toward opposing fracking."

Rouse's smile wavered. "Well, I don't have the actual grant percentages at my fingertips. But whatever they are, I suppose that is to be expected. After all, fracking constitutes a rapidly growing share of the carbon-energy market, and it therefore represents the greatest threat to our health and the environment."

Two minutes in, and the lisp was already grating. Hunter found himself gritting his teeth.

"I also noticed that the single largest share of your grant-making is channeled through the Currents Center." He nodded toward Ratzenberger. "In turn, you use the money to set up nonprofit advocacy groups and campaigns, giving them the benefit of your organizing experience and offering them the shared legal benefit of your own tax-exempt status."

Ratzenberger studied him a few seconds before responding.

"That's correct. The Center acts as a kind of incubator. We help get these groups launched, and then we do our best to make sure that they can function independently and successfully."

Hunter made a show of squinting at a page. "One of those organizations is the Caring and Sharing Alliance, is it not?"

The appraising look became a scowl. "What of it?"

"It's one of a number of groups you fund, assist, and shelter under your tax-exempt umbrella for ostensibly 'educational' activities."

"What do you mean, 'ostensibly'?"

"I mean they appear to be engaging in overt politicking."

Rouse completely lost his smile and started blinking. Ratzenberger unfolded his arms, wiped his palms on his trousers, and leaned in.

"That's absolutely false. The Alliance's activities are purely educational."

Hunter shook his head. "Exactly one month ago my own eyes and ears told me otherwise. I was visiting Roger Helm's headquarters for an interview when I encountered a host of demonstrators from the Alliance. They were chanting against his candidacy, not about specific policies. They've also been holding news conferences and issuing reports criticizing his personal wealth and targeting his campaign contributors—even picketing their homes and committing vandalism against their property. That seems pretty political to me."

Rouse cut in. "Nonprofits are allowed to engage in a certain percentage of political lobbying activities," he said, his lisp now sounding more like a serpent's hiss. "But as for your specific claims: After a group is established, Currents cannot be held responsible for everything it may choose to do in the future."

"Perhaps. But it's not as if you set them up, then wash your hands of them and go away. In fact, I discovered that you maintain active oversight, through Vox Populi Communications. That's the consulting firm you hired to manage media for Currents and for your network of nonprofits—including the Alliance."

"Those are all independent arrangements and contracts," Ratzenberger snapped.

"Mr. Ratzenberger, I've looked into your financial reports and theirs. Your grants show up as line items on the forms, explicitly listing Vox Populi as running media campaigns for all those groups. So, in fact, you pick up that tab for its work. And—by strange coincidence—Carver also serves as the chief political and media consultant for Carl Spencer's presidential campaign."

"All right, enough of this! Just what are you driving at, Mr. Hunter?" Ratzenberger's face was red and his fist lay clenched on his lap.

"Just this. I see big, tax-exempt grants from the personal foundation of Avery Trammel—a wealthy, 'alternative energy' investor—flowing into Currents, supposedly for perfectly lawful, tax-exempt educational purposes. But then I see Currents pouring that so-called 'educational' grant money, plus its other resources, into groups and individuals engaged directly in partisan political campaigning—attacking a pro-fracking presidential candidate on behalf of a rival who's pushing 'alternative energy' policies that Mr. Trammel favors. If I have that wrong, I thought you might want to clarify things for me, before I publish some articles to that effect in the *Inquirer*."

Ratzenberger appeared about to explode as Rouse, looking on the verge of panic, jumped in.

"Oh, don't do that!" he said, waving both hands. "You've got it all wrong! This is a huge misunderstanding." He stood. "Before you do a thing, Mr. Hunter, please let me make a few calls. We'll be happy to help clarify everything for you."

"Wallace, can't you see it's a waste of time?" Ratzenberger said, also rising. "We warned you about this guy."

Hunter pocketed his notepad and got to his feet, too.

"'We?'" he prompted, raising a brow.

"This meeting is over, Mr. Hunter. If you write any defamatory nonsense along the lines you've described, you and the right-wing rag you represent will be hearing from our attorneys."

"Wow. Well, in that case, I sure don't want to seem uncooperative."

He pulled out a business card. "Here—let me make it easy for your lawyers to reach me."

He dropped it on the coffee table.

"Tell them I look forward to our chat."

2

"What is wrong, my dear?"

Julia faced away, looking out the tinted window of the limousine. Rain from dingy piles of clouds misted across the rural Virginia countryside. He saw a brief shake of her head.

"Seriously, now. Something is troubling you."

"I'm all right. Just tired."

She did not look at him. Just as she had barely looked at him this morning, or during the ride from the Watergate to the Mayflower. Her remarks at the Democratic National Committee luncheon had felt perfunctory, lacking her usual passion.

"I hope you are not still holding against me that I had to miss your award dinner earlier this month," he ventured.

Another shake of the head.

"You know how sorry I am about that."

"Honestly, I'm just tired."

He wondered about that.

"You seemed to be sleeping soundly when I came in."

"I was," she said. Then she added, a shade too quickly: "I mean, I must have been. I didn't hear you."

A lie. He had known her far too long to miss the nuances of insincerity.

He turned away, closing his eyes.

So, then. She suspects. Or perhaps she knows . . .

There had been other women during their two decades together, of course. But he had been discreet, and he did not believe she ever even suspected.

This complicated things. And complications were the last thing he needed right now . . .

He thought of how they had first met, almost twenty years earlier. He had already amassed much of his fortune and was widening his sphere of social and political influence when they shared the dais at some feminist conference in New York. Then in her early thirties, and in contention for her second Academy Award, Julia Haight was the star and keynoter of the conference, lending Hollywood glamor and media attention to the festivities.

Eyes shut, he could still easily recall the way she looked on the stage that night: the wavy auburn hair, the large dark eyes, the aristocratic cheekbones, the elegant body, the showgirl's legs. He had enjoyed many talented and beautiful women in his life; but what arrested him about her was the sheer intensity of her idealism. She gave a fiery speech defending women's empowerment in the workplace. She mesmerized him. He could not remember a single word she said; but he never forgot the image of her striding across that stage, mic in hand.

It was after the dinner, over private cocktails, that he caught the first faint hints of her insecurities. It was only much later that he learned their depth.

The daughter of a famous actor, whom she worshipped, Julia had suffered his cold, remote inattention throughout childhood. Still a girl, she threw herself into acting, striving obsessively to prove herself worthy to attract his love and respect. Her talent, looks, and raw ambition were undeniable. By her early twenties she won starring film roles, and soon, the adoration of millions. Yet she never won the one love she craved.

So she sought it elsewhere, allowing herself to be used and abused by powerful men in the movie industry. By age twenty-eight, her career was soaring, yet her self-esteem was plunging. It hit rock-bottom when her father died that year. She emerged from a substance abuse clinic searching for meaning, and found it in liberal politics. It became her new obsession, her new substitute for authentic self-esteem.

When Trammel met her that night, the attraction was instant and mutual, though only he fully grasped the reasons. He was a father figure who—powerful, reserved, even forbidding—showed her the love and respect she had sought so long and desperately. As for himself, in addition to her intelligence, beauty, and talent, Julia also offered a ticket of admission into the world of celebrity—and a whole new sphere of influence and power. Their complimentary roles carried over into their sexuality: his dominance and her submission were intoxicating to them both.

Or had been . . .

His eyes opened onto the bleak landscape. The realization of his growing estrangement from her felt of a piece with the feeling of foreboding that had been gathering around him for the past several months. He wondered why, on the threshold of his ultimate triumph, he felt so bleak.

He put his hand into the pocket of his trousers, his fingers seeking reassurance from the cool metal surface of his father's pocket watch. He reminded himself what this was all for, trying to recapture the old fire, the sense of mission . . .

. . . when, in his jacket, he felt the vibration of his phone.

He took it out and saw who it was.

"Yes, Wallace." He listened for a moment, phone pressed to his ear so that she could not hear the conversation. "I see. All right, give me his number . . . No, there is no need to apologize. You and Paul did exactly what I asked. At least we now know where we stand with him. Just go about your normal business. From this point, I shall deal with him myself."

3

The call Hunter expected came through on his burner while he was driving back to his Bethesda apartment. It had been forwarded via the spoofing site and the second, hidden burner.

"Yes?" he answered.

"Would this be Mr. Hunter?"

He recognized the distinctive voice.

"Ah, Mr. Trammel. I've been expecting your call."

"Have you, now? It seems you have been a busy fellow. And a nosy one."

"I am cursed with boundless energy and curiosity."

"Apparently so. And utterly misdirected. Mr. Rouse told me of your visit with him and Mr. Ratzenberger. Your groundless speculations left them in a bad frame of mind."

"Please tell them I am grieved and beg their forgiveness."

"There is no need for the testy attitude, Mr. Hunter. You and I have been working at cross purposes for too long."

"Given what I know of your purposes, I hope I am."

"Perhaps there are misunderstandings about that. Or perhaps we can reach some accommodation. In any case, I believe it is time we finally meet and have a discussion."

"Gee, I can't wait. Name a time and place."

"Normally, I would prefer to meet in the city. However, my wife and I have just arrived at our home in Virginia. We shall be hosting a charity event tomorrow evening. I suggest you come here tomorrow morning—say, ten o'clock."

"Ten is fine."

"Excellent. Let me give you the driving directions. From the city, take Route 66—"

"That's not necessary. I know where you live, Mr. Trammel."

"My, my. You *have* been doing your homework about me."

"Oh, I'm just getting started."

TWENTY-NINE

About a mile down the narrow country lane, Hunter encountered a four-foot-high brick wall that bordered the road and established the perimeter of Trammel's estate. Driving on, he reached the entrance and turned into the driveway. He noted the security camera atop the gatehouse as he pulled up and lowered his window.

The uniformed guard who stepped out of the booth was tough-looking and packed a Glock on his right hip.

"Name, please?"

"Dylan Hunter of the *Capitol Inquirer*, here to interview Mr. Trammel."

The guy nodded. "I have you on list. Show me ID, please?"

The accent was unmistakably Russian. Hunter presented his driver's license. The guard gave him instructions to the parking area near the house. Then the gate slid open in front of him as the man spoke into a walkie-talkie to announce his arrival, also in Russian.

On the drive in, he observed and memorized details of the grounds and the looming mansion, comparing the current reality against what he'd studied in online archives of satellite imagery and old real estate photos. He spotted two more security cameras along the driveway, then three more on the house itself—one atop each wing, and one over the covered front entrance. There, a blond-haired guard watched as he looped the central fountain, whose spray left shimmering rainbows in the dazzling morning sunshine.

He locked and left the Forester in the parking area, setting the alarm to warn him if anyone tried to search it. The last thing he needed was for Trammel's people to find his hidden weapons or electronics. He walked back along a covered walkway. Of the six garage bays, only the one nearest the house entrance stood open. A black Cadillac stretch limo occupied that space, and a man was busy vacuuming its interior.

Outside the front door, the guard had been joined by dark-haired one holding a security wand.

"I'm clean," Hunter said, prompting the guy to say something.

"We search, anyway. Rules."

He raised his arms, letting him wave the wand around his body.

"I think I detect an accent," Hunter said, grinning. "Norwegian, right?"

The blond snorted. *"Pridurok,"* he said to his partner. *Moron.*

"Amerikantsy," the other chuckled, shaking his head.

"So, was I right?" Hunter said, keeping the grin.

"Yeah," the guy with the wand answered. "You very smart man."

A very smart man would not let them know he understood Russian. Maybe they would inadvertently reveal something.

They brought him inside, into the stunning foyer. Hunter had already seen realtors' photos of the interior posted online. But he spun around, expressing amazement—while committing more details to memory. On the balcony above, a middle-aged woman carrying file folders walked toward the north wing. It told him Trammel's offices were probably back there somewhere.

The pair led him toward a corridor beneath the stairs while they continued to mumble to each other in Russian.

"Trammel says this guy's trouble."

"He doesn't look like it. Look at him, grinning like an idiot."

"Da. The old man seems to be getting paranoid lately."

"Maybe wife trouble. She looked upset yesterday."

"Could be. Irina told me Julia barely said a word to him at dinner last night."

"Shhhh!" the blond guard hissed. "She's here."

They entered a huge, ornate drawing room. Julia Haight, in casual blouse and slacks, stood in its center, overseeing a crew of decorators arranging tables for the evening social event. She looked at him quizzically as they neared.

"Ms. Haight," he said, nodding politely.

"And you are?"

He stopped.

"Dylan Hunter, *The Capitol Inquirer.* Here to meet with your husband."

She raised a brow. "Wait. I remember seeing you. Aren't you the one . . ."

"Probably."

"This way." The blond guard snapped his fingers.

He smiled at her and nodded again, then continued after them.

2

They passed into a dazzling solarium. Across the room, in a navy sports jacket and cream-colored slacks, Avery Trammel stood framed against a tall, sunny window, his back turned to them. A staged pose.

"Sir—" the blond guard began.

"Leave us."

They retreated. Hunter listened to their echoing footsteps fade behind him. Trammel didn't turn or speak.

"Gee, what ever happened to good old Southern charm and hospitality?"

At that, Trammel turned.

"You are not amusing, Mr. Hunter."

"I don't write for the entertainment section."

Trammel glared at him. After a few seconds of silence, Hunter crossed his arms and began to tap his foot.

"Did you invite me here to watch you die of old age?"

Trammel glanced toward the drawing room, then back at him.

"It is a beautiful morning. Perhaps for privacy we should converse outside."

He turned and walked toward a set of French doors. Hunter followed him out onto a small balcony, then down a set of stairs into the yard. Hands jammed in the pockets of his trousers, Trammel set out on a flagstone path leading across the vast green lawn. They passed between a small greenhouse on the left and a tennis court on the right, heading toward a pond with a gazebo at its center. Somewhere in a nearby maple, a mockingbird twittered.

Hunter looked around at the grounds and back at the massive home.

"I must say, in spite of your 'green energy' losses, it looks as if the rest of your investments are still keeping you in chips."

"Why are you exerting so much effort to insult me, Mr. Hunter?"

"Trust me, it's no exertion at all."

Trammel stopped and faced him.

"Seriously. What are you hoping to accomplish?"

"Seriously? I'm hoping you might answer the same question."

Trammel took a long, slow breath.

"Mr. Hunter, you are an intelligent and ambitious man. Your newspaper could not possibly be paying you what you merit."

"How true. But what newspaper could possibly afford what I deserve?"

"Joking aside, you could do much better for yourself."

"Could I now."

"I am confident that employment and compensation far more appropriate to your obvious talents could be found and arranged."

"By whom?"

Trammel smiled. "Let us be candid. You have been a growing distraction for me. Distractions cost me time. And time is money. I have extensive connections. If you are willing to abandon your campaign of harassment, I could look into new arrangements for you that would redound to our mutual benefit. A 'win/win' situation, as they say."

"That is your idea of a 'win/win' arrangement?"

"Is it not?"

Hunter laughed. "Is *that* what you think I came here for?"

Trammel's smile vanished.

"Not really. Still, I had hoped you might be open to a generous offer."

"What you want to buy isn't for sale."

"I could make it more than worth your while."

"Nobody is that rich."

Trammel fixed Hunter with a cold stare. He grinned back.

"You know, somebody probably told you that if you stare at people without blinking, you can intimidate them. As you see, that advice is overrated. So why don't we get down to the real reason you asked me here?"

Trammel nodded slowly.

"Yes. Let us do that." He began to walk along the path again. "Mr. Rouse informed me you were questioning my donations to the Currents Foundation."

"I was curious about where those donations are being channeled. As I told him, it seems grants from your personal foundation to Currents have focused on funding groups and campaigns trying to stop fracking—a cause in which you stand to benefit financially."

Trammel moved off the path toward a budding weeping willow overhanging the edge of the pond. Bordered by flat rocks and lush vegetation, the oblong pool looked to be four or five feet deep. At one end a small waterfall flowed over several stone shelves; at the other, grasses poked through the surface here and there among lily pads. On a tiny island in the middle stood a white, octagonal gazebo with a peaked roof, decorated gaily with hanging wicker flower baskets. It clung to the rest of the lawn by an arching wooden bridge.

"As you must know," Trammel finally answered, "there is nothing illegal or deceptive about donating to organizations that share one's own views on such issues."

"No, there isn't. The First Amendment protects that. But it seems tax-deductible grants from you into the Currents Foundation are funneled through their Currents Center into direct political action—which does raise legal issues with the IRS."

"That is simply not true."

"No?"

Trammel stepped to the edge of the pond. Beneath the green water a group of large koi fish, mottled orange-and-white, glided toward him and massed near his feet. He reached into a nearby covered pail and scooped out a small quantity of fish food, which he began to sprinkle amid the now-roiling mass. Hunter knew he was stalling, choosing his next words carefully. He waited him out.

"No. My foundation contributes to the Currents Foundation for the educational purposes specified," Trammel replied, continuing to pay attention to the fish. "I have no knowledge of or, frankly, interest in what they do with money from other donors."

"Well, that seems implausible, since you sit on the board of the Currents Foundation and ought to know where all the money goes. I also discovered that, besides your foundation's general 'educational' grants to Currents, you also set up a 'donor advised fund' with them, into which you pour even greater sums. That financial gimmick lets you channel your cash to specific groups and causes, while remaining anonymous. Why, it may even be funneled into political lobbies and groups like the Caring and Sharing Alliance, to attack Roger Helm."

Trammel threw the remaining fistful of food into the water and spun to him.

"Obviously, you do not know the regulations governing such funds," he snapped. "By law, I may offer only nonbinding recommendations about where my contributions might go. But as the fund's sponsor, the Currents Foundation has complete autonomy to ignore my suggestions."

Hunter sauntered over to him.

"Come on, Trammel. Your private foundation provided the seed money for the Currents Foundation. You're on its board. You arranged for the hiring of Rouse and later recommended Ratzenberger to run the Center. And you are telling me you don't select which groups get your money?"

"That is *exactly* what I am telling you. Nor is there a shred of evidence for your libelous insinuations. And if you choose to publish such rubbish, I shall take legal action."

Hunter smiled. "Rest assured I would never publish anything without supporting evidence. Meanwhile, there's another aspect of this you might clear up for me."

"And that is?"

"Lucas Carver."

Trammel's raptor eyes became slits. "What about him?"

"He and his company, Vox Populi, ran the anti-fracking campaign you were involved in a few months ago, and he enlisted your wife as its national spokesperson. In fact, you serve on Vox Populi's board. Vox Populi handles the media work for the Currents Center and for most of the groups that the Center has set up, including political lobbies." Hunter shook his head. "All these cross-memberships in groups and boards . . . why, it's incestuous."

"It is both legal and rational for individuals of like mind to associate. That too is protected by the First Amendment."

"But Carver is chief media strategist for Carl Spencer's campaign."

"Also completely legal. He is paid by the campaign, not Currents. There is no co-mingling of funds, if that is what you are driving at." He paused to smirk. "So, Mr. Hunter, you have nothing. I, on the other hand, do have something."

"Which is?"

"Which is the knowledge that you are not the man you say you are. There is no such person as 'Dylan Lee Hunter.'"

Hunter had long expected this day—even wondered why it had taken this long for someone to notice.

"The Social Security Administration, the Department of Motor Vehicles, and a number of police agencies will tell you you're wrong. Want to see all my IDs?"

Trammel waved dismissively. "However you obtained those documents, there is no record of 'Dylan Lee Hunter' going back more than about four years."

"Did it ever occur to you that maybe I use a pen name? Or that perhaps I changed my name?"

"It did. But legal name changes are recorded in state archives. I had people check, and there is no record of that occurring anywhere in the United States. They even checked Canada, to no avail. Yet somehow you possess government-issued ID cards as 'Dylan Hunter.' How do you explain that?"

"To you? I don't."

"To anyone, then."

"Those with a legitimate need to know either have or will be informed."

"Oh, quite soon *everyone* will know. You see, I suspect you are hiding something behind that pen name of yours. For I can imagine only a few explanations for those ID cards. And if you insist on pursuing your invasion of my privacy, then I shall have no recourse but to inform the media of my suspicions. You have made many enemies in the press, and I think they would be eager to dig into the mystery that is 'Dylan Hunter.'"

Hunter shrugged.

"They are welcome to try. But speaking of hiding something, Trammel, I've found mysterious omissions in your personal history, too. Try as I might, I can find no birth certificate for 'Avery Trammel.' It appears that your life under that name began abruptly during your teen years. Then, after a college career of militant Marxist activism, you had a sudden, almost overnight change of interest toward capitalism, followed by an unlikely, meteoric rise to vast wealth. Almost magical, really. So, I think I should continue to poke into that. And also dig a little deeper into Currents, and the nasty things the groups it spawned are doing to manipulate this election."

Fury crossed Trammel's face. He pointed a thin finger, jabbing the air to make his points.

"Perhaps you are willing to sacrifice your own career and reputation. But just remember: Exposure of the truth about you might hurt those close to you. Friends, family . . . perhaps that pretty lady I saw you with."

Hunter stepped in, getting right in his face.

"Trammel," he said quietly, "that was the one thing you shouldn't have said."

He saw a flicker of fear and surprise in the billionaire's eyes.

Then he turned and walked back toward the house.

3

Entering the French doors of the solarium, Hunter was surprised to see Julia Haight standing in the curve of the bow windows.

"Hello, again," he offered, closing the doors behind him.

"I remember," she said, walking toward him. "I saw you after the candidates' debate. And before that, a couple of months ago, outside the EPA."

"That's right. I'm afraid I left a bad impression on both occasions."

"You did, Mr. Hunter."

"I'd like to remedy that, so I hope you don't carry grudges."

A faint smile. "We'll see."

"Do you prefer 'Ms. Haight' or 'Mrs. Trammel'?"

The tiniest tug of bitterness at her mouth, masked quickly with a forced smile.

"Julia will be fine."

He answered her smile. "It's Dylan, then."

Her glance darted toward the windows. "I hope you don't mind my spying, Dylan, but you were the last person I expected to see here. So I was curious. You two looked as if you were arguing."

Hunter nodded.

"What about?"

Outside, Trammel was on his phone, gesturing. Already telling someone about their encounter. He weighed how much he should say to her.

He turned back to study the famous face, up close. Though just past fifty, Julia Haight had aged well and remained stunningly beautiful. Large, dark brown eyes; full lips; high cheekbones; auburn hair aflame in the slanting rays of morning sun; toned legs revealed by snug slacks.

Yet also in her face, the tightness of stress; in her eyes, flickers of worry—and redness, as if she had been crying.

He recalled what the guards had said. Seeing no one within earshot, he decided to gamble.

"I came here to chat with your husband about his political contributions and associations. His donations and business investments appear to be entangled with individuals and groups whose activities—well, let's just call them questionable."

"I read what you wrote about CarboNot, and the things going on with fracking in Pennsylvania. You made it all sound criminal."

"I'm afraid it was. And your husband was a substantial CarboNot investor. I have strong reasons to believe he and others were involved in a 'green energy' investment scheme to make millions by getting the government to shut down the fracking industry."

"Well, fracking *is* dangerous. It's—"

He raised a hand. "Look, I don't want to argue the merits of the technology. I'm only talking about powerful people, inside and outside of government—including your husband—conspiring to manipulate the federal regulatory process in order to make a killing in the stock market."

She wet her lips. "And you have proof of that?"

He thought of the secret recordings from his wiretaps and bugs, and the other illegally obtained evidence he could never use or write about.

"Let's just say I'm very sure of it."

She lowered her eyes. "Will he face arrest?"

"For that? I doubt it. The scheme failed, and the participants lost a lot of money. Senator Conn was the central player, and when he died, I think a lot of their secrets died with him. Besides, that's not what concerns me now."

"Then what?"

He saw what looked like sincere bewilderment.

"A lot of nasty things have been happening lately that I can't yet explain or tie together. To be honest, I only have pieces of it. But somehow, a network of groups your husband is involved with seems to be at the heart of it all. Do you know anything about his association with the Currents Foundation?"

"Well, I know he gives them money and he's on their board." She looked off into space, chewing her lower lip. "I know they fundraise for progressive groups. And I believe Lucas Carver is heavily involved with them."

"How well do you know him?"

"Not well at all. He's Avery's friend, really. Probably his closest friend. The two of them go way back." She glanced again out the window. "Oh—he's coming."

Hunter saw him striding down the path toward the house.

"I should go now. I appreciate your talking with me . . . and I'd be grateful if you didn't mention our conversation to him."

She met his gaze for a moment. Then nodded.

"I won't."

He read her expression and believed her. What was in that expression also prompted him to take another chance. He pulled out a business card.

"Julia . . . I don't mean to be presumptuous or intrusive. But I sense you're troubled about something. Look, we're complete strangers, so you have no reason to trust me. But if you ever feel the need to talk about—well, whatever's going on here, feel free to give me a call."

He extended the card and a smile.

"After all, I'm a reporter," he added. "I protect the privacy of people who tell me things."

She searched his face. Her eyes told him she felt alone and needed someone she could trust.

"Thank you," she said softly, taking the card.

"I'll find my way out." He nodded again and turned away.

Hunter felt her eyes following him as he left.

THIRTY

Trammel pushed aside the plate bearing the remnants of his omelet. His eyes moved around the table, pausing briefly on each of his three breakfast companions.

It had been six days since he, Lucas, Sid Cunningham, and Carl Spencer had met at Vox Populi. He selected the Lafayette Room at the Hay-Adams for this, their Monday morning follow-up meeting, not only for its elegant ambiance, but as an unspoken reminder to the candidate of their previous encounter here. Spencer's sullen expression told him he got the message.

"Why so gloomy, Carl?" he needled, just to emphasize his control over him. "I hear from Lucas that all the news today is positive."

"It certainly is." Carver's mood was buoyant. He sipped from the second screwdriver the waitress had brought him, then lowered the frosty glass. "Gallup's weekend survey has us closing to within seven points. Which is a pretty damned amazing turnaround in just one week."

"Excellent. Lucas, you appear to have delivered on your promise to enlist the media against Helm."

Carver tried and failed to suppress a smile. Still, his smiles never reached his eyes.

"They are coming through for us, for sure." He leaned in, lowering his voice. "And a real biggie is on the way. This weekend I reminded Schindler at the *New York Times* about some of the past employee complaints at Helm's company. Wage discrimination against women, hiring discrimination against minorities—that sort of thing. First he said they wouldn't bother pursuing that old stuff anymore, not without some fresh angle. So then I told him the Civil Rights Division at Justice was about to announce an official investigation of those complaints, and that my contact agreed to give the *Times* the scoop. *That* got his attention."

Cunningham frowned. "Why is this the first *I'm* hearing about it?"

Carver spread his hands. "It's just timing, Sid. I've been working on it for weeks, through the White House press secretary. He took my suggestion about investigating Helm's business practices to the chief of staff, to run by the president. Glover liked it and told the A.G. on Friday to pursue an official investigation. I told Schindler about that on Saturday, and he called me back late last night to say the *Times* will run a story tomorrow." He chuckled. "That will really put Helm on the defensive."

"Thanks to you, Lucas," Trammel said, "he is already on the defensive."

Carver feigned a modest shrug. "But it was still your idea to tell Carl to go after Muslim terrorism at the debate. I'm keeping that issue alive in the press, too—reminding everyone how prescient Carl was, and how Helm got caught flat-footed."

"Yet it was *your* idea to have Carl take a week off the campaign trail to attend victim funerals. The public response has been overwhelmingly positive." Trammel turned to Spencer. "I watched the televised coverage, Carl. Your remarks at yesterday's memorial service for that lady and her baby were particularly well-crafted. You hit all the right notes; in my opinion, it was pitch perfect."

Spencer, who had been staring into his coffee cup, raised angry eyes.

"My God, Avery. That is *cold*. That 'lady' had a *name*: Patricia Wright. And her baby girl was named *Allison*. And my remarks weren't 'crafted,' damn it—they were off the cuff, straight from the heart! Facing her husband and their little boy yesterday was one of the hardest things I've ever had to do."

Trammel cursed himself for stupidity. Spencer already hated him, so this choice of venue needlessly poured more salt into his ego wounds.

He had humiliated the man, and if he kept reminding and threatening him, it might provoke a disastrous rebellion.

"Carl, I sincerely apologize for my grossly insensitive choice of words. They by no means reflect my true feelings. I cannot imagine how difficult that tragic occasion was for you."

"So were all the others I attended!"

"Come on, you two," Carver jumped in. "This is a good morning. Let's not spoil it with misunderstandings. Avery, I went ahead as you asked and contacted the 'RT' network producers. They're eager to do a televised segment with Carl tomorrow afternoon. But what exactly do you think an interview there can accomplish?"

Trammel picked a tiny piece of lint off the charcoal cuff of his suit jacket.

"Since the debate, you have all said we must reassure progressives that Carl has not embraced a right-wing foreign policy. Appearing now on Russia's international television network gives him an ideal platform to make that case. As you know, Moscow has its own worries about the spread of Islamist violence. Carl's message tomorrow on RT should be that he wishes to cooperate with Putin to fight Islamic terrorism, *but* with the hope that it will lead to wider peaceful cooperation between our two countries on a range of issues—such as initiatives to reduce our respective nuclear arsenals."

"I love it!" Cunningham exclaimed, slapping the table.

"I'll second that," Carver said. "On the one hand, it will remind independents and even Republicans that Carl warned about Muslim terrorism at the debate, while on the other hand, it will let liberals know he's still committed to a peace-oriented foreign policy vision." He turned to Spencer. "How about you, Carl. Does that sound like the right angle?"

Spencer was looking at Trammel and didn't reply for a few seconds. At last he said, "It makes sense."

"Well, then, don't look so sour about it," Cunningham said, laughing. "It will definitely continue your momentum in the polls." His eyes drifted around the noisy restaurant. Then he pointed toward the entrance. "By the way, seeing your private security guys over there reminds me: It's way past time you accept Secret Service protection."

"I just don't like the idea of a team of people following me wherever I go."

"I understand, Carl, but you know it comes with the job. You want to be president, you give up a lot of your privacy."

Spencer shot another look at Trammel. "I suppose so."

"Good," Cunningham said, picking up a half-eaten wedge of toast. "I'll contact them later today."

"I meant to ask," Carver said, "how's Stu Kaplan working out for you?"

Cunningham chewed and swallowed, then gestured toward Trammel with the remaining piece of crust. "Avery, your suggestion that we hire Conn's chief of staff was brilliant. It's like an official passing of the torch, from Ash to Carl. That's how everyone sees it."

Trammel's memory went back to that day in the CarboNot conference room, when he first met the man whose eyes reminded him of a barracuda's. "Lucas and I met Mr. Kaplan some months ago," he said. "We were both favorably impressed. I am pleased he is proving himself to be an asset."

"Oh, God, yes! I have Stu working the Hill, because he knows everybody. He's getting Conn's last diehard supporters to come around to us. From what he tells me, we shouldn't see any of them defect to another candidate. So it should be clear sailing for us through the convention."

Trammel saw an opening.

"Speaking of Mr. Kaplan reminds me of another matter. It goes back to the 'fracking' controversy and the *Inquirer* articles by that right-wing reporter, Dylan Hunter. He is the one who spun all that conspiracy nonsense about Ash Conn."

Spencer nodded. "That guy smeared the reputation of a good man. He's lucky Ash died before he could file a lawsuit for defamation."

"Well, I am sorry to report that Hunter is at it again. And this time, it appears that *we*"—he nodded at each of them—"are his new targets."

"What?"

"I am afraid it is true, Carl. In fact, he has interviewed some of my associates, and he even visited me late last week. He is tracking the flow of contributions into our campaign and drawing outrageous inferences."

"Such as?" Carver asked.

"Such as the fact that you work for this campaign, Lucas, and simultaneously for various political advocacy groups that attack Helm—groups funded through the Currents Foundation, to which I contribute. Hunter finds something sinister in all this. It is the usual conspiracy-theory tangle of ridiculous insinuations and paranoid speculations. However, their validity is not the point. The point is, he has established for himself a high-profile media platform, and a lot of people believe his rubbish. If he is not dealt with, pro-actively and soon, I fear that he may force us on the defensive and kill the momentum we have been building."

"What can we do about it?" Cunningham demanded.

"Your mention of Mr. Kaplan reminded me that he and my own staff investigated Hunter's background during the fracking controversy, and discovered an intriguing fact: All records about him go back no more than three or four years. They learned that there is no such person as Dylan Hunter. And yet he possesses authentic ID cards under that name."

Carver looked surprised. "How is that even possible?"

Trammel interlaced his manicured fingers and rested his hands on the table.

"One possibility, accepted by my sources, is that this man is an employee of some government spy agency, or perhaps a hired contractor working undercover. We think he is trying to disrupt political candidates and causes that his 'handlers,' whoever they may be, consider to be a threat."

"That sounds crazy!"

"Not if you trace his activities, Carl. Last year his articles successfully targeted the MacLean Foundation and a network of organizations and individuals striving to bring progressive reforms to the criminal justice system. Next, he attacked the alternative energy movement and its champion, Senator Conn. His articles successfully stymied efforts to halt fracking, created chaos within the environmental movement, and smeared a Democratic presidential candidate. Now, he is coming after progressive foundations and nonprofits generally, and a second Democratic candidate specifically. But before you ask—no, I do not believe the Republicans are behind this. I think it may be a faction deep within the intelligence community."

"If what you say is true," Carver said, "then why can't we just expose him?"

Trammel pointed at him and smiled.

"Exactly, Lucas. This 'Dylan Hunter' or whoever he is, and the forces behind him, have been succeeding only because they operate in secrecy. But even though my people have not been able to find out who he really is, we possess some crucial advantages over him. He already has made many enemies among fellow reporters. They would be eager to investigate this man's real identity. The best case for us is that they will uncover something unsavory and scandalous. At very least, they will force him onto the defensive or into hiding. Either way, exposing his phony identity will stop his attacks on this campaign and our network of supporters."

"So where, when, and how do we begin?" Cunningham asked.

"You and Carl should proceed with the existing campaign plan," Trammel said. "Meanwhile, I shall share what I have learned and suspect with Lucas. After that—"

"—leave things to me," Carver finished, with the smile that never reached his eyes.

2

Emmalee put the plates and silverware from her breakfast into the dishwasher. Though it wasn't full enough to run yet, she turned it on anyway.

Some noise to break the endless silence in the empty apartment.

Restless, she moved to the living room. She had already checked the morning TV listings, and nothing appealed, so the big wall screen hovered dark and empty. Scanning the bare walls, she reminded herself she needed to make another shopping trip for some prints. Maybe a colorful throw rug for the center of the floor, too. And a few cheery pillows for the bland beige sofa, where bulging plastic bags from her Saturday excursion to Georgetown shops still waited for her attention. Avery had given her a healthy checking account and paid off her credit cards, so she could get whatever she liked.

She eyed the sound system, but turned away. It had been playing non-stop for the past week, and it only deepened her depression. Music excited her, made her want to move, made her want to be with people. The sound of it here, now, would just remind her that she was alone.

Still in her bathrobe, she folded herself into a big upholstered chair, drew up her legs, wrapped her arms around her knees. Being alone was a feeling she had never gotten used to. She'd never had to. From childhood, she was always complimented for how pretty she was, and her looks had won her constant attention, many friends, and later, many boyfriends.

Seizing the attention of boys, then men, was easy. Skirts and dresses that displayed her showgirl legs and ass never failed to catch their interest. Then, just widening her eyes a bit would hold them like a magnet. They always told her how cute she was when she wrinkled her nose, so she did that a lot, too.

God, men were so easy.

Or had been. Now, not so easy. Easy to bed, sure, but not easy to keep. She still had her looks, and she could still get laid anytime she wanted, just by sliding onto a hotel bar stool. But she was no longer a hot young dancer, and the city was filled with hot young women on the make. The men who counted wanted their arm candy to be young—girls in their twenties. And she'd just had her thirty-ninth birthday. Women like her were just a one-night stand.

She hugged her knees tightly. Losing Ash, she had been thrown back into the market—and things were so different now. For the first time in decades, she was alone. And scared.

When Avery swooped in so unexpectedly, it seemed like a miracle. He was impossibly rich and powerful. Despite his age, he was in decent shape and horny as a goat. The only problem was, he was married to a famous movie star. And she didn't want to be his Other Woman. There was no future in that. Maybe not even much of a present, either. It had been a week since Avery had been with her—last Tuesday, the day after all that horrible terrorism.

That Monday morning she had heard an echoing *boom* and went out onto the balcony, where she saw drifting smoke and heard gunshots and sirens all over town. She'd spent the rest of the day watching the nightmare unfold on TV. The Metro was shut down and the streets blocked off, so she couldn't go anywhere, and she was frightened because Avery wouldn't answer his phone or return her calls. Not until Tuesday morning, when he phoned to explain he had been tied up in meetings and the chaos, but wanted to see her that night.

He arrived in a great mood, bringing her flowers and two bottles of Dom Perignon—the special Charles & Diana edition, which she later learned was incredibly expensive. He was cocky and boastful; he said he'd "finally closed the investment deal of a lifetime, which was about to pay off handsomely," and told her he wanted to celebrate. So they did.

But even though he promised to see her again this past weekend, she hadn't heard a peep from him since. He hadn't even bothered to answer her calls or text messages.

Shopping binges hadn't lessened her loneliness or anxiety; they only seemed to make them grow. And the gnawing fear now made her mind race. Had she done or said something wrong? Maybe his wife had found out about them. Or maybe he had some kind of problem with Carl Spencer, after *that* little episode. That bothered her, too. She'd given the senator a great time—and her phone number. So why hadn't *he* called, either?

Almost a week, now. She hadn't been alone this long in years.

What the hell was going on?

She unfolded herself from the chair and padded over the cold wooden floor to where she'd left her cell phone on the dining room table. There were no replies to her messages.

She tapped in his number. Finally, he answered.

"I am with some people and cannot speak to you right now." His tone, cold and remote.

"But you haven't answered any of my texts or—"

"I shall call you when I can."

And then he was gone.

She stared at the blank screen. Then set the phone down on the table. Then sat down there herself, growing even more fearful.

After a while, the fear began to turn to anger.

3

Cronin finished the call with a lieutenant from the Pennsylvania State Police barracks in Clarion, then rolled his chair back from his desk. He tapped the notepad in his lap with his pen, thinking about what he had learned.

The grotesque bindings that were used to nail Boggs's forearms to the tree kept just scraps of his arms and hands intact, which explained how the neighbor's dog had found his hand. Besides that, there wasn't much left of the corpse. Bear and fox tracks were all over the place, so the exact cause and time of death were unknown.

However, just beyond the clearing where the body was discovered, they found ATV tracks—at least a few that hadn't been obliterated by the spring rains. The staties figured out the tire model from the tracks, then checked out which models of ATVs used those. The lieutenant told him they had just compiled a list of customers in the area who during the past five years had bought ATVs bearing that brand of tire.

On a hunch, Cronin asked, and the lieutenant promised, to fax him the list of customer names.

He checked the time. Two ten. He rubbed his eyes, then got up from his desk and headed to the break room to grab a cup of coffee.

When he returned ten minutes later, somebody had dumped the fax on his desk.

He sat, took a sip, then removed the paperclip holding on the cover sheet.

The list of names wasn't long, maybe forty or so. He scanned it idly, with no expectation that any name would jump out and mean anything to him.

Then his eyes paused on a surname that tickled his memory.

Where had he seen the name "Adair"?

He had a vague recollection that it was related to something in one of Hunter's articles.

He took another big gulp, then opened a desk drawer and pulled out the fat file folder containing the reporter's various newspaper clippings. He started reading.

Forty minutes later, he felt the tell-tale tingle that a cop always gets when he hits paydirt.

He thought about how he should proceed with this. That took another half hour.

Just after three-thirty, he wandered over to Erskine's cubicle.

"Paul, I just got a message from home. Looks like there's a situation I need to attend to."

Erskine spun around in his chair, a look of concern on his broad face. "Somebody sick?"

"No, nothing like that. And it's not the marriage or anything. It's . . . just complicated. Anyway, I have some vacation days due, so I can afford to take a little time off. Can you cover for me for a few days while I'm out? My current case files are on top of the desk."

Erskine pulled his bulk out of the chair and slapped him on the shoulder.

"Sure, buddy. I'll have them route your calls to me. Take whatever time you need. Hope it's nothing serious. Call if you want to talk."

"Thanks, Paul. I owe you one."

As he walked away, Cronin felt like hell. Again.

He wondered why he felt he had to keep this stuff private—why he didn't want to share with his partner what he was learning. Paul was such a great guy. He didn't deserve this disloyalty.

He stopped back at his desk to retrieve Hunter's file, then headed for the exit.

Once he got home, he'd have to gas up the car, then check and see what kind of motel reservation he could get around the Allegheny Forest.

THIRTY-ONE

It was the end of a long day, and Avery Trammel sat enjoying a glass of brandy in the study of his Watergate apartment. He felt fatigued but content.

One week after the attacks, it appeared the official investigations were concluding that the four terrorists were a homegrown Islamist cell radicalized via the internet. The captured terrorist had clammed up under the counsel of his lawyer. No one had yet made any link between them and Shishani. Even if they did, the Chechen had no direct connections to the SVR or Moscow. The few media reports so far indicated the police suspected him of being a drug courier, killed in some transactional dispute. With luck, his murder would not rise to FBI scrutiny; they were too preoccupied looking into the terrorism.

As for the campaign, it was finally getting traction. *Maestro* was superb at orchestrating media responses, and the press were giving Spencer lavish praise and attention. They had been hostile to Helm from the beginning, but now, under Lucas's subtle guidance, their criticisms had risen in a crescendo.

The main weakness was the candidate himself. Lucas and he wished that Spencer had more credibility as a committed progressive. If he could arouse the base, they could easily close the gap with Helm in the polls. But they had to work with the candidate they had, and so far, things were getting back on track.

As he felt the brandy blaze its course down his throat, Avery Trammel finally dared to think his lifelong mission just might succeed.

Over the decades, as he meticulously planned and brilliantly executed each step of the plan, he often wished he had someone in whom he could confide fully. Sokolov knew of his activities and appreciated him, but strictly as a fellow professional. Lucas was a close friend, but there was too much he could never be told. That was even more true of Julia.

So he felt lonely. Never more so than now, after his recent string of spectacular successes. He had salvaged the election from the catastrophe of Ash Conn's murder, and then—through unthinkable daring and risk-taking—had rescued the campaign of his lackluster successor. If only there were someone who could appreciate him for it all, emotionally and with full understanding.

And who could respect his motive . . .

That thought prompted him, as it so often did, to press the hidden latch under his desktop. The side panel popped ajar. He rose, opened it, and then the interior safe. Ignoring the other contents, he slid out a large, heavy metal box from the bottom shelf and hauled it atop his desk.

Inside were the archives of his life: a photo album; scrapbooks containing faded newspaper clippings, documents, official records; bundles of correspondence; personal mementos; several books; and a leather case.

He opened the photo album first. The very first photo, preserved beneath a sheet of clear plastic, was a posed black-and-white studio portrait of him as a small boy, standing before his seated parents.

These, their images, had been his only constant companions throughout the years, the indelible reminders of the vow he had taken as a child. *They* would have understood—and taken enormous pride in the course of his life.

He paused on the photo for a long time, until the familiar sting of tears made it impossible to see the faces clearly. Wiping his eyes, he closed the album and moved to the leather case. He opened it carefully, knowing its age rendered it fragile.

Inside, a medallion hung on a folded red ribbon edged with twin gold stripes. It was a complex thing: roughly round, with a gold border broken on the right by a curling red banner; on the left by a red star; and on the bottom by a crossed hammer and sickle. Inlaid at its center was a circular platinum disc featuring the face of Vladimir Lenin.

The Order of Lenin—the highest civilian honor bestowed by the former Soviet Union.

The medallion rested on a red document booklet, printed in Cyrillic script. He did not open the delicate item, nor did he have to. He had read it many times before. It announced that the honor—for meritorious services to the Soviet state and society—had been granted posthumously to his father, John Avery Tremills.

He was relieved his father did not live to see what happened to the cause for which he had sacrificed his liberty, his health, and ultimately his life. The award was a bittersweet reminder of the ideals that had once animated millions, across several generations. His father had remained true to those ideals until his premature end in ignominious captivity.

Trammel knew better. Communism was indeed "the God that failed," as a disenchanted follower once put it. It no longer merited undying loyalty.

Yet, his father's life did. His commitment and character deserved to be honored, even if his cause did not. And not with medals from a dead and corrupt empire; but with action against the society that had destroyed the man's precious life, as well as that of his loyal mother.

He was slipping the medallion back into its leather case when his phone chirped. He took it out, looked at the screen, and sighed. He was tempted to ignore her once again, but he knew that she would continue, and there was no point in putting her off any longer.

"Yes, Emmalee. I was intending—"

"No you *weren't*, you bastard!" she shouted. "You were gonna juss keep ignoring me, an' you know it!"

Drunk. The last thing he needed right now . . .

"Emmalee," he said carefully, "that is not so. I just got home a few moments ago. I was about to—"

"*No.* What you're gonna do is get your ass *down* here, *right now*. Because if you don't, like, in the next three minutes, I'm gonna swallow this bottle of pills"—he heard a rattling noise—"an' leave a note all about you. An' if you think I'm kidding, juss try me!"

He shot to his feet.

"Emmalee—please, take it easy. All right, I understand you are upset with me. We do need to talk. I can—"

"Right . . . now!" she shouted.

Then broke the connection.

A jolt of panic hit him. *She sounds serious . . .*

He rushed to the door, grabbing his sports jacket from its wooden hanger on the wall hook. He heard the hanger fall and bounce on the marble as he flung the door open and trotted down the hallway.

He spotted Julia in the living room reading something as he passed. She looked up.

"Good God! What's wrong? You look—"

"Sorry. I shall be out for a while and will explain later."

He threw open the front door and headed toward the elevator—then, knowing it would be faster, the stairwell.

2

Julia stared at the closing entryway door, dumbfounded by what she had just witnessed.

Avery, always in icy control of his emotions—looking completely unglued.

She had never seen him ruffled, let alone in a panic, and had no idea what had happened to bring him to this. Yes, he had been sullen after his CarboNot stock crashed, and she knew he was angry over the destruction of his Gulfstream. But on the surface he was always unflustered, never raising his voice or projecting worry. Even after last week's terrorist attacks, while she and everyone else were horrified and distraught, he remained a calm and reassuring presence.

Which made this all the more shocking. Like his recent coldness toward her, and his affair with the unknown woman, this behavior was unprecedented. Her husband was becoming erratic—and it frightened her.

A week ago, her doctor had prescribed diazepam for her anxiety and insomnia. She knew she needed one now. Tossing aside the latest issue of *Variety,* she left the parlor, heading for her bathroom medicine cabinet.

Halfway there, she stopped.

The door to his study stood ajar, blocked open by a wooden coat hanger lying on the floor.

He had never permitted her to enter this sanctuary, not since they had first moved in, when he asked her to help choose the furnishings and decor. And he *never* left it unlocked, let alone open. Yet he had left here in such a rush that he didn't make sure the door closed and automatically locked behind him.

Maybe the reason for his panic could be found inside.

And—*damn it!*—as his wife, she had a *right* to know what it was.

He wouldn't be back anytime soon, not the way he looked. So, heart thumping, she pressed her fingers on the door and pushed it open.

The interior was much as she remembered from years ago, except now the beautiful cherry bookcases were loaded with hardcovers and leather-bound sets that looked old and collectible. In the center of the room, the crystal chandelier blazed above the huge cherry desk that he'd had custom-designed years ago.

Then she noticed that the entire side panel of the desk was open, like a door—and that an *open safe* was hidden inside.

Leaving the door to the room propped half-open by the hanger, she went to the safe, bent, and peeked inside.

Then felt something cold crawl across her skin.

A *gun.*

Next to it, *ammunition.*

On the shelf below, two big stacks of money.

On the lower shelves, what looked like some kind of radio, and a walkie-talkie or something, and a bunch of phones and batteries, and other gadgets.

She spotted a stack of little booklets on the shelf next to the money. Curious, she reached inside to retrieve them.

They were passports, four of them. Puzzled, she opened the top one. Inside was a driver's license, too. The matching photo on both documents was of Avery . . . but with *dark hair and a mustache*. And the name listed on them was *Harold D. Felton.*

She stared, uncomprehending. Closing it, she slid it to the bottom of the stack, then opened the next one.

Again, Avery's face stared back at her from the passport photo and a second license . . . but this time sporting longish, light-brown hair and a goatee. The name on these was *Richard T. Dieter.*

She shuddered. She had to struggle to keep a grip on the passports as she shuffled them again to the final two.

In the third, Avery was transformed into a balding man with wire-rimmed glasses, named *Melvin A. Rothstein.* In the last, he was a red-haired, broad-nosed fellow named *Sean Ryan Mallory.*

"*Oh God,*" she heard a strange voice saying, again and again, before she realized it was her own.

She sank slowly to the floor. Her brain could not make sense of this—except to realize dully that her husband of eighteen years had a secret life she knew nothing about . . . and that whatever he was, and whatever he was doing—*it was wrong.*

After a moment, she got to her feet. She noticed a large, open metal box on his desk, and moved in for a closer look.

On the desktop beside it lay a medallion. Bending over it, she saw the face of Lenin, and a hammer and sickle.

And finally knew what this had to mean.

Who the hell are you, Avery Trammel? If that's your real name . . .

A photo album also lay on the desk. She opened it to the first page: an old black-and-white photograph of a man, a woman, and a little boy. The man's face, so much like Avery's . . .

She realized who they had to be.

Shaky, she eased herself down into his desk chair, still clinging to the passports.

Her brain was numb. Everything she thought she knew about the past two decades of her life had been a lie, blasted to pieces in just five minutes.

She tried to pull together the torn scraps of her thoughts. She knew she had to do something, but had no idea what. Should she report him to the authorities?

Well . . . for *what*, exactly? And *which* authorities?

And besides, who would ever believe her?

The items on the desk, in her hand . . . it was evidence of something terrible going on. But she could hardly steal any of it without him noticing. He was incredibly smart, and ruthless.

She remembered the gun—and her mouth went dry.

The evidence could not go with her. Everything in here had to stay exactly as—

Then she thought of the obvious solution.

She left the passports on the desk and hurried to the door. Making sure to keep it propped open, she ran to the bedroom for her purse. Fetching her phone, she rushed back into his study.

She spread open the passports on his desk, laying the corresponding driver's licenses alongside. Then she stood above them with her phone and started taking photos, including close-ups of each item.

Next, she moved around to the safe, adjusted the camera for flash, and started tapping away. First, from a distance, to show the open panel. Then successively closer, to reveal the contents.

Then, close-ups. The guns and ammunition. The twin stacks of cash. The strange-looking radio and the other gadgets. She pulled some of them out, placed them on the floor, and got good close-ups before replacing everything as it had been.

Finally, she went back to the desk to photograph the medallion and the accompanying booklet in that strange Russian writing. She was busy taking shots of the photo album when she spied the scrapbook still lying within the metal box.

She lifted it out and carefully opened it. Began turning pages.

The shock she had experienced so far could not match what she now felt.

As she took photo after photo of its contents, it was hard to keep her hands from shaking, harder still to focus through the welling tears. There was so much, *too* much. She kept it up as long as she dared, then replaced the scrapbook in the box.

She spent her last moments in the room arranging everything exactly as she first saw it. Then, as she went out, she realized he probably hadn't noticed that the hanger kept the door from closing, so she kicked it aside and let it click shut and locked.

Outside, she felt nauseous. She had to lean against the wall to keep her balance.

Now, she had to think about what to do next.

The ugly image of that gun, and what it implied, loomed in her mind.

Gripping her phone tightly in both hands, like a drowning person clutching a life preserver, she stumbled down the hallway and into her own office.

She made sure to lock the door behind her.

THIRTY-TWO

Trammel rang her bell. And waited, growing more anxious by the second. Then rapped on her door. He did not dare call out, for fear of attracting the attention of neighbors.

Finally, he heard the lock being unlatched. The door opened.

She stood there in a short, pale-blue satin bathrobe, barely tied shut. It would have been any man's sex fantasy—save for her bleary red eyes and the slackness in her lips.

"Soooo. He actually came."

"Of course. Let me in, please."

"Sure . . . come on in, make yourself at home. After all, it *is* yours, you're payin' for it. Like you're payin' for me, right?"

He nudged his way past her and closed the door.

"Come, let us sit down, Emmalee. Here, let me help you to a chair."

"Oh, how gallant!" she said, smirking, but grabbing his offered arm.

He steered her on an unsteady path toward a stuffed chair, but she shook off his hand and flopped on the sofa. Her bathrobe rode up and came almost completely undone. A near-empty Chardonnay bottle stood on the coffee table next to her phone, an almost-empty wine glass, and a box of tissues. Crumpled tissues were scattered across the table and on the carpet near the sofa.

"Emmalee . . . dear. I am worried about you," he said, hanging his jacket on the back of the chair opposite and sitting. "Tell me what is wrong."

Her mouth twisted into a sneer. "'Emmalee dear.' Oh, he's so *worried* about you, Emmalee. How nice. Well, mister big shot, you sure have a funny way of showin' it."

"Whatever do you mean? Have I not—"

"You think you can just waltz into my life an' buy my ass, like I'm some kinda cheap whore. You set me up here an' then you pimp me out . . . No, wait, don't you deny it, it took me a while to figure it out, but that's what this is, isn't it? Except I don't get paid by the hour, I get paid by the month, I getta monthly allowance in my checking account, an' this fancy pad, where I turn tricks for you, so that—"

"My God, Emmalee! Is that what you think? Please, stop and listen. Carl Spencer—darling, that was for *us*. I thought you would enjoy it—you told me you would, and afterward you said you did. It excited me, too, secretly watching you—and I filmed it so we could watch it later, together."

She eyed him suspiciously. "He didn't pay you, or do you some kinda favors in return?"

"Absolutely not! He had no idea you and I planned what happened . . . or that he was being watched and filmed. I only told him you needed a job, and he agreed to meet you to discuss it. *You* did all the rest." He forced a smile. "Look at you. No wonder he found you irresistible."

Her eyes tracked down her exposed flesh. "Really?"

"Of course! How could you think otherwise?"

"Because you an' he have been totally ignoring me, ever since. You don't answer my calls, you stood me up this weekend. An' he won't take my calls, either, even though he promised me a job."

"You . . . called him?"

"A *bunch* of times. I left messages, too, on the number he gave me. But after he got his jollies, now he doesn't have the time of day for me."

Trammel had to clench his teeth.

"Emmalee—you must be reasonable. Think about it. Carl Spencer is a presidential candidate. His schedule is completely booked, and everyone is watching his every move. His enemies would just love to find out about you. Did you honestly expect anything more than what happened that one night?"

"I expect him to at least keep his goddamn promise and give me a goddamn *job*. Like I expect *you* to keep your goddamn promise when you make a date for the weekend."

"I am so sorry about that. But you know I am advising his campaign. And after the terrorist attacks, you cannot imagine how busy we have been."

"But you coulda *called*, at least, insteada keepin' me waiting here."

He clenched his fists. "You are entirely right, my dear. It was inexcusable of me."

"Yeah. An' when am I gonna meet Julia? You said we'd do things together, and you haven't even introduced us yet."

This was getting way out of hand.

"You are right about that, too. Julia and I have been so busy that we barely see each other these days. But I shall speak to her as soon as possible to arrange dinner together."

She seemed mollified at that. Then her lips began to work.

"I thought . . ."

"What did you think?"

Tears began to puddle. "I thought you were gonna abandon me."

"Emmalee! How could you—"

"After Ash, I couldn't take that. I'd be all alone again. Back out on the street, without no money and no job, and—"

She began to wail.

He moved to the sofa, put his arm around her shoulders.

"You should have known better than that. I told you I would take care of you, did I not?"

She looked up at him, the tears laying fresh tracks of mascara down her cheeks.

"You're so strong, Avery. An' look at me. I'm a mess. Since Ash died, I'm nothing."

"Now, you truly are being silly. You are intelligent, and talented, and beautiful." He kissed her forehead.

"You think I'm still beautiful? I was, once. I could get any damn man I wanted."

"You are gorgeous. Any man would be lucky to have you. Remember how Carl wanted you?"

She giggled. "Yeah. He did."

"Here, let me get you a tissue."

She wiped her eyes and nose. Looked up at him again.

"You still want me, too, right?"

He squeezed her shoulders. "Of course I do."

"Prove it," she said, opening the bathrobe.

For Avery Trammel, the lies, and those implied by his actions, came easily.

2

Julia spent the next hour downloading the photos from her phone to her desktop computer, into an innocuously labeled file folder, and then uploading a copy of the folder into a cloud storage service. She made a third copy on a thumb drive, and hid it in a purse in the back of her closet.

During the entire time, she couldn't stop thinking about what she had seen in his study.

Especially the gun.

She no longer knew him. A man who could deceive her so enormously and for so long had to be a psychopath, or something. He could be capable of *anything*.

At least now, if anything ever happened to her, somebody eventually would find the photos.

But that was little comfort. For the time being—until she could figure out exactly how to use them—she had to make sure nothing *did* happen to her.

She rose from her desk and began to pace the room.

Avery was a driven man. All right—*ruthless*. It was time she admitted to herself what she had seen but ignored for so long. He would go to any lengths to get what he wanted, or to defeat an adversary. He would stop at *nothing* to keep secrets like these.

And he was no fool. He had already asked why she had been upset lately, and it was obvious he wasn't buying her explanations. He would assume she suspected or knew he was seeing someone else. For all she knew, that affair might even have something to do with his other secrets. He would naturally think she would start to spy on him.

If he did, she might be in danger.

She had to make him think she really *didn't* think he was having an affair.

With that thought, she stopped pacing.

No, he would never buy that. It would require a complete change in her demeanor. Which wouldn't ring true. It would make him even more suspicious.

It had to be a different approach.

Standing helplessly in the middle of the room, she raised her eyes to the office walls. To the empty comfort of the posters and framed photos of her stage and film roles.

To the photo of herself and Avery, nineteen years ago, at the celebratory all-night party held after her second Academy Award triumph. They had just started dating. In the photo, they were posing, he proudly holding her in the circle of his arm, she proudly holding her golden statuette.

The sight of it made her sick, and she looked away.

Then it sunk in.

You are one of the world's greatest actresses.

Her gaze fixed back upon the photo.

He has been playing a role with you, all these years. Now, you have to play a role with him.

And you are much better at role-playing than he could ever be.

But what role, exactly?

It had to seem authentic. That meant her character had to have a plausible motivation—something consistent with the kind of person he knew her to be, and with her recent behavior.

She moved around the room, visualizing it.

Making it real.

Getting into character . . .

3

He checked his watch as he entered the apartment, and winced. It had been almost three hours.

Maybe she had gone to bed.

But when he stepped through the foyer, he saw her in the parlor, rising from a chair.

"Avery, dear!" she called out, her dark eyes wide with concern. "Are you all right?"

It surprised him. He had prepared himself for an angry scene.

"Yes. I mean . . . I had to attend to an emergency."

She rushed over to him, arms open. Astonished, he let her embrace him, and he wrapped his arms around her.

"My God," she whispered, trembling. "I was so worried! The way you looked when you ran out . . . I didn't know what to think."

"I am so sorry I frightened you, my dear," he said, raising a hand to stroke her hair. "I received a call that an old friend—no one you would know—had been in a terrible auto accident. I had to hurry to the hospital," he added, offering the explanation he had invented.

"Oh, I'm so sorry! Is he going to be all right?"

"Fortunately, the doctors say it was less severe than it first appeared. For a while, they were worried he might have suffered a spinal injury. But it is merely severe whiplash."

"You must be so relieved." She drew back, looked up at him, smiled. "You look exhausted. Why don't you join me in the parlor? I'll pour us some brandy."

"All right."

He went to his favorite armchair, and in a moment she returned with two glasses.

"There. Maybe that will relax you," she said, claiming her own chair.

"Thank you. I needed this."

She nodded as she took a sip from her own glass. She wore green lounging pajamas that complemented her long auburn hair.

"Me, too." She hesitated, casting her eyes down for a second, then looked back at him. The worry was there again, but of a different kind. "Maybe I need it more than you do . . . Avery, I don't like what seems to be happening between us lately."

And now it begins. He pressed his brows into a look of concern. "What do you mean?"

She took a deep breath. She looked at him directly. Sincerely.

"Dear, you don't have to say anything you don't want to. Actually, I'd prefer that you just listen. You and I, we've been married almost twenty years. We've had good times and bad times, but a lot more good than bad. We know each other about as well as two people can. But these past few months, you haven't been yourself. I sense you have been under a lot of stress."

She paused, expectantly.

He nodded slowly, cautiously. "That is true. I have been going through a rough patch. With work."

"With work, and I suspect with other things . . . No, don't say anything, not yet. Please, just hear me out, okay? . . . Look, a marriage that's endured for as long as ours is also going to be stressed from time to time. And busy people like us, who are around a lot of other interesting people during stressful times—well, the marriage is going to be tested." She took another deep breath. "And sometimes, under pressure and confusion and God knows what, maybe we'll make a mistake."

He could not say or do anything, except to keep his gaze riveted on her face and listen.

"If and when a mistake happens, the other person has to decide what to do about it. Whether to let a long and happy marriage come apart, just because of a mistake, maybe committed under pressures and frustrations."

She put down her drink on the table next to her, stood, and walked over to him. Then knelt on the floor, at his feet. She took one of his hands in hers. Raised it to her lips and kissed it.

"Avery, dear, you are a private man, and I have always respected and allowed you your space. I also want you to know that I allow for mistakes. Because I'm sure I am a contributing factor. I'm busy, too, and haven't always been around for you when you needed me. But I want to change that. Avery, I want us to be closer."

He saw the beginning of tears as she continued.

"I still want to be the one and only woman in your life—if that's what *you* want."

It astounded him. It was the last thing he expected. He raised the hand she held and brushed it across her cheek. Felt the smoothness, the warmth.

"Julia . . . dear . . . there are days I realize I do not deserve you—and this is one of those days." He said it sincerely, and in wonder, realizing that it was one of the only fully honest things he had said to her, or anyone else, in a long time.

"Perhaps we can both do better," she said.

He swallowed hard.

"I could not ask for a better wife. But from now on, I promise to be a better husband."

Avery Trammel said it knowing he was already lying again.

4

After apologizing, Trammel kissed her and said he had to wrap up a few things before coming to bed. He headed back to his study, tapped in the keypad code, and entered. He almost tripped over the hanger lying on the floor. He frowned—then remembered what had happened during his hasty exit. Draping his jacket over it, he hung it back on its wall hook.

The next quiet moments were spent toying absently with the items he had left out on the desk. His mind was far away, however, brooding over the unsettling events of the evening.

He was close, so close to achieving his objective. But formidable threats still stood in his path.

The unpredictability of Carl Spencer.

The continuing popularity of Roger Helm.

The relentless prying of the *faux* reporter who called himself Dylan Hunter.

But perhaps the foremost threats he faced came from the two women in his life: from the emotional volatility of one, who saw and understood nothing about him; and from the disquieting awareness of the other, who had seen and perhaps understood too much.

He considered each of them in turn, weighing what to do about them. Because something clearly had to be done. Being a decisive man, once again he did not take long to reach conclusions.

Trammel got up, bent over his safe, retrieved and prepared a burner, then sent out the usual text message. He removed its battery and SIM card again, returning it to the safe, and emerged with the satellite phone, which he powered on.

Lasher's answering call came through within two minutes.

"Yes, sir?"

"I have more work for you," Trammel said quietly. "It will be complicated. It also will have to be handled delicately."

Down the hallway, in the guest bathroom, his wife pressed a cold washcloth to her face and neck after throwing up into the toilet.

She rinsed her mouth, then stood, wobbly and shaky, before the vanity mirror. Her complexion was ashen, her eyes dark-ringed. She would have to do something about that before joining him later in the bedroom.

Julia Haight recalled the celebratory photos and publicity posters on her office wall, and the twin golden statuettes on the mantelpiece in the parlor. However, the stellar performances they honored were nothing compared to the one she had just delivered.

She knew her life would now depend on the answer to a single question:

Had it been good enough?

THIRTY-THREE

"*Avery Trammel: billionaire investor and progressive philanthropist, whose power is felt at the highest levels in Washington.*

"*Lucas Carver: influential media strategist and leftist political consultant, whose publicity campaigns shape the 'narratives' you encounter every day, on television and radio, in newspapers and magazines.*

"*Trammel and Carver: old friends and political allies—now colluding through a tangled web of tax-exempt foundations and nonprofits.*

"*Their plan: to use that 'charitable, educational' network—and its millions of dollars in tax-deductible donations and resources—to affect the outcome of this year's presidential election.*"

On the other end of the phone line, Bronowski stopped reading aloud and whistled.

"Dylan," said the *Inquirer's* editor-in-chief, "*please* tell me you can back all this up."

"You wouldn't be reading it if I couldn't, Bill. You'll find my source notes at the end of the piece. Remember—you asked me to look into the organized campaign against Roger Helm. What you're reading in this first installment barely scratches the surface. I'm uncovering more every day."

"Well, I sure won't need a second cup of coffee this morning. Damn, I can't wait to finish reading this. So, what can I expect from you down the road?"

"I interviewed Trammel and a couple of his associates in the Currents network—it's in the piece. I know how to read people," he said, thinking of his CIA training, "and I could tell they were hiding something. In Trammel's case—judging from his personal threats against me—it has to be something big."

"He *threatened* you? How?"

"I said it was personal; let's leave it at that for now. But a man in his position wouldn't try to scare off a reporter lightly."

"Damned straight. I've been a reporter and editor for decades, and the only people who ever threatened any of us were mobbed up. Who the hell *is* this guy, anyway?"

"There are things about Trammel's background that remain murky. Perhaps deliberately hidden. That's part of what I'm looking into."

"I should put our I-team on this to back you up. You need—"

"Thanks, but no thanks, Bill. You know I work solo. I have my own resources to call on for help, if I need any. Besides"—he thought of Julia Haight—"I have to tread carefully with certain confidential informants, to avoid spooking them. They are in positions to blow things wide open."

"All right, then," Bronowski said, sounding dubious. "Play it your way. I trust you, you've always come through . . . So, what *do* you need from me?"

"Just publish the pieces as I submit them. I'll email them to you, on no particular timetable, as I learn more. Of course, you want the staff to dig up appropriate photos and graphics to accompany them."

"Sure. We've been headlining nothing but the terrorist attacks for the past week. This will be a change of pace for the readers. And of course, none of the other papers in town are going to touch this story, so we'll own it . . . I'm excited about this, Dylan. I don't want to waste a day or two teasing it. I'll hustle it over to the fact checkers right now, see if we can get it out on the front page tomorrow."

"Great. You'll hear from me again very soon."

"Can't wait."

2

"I am so sorry," Avery said. "Considering how I disappointed you, I was hoping to make amends by showing you a splendid time this evening. But New York just called, and I have to be there in three hours for an unscheduled dinner meeting. I am at Reagan now, waiting to board a shuttle flight." He sighed. "The meeting is unlikely to break up until late, so I shall have to stay in Manhattan overnight."

"I understand." She squeezed the phone tight, wondering whether to believe him. Then she heard a flight gate being called somewhere in the background, and felt a wave of relief. "Really I do."

"The frustrating thing is that I managed to get seven o'clock dinner reservations for us tonight at that new place in Georgetown, Petit Plaisir."

"I've heard about it. But it's all right. We can go another time."

"No, it is an opportunity wasted. Because of the review in the *Post*, it is already such a huge hit that reservations are almost impossible to come by. I was fortunate that someone cancelled. But now . . ."

"That's too bad. I do love French food."

She heard him sigh again. "I suppose you could always go without me. After all, there is no point in wasting the reservation."

"You mean go alone?"

"You could . . . But what am I thinking? That is silly. You should have an escort."

"Right. I couldn't show up by myself at a place like that."

"Of course not." He paused. "You know . . . I just had a thought. Have I mentioned that I just hired a new driver? A real gentleman—well-traveled, speaks a number of languages, an amusing *raconteur*. He tells me he is working on a novel. Anyway, he is returning home after dropping me off. I could call and have him come by with the limo later this evening, and then escort you to dinner."

With what had happened between them so recently, she immediately felt wary.

"Dinner, with a complete stranger? Avery, that seems more than a bit bizarre."

"Not at all. The last thing I wish is for you to be stuck in the apartment and miss out on another good time, just because of me. Besides, you can act as my scout—let me know whether the food is as grand as they say."

"Honestly, I should just stay here and—"

"Nonsense. My dear, I truly want to do this for you. You deserve it. Let me call ahead and tell them to put everything on my account—anything you want. My present to you. And please, do not worry about your escort. I had him carefully vetted."

She pondered it for a moment. The driver would pick her up in Avery's limo right here, at the Watergate, drive her straight to the restaurant; they would eat for a couple of hours, then return directly back home. Under the circumstances, it seemed unlikely anything unpleasant could happen.

Besides, she was tired of the long days and nights of fear and worry. Her spirits could use a boost, and—all things considered—yes, she *did* deserve it. After everything she had been through, the least Avery owed her was a spectacular dinner.

"All right," she said finally. "It sounds special. Thank you, Avery."

"Thank you for accepting. I am delighted to do it for you. You will have to tell me all about it tomorrow."

"So," she asked, "who is this remarkable driver I should be expecting?"

"His name is Ray," he answered. "Ray Lasher."

3

From his latest hotel room, Lasher called her on the phone number that Trammel had provided. When she came on the line, he greeted her in as warm and charming a tone as he could muster, before explaining the slight change of plan.

"I'm really sorry, but on the way back from the airport, Mr. Trammel's limo broke down. I had to have it towed to the shop to be looked at. I hope you don't mind if we take my car to the restaurant. It's not much, I'm afraid."

"Oh, that's all right. I'm not fussy."

"I'm relieved. *Please* don't tell him I picked you up in a Taurus, okay? He'd be furious."

She chuckled. "Don't worry. It will be our secret."

"Thanks. I'll be there at six forty-five sharp. Do you want to meet me out front, or in the lobby—or should I ring for you at the desk?"

"I can be down in the lobby. What do you look like?"

He laughed as he finished applying the spirit gum to his upper lip.

"Please don't ask me to describe myself. I don't want you to change your mind. I know what *you* look like, of course, and that's all that matters."

She laughed, too. "All right, Mr. Lasher. You can surprise me. See you at six forty-five."

He put down his phone on the counter next to the sink. Then picked up the goatee and carefully pressed it in place for about a minute. Then inspected the results in the mirror.

The dark hair and brows, along with the facial hair and brown contact lenses, completely transformed him. Even his own mother, bless her soul, wouldn't have recognized him.

Lasher didn't use disguises for everyday life, but they were mandatory on ops. Cameras everywhere these days. Hell, you could be photographed even passing by an ATM. And tonight he'd have to be especially careful. After all, he'd be going to the Watergate, then to a fancy restaurant filled with politicians and celebs, and with a famous woman who would turn lots of heads. People might stop over to greet her. They would remember him, wondering what *he* was doing with her tonight.

The very thought of being with her excited him. Every man who saw them tonight would wish they were in his shoes. They'd be curious about their relationship. Wonder if he was going to get laid.

The strange, dark face in the mirror was grinning back at him.

They had no idea.

4

As promised, she was waiting in the lobby. People stared at her, of course—how couldn't they? She looked stunning. Short fawn-colored cocktail dress, dark brown jewelry, and holding a long brown cashmere coat that had to be worth five grand. He was glad she wasn't wearing it yet; it gave him a chance to take in her incredible legs.

"Hello," he said as he approached with a smile. "It's me."

"And hello to you, Mr. Lasher," she said, extending her hand and looking him up and down. He could tell she was pleasantly surprised by his appearance. His looks usually had that effect on women. Even in disguise.

He took her hand and nodded over it, then released it—reminding himself of the role he was playing.

"I left our chariot out front. Here, let me help you on with that."

He took the coat from her, opened it, and let her scoot around and slide inside. As his hands rested on her shoulders, ever so briefly, he glimpsed the arc of soft flesh within her neckline. Her perfume was a magnet.

"Shall we go?" he said, grinning and offering his arm.

She smiled. "Let's."

He led her out, over to the waiting green Taurus he had stolen hours before.

5

On the drive to the restaurant, she asked how "a man like you" found himself in Washington, driving limos. He told her the legend he and Trammel had invented for the occasion. She seemed fascinated by his tale of a Green Beret career that took him around the world, which led to a failed marriage and a teenaged daughter, Susan, living with his ex in Boston.

She had unbuttoned her coat in the car. It was an act of will not to glance down at the exposed thighs in his peripheral vision, flashing rhythmically under the passing streetlights.

Ten minutes later, he rolled up to the front of Petit Plaisir. He helped her out, handed a twenty to the valet, and they went inside. Lasher felt lots of eyes tracking them as the hostess led them across the elegant dining room and seated them at an isolated window table.

Because he knew exactly how this evening would end, the next ninety minutes were among the most exciting of his life. Role-playing was a game he was used to, and toying with her was a thrill. Warned by Trammel about sensitive topics, he steered away from questions about the marriage and her past, instead letting her ask about himself. He had to make up some things on the fly, but stuck closely to the basic legend. Her questions about his "novel in progress" were especially persistent; she said she was fascinated by the writing process. To sound plausible, he had to draw from a TV interview he saw once with Stephen King. He could tell she believed him. Hell, maybe he *could* write fiction.

It was a relief when the wine and food arrived. It gave him something safe to discuss with her. He asked her how she liked the Watergate, and listened attentively to her go on about the social side of life in Washington. She obviously needed to talk, and to relax. She didn't stop him when he filled her wine glass several times, and he ordered a second bottle.

As the wine took hold, he caught her looking at him, then looking away. It thrilled him even more, knowing that he could probably get her into bed willingly. But it would have to be different tonight.

After they ordered dessert, she excused herself to go to the ladies room. He helped her out of her chair and watched her walk off, just a bit tipsy. Moving away, her ass looked fantastic.

He glanced around. No one was looking. He raised the wine bottle to top off her glass.

No one saw him drop the pill into her drink.

She returned just after the desserts arrived.

"Let me offer a toast," he said, raising his glass. "To a great lady and lovely dinner companion."

She smiled. Touching glasses, then holding his eyes, took a long sip.

"Ray, I want to thank you for a wonderful evening. Things have been so difficult lately. I can't tell you how much I've need to relax like this." She took another sip, looking down at the table. "Maybe I shouldn't say this, under the circumstances, but I've been feeling pretty much alone. No longer sure who I can trust, and what to believe."

He nodded, heart pounding. "It must be so hard, being in your position."

"It is. The kind of life I've had, in the public spotlight all the time, married to a rich, powerful man—it can swallow you whole."

"I can only imagine." He resisted the impulse to put his hand on hers. It would be too much. He had to control himself now.

She sighed. "Oh, well, I'm just feeling sorry for myself." She forced a smile. "We should probably go."

Her glass still had a lot of wine left.

"But we haven't finished our wine," he said. "Avery would never forgive us for wasting such an expensive bottle of Chardonnay." He raised his glass again. "How about another toast? To better days."

She smiled, shaking her head, but picking up her own. "You're a nice man, Ray Lasher." She took another long swallow.

Fifteen minutes later, her eyes had grown dull.

"Whoa," she said, her hands fluttering, as if waving something away. "All that wine . . ."

He leaned forward. "Are you all right?"

"Just . . . real dizzy, alluva sudden." Her head was rolling a bit. "I gotta lie down."

"Sure. We'll leave right now."

He got up, hurried around the table, helped her to her feet.

"Here, lean on me . . . That's it. Let's go get your coat."

By the time they reached the entrance, she could barely stand. He handed his claim ticket and five bucks to a passing waiter, asking him to have the valet fetch the car.

"No, she'll be okay," he responded to the pretty hostess's question. He grinned. "She's been sick, and I think the combination of wine with her meds was a little too much."

6

From somewhere under deep layers of fog and confusion she felt a sharp, terrible pain. She shrieked and forced her eyes open.

In the smear of spinning lights and shapes she saw a steering wheel before her eyes closed again.

"Ahhhh!" she gasped again.

This time her eyes opened onto a face . . . a man with a beard and dark hair and burning black eyes, and she tried to remember who he was. His face floated above her, snarling . . . and *what was he doing?*

"Stop! What . . . are you . . ."

Then she began to remember . . .

Avery . . . how he looked the last time she . . .

Another piercing shock.

"Oh God stop! *Please* stop!"

Avery . . . you sent this man to me . . .

And then she knew terror.

"Ray! Noooo!"

She pawed at his face, her arms rubbery and weak. Tangled her fingers in his beard . . . and it came off in her hand.

"Bitch!" he spat out.

Then put a gloved hand over her mouth.

The black eyes, inches away, bored into hers.

Then something banged against her head.

7

Lasher got out of the car.

Let his breathing and heart begin to slow.

Put the goatee back on, pressed it into position.

Waited for his eyes to adjust to the moonlight and the dark, desolate structure nearby.

Miles from downtown, the parking lot of the abandoned warehouse had become a dumping ground for the local low-lifes. Scattered in the weeds around him were the dark shapes of crushed beer cans, rotting cardboard boxes, worn tires, a moldering sofa.

Now, in their midst, a late-model stolen Taurus, wiped clean of prints, and bearing the battered, half-naked corpse of a famous woman.

Filled with an intoxicating sense of power, Ray Lasher set out striding down the wooded path back toward the main road, to the Metro parking area a mile away, where he'd left his own Grand Cherokee this afternoon.

Ten minutes later, he was driving toward the city, and on his sat phone with Trammel.

"It's done," he said.

"Please tell me there were no complications."

"None at all. I'm heading back now. I'll spend the rest of the night taking care of everything else."

"See that you do."

THIRTY-FOUR

"I tried to warn you, Lucas," said Avery Trammel during a brief pause in Carver's obscenity-laced phone rant. "I said you had to go after this Hunter character pro-actively—demolish his credibility *before* he published anything."

"Yes, yes, I know you did. And it *was* on my schedule. But in case you haven't noticed, I've been just a wee bit preoccupied running the entire goddamned media effort for the campaign."

"Which is exactly what he has targeted: the entire media effort," Trammel replied. "Now it is *your* credibility—actually, *ours*—under challenge, instead. He struck first. And if I have learned anything from your sermons about 'narrative control,' it is: 'He who first frames the story, controls the news.' He has put us on the defensive. My staff has been fielding media inquiries all day."

"Here, too." He could visualize Carver pacing his office, as he always did when excited or worried. "Spencer is having fits, and Cunningham is beside himself. It'll be no good trying to answer each reporter's questions, one at a time. That would keep us playing defense for days."

"Until his *next* article, when it would begin again." Trammel spun the silver pocket watch on his desktop.

"You're right. He'll own the news cycles." Trammel heard the noise of a keyboard clicking. "Okay . . . I'm about to send an email to my staff, here and in New York. I'll get them researching his claims. We'll have to release a statement, a point-by-point rebuttal, no later than tomorrow. We'll label his article as a classic example of 'fake news.' That can be the theme: '*The Inquirer* is peddling politically biased fake news.' Our friends will be happy to give it a lot of coverage."

He sighed. "Lucas, you do realize that will not be nearly sufficient."

"I know, I know. But that's just step one. Step two—and this is crucial—*simultaneously* we have to go after *him*, personally, just as you suggested. Turn public attention away from whatever Hunter says in his articles; instead, make the story all about *him*. Attack his credibility by questioning his background. Get everyone asking, 'Who is Dylan Hunter?' What is his real name? Where did this guy come from? Is he working for someone? If so—who? Why the secrecy? What is he trying to hide behind that fake name? . . . Hey, *that's it!*"

"What is 'it'?"

"Our *meme*, Avery: 'Fake news from a fake reporter.' We headline that in all our statements. That, and 'Who is Dylan Hunter?' The press will eat it up—they'll put reporters on it, looking into his background, hounding him with questions wherever he shows his face. We'll enlist a congressmen or two to do the Sunday shows—suggest maybe Hunter is a hired gun working secretly for Helm."

Trammel found himself smiling. "You truly are a genius about framing media campaigns, *Maestro*."

"Yeah, well, I only wish I had listened to you and done this sooner. Pre-empted him. Maybe we can blunt what he's doing, but we won't be able to distract *everyone's* attention away from whatever issues he raises. And that still worries me."

"As it does me."

"So, how much do you think he knows about the flow of contributions through the Currents Foundation?"

Trammel gave the watch another spin. "We shall have to proceed on the assumption that he knows, or will soon discover, everything. That may be unavoidable at this point."

"I hope not. Last thing we need is for the IRS to start questioning if tax-deductible donations are being used for political purposes."

"Agreed. However, whatever revelations emerge will not matter a few months from now, after the election." He picked up the watch, turned it over. Studied the inscription on its back. "After this election, nothing will matter anymore."

"Sorry, I couldn't hear that last part. Could you repeat it, louder?"

"Never mind," said Avery Trammel. "It was nothing important."

2

Ed Cronin turned off Higgins Hill Road and drove up the steep driveway, to the impressive house at the summit of the hill. It was a modern combination of wood and glass. Its western end was a triangular, glassed-in porch, like a ship's prow, extending as an outcropping over the edge of the bluff. The house made him think of Noah's Ark coming to rest on a mountain top.

He got out of the Crown Vic, and took a moment in the crisp breeze to admire the sunset view. In the distance, the Allegheny River cut through the hilly forest that claimed its name. He collected his thoughts from the past day, spent with the state cops and at the crime scene out in the forest. Then went to the front door and rang the bell.

It opened on a pretty little brunette in her forties.

"Yes?"

"Sorry to bother you, ma'am." He showed his badge credentials. "My name is Sergeant Ed Cronin. I'm a detective in the Alexandria, Virginia, police department, and I'm working a case that's taken me all the way up here. Would you be the wife of Dan Adair?"

The look of curiosity turned to one of concern. "I am Mrs. Adair, yes. Your case involves my husband?"

"Not directly. It's complicated. But he may be of help to our investigation. Does he happen to be home right now? I'd like to have a few moments with him, if possible."

"We're about to sit down to dinner. Could this wait till tomorrow?"

He spread his hands apologetically. "I'm afraid I'm on a deadline to get back to Virginia. So if I could see him now, I promise it won't take long." He smiled. "I sure don't want your dinner to get cold."

"Well . . . I suppose so. Come on in."

She led him through the foyer into the den. An older man in a recliner put aside his newspaper and stood. Across the room, a young man watching television remained seated, but turned at his entrance.

"Dan, this gentleman is a detective from Virginia."

He heard a slight emphasis in the way she said it, and the man's eyes and lips narrowed as he approached. Cronin offered a smile and his hand.

"Mr. Adair, I'm Detective Sergeant Ed Cronin with the Alexandria P.D. But I'm also on a task force investigating a wave of crimes in the D.C. area."

"Dan Adair," the man replied. He was tall and lean, with sandy-gray hair and beard, and a firm handshake. "Nice to meet you, Sergeant. Over there's our son, Will."

"Hi," the twenty-something kid said, looking wary. He turned immediately back to the TV.

Adair gestured toward an empty club chair. "Have a seat. Anything to drink?"

"No, I'm fine," Cronin said, taking the chair. The Adair couple settled onto the sofa facing him. "As I told Mrs. Adair, I hope you might be able to help us in an investigation. Your company was targeted by that ecoterrorist group, WildJustice. The bodies of its two leaders, Zachariah Boggs and Rusty Nash, were found near here recently. Both murdered."

He saw her move her hand to his thigh, like she was clutching it.

"We know," Adair said, his voice and eyes hardening. "Everybody around here does. And it couldn't have happened to two more deserving people, either. Those thugs threatened my employees, vandalized my work sites, then murdered a scientist I hired." He rested his hand on his wife's, gave a little squeeze. "I bet they'd have gone after me, maybe even my family, if they'd had a chance."

Cronin nodded. "It had to be a nightmare for you."

The woman swallowed hard and looked down. Adair looked straight at him, unblinking.

"So what exactly are you investigating?"

"You may have heard there were possible connections between what their group was doing up here, and some things going on in Washington. I'm looking into that."

"I'm glad you are. Personally, I'm sure there was a conspiracy going on to stop fracking. I think these ecoterrorists were involved with people in government, like EPA, and their political cronies in 'green energy' companies. Some of it was written up in one of the papers down there."

His opening. "Oh, you mean that *Inquirer* series."

"Right. That laid it out pretty well."

"I saw you were mentioned and quoted in those articles. So, did the reporter interview you in person?"

Saw the slight tightening of his lips. And of her hand on his leg.

"He did. Since you read the series, you probably know he came here, talked to me and my people, visited one of our drill sites. He was curious about the hydraulic fracturing process—what everyone calls 'fracking.'"

"How well did you get to know him?"

A slight smile. He realized the guy was catching on to his real purpose.

"Dylan Hunter? I did get to know him a bit. A very dedicated reporter." He glanced at his wife. "In fact, we invited him here for dinner, to meet with a few local people being harassed. He also met with Adam. Dr. Adam Silva—the toxicologist that Boggs later murdered."

Now *that* was interesting. "So he met the murder victim?"

"Attended his funeral, too," Adair answered, an edge creeping into his voice. "We went there together. Met his widow and kids." He broke eye contact. "One of the hardest days in my life."

Cronin paused, absorbing it. He considered the nervous behavior of Adair's wife and son.

"So Mrs. Adair—you also met him at dinner."

She nodded. "I did." She added, unnecessarily. "And he seemed like a very nice man."

Cronin looked across the room. "How about you, Will? Did you ever meet Mr. Hunter?"

The kid turned to face him. He was skinny with light hair and evasive eyes.

"I think so. Well, yeah. When he and the lady came to the drill site. I met him out there."

"Lady?" Cronin asked.

The kid's eyes flashed to his father's, looking trapped.

"Yes," Adair interjected. The hard expression had returned. "He was accompanied by a young woman that day. A friend."

Cronin smiled. "Ah. Probably his girlfriend, Ann Woods."

"I believe that was her name. Yes."

"Lovely person. Did Mr. Hunter ever return here at a later time?"

Adair frowned. "Not to my knowledge. You seem focused on him, Detective. Mind if I ask why?"

Cronin sat back. "Hunter and Boggs appear to have had some personal issues between them. In fact, Boggs sent a bomb to his newspaper, intended for him. I was with Hunter when he got the message about that. He was extremely upset."

"Who wouldn't be?"

"Exactly. Who wouldn't be?"

"Look, Detective, I'd really like to help you, but I don't understand exactly where this is going."

"Mr. Adair, I spent yesterday with the state police here, going over the crime scene evidence in the deaths of Mr. Boggs and Mr. Nash. Nash had been stabbed repeatedly, and his body was found inside his own car, abandoned off a road a couple of miles from here. It was clear that he had been murdered elsewhere, though, not in the car. Whoever did it transported him to that spot, then wiped his vehicle clean of any fingerprints. As for Boggs, his remains were located in an isolated area of the forest. There wasn't much of him left, but it looks as if he may have been tortured before he was murdered."

He paused. Watched her swallow and grow pale. Adair was good, though. He actually smiled.

"You don't say. I'm glad to hear it. 'Live by the sword,' and all that."

"Yeah, well, I'm not saying he didn't deserve it. For a while, we thought he killed Nash, but it no longer looks that way. Looks like somebody else killed them both."

"Looks to me like that 'somebody' deserves a medal."

"Now, you know it doesn't work that way, Mr. Adair. We can't have people taking the law into their own hands—if that's what this was. But it could be somebody else in their gang did it. In which case, we have another nutjob killer out there."

"That's a scary thought," the woman said. She didn't sound that scared.

"However, there *was* some interesting evidence near the place where they found Boggs's body."

Cronin paused. Saw her swallow. Adair waited him out, expressionless.

"There were tire tracks out there," he continued, "from an all-terrain vehicle. An ATV."

She looked even more uncomfortable. Adair nodded.

"Yes, Detective, we know what an ATV is. I own one myself. A lot of people around here have them."

"That's what I found out. And when they checked the tire prints, they were able to tell they came from a specific kind of ATV. A Kawasaki Mule. They put together a list of everyone around here who's bought one of the models with that kind of tire on it. And—"

"—and they found out I own one. So *that's* why you're here."

Cronin shrugged. "You have to admit, it's an interesting series of coincidences. You are threatened and targeted by Boggs and his group. Then he and one of his pals are found murdered, in particularly nasty ways, within a few miles of your home. Then tire tracks from an ATV like the one you own are found close to the crime scene where Boggs was killed."

"Just a minute!" the woman snapped. "My husband wouldn't—"

"Easy, Nan," Adair said, patting her shoulder. "You and I both know the detective here is way off base."

"I am?"

Adair actually smiled. "And you know it, too, Detective. Because if the state and local cops really thought I had anything to do with those murders, and had any evidence, *you* wouldn't be here; *they* would." He turned to his wife. "Nan, he's not after me. He knows I had nothing to do with this."

"If that's true, Mr. Adair, you could clear things up for us right now, by letting me have a look at your ATV."

"Be glad to," Adair said. "It's right out in the garage. Honey, why don't you take the roast out of the oven. You and Will can start in, if you want. This shouldn't take long."

Adair led him out there, past a couple of cars, to the far bay.

"It's a bit dim over here," he said. "Here—have a flashlight." He grabbed one off his tool bench and offered it to Cronin.

"Thanks."

Adair pointed to the vehicle. It was several years old and bore some scratches and dents. But it looked almost new. Getting near, Cronin saw it had been washed and thoroughly cleaned. He bent over the rear bed and inspected it closely. It looked spotless. He pulled out a couple of photos of the tire tread from his jacket pocket—a shot from the crime scene, and a manufacturer's photo of the tire model—then squatted down and directed the beam at one of the rear tires.

It was brand-new. He flicked the light toward the front tire. Also mint.

He rose to his feet, snapped off the flashlight.

"So you replaced the tires. And also went out of your way to get this thing immaculately clean. What owner does that to an ATV?"

Adair crossed his arms over his chest. "How about an owner who has put his ATV up for sale? Want to see the newspaper ads?"

Cronin had to admire him. He was one cool bastard. Like the guy he was protecting.

"Come on, we both know this isn't about me," Adair went on, shaking his head. "Like I said, if it was, I'd be talking to the staties. A cop from the Vigilante Task Force in D.C. wouldn't come up here unless what happened to Boggs and Nash had something to do with whoever you're after."

"You're a smart guy, Mr. Adair. No wonder you're such a successful businessman."

"And you're a smart cop, Detective Cronin. But if I'm guessing right about what you suspect, you're making a big mistake."

"So, what big mistake am I making?"

Adair glanced down at his watch. Unfolded his arms.

"My dinner is getting cold, Detective. Here, I'll open the garage door and let you out."

3

"You were right." Adair's gruff baritone was loud in the phone at his ear. "This guy Cronin was definitely interested in you, and also in the ATV tracks. Glad you warned me, so I was able to change the tires and clean it up before he came sniffing around asking questions."

"Actually, it was Annie who warned me some time ago about the possibility of tire tracks," Hunter said. "She saved our butts. Did you get any sense of what else he knows or suspects?"

"I think he suspects a lot more than he knows, or can prove. I'm sure he noticed that Nan and Will were nervous—I did. But lots of people are nervous talking to cops. The only thing he probably didn't know before, but slipped out, is that Annie was up here with you when you visited our drilling site."

Hunter didn't like that. It could make her a possible suspect in what happened to Nash. But they had no evidence she was there at his time of death.

"Not a big deal," he said. "I'm more concerned that the state cops might pursue the ATV angle. It's all they seem to have as physical evidence, but you also had a motive."

He heard Adair's chuckle. "Well, Cronin will tell them they no longer have any ATV evidence. As for motive—hell, ninety percent of the folks around here hated those ecoterrorist bastards, too."

"Still, be careful. I know Cronin. He doesn't give up. You might see him again. You should expect it, and tell Nan and Will to expect it, too. You don't want to be caught off guard and reveal something you shouldn't."

"Right. I'll talk to them. Don't *you* worry. It'll be okay. We got your backs."

He caught the plural. "Thanks. I can't tell you how much we appreciate it."

"And I can't tell you how much we owe you. Tell you what: You get your ass here in November, I'll take you deer hunting. You ever done that?"

He smiled to himself. "Sure. I told you my dad used to take me to the Allegheny Forest to hunt."

"That's right. You did mention that. Did you enjoy it?"

"I'll never forget it."

THIRTY-FIVE

Annie headed down a seventh-floor corridor of the Old Headquarters Building, holding the last three sealed envelopes she still had to distribute today.

They had narrowed the suspect pool considerably, and surprisingly fast. Grant had just run a clever check on his own boss—Director of Operations Les Sisler—and cleared him. In truth, Sisler had never been high on their list. Though Grant described him as "a weenie," Sisler had never tried to impede his work over the past decade.

Meanwhile, her own bait, circulated throughout Ops, had generated no discernible reactions from Moscow. If the mole were in that directorate, she and Grant were reasonably sure their efforts would have provoked a noticeable response. So, tomorrow, they'd have to circulate "corrected" memos, to undo any problems arising from their fake ones.

Since this morning, she'd begun to work her way through the Directorate of Analysis. She still had two stops to make there—plus one with someone they hadn't been able to vet so far: Wesley Burroughs. As right-hand man to the DCI himself, the former analyst had unlimited access. Which meant if he were the mole, he had been doing incalculable damage.

Annie entered the "front office" area that housed the executive staff, stopping first at Analysis. She went through the clearance rituals with the executive assistant, a gruff, forbidding woman. From previous experience, Annie knew her favorite word was "can't." Insisting that the SCI document from Garrett *had* to be hand-delivered, she finally wrangled permission to enter the directorate's inner sanctum.

Agnes Headley reminded Annie of the actress who had played "Nurse Ratched" in the old movie "One Flew Over the Cuckoo's Nest." In her early fifties, Headley wore her medium-brown hair pulled back tightly. Her broad, flat face always looked expressionless, but up close her pale eyes betrayed flickers of constant scheming. Grant had warned Annie that the woman's M.O. was passive-aggressive manipulation.

Headley sat behind her massive desk, staring down at papers and ignoring her entrance.

After twenty seconds of this, Annie strode to the desk and plopped the sealed envelope atop the stack of papers she was reading. Headley jerked back and looked up.

"This is from Mr. Garrett," Annie said, "your eyes only. Not to be circulated more widely." She turned on her heel and headed back toward the door.

"Just what in hell do you think you're doing, marching in here and—"

"My job," Annie said, without turning.

Her next stop was just down the hall. This time she got right in without a hassle; Grant had called ahead, notifying Wesley Burroughs to expect her. He actually stood and came around the desk to greet her with a handshake and a grin, all teeth. The handshake lasted three seconds too long, and he looked her up and down as he accepted the envelope.

Burroughs squinted at the security markings on its exterior. "So, what's this all about?"

"I haven't the foggiest, sir. Mr. Garrett just said it was important for me to hand-deliver it to you, and *only* to you. He also said it should be secured in your safe after reading."

"Interesting," he said, looking at her, not the envelope. "How mysterious."

"That describes pretty much everything in this building."

He laughed, again showing lots of teeth. Though his swarthy face made her think of a street hood, Burroughs dressed nattily and wore custom wingtips with extra-thick heels, to compensate for his diminutive stature. At this proximity, she also could tell he dyed his hair dark brown.

"You're funny, Ms. Woods. And smart. I recall your work on the Muller investigation. Really brilliant. Tell me . . . do you like your current position?"

"Best job I ever had." She fixed him with a blank stare. "I wouldn't trade it for the world, sir."

"Are you sure? I have an opening coming up in my office, and someone like—"

"As I said, I'm perfectly happy where I am." She waved the third envelope in her hand. "I have to deliver this downstairs, right away. So I'll be on my way, sir."

"Oh. Sure, all right." The disappointment in his face was obvious. "Thank you so much for this . . . and for being so conscientious. You're a real asset here, Ms. Woods."

"I appreciate that, sir."

She turned and walked away, quickly, knowing he was watching her ass and legs. It made her grit her teeth and hope he was the mole. She'd enjoy seeing Burroughs doing a perp walk in cuffs outside a courthouse.

Her last stop was several floors and a hike away. En route, she had to consult a posted wall map. The layout at Langley was chaotic, with various divisions within the four directorates scattered between the two headquarters buildings, Old and New. She was glad the mission centers weren't yet up and running: Drawing from all elements of the Agency, they would have made an investigation like this infinitely more complicated.

She finally found the Office of Russian and European Analysis and was buzzed into the secure vaulted area. The room was filled with cubicles where analysts hovered behind large computer screens and stacks of documents. The guy at the entrance pointed her in the right direction. She meandered through the room to an office along the wall. The door was closed and locked, so she knocked and waited.

After a moment, Kurt Spitzer opened it part way and stuck his head out.

"What is—" His face brightened as he saw her. "Oh . . . hi. May I help you?"

"Mr. Spitzer, I'm Annie Woods, from Ops. I work with the deputy director. He asked me to hand-deliver this. As you can see, it's SCI. Only for you, as Russia House chief, and not for further circulation or discussion."

Spitzer stepped outside to accept the envelope. He was tall and not wearing his suit jacket, which revealed he spent a lot of time in the gym. He grinned and eyed her the way Burroughs had—a reminder they'd been fraternity brothers at Yale. But where his pal sported short dark hair, Spitzer's was blond, and worn at a length fashionable twenty years ago, while he was still in his thirties.

"Of course." He smiled down at her and crossed his arms, to make his biceps bulge more. "'Woods . . . Woods.' Why is that familiar?"

"It's what you see when you look out your window. Have a nice afternoon, Mr. Spitzer."

She left him with his envelope and his leer.

2

On Thursday morning, Hunter devoted most of his workout at the Silver Spring dojo to sparring with a guy who, like himself, had trained for years in krav maga, the Israeli self-defense system.

His own martial arts experience over two decades had been eclectic. It started in college with hapkido, in which he earned a black belt. In the CIA, he discovered krav maga, impressed by its self-defense practicality and brutal efficiency. But Hunter knew real-world fights required the ability to absorb punches and kicks, and they usually ended up on the ground. So, seven years ago he started MMA training, to get used to full-contact sparring and learn jiu-jitsu grappling moves. To keep himself sharp he also tried to get in some dojo time each week, in addition to his gym workouts.

This morning's sparring session ended with a half-hour of grappling on the mat, practicing various chokes, pins, and escapes. He hit the shower exhausted but satisfied.

Back at the apartment, he powered up a burner, checked his phone account through the spoof site, and was surprised to find it loaded with waiting messages from Danika. Which couldn't be good. He called back at once.

"It's been crazy, Mr. Hunter! I don't know what's going on. Three urgent messages from your editor, Mr. Bronowski, one from a Darrell Ellis at WTOP, two from Nancy Lafferty at the *Washington Post*, another from Shelly McIntyre at CNN, then Erik Greenwald at the *New York Times*..."

"Whoa! Easy, girl. Let's do this: I'll contact my editor first and see what's going on. Then I'll call you back and collect all the other messages, okay?"

"Okay... Oh, here comes another call."

"Take it. I'll be back to you in a little while."

Hunter thumbed in Bronowski's direct line.

"Yeah?"

"Bill, it's Dylan. What's going on?"

"You don't *know*? Where've you been, Antarctica?"

"I've been out this morning. Tell me."

"This group you've been investigating, Currents, and their media guy, Carver? They held a news conference at ten. They issued a rebuttal statement to your article—and then they went directly after *you*. Remember how last year I said I'd Googled your name, but couldn't come up with anything about you more than a couple years old? Well, they checked into your background, too, and they're saying 'Dylan Hunter' doesn't even exist. That your identity is fake."

"Bill, I've hinted to you before that I operate under a pen name."

"Yeah, I figured. But they're saying there's more to it than that. They say you've shown people valid government IDs issued to the name 'Dylan Lee Hunter'—just as you did here, by the way, when I hired you. But they say no birth records anywhere connect that name to the listed birth date. According to some attorney at the news conference, the only way that could happen is if you had a legal change of name, from your birth name to this one. There would be records somewhere that tie the two names together. However, they say they checked—and there aren't."

So, Trammel made good on his threat . . .

He had anticipated this moment and what he'd say when it arrived.

"Bill, I know it seems strange. There *are* possible explanations, though. For example, there is a way for the government to change somebody's name, if they're trying to protect him from harm."

Bronowski fell silent a moment, processing it.

"What are you telling me—that you went into *hiding* or something, and you're operating now under this new 'Dylan Hunter' identity that the government cooked up?"

Hunter didn't want to lie. So he didn't.

"Now, *you* said that, Bill—I didn't. I'm not going to say anything more. I can only tell you, honestly, that if my real birth name came out, there would be serious danger to me, and perhaps to others, too. So, I had to go to great lengths to make sure that won't happen."

"How is it possible you left no tracks? Or that somebody from your past doesn't recognize you when you're on TV?"

"I know. It's a real mystery, isn't it?"

"This isn't a joke, you know."

"No, it isn't. I'm telling you, bluntly and candidly: This is all about protecting my personal safety. If certain parties knew who Dylan Hunter used to be, the next time my name appeared in the *Inquirer* would be in the obituaries."

He listened to Bronowski breathing heavily for the next half minute. It ended with a long breath that turned into a sigh.

"All right," he said, his usual strident tone gone. "Given the kind of investigative work you do, I think I get it. Something you wrote in the past pissed off the wrong people, and you had to go off the grid and become somebody else."

"I told you I won't say another word about it."

"Okay, then. But how the hell do we handle this feeding frenzy? I'm watching my phone buttons flashing like Fourth of July fireworks."

"Obviously, we issue a statement right away, along the lines I just told you—but saying even a bit less. I'll draft something for you shortly, and you can put it out under my name."

"That won't satisfy them."

"Of course not. We both know the rest of the press hates the *Inquirer* and are especially gunning for me. They'll keep digging. But between you and me, I've covered my tracks well. I'm confident they aren't going to find a thing. It will drive them crazy, but after a while I think they'll lose interest."

"Yeah, yeah, but what are we going to do in the meantime? We have these bombshell articles from you scheduled, but this will be a big distraction. *You've* become the story now. This outfit at the news conference is brushing off everything you say as 'fake news from a fake reporter.' People will see your byline, then stop reading and ask instead: 'Who is Dylan Hunter?'"

Since his confrontation with Trammel, Hunter had prepared for that, too.

"Which is why you're not going to get any more articles about this from Dylan Hunter."

"*What?* After we teased all these upcoming—"

"What you'll get are unsigned pieces that you'll instead attribute to an 'undercover' *Inquirer* special investigative unit—unnamed."

"Oh, come on! We'll never get away with that. They'll *know*."

"Sure they will. But they won't be able to prove it. Meanwhile, another thing will swing the attention back in our favor."

"And what's that?"

"The coming stories *will* contain blockbuster revelations nobody will be able to ignore."

3

When Hunter ended the call, he phoned Danika, telling her to inform all media people trying to reach him that the *Inquirer* would be issuing a public statement shortly in answer to their questions.

Next, he responded to a text message from Wonk, reassuring him that everything would be fine.

Finally, before drafting the short statement he promised Bronowski, he called Annie to answer the worried voice mail message she'd left. He spent the first minute calming her down.

"But now *everyone* knows you're not who you say you are!"

"Annie, that was inevitable. I've been prepared for this day for a long time. And I can get past it, too." He told her his plan to issue a cryptic statement hinting that, due to past threats, he had to change his identity.

"Dylan, you know that will make them even *more* curious about you. They'll try to follow you and look into every nook and cranny of your life. We—"

She stopped.

"I know," he said gently. "I've been thinking about that. If we go public about our relationship, it will make things a lot harder. Mostly for you."

There was a long silence. When she spoke, it sounded as if she were trying to control anger.

"You said 'if.' And you said 'relationship'—not 'engagement.'"

"We need to think this through, Annie. Figure out the best way to proceed."

"I thought that was settled when you gave me the ring. And then, after I returned it, *you* insisted and finally persuaded me to put it back on."

"I know. Look, this is a mess. We're both distracted with work, and we can't resolve this over the phone. We'll do that next time we get together. But right now, I have to issue the statement."

"*Then* what?"

Trammel's smug face swam into Hunter's consciousness.

"Then, Annie, I go after these sons of bitches and shut them down."

THIRTY-SIX

"It's not working," Carver said grimly, waving a sheet summarizing the latest public opinion surveys.

They were back in the Vox Populi conference room, the four of them, in an emergency strategy session.

"The daily tracking polls tell the tale," Carver continued, his voice uncharacteristically subdued."One week ago, the night of our news conference exposing Hunter, we saw the beginning of slight movement our way. The next two nights, Friday and Saturday, were better. We definitely started closing the gap with Helm.

"But Sunday the *Inquirer* hit back with that big story about Currents, tracing its funding from Avery's foundation, and then showing Currents, in turn, funding anti-Helm groups. And on Monday they came out with the follow-up on me and Vox Populi, tying us to all of it. The articles are cleverly building a narrative that Carl's campaign is part of a big conspiracy to violate campaign funding laws—that we're illegally benefiting from charitable, tax-deductible contributions."

He tossed the sheet onto the conference table. It spun into a water glass.

"Our momentum in the polls stopped Monday night. Tuesday, two different tracking polls showed us headed back down again. Last night, the same. Bottom line: We're about ten, eleven points behind Helm, and the vector continues to point the wrong way."

Sid Cunningham's mouth was set in a grimace. "I thought your big, fancy media campaign was supposed to counter all that—make *him* the story, not us. Why isn't it working? I saw negative stories about him all over the place this weekend—the *Post*, CNN, MSNBC—"

"First of all, Sid, the *Inquirer* was clever to take his name off the bylines of those hit pieces, so that he won't continue to be the central focus."

"Damn it!" Cunningham exploded. "Everybody *knows* Hunter wrote those pieces. The *Inquirer* is just giving him cover by saying they're by a team of reporters."

Spencer was hunched over the conference table, scowling at the sheet of paper. "Exactly. I don't get it. He and his rag have zero credibility."

"Well, I'm afraid I *do* get it," Carver replied. "The *Inquirer* may have no credibility among people like us, Carl, or any educated people, for that matter. But its readers represent a different demographic. And it's a big one. Those kinds of people eat up conspiracy theories, and that's what Hunter has spun for them. These front-page *Inquirer* stories have social media and radio talk shows buzzing.

"And to answer what Sid said, it doesn't *matter* that we had our surrogates all over the Sunday talk shows. Nobody watches them, or believes the people on them, not anymore. Millions of people think the news media is being manipulated—"

"—by people like you," Spencer interjected, looking testy.

"Whatever," Carver replied, shrugging. "The fact remains, they don't buy anything they read or hear in the media. But they do buy what Hunter is giving them, because, as I say, he's created a compelling conspiracy narrative. And in a choice between believing him or the regular media—he's winning."

Trammel sat listening, studying his manicured nails with a mounting, queasy feeling of anxiety. He cleared his throat.

"So. What do we do about this, Lucas?"

He saw his own anxiety reflected in Carver's eyes.

"Don't worry," the strategist said, forcing a smile. "We can turn this around. We have a lot of time. We're still over two months out from the July convention. Even a week is an eternity in politics, because all sorts of unplanned events intervene. For one thing, every big media organization is investigating Hunter's background, now, and something ugly is sure to surface soon. For another . . ."

Trammel stopped listening. He realized right then that Lucas had no good answers, and that his words were mere public-relations spin, empty clichés meant to reassure his paying clients and keep the cash flowing into his company.

Like the *Maestro*, Trammel had studied politics for decades. He might not have Lucas's nuanced grasp of marketing tactics, but he understood the basic principles. One thing he knew is that you could not successfully sell a fatally flawed product—not in a marketplace with more attractive options.

He looked at the candidate sitting beside him. A mere pretty boy, consumed with the desire to be popular. Intellectually vacuous. Uninspiring. Fundamentally incapable of winning a head-to-head competition against a self-confident, intellectually robust visionary such as Roger Helm. Perhaps not even against a stupid, demagogic celebrity such as Tom Waller . . .

In that searing instant of realization, Avery Trammel shuddered, because he saw his lifetime dream dying. The queasy feeling increased.

He rose to his feet, unsteady, interrupting Lucas's blather.

"I am afraid I am not feeling well," he announced.

"Yes, I can see that," Carver said, alarmed. "Avery, you're shaking. Can I get you something, or call—"

Trammel waved a hand. "No, no. My driver is waiting downstairs. But I should leave. We shall have to continue this discussion later."

Carver escorted him to the elevator, steering him by the elbow. They waited a moment before the door opened. Trammel stepped inside.

"God, Avery," Carver said, grave concern on his face, "I hope it's nothing serious."

"I hope so too, Lucas."

2

Avery Trammel sat alone, secure behind the locked door of his study, huddled with his private things.

Once again, the album lay open on the desk before him, open to that first of so many treasured photos of his youth. It was the one of himself as a small boy with his parents: black and white, slightly faded, almost sixty years old. It had been taken in some studio, long forgotten: he, standing in front, skinny legs in short pants, white socks, dark shoes, and a checkered shirt; his pretty mother seated behind him, slightly to one side; his handsome father towering behind them both. They each had a hand on him: hers, around his little waist; his, upon his shoulder.

He was smiling in that photo. The expression always looked so alien to him, because he could never find photos of himself smiling in his later youth or adulthood.

Avery Trammel came here often to look at this photo, and the others of his childhood with his parents. It felt like a quest to discover, or rediscover, something missing. He was self-aware enough to understand what he sought, of course.

It was only in these moments that he could summon, if only faintly, any memory of the feeling of love.

In more than a half-century since the photo was taken, he had been surrounded by many people. They made their presence felt upon him in many ways, just as he made it a point to stamp his own presence upon them. He interacted with people constantly—commercially, socially, sexually. However, not emotionally. Not deeply so, in any case. Since his youth, there remained a sort of barrier between himself and others, leading to a superficiality of interaction, an absence of intimate connection, which left him feeling distant. A part of him, the dominant part, had long ago become a remote observer of others, and not a full participant with them.

He was also sufficiently self-aware to understand why.

If the photo album reminded him of his last connection to the feeling of love, the scrapbook beside it reminded him why hatred had taken over in its place. For the loss of love and the birth of hatred were of a piece.

Avery Trammel slowly turned the pages of both volumes, pondering the course of events that had, at last, brought him so close to the end of this long journey.

He began life as Avis Tremills, son of an English-born father, John Avery Tremills, and his American-born wife, Eileen Rogers Tremills. John Tremills's parents had immigrated to the United States when his father was assigned to manage the New York office of a London-based bank. But like so many, the bank was hit hard by the Depression. The Tremills family suffered long unemployment and grave financial hardship. Though extremely intelligent and an exceptional student, young John could only afford to attend City College of New York, where he studied civil engineering.

There—like thousands of bright young men and women traumatized by the economic brutality of the Depression—John became radicalized and joined the Communist Party. At age twenty-five, during a demonstration, he met a fellow Communist, Eileen Rogers. They eventually married and, not long after the end of the war, their only child, Avis, was born. The family moved into a little ranch house on Long Island, where John had found a job with a small defense contractor, while Eileen taught high school history.

With the move to Long Island, John and Eileen stopped attending Party meetings and demonstrations, or even arguing politics with family and co-workers. To everyone's surprise, they abruptly became completely apolitical, it seemed, and began to spend far more time socializing with neighbors, many of whom were John's co-workers at the company.

For little Avis, it was an idyllic childhood. Their suburban neighborhood had plenty of boys his age to play with. His parents got him a caramel-colored cocker spaniel puppy that they named Taffy. His parents also liked to travel. They often took weekend family trips to a camp in the Adirondack mountains, where they met and befriended other families and their children. His father took him fishing in a little boat on a blue lake, while his mother prepared picnics that they enjoyed afterward on its shore, cooking their catch over a campfire. Sometimes, Avis got to take exciting train rides with them, too, accompanying his father on business trips to big cities like Chicago and Boston and Washington. Whenever John had to hurry off to some meeting, Eileen would take Avis to art museums and libraries. Sometimes, in the evenings, they even attended plays and symphony concerts.

From his earliest years, his mother had introduced him to music, then reading and the world of books and music. Astonishingly precocious, by age four he had learned how to read and do simple arithmetic, and he could identify pieces of classical music and name their composers. Eileen Tremills was a wonderful mother and teacher, and Avis loved her dearly.

But he idolized his father. John Tremills was a tall, masculine presence who taught him to throw and hit a baseball, took him to Yankees games, showed him how to use tools, and explained the inner workings of radios and early television sets. John also took up a hobby, becoming an avid, skilled amateur photographer. He showed Avis how to take pictures with the funny, heavy box camera he had acquired. Then he bought a lot of chemicals and equipment and built what he called a "darkroom" out in their garage, where he developed the pictures. He installed a heavy metal door on the darkroom, and secured it with a large padlock, explaining to Avis that he had to prevent anyone from coming in and ruining his pictures.

One evening while playing with Taffy in the back yard, he heard his father's car turn into the driveway, returning home from work. He ran around the garage to find his father lifting a strange-looking contraption from the trunk of their big Buick. Entering the garage behind him, he asked what it was. His father, startled, turned and told him it was just a piece of testing equipment for a machine at work. He took it into his dark room and locked it away, because he said it was expensive and he did not want it to be stolen.

They enrolled Avis in a local elementary school when he was five. By then, he was already so advanced that the school was compelled to let him skip first grade. He still knew more than his classmates, though. To keep him from becoming bored, his mother would give him extra lessons at home, then send him to his room with homework. He would finish quickly and bring his work downstairs for her to check. Sometimes he would interrupt them in quiet conversation in the dining room, and they would look up, surprised. "Don't sneak up on us like that," his father would say, and then they would all laugh.

But sometimes he would hear them whispering in nearby rooms, or, waking up late at night, he could make out their voices behind the closed door of their bedroom, saying things he could not quite understand, in tones that seemed either harsh or worried.

Then came that cold, terrible November night . . .

He remembered it was November because it happened just before his eighth birthday, which was November 28. He had been asleep in his room when sudden, loud banging downstairs jolted him awake.

He jerked himself upright when he heard loud men's voices shouting *"FBI! FBI! Hands where I can see them!"* Then his mother's voice, screaming from her bedroom—the sound of her feet in the hallway—and then his door bursting open and she rushing to him in her nightgown, her eyes wild, shouting *"Avis! Avis honey! Come to me!"* and grabbing him and hugging him, so tight he could not breathe, while blue lights flashed outside his window and other lights flared outside his room and heavy feet pounded up the stairs—

—and then two big men in dark suits and hats spun around the doorway into the room, crouching low *and pointing guns right at them* and yelling *"FBI! DON'T MOVE! GET THOSE HANDS UP!"*—and his mother squeezing him and saying in his ears, over and over, *"It's all right baby, I won't let them hurt you, don't be afraid Avis, it will be all right dear"*—and then one of them grabbing her arms and trying to pull her away from him as she screamed *"NOOOO!"* while the other grabbed *him* and yanked him in the other direction, and he felt like his bones were breaking and he screamed and then the man jerked him away from her and down onto the bed—

—and then he saw his mother being shoved to the floor, and the other man jumping on her back, and then his terror turned to rage—and howling he flung himself at the man above him and started hitting and clawing and biting like a wild animal, until his teeth found the man's hand, the one without the gun, and he clamped down hard and the man yelled *"AHHH!"* and then his other hand, the one with the gun, came whipping around and crashed into his head and he knew nothing more . . .

The night that John and Eileen Tremills were arrested by the FBI, Avis was ~~only~~ almost eight years old.

Only when he was much older was he able to process what had happened. He learned that his father had never left the Communist Party, but had been groomed by Party officials for recruitment into a Soviet espionage ring. On those wonderful weekend family excursions to the rustic, innocuous-looking camp in the Adirondacks, he was actually being trained by KGB handlers there to become a courier, "talent scout," and recruiter. With his engineering background, John Tremills was assigned to a cell in the New York City area tasked with stealing highly classified technological developments from university and defense contractors.

His parents' were held without bail. That period, and the subsequent espionage trial, lasted two years, during which time Avis was sent to live with his mother's divorced sister and her daughter. It was an endless period of further terror and fury for the child. He did not understand what had happened, or why, and no adult wished to explain it, or tried to. Later, he understood: How could one explain arrests and trials for espionage and treason to a small boy? He knew only that the two people he loved and depended upon most in the world had been violently ripped away from him, overnight, leaving him scared and angry and alone—and that the men who had committed this terrifying act were *from the government.*

He did not see his parents again for those two interminable years. He learned later that he would have been permitted visits, once a month, to the prison where they were held—but that *they* had not wanted him to see them there, behind walls and barbed wire and a thick plastic window, where he would talk to them on a phone with armed guards hovering nearby. They thought it would be worse for him, that their sensitive child had already experienced enough trauma.

Or perhaps not. During those two years living with his divorced aunt, Avis was an alien in a new neighborhood, a new school. He felt completely isolated. He could not focus on anything but the haunting memories of what had happened, memories that caused him to wake up screaming. His school grades suffered terribly, and he lost the grade level he had been advanced to. Counseling did little good; no one then understood PTSD, especially in a child.

And through it all, he had to endure the malicious hostility and bullying and insults of his peers and classmates, chants of *Communist* and *Traitor*—words spat with blind hatred, but whose meaning neither they nor he could begin to grasp.

At the end of the two years, John Avery Tremills was convicted for espionage and sentenced to life in a federal prison. Eileen was acquitted for lack of sufficient evidence of direct knowledge and complicity. Avis was ten years old when she came back to him. That day, they cried for hours in each other's arms on his little bed in his aunt's house. His mother rocked him, petting his hair, trying and failing to explain why all this had happened to them.

And why his beloved father would never be coming home to them.

For the next two years, things only got worse.

No school would hire Eileen. Nor would any decent-paying company. Though highly intelligent and educated, she was reduced to taking the most degrading and menial of jobs, at places where no one asked many questions about one's background. After a few months, her own sister could not take the pressure of her indignant neighbors, and they could no longer stay with her. They were forced to move into a two-room dump of an apartment in a run-down neighborhood. They lived off what little income Eileen could earn working long hours as a maid in cheap motels, or folding clothes in a laundromat—supplemented by the charity of her sister and a local Unitarian church.

Avis watched his mother deteriorate from a lovely, lively, educated woman, into a lonely, embittered woman aging rapidly before her time. Her anger toward the United States government was boundless, endless—and of course he absorbed it without question. Her rants confirmed his experience of that horrifying night and the hideous years since.

They had locked his father away in a cage forever. They had reduced his mother and himself to an animal existence.

In time, he no longer experienced the bottomless fear.

In time, the fear became a towering rage.

Avis Tremills was twelve years when he made a vow to himself.

He made the vow when he heard his mother, behind the closed door of the bathroom in their shabby little apartment, sobbing uncontrollably.

He stood outside the door, fists clenched, shaking. And in that moment, he made the silent vow.

He did not know when, or how, he would make good on the promise. But he knew then that he now had a mission that would define the rest of his life.

The mission was revenge.

He closed his eyes and made the vow.

The goddamned United States of America will pay for this.

Only one thing kept Eileen Tremills from hitting rock bottom—from turning to drugs, alcohol, or prostitution. That was her brilliant, beautiful boy. If there was only one thing she could salvage from this nightmare, it would be her Avis.

But to do that, she decided, he needed to be severed from any association with the widely hated name *Tremills*. In the McCarthyite Era, that name had become the modern equivalent of the Scarlet Letter. It would only taint her boy's future, denying him the opportunities that his genius merited.

So, just before he turned thirteen, she scraped together the money to file the papers to have his name legally changed. They chose his new name together. In honor of his father, he chose his middle name, *Avery*, to be his own first name. At his mother's request, her maiden name, *Rogers*, became his middle name. And *Trammel* was an alteration of Tremills—with the added symbolism that it meant harnessed or shackled, an enduring reminder of their family's oppression by the fascist federal government.

Having shielded him from further persecution with the new name, she enrolled Avery into a new school, too, several miles away, where no one knew of his past.

Burning with a fierce new purpose, Avery Rogers Trammel made the most of the opportunity.

He tackled his schoolwork with missionary zeal. His talents, long lying fallow, once again took root and blossomed. He soon proved himself a brilliant and eager student. Encouraged by his mother's doting, and weekly letters of encouragement from his imprisoned father, Avery performed spectacularly. By the end of his first year, he stood academically at the head of his class. And never lost that standing.

He graduated the class valedictorian. His speech was a daring call for his peers to go out into the world and fight for social justice.

He mailed a copy, and a photo of himself in cap and gown, to his father—who still could not bear to have him come and visit in person. He received a tear-stained reply a week later, which he kept inside a growing scrapbook.

Days after his June graduation, Avery traveled into New York City and tracked down a name he found in one of the newspaper accounts of his parents' trial. The man had been implicated in the espionage ring, but never charged, for lack of evidence. After a long conversation to convince him of his identity, he was given only a phone number. The phone number, which he dialed from a public booth in a drugstore, led to a brief meeting in Central Park. That meeting led to three more, in different places, with different individuals, over the course of a week. A message left inside a locker at Penn Station dispatched him to Washington, and yet another meeting in the rear corner booth of a busy steakhouse.

After a month of careful vetting, Avery Trammel found himself recruited by the KGB and assigned a handler. He did all this without telling his parents. After their ordeal, they would have been worried sick and warned him off.

In exchange for his future services, Avery insisted to his handler that his mother, who had suffered so much for her loyalty, deserved some help. His handler forwarded the request to the Center, which approved a modest stipend, routed circuitously to Avery. He gave it all to his mother, telling her he had gotten a part-time job. That, coupled with her own meager income, allowed her to move into a better apartment in a different town.

Trammel's academic excellence had won him a number of scholarship offers. He selected George Washington University School of Government, Business, and International Affairs, in Washington, D.C. It was another major stepping stone to his objective.

It was the 1960s, a time of revolutionary fervor and upheaval. His handler warned him to keep a low profile. He was to be a "sleeper," an illegal slated for long-term training and development. He spent vacation time traveling to safe houses and rural sites where he could be trained. But hot-headed and angry, Trammel was impatient. Behind the back of the Center, he began associating with campus Maoist revolutionaries. Over the next two years, he participated in disruptive street protests. Later, he secretly joined a violent underground cell. He became involved in their campaign of bombings, until an FBI informant exposed their plot to bomb the Pentagon. Trammel and two members of his cell narrowly escaped discovery and capture.

At that point, Trammel realized that while he had been venting years of pent-up anger, he had been making little progress toward fulfilling his mission. He could remain a revolutionary insurgent, or choose to play the long game with the Russians. He pondered which course was most likely to wreak the greatest havoc.

He chose the Russians.

Avery Trammel studied both business and government, eventually graduating *summa cum laude*. He then pursued his Master's, again graduating near the top of his class.

Over the next fifteen years, he began his climb up the ladder of wealth and power, aided each step of the way by Moscow. They had realized his enormous potential at the outset, and invested heavily to help him become the consummate "agent of influence": an operator at the highest echelons of American business, government, and society. He possessed advanced degrees in international finance and government, formidable intellectual powers, unshakable self-confidence, and relentless drive. To all this the Center provided timely infusions of substantial investment cash, and strategic assistance in international currency manipulations. Trammel's rise was meteoric. Moscow backed him just as they had other prominent financiers over the decades, directing these agents into critical positions of influence and decision-making.

Until 1989. The disastrous collapse of the Soviet Union and the cause of international communism left Trammel without his support system. However, he had long been disenchanted with Soviet corruption, and, in truth, with communism. Besides, deep down, Marxism had never been his core motivation—only the intellectual rationalization for his festering hatred.

That is when he made his next strategic decision. As the Soviet Union began to reconstitute itself as an imperial oligarchy, Trammel decided that he would continue to avail himself of their resources—but for his own personal objectives. With Russian money, he would build a network of cultural and political advocacy foundations and groups, then employ them to manipulate American politics and policy. With Moscow's cooperation, his network would pursue the strategic, long-term goal of installing a puppet in the White House.

But at the right moment, the Kremlin would realize that the puppet was not theirs.

In the end, the puppet would dance to the strings held by Avery Rogers Trammel.

3

Careful to preserve the fragile pages, Trammel closed the photo album, then the scrapbook. He stacked them inside the metal box, then returned it to the safe inside his desk.

He remained kneeling there, understanding why he had to revisit these reminders of his past today. It was the same reason that had driven him from the meeting.

At age sixty-four, this year would likely be his final opportunity to fulfill his vow to his parents. Yet his mission now stood in grave peril.

For lack of character, Ashton Conn had failed him. For lack of substance, Carl Spencer was destined to fail, too. The man could not possibly compete against Roger Helm.

Yet Spencer could not be *permitted* to fail. Nor could he allow *himself* to fail to keep his solemn promise. Not after having come this close to succeeding.

He had revisited these mementos to steel himself for the grave thing he was preparing to do. The odds of succeeding, he knew, were not high. But they were far higher than inaction.

His hand groped for the old silver watch in his pocket. It had belonged to his father, who had sent it to him the day he went on trial. It had not kept time for decades. But during the childhood period when he was alone, it was the only thing that had kept him sane. And ever since, the timepiece buttressed his resolve during times of difficulty.

This was such a moment.

He drew it from his pocket now, turning it over to read the faded but still legible inscription etched onto its back. It was a famous phrase from Virgil's *Aeneid*—his father's favorite quotation—and beneath it, John Tremills's own initials:

Audentis Fortuna Iuvat

J.A.T.

"Fortune favors the bold," he whispered.

Seeing it, saying it, gave Avery Trammel the strength to reach into the safe for the satellite phone.

THIRTY-SEVEN

Located next to the Central Library, the baseball field at Quincy Park in Arlington, Virginia, was not a large venue for a presidential candidate's outdoor event. It wouldn't have been adequate later in the campaign season, when crowds would get much larger. But it was sufficient at this stage of the primary season.

Besides, this was not officially a campaign event. Roger Helm had first agreed to show up months earlier, because the locals wanted to honor him for his years generously supporting northern Virginia youth baseball leagues. When his campaign manager, "Cap" Moyer, tried to have the event double as a campaign rally, Helm exploded, saying that would "politicize" the award and "dragoon innocent children" into his campaign. It took phone calls from league officials and coaches to persuade him, reluctantly, to attend, but he agreed only on condition that there would be no political speeches, local politicians, or campaign signs present.

The Secret Service disliked outdoor events, and they hated this particular venue, especially in the wake of the terrorist attacks. With limited manpower, they had too large a periphery to control. Quincy Park was surrounded on all sides by roadways. The nearest to the ball field was North Quincy Street to the west; it ran parallel to the first base line, not sixty feet from home plate, where the ceremony would take place. In addition, only a few sections of the ball field and park were fenced in.

But the protective detail worried most about the many massive, high-rise apartment buildings along Fairfax Drive, barely four hundred meters to the south. Hundreds of windows and balconies overlooked the library and had a clear view into the ball field beyond.

Preparations began the night before, when agents and local police cleared the park, then trucked in and erected metal barriers around the periphery, to funnel the crowd through metal detectors. They suspended tarps on the backstop and nearby fences to block rear and side views of the candidate. A truck arrived to empty the recycling bins in the small parking lot behind the backstop, and the bins were then padlocked shut. That was where the Helm motorcade would arrive, and it now was limited to Secret Service and police vehicles. His close protection personal security detail would escort him directly from his armored SUV into the field, then take up positions near him during the ceremony.

At nine a.m. on Saturday, police closed the surrounding streets, diverting traffic. Those wishing to attend the event would have to park in nearby lots and walk to the field. Meanwhile, the candidate had personally donated ten thousand dollars to the Arlington Central Library to remain closed until after the event. Police cars and officers were stationed at close intervals along the roadway sidewalks. A second line was stationed inside the ball field, along the outfield fence and the newly erected barriers, to keep the gathering crowd flowing toward the metal detectors. A bomb-sniffing dog then checked out the team dugouts, and the nearby vehicles and recycling bins.

In addition, the Secret Service posted agents to watch the apartment complex just across North Quincy Street, plus two counter-sniper teams atop one of the buildings there—one to watch the ball field, the other the buildings on North Nelson Street, which ran along the opposite side of the park to the east. To the south, they stationed two more counter-sniper teams on the roof of a ten-story office building on the north side of Fairfax Drive. Their mission was to scan all those apartment windows and balconies rising above them on the opposite side of the street.

It wasn't ideal, but it was the best they could do. They'd be glad when it was over.

2

When he first saw news of the event posted on the candidate's website, Lasher headed to Arlington, then drove the streets around the park, studying the area. He couldn't believe the Secret Service team would permit their candidate to appear in a place this exposed. If Helm and his people insisted on coming here, they were suicidal idiots.

He returned the next day in disguise, in case any advance team was keeping an eye on the area. While kids played in the sports fields, he pretended to be a bird watcher, using a camera and tripod to snap photos of birds—and of the various buildings in the area, lines of sight, obstructions. He had plenty of options about where to set up, but that depended on where, exactly, they would position Helm.

The safest place for him would be in the small parking area bordering the north wall of the library. With the building at his back, Helm would be protected from any sniper perched in the tall structures to the south. But Lasher didn't think it likely they'd hold the ceremony here; small trees bordering the parking lot would block the crowd standing in the field from seeing him clearly.

No, the ideal spot for visibility to his followers also would be the worst from the security standpoint: at the far northern end of the park, in the baseball infield, where VIPs could sit in the bleachers behind him while he spoke. His speculation was confirmed the same evening, when he read in a local paper that Helm would throw out the first pitch of the new Little League season.

Lasher showed up for a third day, Wednesday, this time in jogging clothes. He spent the first twenty minutes trotting around the park grounds, pausing briefly to flirt with a soccer mom watching her kid on the field, and otherwise looking normal, before wandering over to sit on the bleachers and sip from a water bottle. He lounged back, breathing deeply, resting his arms on the riser behind him, his sunglasses turned up toward the sun—and the high-rises just a few hundred meters in the distance. He noted which balconies and windows in which buildings afforded the best possibilities for concealment, and which had the line of sight blocked by trees. He took out his cell phone and pretended to place a call, then paced around the area near home plate and the bleachers while he surreptitiously snapped photos of the distant buildings.

After half an hour, he drove back to his latest hotel room with the sketch of a plan in mind. He had a lot of preparation ahead of him.

3

Hunter had more than enough to preoccupy himself when Bronowski called late Friday, begging him to do a follow-up interview with Roger Helm, to run as a sidebar with his Sunday story. He wanted Helm's response to the recent terrorism and to the growing scandal in the Spencer campaign.

When Hunter phoned the campaign's press secretary, he was told the candidate had no time Saturday for a phone interview, but that Hunter was welcome to join him at a noon ceremony in Arlington, then interview him afterward in his car, en route to his next campaign stop in downtown D.C.

To reach the ball field, Hunter had to park on 11th Street and walk over, crossing North Quincy. It took ten minutes for two lines of cops, then a couple of Secret Service agents, to verify his press credentials and the faxed invitation from Helm's press secretary, then send him through a body scanner set up in the parking area behind home plate.

Out on the field a rope line, manned by cops and Secret Service agents, had been strung along the base paths, and a crowd of at least fifteen hundred was already there, with many more arriving. TV camera crews had set up between the pitcher's mound and second base, to get promised shots of Helm tossing a pitch to a Little League catcher.

Just to the right of home plate they'd put a small platform with a lectern; it blossomed with spiky microphones, like a cactus plant. A couple of large speakers attached to tall metal stands aimed toward the crowd. About a dozen boys in Little League uniforms stood near the first-base dugout with four men who must have been their coaches. Just beyond, on the bleachers, members of a local school band, dressed in smart navy-blue-and-white uniforms, were tuning up.

The print press, about two dozen, milled on the third base side. Hunter joined them reluctantly, knowing what was coming.

"Well, well, well—if it isn't the international man of mystery."

"The fake reporter has arrived to gather more fake news."

"Did the Marshals Service give you a furlough from your witness protection?"

"Careful, now, don't piss him off. He could be a mobster under alias."

"That face . . . he *does* look like a Mob enforcer, doesn't he?"

"Or maybe he's a spy."

"Yeah, but for what country?"

"Come on, the last Nazi spies died years ago."

He ignored them. He'd been trained to undergo far worse than verbal harassment, and knew that after failing to provoke a response, they'd soon lose interest. Besides, the terrorism attack had reminded him always to keep his situational awareness focused on what was happening around him.

Hunter hated crowds. Here, in the open and without a weapon, he felt naked. He stepped toward the third-base dugout, to have a bit of a protective barrier at his back.

Eyes hidden behind sunglasses, he surveyed the crowd, the expansive field beyond, and the line of apartment towers barely a quarter mile away, under the bright midday sun. Those buildings especially bothered him. He spotted counter sniper teams on several rooftops, but they had way too much to watch.

Who in hell approved this event location, anyway?

THIRTY-EIGHT

Four hundred twenty-five meters south on North Quincy Street, a large apartment building soared into the clear May sky. It towered behind a low, single-story commercial building that occupied the corner of North Quincy and Fairfax Drive. Because of that, the high-rise—unlike its neighbors—was set back about three hundred feet from Fairfax. And that setback allowed a neighboring building to block it from the view of the Secret Service's rooftop counter-snipers, who were positioned farther down Fairfax.

All along the broad front of the massive building, balconies faced Quincy Park. These stood exposed to the eyes of agents in the park, who were watching the buildings through binoculars. However, another set of balconies, much harder to see, clung to the eastern side of the building above North Quincy Street. These offered only narrow, end-on views toward the park.

For Lasher, though, their three-foot width was quite enough.

He lay prone on the seventeenth-floor apartment balcony, which he'd made a little more comfortable with pillows taken from the bedroom. He had hung large brown bath towels over its railings to obscure his presence. In hands covered by shooting gloves was his newest toy: a Desert Tactical Arms SRS—a compact, bolt-action sniper rifle in .308 Winchester. He had zeroed and fired it at a local range, delighted that it lived up to its impressive accuracy claims. The weapon rested nice and steady on its front bipod as he tracked across the baseball field through a Schmidt & Bender 5-25x scope.

Trammel sure had a right to worry about Helm's popularity. Thousands had shown up to see him, mostly families and their kids. They flowed like a slow-moving amoeba up to the rope line, where dozens of cops and Secret Service agents stood to keep them back. Up here, he could hear the band in the bleachers clearly, their brass and drums reverberating off the walls of the buildings around him. On the platform to the left of home plate, an American flag flapped in the breeze. He'd have to pay attention to that, although at this distance, and with the accuracy of the rifle, a little wind shouldn't make more than an inch of difference.

Before selecting this building from several options, Lasher had checked online apartment review sites and found out security here was lax. Wearing a disguise and a well-known delivery company's uniform, which he'd bought second-hand on eBay, he carried his box, covered with all the right shipping labels, right past the guy at the front desk. He started his search for an appropriate apartment on the top floor, knocking on the doors of those with balconies overlooking North Quincy. If the unit was occupied by a family, he pretended he'd gotten the wrong address and left, going down one floor and trying again. On the 17th floor, an elderly man opened the door. Once assured that the old gent was living alone, Lasher raised his silenced pistol to the man's face and shot him.

Inside, he dragged the body into the bedroom. Next, he set up his firing position on the balcony. Back inside, he opened the box and retrieved the rifle, scope and bipod. He took his time preparing and checking it out. At 1100 hours, he wrapped it in a blanket, carried it outside, and settled down into position.

He had told Trammel that—given the risk, plus the likelihood that he would be hunted for the rest of his days—this job would be the last of his career. For that, he required an amount sufficient to make it worth his while. They negotiated for a while and finally settled on a price. Two days ago, half his fee was transferred into one of his offshore accounts. That sum alone was many times greater than anything he'd previously received for a job. When he received the rest afterward, he knew he'd be set for life.

Lasher spent some of the hour before noon fantasizing about how he would invest and spend thirty million dollars.

2

At twenty before noon, the school band broke into a medley of Sousa marches. Hunter thought the kids were really good, and so did the crowd, which cheered and clapped after each selection.

At ten minutes before noon, the band stopped and some guy who identified himself as a local radio personality took the platform as the event's emcee. He offered a boisterous welcome to the crowd, which had now swelled to around five thousand. Hunter tuned him out, focusing his attention on the crowd and all those distant windows and balconies.

He couldn't shake that tingly feeling—the one he often used to get during ops, when something wasn't quite right.

At five minutes before noon, over the voices from the platform and the chatter of the crowd, Hunter heard a commotion in the parking lot. Secret Service agents were moving about back there and calling to each other. Out on Washington Boulevard, a couple of motorcycle cops, strobes flashing, made the turn onto North Quincy and rolled past the lot entrance. Behind them, a procession of three black Chevy Suburbans turned in and pulled up behind the tarp-covered backstop. Agents from the lead and follow cars emerged and swarmed around the middle vehicle.

Lasher watched the line of vehicles approach the site from the north along Washington Boulevard. He lowered his head to the scope again, tracing what would be their route entering the parking lot behind home plate, then his target's path on foot around the backstop to where the ceremony would take place. The scope's reticle marks crawled across the faces of the waiting Secret Service agents, then over to where the media had gathered, then back toward—

He felt a jolt of recognition—then swept the scope back toward the cluster of reporters, settling on a face.

"Oh . . . my . . . God," he murmured aloud.

His breathing quickened. This was just too good to be true.

Roger Helm *and* Dylan Hunter.

He would get a "two-fer". . . and so would Trammel. Maybe he could even talk the old bastard out of a few more millions, as a bonus.

He had to adapt his plan on the fly. During the coming moments, it would be necessary to keep track of the relative positions of both targets. His primary objective was Helm, so it was crucial to take him out first. Then he'd have to immediately swing over and fire at Hunter, before the man realized what was happening and could react. With luck, though, the horror of what was happening would just begin to dawn on Hunter when he, too, would feel a round smash into him. That would be *perfect.*

Lasher suddenly wished he had selected a semi-auto sniper rifle rather than the bolt-action SRS. Fast as he was, chambering the second round by hand, then re-aiming and firing, would slow him down a bit. Maybe a second between shots, or even a tad more.

He raised his head, watched the black Suburbans enter the lot and disappear behind the tarp they'd hung on the backstop. He readjusted his ear protectors. Lowered his eye to the scope once more. Established a firm cheek weld against the stock. Worked on steadying his breathing.

That's right . . . breathe . . .

He had to remain calm, now. There would be years to savor this moment, the greatest of his life—the moment he not only changed history, but finally beat his hated rival . . .

He moved the scope to where Roger Helm would emerge from behind the backstop and enter the baseball field.

Flicked off the safety.

Moved his index finger from the side of the trigger guard and onto the trigger . . .

"And now, everyone, the moment you've been waiting for. On behalf of all our teams, their parents, and every one of you who enjoys America's pastime, I'm honored to introduce a friend of our community and a great benefactor of our youth . . . ROGER HELM!"

At this, the band struck up some fanfare Hunter didn't recognize, and the crowd began to cheer and applaud enthusiastically. He stepped forward to the near end of the dugout to see better. Surrounded by a knot of agents, Helm emerged from the back door of his SUV, and together they strode briskly toward the pathway around the backstop. Two agents moved in front of him as they emerged onto the field.

The reporters and photographers clustered just behind Hunter suddenly surged forward, and he found himself in their midst.

"Damn it!"

Lasher watched helplessly as the target stepped out from behind the tarp with two agents in front of him. As the man waved to the crowd and made the turn for the platform, a third stepped up beside him and kept pace.

He didn't have a clear shot.

He swung the rifle a few degrees, noting Hunter's new, closer position at the end of the dugout, then swept it back onto the candidate. He was still blocked by the agents.

He fought to keep his frustration in check.

Patience . . . just a few more seconds . . . right after he steps onto the platform . . .

Jostled by the mob of reporters, Hunter moved back a few steps to let them to pass. Unable to shake his feeling, he watched the emcee move to the edge of the platform to greet Helm as he approached. Then the protective detail split off to take their posts. The candidate hopped up onto the platform and into the immediate embrace of the emcee. They separated, shook hands, and the host swung him around to face the crowd, raising his arm in triumph, like a referee declaring the winner of a boxing match.

Roger Helm stood there, every inch a leader—tall, commanding, vibrant, handsome in his dark suit. He turned his gray-blond head—then somehow spotted Hunter standing in front of the dugout. His grin broadened as he pivoted and pointed at him.

Hunter smiled and was raising his own hand in response when the shot rang out.

Lasher watched the target hop up on the platform, and he was about to fire when the host stepped forward to grab him in a bear hug.

He clenched his teeth. Drew a breath, let half of it out, held the rest.

Wait . . .

The two men separated, and the host spun him and raised his arm.

Steady now . . .

The scope's crosshairs settled in the middle of the target's chest as he turned his head to the right.

Squeeze . . .

He felt the trigger snap and the blast. Not waiting to watch the hit, he worked the bolt to chamber a new round as he swung the muzzle toward the end of the dugout . . .

Hunter wasn't there.

He swung farther right and found him a few steps away, in front of the dugout.

The crosshairs settled on his head.

Squeeze . . .

Hunter saw Helm take the impact, then heard the distant *crack* above the din.

Only because the disquieting feeling had put him on edge did he know at once what was happening, and immediately stepped toward the platform.

That motion saved him. A second shot sizzled just inches past his head to strike the top of the dugout behind him. Already in motion, he dropped instinctively, a habit instilled during firefights while embedded with operators in Afghanistan. A third shot whistled by in front of him—right where he would have been had he continued moving forward—and smacked into the cinder block interior wall of the dugout.

Without thought, he rolled to his right, tumbling down the dugout steps as a fourth shot kicked up a dirt geyser where he had been half a second before.

He pressed himself as flat as he could against the bottom step while screams filled the air outside. It took several seconds for his conscious brain to catch up with his subconscious and realize that *he* had been targeted, too—

—and several seconds more to realize what that meant.

3

Lasher cursed as his second target vanished from view into the dugout.

But he had no time to waste on anger. He'd fired four rounds, and amid the panicked, stampeding mob out there, highly trained agents would waste no time heading this way and blocking all escape routes.

He had to exfil, fast.

Staying low, he scrambled back through the open door of the balcony. Inside, he leaped to his feet, popped off the bipod, and tossed it, his ear protectors, and the rifle back into the box he'd left open on the sofa. He tugged the uniform jacket down in the back to cover his Glock. Holding the box shut, he left the apartment, walked quickly to the stairwell exit, then rushed down as fast as he could. His legs were burning and he was breathing hard when he emerged on the ground floor. He walked as steadily and coolly as he could toward the lobby entrance.

"Have a nice day," the guy at the desk called out from behind him.

"You too," he managed, not looking back.

Outside, he walked another block south, into the underground garage where he'd left his rental. He tossed the box onto the back seat, pulled the Glock from its holster and left it under a towel on the passenger seat.

He exited the garage and turned west. Around him the streets echoed with the wail of sirens. He drove cautiously, obeying all traffic rules, listening to the police scanner on the passenger floor, following his pre-planned, circuitous route to the chain hotel near Bailey's Crossroads.

Back in his room, he turned on the television.

Only then did he learn that Roger Helm, though gravely wounded, was still clinging to life.

PART III

THIRTY-NINE

"What are *you* doing back here?"

Dan Adair stood in his doorway, hands on hips.

Cronin was tired. The long drive back here from Alexandria had begun at six a.m. Saturday was his day off, so he was off the clock and not getting paid for this, and he was in no mood for attitude.

"I have more questions."

"Well, Detective, that's too damned bad, because I have no more answers." Adair started to close the door on him.

"It's about your son, Will."

Adair stopped in mid-motion.

"What about him?"

"Let me come in and I'll tell you."

Adair appraised him for a moment.

"All right."

"If they're here, you might want to have Will and your wife sit in on this."

Adair summoned them, and they settled in again in the den, in the same seats as before. A cup of coffee and pages of a newspaper lay on a table next to Adair's recliner, and the TV was on in the background, muted.

"You had something to tell us about Will," Adair said, his voice stern. He didn't lounge back in his recliner, but sat forward, sinewy arms folded across his chest.

Cronin glanced at the kid, whose eyes widened.

"Digging through files, I found notes I tracked back to a federal prosecutor who was investigating WildJustice. When I contacted her office, I found out they had questioned Will about his involvement with Boggs and his group. Which surprised me, since that connection never came out in any court filings or in the media. Turns out she was itching to prosecute your son here as an accessory to a criminal conspiracy. So you hired an attorney, and he cut a deal with her—that Will would tell the feds everything he knew about WildJustice, in exchange for immunity from prosecution. They also promised to keep it out of the papers."

Nan Adair looked panicked. Will looked stricken.

Adair looked mad.

"What of it?" he snapped.

Cronin nodded toward the young man. "So on top of everything we discussed before, now I find out your kid was in up to his eyeballs with Boggs and his group—the very same people who were threatening you. But now the feds are protecting him. Seems to me that a lot more is going on here than you told me, Mr. Adair."

"Then why don't you go ask the feds about it?"

Cronin had come here to press hard and get answers, and now was the time.

"Look. Let's stop playing games. You all know why I'm here. We just haven't said it out loud. *Dylan Hunter.* Our task force has been investigating his possible involvement with the vigilante killing spree around D.C. since last year. Hunter was writing about the criminals who later turned up dead, and his articles were left at the crime scenes. Then he starts writing about Boggs and his gang. And he comes here and meets with you people, who Boggs was threatening. And you introduce him to the scientist who Boggs later blew up. Hunter attends the funeral—and then Boggs tries to blow *him* up. All of a sudden, Boggs and his pal are found murdered, too, and the tire prints out there match the same model ATV you own."

He watched them exchange glances, and pushed on.

"Know what I think? I think you know all about him, and you're covering for him. Dylan Hunter was here—you admitted that—and I think that to protect you, and to avenge that murdered scientist, he went after Boggs and Nash. I think he borrowed your ATV to go out in the woods and kill them. And I think you helped him—which makes you accessories to murder."

"That's crazy!" Adair shouted. "And you don't have a lick of evidence to support your—"

"Here's what I *do* have, Mr. Adair." He pointed at Will. "I have access to files proving your son was conspiring with those terrorists and murderers. The feds promised to keep that stuff quiet and out of the papers. But *I* didn't."

Adair leaped to his feet.

"What kind of bastard are you? You barge in here and threaten us, and for what? Why aren't you doing your job and chasing real killers?"

"That's exactly what I'm doing. Chasing a real killer. And to protect him, you've been stonewalling me, lying to me. So if you don't want me—"

He heard Nan Adair gasp. She was looking toward the TV screen, her hand raised to her mouth.

Cronin looked, too. Felt his own shock.

Adair grabbed the remote from the table beside his chair and turned up the volume.

2

They sat paralyzed for the next ten minutes, not moving or speaking, just watching and listening. Reporters described the chaos on the baseball field after shots were fired, striking candidate Roger Helm. He had been rushed away by ambulance, and early reports from the hospital weren't good. They began to show cell phone videos of the chaos—the crowd panicking and stampeding, people falling and getting trampled, parents huddling protectively over kids, agents drawing weapons, reporters diving for cover.

The network news anchor narrated the reports coming in.

"*After the first shot hit the candidate, the next three apparently were aimed at members of the media. Multiple eyewitnesses report that those shots seemed to strike near the third-base dugout, where reporters had gathered. We have an unconfirmed report that the shots narrowly missed one journalist, tentatively identified as Dylan Hunter of the* Capitol Inquirer . . ."

The Adairs gasped. Nan whimpered, "Oh no!"

Cronin could only stare.

"*. . . appears to be unharmed. Incredibly, despite injuries arising from people being trampled in the panic, we have no reports so far that the shots hit anyone other than Roger Helm . . .*"

Cronin finally spoke.

"Excuse me. I know this timing is terrible. But I have a long drive ahead of me. We need to finish our conversation."

Adair looked at him. "You're right. We do need to finish this. Nan, Will, would you excuse us, please? Maybe continue watching this in another room?"

They got up without a word and left, seeming eager to.

Adair muted the TV again and rocked back in the recliner. He hooked a thumb toward the screen.

"You want the truth about that guy? The *whole* truth?" His gaze tracked around the den. "All right. I'm a pretty good judge of character. I sense you are a fair man, Detective. My gut tells me justice matters to you. So I'm going to gamble on your character. I'm going to take the risk that after you hear me, you're going to do the right thing. Let me tell you the truth about Dylan Hunter."

And he did.

Twenty minutes later, Adair finished.

"So there you have it, Detective. Right here, in this room, this so-called *murderer* you've been hunting risked his life to save my family and me. We all came within seconds of being blown up. He and Annie, both of them, almost *died* saving us. They put it all on the line for us, when the entire goddamned government was out to get us, and when nobody in law enforcement did a goddamned thing to help us.

"But here you are, still trying to nail him. And for what? Because this man who saved our lives killed a *terrorist*—and maybe some other cold-blooded murderers, too."

He snorted, shaking his head with contempt.

"All right, I promised you the truth, and there you have it. As for what you do with it—again, I'm gambling on your character. But I won't promise you the same truth if you try to drag me into a courtroom. No, I'll lie through my teeth to protect Dylan and Annie. So will my family. And we'll do it without the least bit of guilt, or any fear about what might happen to us. Because, far as I can see, you still have zero evidence against him. All you've got is what I just told you, which wasn't under oath. And it would be your word against mine, anyway.

"You want to persecute us now for our loyalty to him? You want to threaten to expose Will if we don't turn against him? You think you can get any jury to find Dylan Hunter guilty of anything he's done? Go ahead and try."

Adair pulled himself to his feet. His voice lost its harshness.

"But looking at you, I don't take you for a complete fool. In fact, I think you are basically a good guy, Detective. So I have a sincere piece of advice for you."

Cronin stood, too.

"And what's that?" he asked, quietly.

"Stop chasing other good guys."

3

Back in Bethesda, Hunter disguised himself and took the stairwell down to "Wayne Grayson's" apartment. There he fetched an encrypted sat phone from the hidden vault and, standing near the window, used it to reach Garrett on his own special device. Then told him about his presence at the shooting.

"You saw the whole thing go down, then?"

"Not just that. Grant, nobody knows this except me, yet, but Helm wasn't the only one targeted today. So was I."

"*You?*"

"After the first shot hit him, the next three missed me by inches—and only because I was moving erratically. There was no question the shooter had singled me out and was trying to nail me, too. Which means he almost certainly had to be Lasher."

"Well, well. That puts everything in a whole new light, doesn't it."

"Not really. If you accept that the CAP bombing was instigated by the Russians, then I see them behind this, too, using Lasher."

He heard Garrett's long, low whistle.

"I didn't want to believe that, you know. But I've gotten some background on the Chechen from our foreign partners. It turns out that an MI6 asset in the FSB says Shishani was on their payroll as a confidential informant burrowed in the Chechen Islamist movement. The source claims he even had a hand in the Moscow apartment bombings. Which, if true, explains why he was tapped to coordinate the bombing here in D.C."

"It keeps coming back to the Kremlin, doesn't it? The only thing I wonder about Lasher is when he's doing a job for his Moscow handler, and when he's off the leash, doing things on his own. Like today. The hit on Helm—that had to be ordered up and paid for by his handler. But nobody except my editor and Helm's people knew I'd be there today, so he had no time to work me into the plan."

"You're saying you were just a target of opportunity?"

"Nothing else makes sense. The shooter must have spotted me, then decided on the spot to kill two birds with one stone—so to speak. Which confirms to me it was Lasher. I can't imagine anyone else recognizing me, or being so eager to take me out that he'd fire three times at me."

"I see your point. But think about what that means, Dylan. Leaving aside his personal hatred for you, and assuming his shooting Helm wasn't also just some kind of ego trip, it looks like the Russians are still resorting to desperate measures to affect the election outcome."

Hunter stared bleakly at an empty wall. "From the news reports, it appears they succeeded. On the way home, I heard the Helm campaign has been suspended."

"As unbelievable as it is that Moscow would dare be behind all this, I'm starting to believe you."

"The fastest way to prove it is to find Lasher—then, through him, his handler."

"If he's as good as we think, he's already in the wind."

"Only if he's finished, Grant. But I don't think so."

"Why not?"

"Because for him, I'm unfinished business."

FORTY

She opened her door to him with a worried expression.

"You scared me on the phone when you told me you were there today. Are you sure you're all right?"

"I'm okay. Physically."

He stepped in past her, not stopping for a kiss, and continued on, into the living room.

"'Physically.' What do you mean by that?"

He felt her eyes on his back as he stood there a moment. Gathering himself for this.

Always fearing it would come to this.

He took a deep breath and turned to face her.

"Please come over and sit down."

She obeyed, looking scared. She wore casual clothes, pale blue blouse and slacks. Her face was pale, too, as if she had a premonition about this—perhaps from something in his voice when he phoned ahead, telling her he had been at the shooting, that he was okay, but needed to see her.

He'd decided he had to do this during the interminable moments he lay on the floor of the dugout, crushed tight against the cold cement steps to make himself a smaller target, waiting for the next bullet, the one that could take his life.

"Dylan, for God's sake—what's wrong?"

He sat on the edge of a chair, forearms on his knees.

"Annie . . . this can't work. It can't continue."

She wrinkled her brows, confused.

"Dylan, what are you saying? What are you talking about?"

"I'm talking about us. I'm talking about our future together."

He saw numbed shock in those eyes now. Her lips parted, then closed, as she searched for words.

"But . . . *why?*"

"For the same reasons as before."

"I . . . I thought we had already resolved everything!"

"I thought so, too. Back at the beginning, *you* were the one with the doubts. It took you a long time to make peace with my nature—with me being a 'sheepdog,' as Grant says. But when you started talking about a family, it forced me to think about what that would mean. About what a life with someone like me would really mean for you—and for our kids."

"Dylan, wait! You need to—"

"No, please, let me talk. I have agonized about this a long time, and you have to hear me out. Think about it, Annie. In just the eight short months we've been together, I was nearly killed by Adrian Wulfe—and, because of me, he came within minutes of killing you, too. Then there was Boggs. He almost killed me, and except for you, he would have. But solely because of my involvement with him, he came within a split-second of killing you—and then his partner nearly killed you, too. Two months ago, a guy in Dixon's gang almost nailed me with a shot that missed me by inches. Only three weeks ago, I was nearly blown up by terrorists. And just today, Lasher fired three times at me, and each bullet also missed me only by inches."

"He almost *shot* you?"

He nodded. "Think about that, and all those other times. Think of how you nearly died three times. Think of how incredibly lucky I've been not to have been killed already. Or arrested, with Cronin trying to nail me for murder. Or simply exposed. Now everyone knows I'm not who I say I am, and because of that they'll be hounding me forever, trying to find out about me. And hounding *us*, if we're together.

"Ask yourself what we could look forward to. Having to hide, constantly looking over our shoulders for some new Lasher, or Boggs, or Wulfe, or even a Cronin. You want kids, but what could *they* look forward to? Annie, that is no way to live."

"Damn it, Dylan! If you really feel this way, why don't you just *stop?*"

He gazed at her stunning face, now ravaged by anguish and anger, hating that his words were causing her so much pain.

"Because I can't, Annie."

"You mean, *won't*. You could if you wanted to. But you don't want to. What I want to know is *why*. Why do you want to do this?"

He lowered his eyes toward the floor, toward the tangled grain patterns in the wood.

"You're wrong about that. About me *wanting* to do it. I *hate* doing these things. The only reason I do them, is that I would hate myself even more if I didn't."

He raised his head. Forced himself up into that cold, high place, where nothing mattered except what he had to do.

"Over a year ago, I thought about Muller and the damage he did to me, and to the good people who died because of him. It was intolerable that he was alive, and that the system would *keep* him alive. So I decided I had to do something about that. And after that—with Susie and Arthur, and the Jacksons, and Adam Silva, and the Adair family, and so many more—it was the same. They cried out for justice, but nobody was listening. And I couldn't walk away."

"I know. I understand that. And I accept that, and I love you for it. You are always going to react like a sheepdog."

He shook his head. "But it's become more than just reacting, Annie."

"What do you mean, 'more'?"

"Today I watched a great man take a bullet—precisely because he *is* a great man. Monsters wanted him dead, because he stood in their way. Not long ago, I watched two other monsters park a truck bomb yards from me, almost killing me and a room full of good people. But they did slaughter many others, including a lovely mother and her beautiful baby. I'd just met them on the street minutes earlier. And it only confirmed what I knew—that what I had been doing was not enough.

"It started to change for me when I realized Ashton Conn, and other powerful, politically connected people, were willing to do *anything*, including killing innocent people, to seize and keep power. People high up in our government—and in others. People who are protected. People who are untouchable." He paused to stress his next words. "Or *were* untouchable—before I came along and decided to make war on them."

"*War?* You're making *war?* All by yourself, like some kind of one-man army?"

"I know it sounds grandiose and ridiculous. But actually, I'm just going back to the war I was fighting before I left the Agency. That war had an official seal of approval. This one doesn't. But it's the same war. Because I'm looking at what is happening around us, even today, and I see the country hanging by a thread. Evil people are taking charge, and good people are too terrified and confused and powerless to stop them."

He straightened in the chair.

"Annie, I've had to go back to war, not because I want to, but because it has to be done. Because only a handful of people could do what needs to be done—but they won't. Because I can—and I will." He paused. "And because I'm very good at it."

She stared at him, incredulous. "You're right. It *is* ridiculous. No—it's *crazy*. Because you can't possibly win."

"I know that, too," he said. "I'm a realist. Maybe, if I'm lucky, I can beat them this time. Maybe the next, too. But to survive for long, I'd have to stay lucky and be perfect. No accidents, no mistakes. Which is impossible. I know it can't last."

She stormed to her feet. "So this is a *suicide mission?*"

He shook his head as he rose to face her.

"You know me better than that," he said gently. "I want to live, Annie. I desperately want to live. I look at you, and you're everything a man like me could want to live for."

He saw her lips start to tremble.

"But it will be suicide for me if I *don't* do this," he went on. "Suicide of a different kind—if I think I can make a difference, but choose not to try. I wouldn't be the same man anymore, not the kind of man . . . you could care for."

She began to cry. It became harder to stay in his cold, high place.

"Annie Woods, you are young, and beautiful, and brilliant, and talented, and you have everything to live for. You told me your dreams. You have a right to be with a husband who can make them come true. Who can give you a normal life—a happy home, kids to raise and love, the chance to watch and enjoy them as they play, and learn, and grow. You have a right to savor the looks on their faces when you take them to the zoo and on picnics, and teach them to walk, and read, and swim. To hug them when they get on the bus to kindergarten and school, and to kiss them when they bring home good grades, and to cheer them in school plays and baseball games. To teach them how to drive, and give them advice when they start to date. You have a right to cry when they drive off to college, and cry at their weddings, and cry when they give you grandkids.

"You could never have any of that with me, Annie. There's no way I can pretend to myself anymore that I will ever have a normal family life. I see too clearly where mine is headed, and where it will end."

She stood shaking, now, tears streaming down her cheeks. He stepped closer to her, but didn't try to touch her. He spoke quietly.

"That night, months ago, outside Susie's house, when I asked you out on our first date—even then there was this voice in my head telling me I was a fool, that it was so wrong to do that—that it couldn't possibly work out, that we would only get hurt. But as I looked at you there, under the street lights, it felt magical, and I felt completely helpless. So I refused to listen to that voice. I charged ahead, hoping and pretending that everything would somehow turn out okay.

"Instead, I've nearly gotten you killed, three different times. I just can't risk that anymore. I *won't* let it happen again. And I won't deprive you of the kind of life you deserve."

He had to stop, gather strength. Because the next words were the hardest of his life.

"That's why you have to let me go, Annie."

He knew he had to make the break symbolic, so it would become real for both of them. He held out his hand, palm up.

"Annie," he said softly, "I am so sorry. But you should give me back the engagement ring."

He heard a little gasp. He knew they were both remembering the last time this happened—the night when *she* had tried to end it, and handed him the ring willingly.

She raised her hand slowly, staring at the ring. Then back at him, through the tears.

Shook her head.

"No," she whispered.

"Annie—please," he said. "You need to return the ring. Because our engagement is—"

"No!" She recoiled from him, covering the ring with her other hand, protectively. "No, it's not! *I* have a say in this. *I* get to decide what will make me happy. *I* get to decide what kind of risks I am willing to take, and what kind of a future I want. It's over when *I* say it's over. And no—it's *not* over!"

"Annie, I—"

"I said, *no!* Now get out, Dylan!"

Sobbing and shaking, she turned her back on him.

He opened his mouth to speak. To reassure her that he still loved her, that he always would.

Then stopped, realizing that would be the cruelest thing he could possibly say.

He found his way to her door, through the sudden blur in his own eyes.

Driving back to his apartment, he told himself, again and again, why he had to do this.

Tried to convince himself that it was the only way.

Repeated the lesson he had been taught by his father, Big Mike, so long ago . . .

You have to protect her, Matt. It's what a man does.

A man protects his woman, no matter what . . .

FORTY-ONE

Twenty-One Years Earlier

Like him, she was seventeen and a high school junior. Like him, she was dark-haired, self-confident, and highly intelligent.

Most unlike him, though, she was popular and extroverted.

Still, Matt Malone was smitten by Jennifer Evans.

The initial, natural attraction was her stunning beauty. Jennifer Evans had the face of a budding movie star: long brown hair framing high cheekbones, full lips, and dark eyes that slanted—like a cat's, he thought. Her body was like a work of art. The previous summer, during a vacation journey through New England, he and his parents had visited the studio of the late sculptor Daniel Chester French. Matt stood transfixed before *Andromeda*, French's breathtaking nude statue of the Greek goddess. Jennifer could have been his model.

Another part of his fascination lay in their differences—in the mesmerizing mystery of a girl of cool beauty, who seemed a rare match for him in intellect and wit, yet so different in personality. She, the dazzling center of attention; he, the loner: not shy or socially awkward, just emotionally self-sufficient and comfortably preoccupied with private pursuits. She, the frequent lead in school theater productions and musicals, spotlighted because of her extraordinary looks and angelic soprano voice; he, usually in some private corner, buried in a book, trying to satisfy an ever-raging and wide-ranging curiosity.

Perhaps what intrigued him most, though, was her anachronistic sense of *style*. Jennifer projected sexuality, but not in the typical trashy way. She shunned the heavy makeup, gaudy bangles, hoop earrings, and teased hair of the day, dressing with the classy femininity he associated with French actresses. Her one stylistic concession to youth was her hemlines.

Matt sensed that she was aware of him, as well. It surprised him. Self-sufficient and private, he didn't understand why girls seemed to find him interesting. When he appeared at gymnastic and swim meets, they would cheer and even whistle from the bleachers. During his sophomore year, they began to flirt with him frequently and aggressively; he responded by dating rarely and selectively. But he found he just didn't have much in common with them. His early experiences with the opposite sex, and with sex itself, left him feeling increasingly wistful and lonely.

Until he struck up a conversation with Jennifer during a gymnastics event early his junior year. She had paused not far from him after performing a floor routine, and he sensed it was deliberate. He ventured a compliment, and she surprised him by beaming and complimenting him in return. Conversing with her was easy. She had an intelligent sense of humor and he enjoyed their repartee. Within minutes, they had exchanged phone numbers. Within days, he asked her out.

Within two weeks, they were a couple.

Matt's parents were pleased when, over dinner and somewhat sheepishly, he told them about her.

"About time," his father said, eyes twinkling. Then he went back to tackling his rib roast.

"So, what does she look like?" his mother asked. "Do you have a picture?"

He pulled out his wallet and handed her the small school photo Jennifer had given him.

"Oh! She's a doll!" she exclaimed. "Here Mike, take a look."

Big Mike leaned over. Squinted. Raised a brow. Then glanced at him, mischief in his eyes.

"Way to *go*, Matt!"

"Stop that," his mother protested. "See? You're embarrassing him."

"Oh, come on, Helen. I'm complimenting him. Son, you got yourself a real babe." He shot a playful look at his wife. "Not nearly as pretty as this one, of course. But she'll do."

His mother laughed, dimpling up.

"Mom *is* beautiful," Matt said, meaning it. His mother looked something like that Italian actress, Isabella Rossellini.

"Just be glad you got your looks from her. If you took after me, this young lady wouldn't be giving you the time of day."

2

Jennifer's family, like his own, was wealthy. Their estates were barely a mile apart in Fox Chapel, an upscale Pittsburgh suburb. Her parents owned some horses, and they had given one to their daughter for her birthday. She was taking riding lessons and told Matt she hoped eventually to enter equestrian competitions.

There was a loft above the horse barn, and that is where they secretly met. Lying in each other's arms under blankets smuggled from her room, they talked about their lives, their travels, their interests, their dreams. He was delighted that she knew so much about the arts, and that they could discuss painting, films, plays, and literature. But swept up in the intense, intoxicating infatuation of first love, Matt overlooked the differences in their personal values and priorities.

"You're *such* a bookworm, Matt. You need to get out more and have fun."

"But I like learning about things like history and politics. For me, that *is* fun."

"*Borrrr*-ing!" She wrinkled her nose; it made her look adorably cute. "If you didn't have such a hot body, you'd be no fun at all."

"You're the one with the hot body." He wriggled against her.

"You really think so?" she asked, suddenly serious.

It astonished him. "You are kidding, right? Jen, you are drop-dead gorgeous."

She smiled and snuggled against him. He loved her warmth and the scent of her skin.

"So, tomorrow is Saturday," he said, nuzzling her hair. "I thought we could go see a movie."

He felt her shoulders shrug beneath the thick comforter. "I suppose."

"What, then? How about a concert?"

"Sure. If there's a decent band in town."

"I meant the Pittsburgh Symphony. They've got a great program: Rachmaninoff's Second Symphony, and—"

"The *symphony?*" She giggled. "I used to go with my folks a lot. But these days I'm not in the mood to sit still for two hours in Heinz Hall. Sitting still isn't *me*. I need to *move.*" She narrowed her cat-like eyes and squirmed against him. "Know what I mean, big fella?"

He grinned. "I guess I do."

3

Just before the Christmas break, one of their classmates, a girl named Joan, told Jennifer and a select group of friends that they were invited to a holiday party at her house. Jennifer told Matt she wanted them both to go. He balked at first; he wasn't comfortable at parties, where people tended to become loud, stupid, and obnoxious. Nor was he much of a dancer—at least, not when attempting what passed for dancing these days. But he knew *she* loved to dance, and when she started complaining again about him being boring, he sighed and agreed to go along, just to keep her happy.

Matt had recently gotten his driver's license, and—with savings from three years of summer and part-time jobs—bought a used black Camaro in decent shape. During the days before the party, he spent a lot of time trying to make it look immaculate for her. As for what to wear, he decided on his comfortable corduroy sports jacket over a polo shirt, jeans, and low-cut boots—a combination he knew she loved.

That Saturday evening he picked her up at her home. She came to the door in a short brown skirt, a snug tan sweater, and matching heels. Her parents waved from the living room and wished them a good time.

A few minutes later, they rolled up to an isolated home, large and lavish, also in Fox Chapel. They followed loud music inside, then down into a big basement rec room. It was decorated with red and green crepe paper, suspended paper snowflakes and candy canes, strings of flashing colored lights, an artificial Christmas tree in one corner, and a foam-plastic snowman in another. Food and beverage tables lined one of the walls.

In the middle of the floor, about seventy-five of their classmates were jumping around to the thumping, deafening racket of a local band on the far side of the room, playing what Matt knew had to be a New Wave hit. The bizarre gyrations conjured the sudden memory of a World War One documentary, and a scene showing spasms induced by nerve gas.

Within minutes he was shocked to learn that there was no adult supervision; Joan, laughing, told him her parents had gone out to dinner and would be gone for at least three hours.

Jennifer tugged him out into the room and joined in the frenzy. He stood there, feeling awkward and embarrassed, neither knowing what to do nor wanting to. She frowned at him and yelled *"Come on! Dance with me!"*—her shout barely audible in the din. He shook his head, leaned in and shouted near her ear, *"Can I get you something to drink?"* She shook her own head, scowling at him, and then turned away, bouncing into the middle of the mass.

Matt stared at her, then stepped away, heading for the refreshment table. He filled a paper plate with some fried things he didn't recognize, poured himself ginger ale from a plastic bottle, and then looked around. He saw some empty folding chairs against the nearby wall, and settled into one.

He watched Jennifer gyrating sinuously in the middle of the pack, quickly surrounded by guys giving her plenty of attention, tossing her hair back and smiling at them. He watched, picking at the food on his plate absently, numbly, miserably, knowing he had several hours of this torture to endure.

After a while, during a pause in the music, she came back to him, pouting.

"What's wrong, Matt? Why don't you want to dance with me?"

"Jen, that sort of dancing—it's just not my thing."

She reached down, grabbed his hand. "Oh, come on—just try. You'll get into it."

He pulled away. "I don't want to." He nodded toward the band. "This isn't what I expected."

Her dark eyes flared.

"Well, *I* came here to dance and have a good time. If you want to just sit here, then go ahead."

She stalked back into the middle of the crowd.

Matt sat watching her, watching all of them, feeling like an alien life form. He had never felt more alone in his life.

He noticed that one guy in particular, a big, blond football jock named Chris Lynch, danced over to her and leaned down to say something. She started to smile at him—then dance with him.

She wouldn't look his way.

Matt felt his jaw and fists clenching.

After the first hour, the band took a break. The place had become uncomfortably warm. Everybody started to filter up the stairs and outside into the chill air to cool off.

He watched her go upstairs, followed by Lynch.

Furious, he got up and followed, but was caught behind a mass of people at the bottom of the stairs. It was a couple of minutes before he could get outside.

He looked around. She was nowhere to be seen.

He asked several people, "Have you seen where Jen went off to?" They just shrugged.

His anger was boiling over. He walked down toward where all the cars were parked along the driveway. Then he spotted her with him, leaning against what had to be his car. His hand was resting on her shoulder, and he had just passed her what looked like a small bottle of liquor.

He stalked over.

"All right, Jen. What the hell is going on?"

Lynch straightened and turned toward him. "What's it to you, asshole? Beat it."

"She came here with me."

He sneered, squeezing her shoulder. "Doesn't seem like she's going home with you."

Matt clenched his fists and stepped toward him. She moved between them.

"No! Stop!" She pressed her hand, the one without the bottle, against his chest. "Matt, take it easy!"

"Let him try," Lynch snarled, clenching his own fists.

"Chris, you stop it, too! We all came here to have a good time!"

"*That*," Matt pointed at Lynch, "is what you consider to be a good time?"

"I just want to dance, and you don't, and Chris does."

"Oh?" He tapped the bottle she held. "Looks like you have more than dancing in mind."

Her anger flared up again. "That's not true! How can you say that?"

"You know this guy's reputation. What am I *supposed* to think?"

"You know *me* better than that!"

He stared at her, feeling his world crumble.

"I'm wondering if I know you at all."

He took a step back, shaking with rage, looking at both of them.

"Seems you've made your choice, Jen."

He turned and strode away.

"Matt!" she shouted after him. "Matt, please wait!"

He didn't.

When he arrived home, his mother was in the living room watching TV. She glanced at the clock on the mantel, then at him with a worried look.

"Home so soon?"

He paused, torn between the pride of privacy and wanting to unburden himself.

Pride won.

"I don't want to talk about it. I'm going to bed."

4

He didn't sleep that night. He lay in the dark, suspended between rage and tears, staring at the ceiling as if it were a movie screen, playing the events of the evening over and over. He tried not to imagine what she did with him after he left her there, but he couldn't help it. He knew he was torturing himself, but he couldn't stop.

He dreaded the prospect of going to school on Monday—of having to face her, and him, and their smirks, and the snickers and whispers of everyone else.

Somewhere just before dawn, exhausted and emotionally spent, he decided what he would do.

He would keep his dignity. He would simply ignore her, and him—no matter what they did or said. They, and everyone else, would provoke no reaction from him at all. He would treat this as if it didn't matter.

Even if it did . . .

He met the dawn taking pride in one small victory.

He had not cried. What she had done to him did not make him cry. No woman would ever make him cry . . .

"Matt!"

A hand on his shoulder, shaking him awake.

"What?" He felt punchy, confused.

He rolled over and blinked.

His father's face, looming above. Looking grave.

"Matt, get up and get dressed."

"What's happening? Is Mom okay?"

"She's fine. We just have to talk."

He left the room. Matt scrambled out of bed and into his clothes, then hurried downstairs. He found them both in the living room. His mother was bent forward, her face in her hands. Big Mike stood in the middle of the room, his hands jammed in his pockets. His face looked tight, as if he were trying to keep a lid on a pot about to boil over. He nodded to a chair.

Matt sat, knowing something terrible had happened, and somehow it involved him.

"We just got a call from Jennifer's parents. She's in the hospital."

"What?"

"They say that you left her at the party last night. So she got a ride with some other guy. And he *beat* and *raped* her."

He spat out both words. Each hit him like a slap.

"They want to know what the *hell* happened last night, Matt—and so do your mother and I. We want to know why the girl you took to a party wound up with a *rapist.*"

He couldn't speak. He knew his mouth was open and moving, but no sounds came out. He felt paralyzed, dizzy.

He shook his head once, trying to clear it. Then again. Then again, and again, and again . . .

"*Matthew!*"

He stopped. He stared at his father's accusing, angry face—at his mother, who would not look at him.

And then he heard Jen, from somewhere behind him, shouting, "*Matt! . . . Matt, please wait!*"

And then he cried out and fell from the chair, screaming and beating the floor with his fists until he felt Big Mike's powerful arms seize him and hold him tight . . .

5

Sometime later, he didn't know how long, he found himself huddled on the sofa, and they were sitting close beside him, on either side, and she had draped some kind of throw blanket around him, because he was still quivering and feeling cold, and he felt a big steady hand on his shoulder, and a small soft hand gently rubbing his back, and she made him sip from the hot cup of tea she placed in his hand, and it was laced with something, maybe whiskey, maybe honey, too, and she told him to sip some more, and he did.

And they sat and waited, asking no questions, until eventually he understood that they were giving him time, time to pull himself together. And when he realized that, and when he felt steady enough, he began to speak. He told them all of it: what happened from the moment he picked her up at the house, and after they got to the party, and how she had behaved in front of him, and how it made him feel, and what happened when he followed them outside, and how that felt, and why he left.

"I knew what kind of person Chris was," he said in a stranger's voice, empty and flat. "But by then I was too angry to care. I just left her with him. She called after me. She said, 'Matt . . . Matt, please wait.' But I didn't wait. I didn't stop."

He stared into a blank, endless distance.

"I walked away."

6

Later that afternoon, after he had eaten something and napped for a while, Big Mike took him for a drive.

They headed north on Route 79 from the Pittsburgh area. They did not speak. Matt stared out the window of the big Chevy pickup, looking blindly, feeling empty, not knowing where they were going, not caring.

At some point he realized that the truck had stopped. He blinked. The area was familiar. Then he saw the lake, and the surrounding forest, and recognized that they were in Moraine State Park. He and his parents had come here a lot during past summers. Big Mike would take them out on his boat, and they would fish, then return to shore where they would swim a little, cook the fish, eat the picnic his mother had packed, and walk the quiet forest trails, listening to the birds and the wind stirring the leaves.

He led Matt now from the parking area down to a picnic table under a tree overlooking the lake. A cold sun was shining, and the lake surface looked glassy and brittle, as if the touch of the slightest breeze would shatter it.

Big Mike let Matt face the water, then sat beside him. He was silent only for a moment.

"First thing I want to know, Matt, is eventually you will forgive yourself for this. You can't right now. You can't even think about that. You blame yourself entirely for what happened to her. You're thinking, *If only I had come back when she called after me.*

"But there's no telling it would have made any difference. You were both upset with each other. She was trying to hurt you out there on that dance floor, and when she went off with that creep. And she succeeded. She wanted to make you jealous, to punish you for not doing everything she wanted, *her* way. I suspect she's more than a little bit spoiled, and used to always getting her way. So, yeah—maybe you come back when she calls you, and you talk her into leaving with you. But then again, maybe not. Maybe she likes guys fighting over her. Maybe she was planning to dump you. We'll never know what was on her mind, what she really planned to do. Maybe she didn't, either.

"One thing I know for sure is you had every right to be pissed off at her. You didn't deserve to be treated like that. She hurt you deliberately, and drove you off, so she brought the situation on herself."

He raised his head, appearing to be looking at the trees and sky, but Matt knew he was framing his thoughts.

"Which doesn't entirely let you off the hook, though. I think you know you made a bad choice. Once she got in the car with you last night, she became your responsibility. Women don't like to hear it, but they're a lot more vulnerable than we are, and guided by their feelings a lot more than we are, too. That's why we men can't afford to let our feelings get the better of us, no matter how much we're provoked. We have to think and take responsibility. And when we make a commitment, we have to follow through."

He rested a big, gnarled hand on Matt's arm.

"As a man, you have one big responsibility toward your woman. You have to protect her, Matt. It's what a man does."

He squeezed the arm.

"From now on, you remember that. A man protects his woman, no matter what."

7

Jennifer Evans did not return to their private school. After she was released from the hospital, her parents put her into an outpatient therapy program and transferred her into another private school in Pittsburgh.

Chris Lynch never returned, either. Arrested for the rape, he was held until trial, then sentenced to eight years in state prison.

Matt Malone sold his Camaro. Then he went to the hospital that had treated Jennifer and spoke to their billing office. He told them he wished to pay her bill in full, and explained why. The office manager had to call in an administrator. The woman was astonished, but impressed and sympathetic. When, months later, Jennifer's father inquired about the hospital bill, he was told it already had been paid by someone, anonymously.

Nobody was permitted legally to tell Matt who was providing her outpatient therapy. So he wrote to her parents. He said his failure to protect her had been unforgivable, and no apology he could offer would ever undo the harm he had allowed to happen. He asked only that they let him assume the financial burdens of any ongoing treatment she required, for as long as necessary. But he never heard back from them.

He never told Big Mike he had done these things.

He knew this was what a man does.

FORTY-TWO

"So now that he's out of the race, obviously we're shutting down all the anti-Helm ads and activities," Carver concluded. "From now on, we'll continue to say nothing but nice things about him."

Spencer had remained unusually quiet throughout the conference call. Which concerned Trammel.

"Carl," he ventured, probing for a response, "at the press conference, I thought you addressed his shooting with extraordinary sensitivity and grace."

"I agree," Carver said. "Even though you strayed off the talking points, you did a great job."

"Well, excuse me, Lucas," Spencer snapped, "but somehow I didn't think America would believe I was the least bit sincere if I *read* your canned statement of sympathy."

For a few seconds, everyone was shocked into silence.

"And your instincts were utterly correct, Carl," Trammel interjected, trying to force sincerity into his tone. "It is a credit to you that you chose to place personal authenticity and simple humanity above any other considerations."

"Well, maybe a little bit of Roger Helm must be rubbing off on me, then."

Trammel gave the silver watch another spin on his desk. He knew this sarcasm was a seed of defiance that could not be permitted to grow. Spencer would have to be handled delicately, deferentially, with a great measure of ego-massage.

"I appreciate how upsetting this is to you, Carl," he said soothingly. "We know this is not the way you would have wished to become the front-runner. However, in the face of this terrible tragedy, the nation is fortunate to have another man of character and compassion to turn to. Lucas, I think you always should take Carl's judgment and feelings into consideration when developing his speeches and public statements."

Carver immediately took the cue. "You're absolutely right. And Carl, *you* are absolutely right about authenticity. After all, this is *your* campaign. As candidate, you have to be comfortable with the messaging. I apologize for failing to seek more input from you, and I promise to do better."

Trammel heard a deep sigh.

"Well . . . I appreciate that. This whole campaign has been stressful for me." Another sigh. "I never expected things would turn out like this."

Carver and Cunningham spent the next several moments bolstering his mood by stroking his vanity. Trammel stayed out of it. For the time being, the less he made his presence felt, the better.

The conversation was winding down when he heard the intercom buzzer in the foyer. He excused himself from the call and left the study, pulling the door shut behind him. He hurried to the entrance and pressed the intercom.

"Yes?'

"Mr. Trammel?"

"It is."

"Sir, there are two gentlemen here with the Metropolitan Police Department. They said they need to speak to you on an important matter."

Trammel had been expecting this for over two weeks, wondering why it had taken them so long.

"To me?" he replied, feigning puzzlement. "Have they said what this is in regard to?"

"They have not, sir. They just said it's urgent."

"All right. Send them up."

He stood next to the door, rehearsing his answers to their questions.

2

When he opened the door, two men stood before him in sports jackets and slacks. One was black and stocky and in his fifties, the other white and slim and possibly in his late thirties.

The older man flashed a badge.

"Sir, I'm Detective Floyd Owens and this is my partner, Detective Brian Cushing. We're with the Metropolitan Police Department's Criminal Investigations Division."

"Please come in."

He led them into the living room.

"This is very nice," Cushing said, looking around and clearly impressed.

"Thank you," he replied. "Please sit there on the sofa. May I have our maid get you something to drink?"

"No thanks, we're fine, sir," Owens replied, taking his seat. Cushing took a quick glance at the Potomac through the sliding glass doorway to the balcony, then came over and joined his partner.

"So, what brings you gentlemen here on a Sunday afternoon?" Trammel said, taking his favorite chair opposite them.

"Does your wife happen to be home, sir?" Owens asked.

"I'm not sure. She and I keep such different schedules. Let me check."

He stood and called out.

"Julia! Are you home, dear?"

There was no answer.

"She appears to be out. If you prefer that she be present, perhaps I should call—"

There was a sound at the front entrance. They looked over.

"Ah," Trammel said. "There she is."

Puzzled, Julia entered the living room, unbuttoning her coat as the men seated in the room rose.

"I'm sorry, Avery. I didn't know you had a meeting planned here."

"No, this was unexpected for me, too, dear." He performed the introductions. She could tell they were delighted to meet her, though they tried not to let on. But she felt unsettled when she learned who they were.

"Detectives?" she said, hanging her coat on the back of her own chair and then sitting. "What is this all about?"

"Mr. Trammel, I asked if your wife was home because this might get a bit sensitive. If you'd prefer to speak privately—"

He waved a hand dismissively. "My wife and I have no secrets between us, Detective," he said, glancing at her with a little smile.

It was all she could do to smile in return.

Owens shrugged. "All right. Mr. Trammel, do you happen to know Emmalee Conn?"

"I do," Avery answered, nodding. "In fact, I consider her to be a friend, as I was with her late husband, Ashton."

"When is the last time you saw her?"

He looked away, his brow furrowing in concentration. "Fairly recently. Three or four weeks ago." He turned back to them. "She called with some questions about the facilities here, so I went down to her apartment to loan her a brochure and explain things."

"She lives here?" Julia asked, surprised.

"Yes," he replied, his voice and manner casual. "Since late March. I had meant to tell you about that, because I wanted to introduce the two of you." His gaze went back to the detectives. "I encountered Mrs. Conn at the senator's funeral. She was in a bad way, and not just from the loss of her husband. The bomb blast that took his life rendered their home uninhabitable. Also, they had experienced serious financial difficulties. So I arranged for her to move in here."

Cushing shot a glance at his older partner, then uncrossed his lanky legs and leaned forward.

"When you say you 'arranged' it, what do you mean—if you don't mind my asking?"

Avery sighed. "Gentlemen, you embarrass me. You see, I prefer to keep certain of my charitable acts private. But it is probably just as well that Julia knows, now." He swiveled his chair to face her. "Darling, because she had no place to stay and very little money, I leased the place for her." He shrugged. "Just until she could get back on her feet."

Even after all she knew of his betrayals, this felt like a knife in her chest. She knew Emmalee Conn's reputation; everyone did. So the secret of his affair was a mystery no more. Once again, it was all she could do to smile and nod.

"That's so sweet of you, Avery!" she said. "I can't wait to meet her." To the detectives, she added, "You may have heard that my husband is famous for his generosity."

The pair exchanged a quick look. Owens turned to them, his face blank.

"I'm afraid it won't be possible for you to meet Mrs. Conn, ma'am. I'm sorry to tell you that she is dead." He waited a beat. "Murdered."

She gasped.

"What?" Avery's eyes were wide and his mouth hung open.

The two men watched him closely, not saying anything more.

"Murdered?" He fell back in his seat, blinking, his gaze drifting off into the distance.

And suddenly she felt as if a cold hand had gripped her heart.

Avery's normal manner, even when surprised or shocked, was tightly controlled and undemonstrative. He was the sort of man who took pride in cool mastery of his emotions. This reaction was excessive, completely out of character—the manner of someone trying to role-play the expected responses in order to convince people of their authenticity.

She was scared—because she *knew* he was not shocked at all.

"Yes, sir. Detective Cushing and I are with the Homicide Branch, and we've been assigned to this case."

"How did . . ." Avery's voice trailed off. He blinked some more and looked at them again. "What happened? Who killed her?"

"We don't yet know 'who.' As for 'what': It appears she was kidnapped and assaulted. Her body was found in a stolen car, dumped near an abandoned warehouse in Maryland. She had been dead for well over a week when her body was discovered. Her purse and phone were gone. It took a while to identify her remains, and after that we've tried to keep it quiet for a bit while we ran down leads."

"Oh, God. The poor woman." He hung his head. "This is horrible . . . unbelievable."

She had to say something.

"It *is* horrible. But I don't understand why you are telling *us* this. Why are you here?"

Owens said, "We have been trying to track her movements since her husband's death. We learned from her email records that she had moved here. Then we discovered that Mr. Trammel had paid for her apartment. We spent some time questioning the staff and some other residents here, and we found out that over two weeks ago she had met a man here in the lobby for what appeared to the witnesses to be a date. While she was waiting for him, she asked some of the staff if they knew anything about a Georgetown restaurant, Petit Plaisir. And that's how—"

"What did you say?" Avery said, jerking his head up. "Did you say Petit Plaisir?"

"That's right. Does that mean something to you?"

"Yes. Yes! She had called me to ask if I could recommend a superior restaurant, and I told her that a *Post* reviewer gave that one a high rating. But I told her it was exceedingly expensive. She sounded disappointed. Again, you understand this was a woman who once could have afforded the best, but had lost everything. So, feeling sorry for her, I told her I would be pleased to make reservations for her, and that if she wished, she could take a friend—my treat."

Julia listened, incredulous—and trying not to show it.

"Okay, that would explain it," Cushing said to Owens.

"To what are you referring?" Avery asked.

"We checked out all the reservations at Petit Plaisir for the past several weeks, sir. We found you had made a reservation for April 28th for Mrs. Conn and 'friend,' billed to your card. Our investigation suggests that a man came here to pick her up on that evening, and that they dined together at the restaurant. But the waiters and hostess recall she seemed to become tipsy or maybe ill, and the man escorted her out.

We've retrieved security camera videos that show the two of them leaving here, then arriving at and later leaving the restaurant, in the same stolen car where her body was found. We haven't been able to identify the man in the video footage, though."

"So *that* is why you are here," Avery said. "You saw those financial links to me."

"Yes, sir. Now, we've found out the man who was with Mrs. Conn doesn't match your description at all. But just to settle things, do you recall where you were on the evening of April 28th?"

"I do. I certainly do. I was at a meeting in my New York office with my staff. They can vouch for my presence. I remember because I phoned Mrs. Conn from Reagan airport in the mid-afternoon, to confirm the restaurant reservations with her. I am sure I can provide you the flight information. Also, I stayed overnight at the Grand Hyatt. That too is easily confirmed."

Owens nodded. "All right, thank you. Did Mrs. Conn happen to mention the name of the person she would be having dinner with?"

He shook his head. "She did not. Or if she did, I cannot recall."

"Look, I'll be honest with you. We're puzzled about the circumstances of her death. Why does a senator's widow go off to dinner with a man driving a stolen car? On its face, it doesn't make sense. Is there anything you can think of or know about Mrs. Conn that might help us?"

She watched Avery looking around the room, as if casting about for answers. Then his expression changed.

"You remember something?" Cushing prompted.

"I—" He stopped. Then continued softly, as if arguing with himself. "No. No, that is just ugly rumor. I do not wish to dignify . . ."

"What is it?" Owens urged.

Avery met his eyes. "It is unfair to say anything negative about people no longer here to defend their reputations. Particularly when it is only rumor. So, please treat what I am about to say with discretion. When I was raising money for Ash Conn's presidential campaign, there were rumors floating about concerning the nature of his relationship with

Mrs. Conn. The scuttlebutt was that they had an 'open marriage' and often sought out other partners, sometimes complete strangers. At the time, I put little stock in any of that gossip; after all, smears are the currency of the political world . . . Still, the rumors *were* persistent."

Cushing looked at Owens again. "That explains what we found on his computer at their house."

"Then it *is* true?"

"It's still all speculation, sir. But, based on what you knew of her, do you think it's possible this man could have been someone she met casually—someone she barely knew?"

"How would I know?" He spread his hands. "It is possible, I suppose."

Avery looked at her again.

"My God. You think you know someone, and then it turns out they were not at all what you thought."

She nodded, but had to turn away. "It's hard to believe."

After they had left, Julia poured him a brandy, but then excused herself. She went to her office, locking the door behind her.

That's when she began to shake, uncontrollably.

His lies had been so fluid, so easy, so persuasive . . . to anyone who didn't know him as she did.

She had no idea how or why he might have been involved in Emmalee Conn's murder. But from what she knew of him, and had seen—hidden in his office, and exposed on his face and lips moments earlier—she had no doubt he *was* involved.

Ever since she discovered his secrets, she had been paralyzed by fear. Now she was more frightened of him than ever. But she was no longer paralyzed.

This changed everything.

She opened the top drawer of her desk and rummaged around.

It took her only a few seconds to find Dylan Hunter's business card.

FORTY-THREE

"What's wrong?"

Startled, Annie looked up from her desk. Grant stood in the open doorway of her small office, hands in the pockets of his gray suit trousers, brows knitted into a look of concern over wintry eyes.

"I'm fine. Why do you ask?"

He stepped in and closed the door behind him.

"Don't lie to me. I've passed by three times today, and each time you've either been staring into space, or huddled over your desk fiddling with your ring." His eyes moved to her hands. "Like now."

She withdrew them from the desktop. "It's personal, Grant."

"No doubt," he said, claiming the visitor's chair. "But not when it starts to affect your work. What's going on with you and Dylan?"

She avoided his gaze. "Just more of the same."

"It looks more serious than that. Come on, Annie. Tell me."

She hesitated for a few seconds. Then, under the weight of his silence and penetrating gaze, she gave it up and told him.

He tapped a fist lightly against an open palm, making little slapping sounds.

"I'm sorry. I thought you two had come to terms."

"It was so out-of-the-blue, Grant. I just don't understand."

"No? You *do* realize the same day he came to see you, he watched a presidential candidate he liked get gunned down, right in front of him, by a shooter who then tried to kill *him*. And before that was the trauma of the terrorist bombing . . . I'm curious: Did he ever tell you about the mother and baby?"

"He mentioned them, yes. But only in passing."

He grunted. "Just like him. Well, I was with him afterward. I can't begin to tell you how much that affected him. He had just spoken with them, minutes before. Afterwards, he found a piece of the baby's doll in the rubble."

"Oh!" She shuddered. "That's . . . hideous."

"You know, every time he remembers them, he's probably thinking about *you,* and any child you might have together. He's terrified that would happen to you, if you stay together. Because it almost did. And he can't allow that."

Her desperate grip on hope began to slip away.

"Grant—what can I do?"

He regarded her steadily. "I don't know, Annie. Because—as a man—I understand how he feels. And I'm not sure he isn't right."

It made her angry.

"I can't accept that," she snapped. "I *won't.*"

His flinty features had sagged. He looked weary, and by more than their words to each other. Perhaps by a job in which tragedy was too often the outcome.

"I worry about you, you know." His gravelly voice was softer. "You were supposed to have a much-needed vacation at his cabin, but it turned into a nightmare. Now you've come back to more of the same."

She didn't respond. She contemplated the light from her desk lamp sparking on her engagement ring.

"Annie, it's clear you can't focus right now. I think you need to take some real time off—away from all of this."

"No!" She rose to her feet. "I'm not going anywhere. I have a job to do right now and, damn it, Grant, I'm going to finish it!"

"See how wrought up you are? You're proving my point."

She took her seat again. Tried to steady herself before she spoke.

"Look, I need to do this. I'm making a lot of progress. Besides, I can't afford to dwell on what's happening between Dylan and me. I need to keep busy. Please, Grant—don't pull me off this. Not now."

He sat motionless, long legs crossed, long fingers steepled, watching her, his pale eyes unflinching, unrevealing.

"All right," he said at last. "You've come this far. You've earned this, Annie."

She sighed in relief. "Thank you, Grant."

"So, what's your next step?"

"I'm cooking up some irresistible bait."

2

It was difficult to meet privately and discreetly in Washington with someone as recognizable as Julia Haight. A restaurant or other public location, where she and Hunter would be seen, was out of the question. A hotel room would afford privacy, but she would be out of place entering any pedestrian hotel.

So Hunter booked a spacious, elegant suite in The Jefferson, one of the nation's finest luxury hotels. He arrived at the three o'clock check-in time, arranged for hors d'oeuvres, wine, and coffee service to be sent to the room, then headed there to wait. Meanwhile, reasonably disguised beneath a broad-brimmed hat and sunglasses, Julia also summoned a cab from her apartment and arrived a half hour after he did. Heads turned as she entered and crossed the ornate lobby to the polished brass elevator.

In the room, Hunter took her hat and coat as she put away the sunglasses in her purse. He noticed the drawn lines of stress on her face, the flickers of anxiety in her eyes. He seated her on the sofa, before a glass-topped coffee table bearing the refreshments, and poured a glass of Pinot Grigio to relax her.

Then he took the armchair at the end of the table and a sip of Cabernet.

"From what you hinted at on the phone, this is a brave thing you are doing, Julia."

She shook her head emphatically, sending ripples through her auburn hair.

"I'm not brave, Dylan. If I were, I wouldn't have settled for a man like Avery. Perhaps there was an excuse back then for an insecure young woman searching for a better father figure—that's what it really was, you know. You see, I had fame and money, but no self-esteem. I still felt like a loser. But Avery was the epitome of a winner. Money, fame, power . . . he had it all." She sighed. "Or so it seemed."

"Don't be too hard on yourself. You were just a kid."

"But there's no excuse for me in the years since them. Deep down, I sensed something very wrong about him. If I were truly brave, I would have asked more questions and demanded more answers. I would have looked for the truth about him, instead of hiding from it and making excuses for him. Now . . ." She gave a little shrug. "Now, I'm terrified of him. Petrified. But after what I've seen and heard, I couldn't live with myself if I kept silent."

"Tell me about that."

She picked up the small purse she'd set beside her on the sofa, opened it, then fished out a gray thumb drive.

"I see you've set up your laptop over on the desk." She handed him the drive. "You need to see what's on here."

They went to the desk; he dragged his armchair over for her. He inserted the thumb drive into the computer and let it auto-launch the photo software.

"I've set this up as a slide show," she explained. "I'll tell you what the images are as it runs."

Within the first two minutes, Hunter knew exactly what he was seeing. The gun and ammo. The fake passports. The burst transmitter and burners. The Order of Lenin . . .

For the next eighteen minutes Hunter sat riveted and numb—barely able to speak or ask questions—while image after image revealed the terrible truth about the man known to the world as Avery Trammel.

When the slide show stopped, he turned to her.

"I was wrong, Julia. When I said that this was a brave thing you are doing. It's way more than that. It's an act of heroism. I can't tell you how important this is"—he stressed the next words—"or how dangerous."

Her lips grew tight. "I figured that much. So . . . am I right that he's some kind of Russian spy?"

"I don't think there can be any doubt."

"But there's more," she said. "I am certain he was having an affair with Ashton Conn's widow. Emmalee Conn—the woman they just found murdered. And I'm just as certain he had something to do with that, too . . . I see that shocks you. Well, imagine how it shocks *me*."

"I thought I'd already reached my capacity to be shocked. Why do you suspect him?"

She spent the next few minutes explaining.

Afterward, he remained still and silent. He was vaguely aware she was watching him while he tried to fit all the pieces together. She broke into his thoughts.

"So, I suppose the next step is to turn him in to the police, or the FBI."

"Maybe," he said, still looking away and mulling it over.

"Why 'maybe'?"

He switched his focus back to her.

"Julia, thanks to you, I think what we have here is more than enough for the FBI to launch an investigation. But I know how long these espionage and criminal investigations take. They'll want to watch him, bug him, trace all his finances and track his movements, find out who all his associates are, try to connect him to other spies. It could take *years*.

"Meanwhile, there are other problems. If the police investigation into Emmalee Conn's murder proceeds, it could interfere with the FBI espionage investigation. Another thing is how you are affected by all of this—and how what you do might affect the investigations."

"What do you mean?"

"I mean you now face a choice. If you suddenly leave your husband, he'll become suspicious about why. He might worry that you learned some of his dirty secrets. That could either put you in immediate danger, or he could get spooked and run. He certainly has the means to take off and vanish. So he'd get away with murder, and whatever else he's been doing. On the other hand, if you stay with him, there's no telling how long the investigations will take. You'd be in constant danger, for a long time. And that's not acceptable to me."

"Or to me!"

"There's one more thing. I am sure your husband is wrapped up in illegal activities involving the presidential campaign—in ways I'm only beginning to discover. Now I see the serious possibility of Russian involvement and manipulation. I have no hard evidence yet, but what you've just shown me throws a whole new light on things. The problem is, the clock is ticking down toward the election, in just a few months. But the official investigations are going to take much longer than that. So it's likely whatever schemes your husband is involved with to affect the outcome of the election will continue, without interference. And I find that unacceptable, too."

She chewed at her lower lip. "So . . . what do you think we should do?"

He considered carefully before answering.

"Whatever we do, we need to do it sooner, not later. Within days and weeks—not months, and certainly not years. I have a few ideas simmering about that. But some would involve your participation, Julia. And I have no right to ask that of you. You've done enough already."

"What kind of participation?"

"Forget about it," he said. Then added, "You have to understand that it's my responsibility to protect you, no matter what."

She regarded him for a moment.

Then slowly shook her head.

"No."

"What do you mean, 'no'?"

"It's not up to you to make decisions like that for me. It's my life. My life is *my* responsibility."

"Julia, I won't—"

She reached out, seized his arm.

"Listen to me, Dylan. Avery—or Avis, or whoever the hell he is—has wrecked my life. He's lied to me and betrayed me for almost twenty years. He's *robbed* me of two decades of my life! The son of a bitch has to *pay* for that. I have to make him pay. It doesn't matter that I'm scared of him. The only thing that matters to me now is *justice*. And if there's anything I can do to help bring him to justice—well, I want you to tell me what it is."

The words struck deep. He had to get up.

He crossed the room, to the window. Her voice, growing angry, followed him.

"So tell me what I can do!"

He looked out over the city. They were on an upper floor, and the window faced south. Above the tops of the buildings he could make out the spire of the Washington Monument. He knew that somewhere between that icon and himself was the White House, invisible and lost, drowning in that vast gray sea of political structures and establishments.

"Don't you give a damn about justice, Dylan?"

He winced. Turned.

"All right, Julia. If you want to help, here is what I think you can do."

3

After she left, he sat on the sofa in the hotel room, sampling the hors d'oeuvres and finishing the glass of Cabernet. From the briefcase in which he'd fetched his laptop, he removed a file folder, and from that, a small stack of pages he'd retrieved from the internet.

He studied them again, trying to connect what they revealed to what she had told him. After about fifteen minutes, he went through his usual security ritual with his latest burner and phoned Wonk.

"Yes, Dylan. May I be of assistance?"

"You may. I need you to do a bit of homework for me."

"And the subject is?"

"Two subjects, actually. The first is Gazprom, the big Russian energy company. I believe their people are actively involved in sponsoring annual conferences in Berlin. Can you see what you can find out about that?"

"Indeed I shall. And the second topic?"

"I need the exact dates and amounts of the Trammel Foundation's grants to the Currents network for anti-fracking campaign and activities. Especially if the amounts are significant."

"When do you need that information, Dylan?"

"ASAP. I need it for an article."

"I shall get on it immediately."

Hunter ended the call and checked his watch. Almost six o'clock. Bronowski probably would be at home, now. He tried that number.

"Yeah, who's this?"

"Dylan, Bill."

"Dylan who? I don't know anybody by that name."

"Ha. Ha."

"Yeah. I don't think it's funny, either. Not only are you causing me headaches over your identity, you're interrupting my supper. This better be good."

Hunter told him.

"Holy crap! Are you sure about that?"

"There may be a lot more, Bill."

"So when can I expect this stuff?"

"Very soon. Days. But here's what I'd like you to do for now. I want you to tease it, for several days. I want you to just hint about what's coming. I'll draft something tonight and email it for you first thing, if you want to start running the promo tomorrow."

"Dylan, my only worry is whether you can deliver what you promise."

"Count on it. And once again, keep my byline off this stuff. Make each of these another 'staff' contribution."

"You know, if these pieces start getting awards, all those freeloading staffers will start asking for raises. Get paid for not working."

"There *are* precedents, Bill. Remember, this is Washington."

"Ha. Ha."

FORTY-FOUR

At six-fifty a.m. on Tuesday, Avery Trammel was sipping coffee in the rear of his limo, en route to Reagan National for another quick New York meeting, when *Maestro's* call came through.

As he listened to the news from his friend, he felt his chest tighten.

"Damn it, Avery!" Carver exclaimed. "Why would they claim such things? Be straight with me, now—is there anything to this?"

"I have no idea what they are talking about, Lucas. This is the first I have heard of it."

"Well, it looks serious. *Really* serious. They're teasing it, saying next week they'll start a new series, all about *you*. They claim it will expose secret connections you have with the Russian government. The first article is supposed to show that money from some Russian energy company is pouring into your foundation."

"That . . . that is *outrageous!*" he shouted. The cup in his hand shook so much that it began to spill coffee onto the floor. He barely managed to settle it back onto the side table without further mishap.

"Outrageous or not, you know where they're headed with this. It doesn't take a genius to connect the dots. They've already tried to trace your foundation grants through Currents into the campaign. Next, they'll try to make a case that your grants include *Russian* money, funneled through you to us."

"If they print any such lies, they shall be answered with a multi-million-dollar lawsuit!"

"It won't matter, Avery. Not to the campaign, it won't. With our lousy poll numbers, this is the last thing we need right now. So whatever we do about this, we'll have to do it fast. Before we talk any more about how to respond, you need to check the *Inquirer* and see exactly what they're claiming."

"I shall do that at once."

He ended the call, then used his phone to go to the *Inquirer* website.

He found the announcement about the coming series displayed prominently, hinting at the promised revelations. As he read, cold dread spread throughout his body, causing him to shiver. He placed the phone down on the seat beside him. Then groped for the intercom button.

"Jeffrey," he said to the driver on the other side of the soundproof barrier, "there is a change of plans. We need to return immediately to the apartment."

Still shivering, he nudged up the thermostat three degrees.

Back behind the locked door of his study at seven forty-five, he checked in with his secretary out at the estate for messages. He tried to quell a rising feeling of panic as she read out the names and phone numbers of all those requesting urgent return calls.

Rouse at the Currents Foundation.

Five different media reporters.

The New York office.

Two investment partners, one in London.

He spent the next hour staring at the list. Thinking about what he would tell each of them.

Pondering how he might stop an impending disaster.

At eight forty-five, he used his intercom to instruct the cook to prepare a pot of coffee and a light breakfast, to be left outside his study on a rolling tray table.

At nine, he made his first call, to his personal attorney. He told the man what he wanted, but the lawyer balked.

"Listen to me, Harvey," Trammel said, stifling a rising anger, "I am not interested in your preaching about 'prior restraint' and the First Amendment. If indeed we cannot ultimately prevail in court, then the objective will be to buy time—at least enough to delay this series from appearing next week. I shall pay you double your rate if, by the end of the day, you file a motion for an emergency injunction to block its publication . . . Good. That is more like it. Now, please get to it."

Next, he spoke to Wallace Rouse. His objective here was soothing reassurance.

"The important thing right now, Wallace, is to keep our wits about us. I have spoken to my attorney, and he is filing a motion for an injunction against the *Inquirer*. He assures me we can block publication of these lies. And of course I shall issue a categorical denial of these defamatory insinuations later today . . . Absolutely not! You have no need to worry that any money from Russia passed through my hands into the Currents Foundation . . . Oh, yes—I have no doubt *he* is the one actually behind this. My team will redouble our efforts to discredit Hunter in the media this week . . ."

It was mid-afternoon before he caught up with his list of calls sufficiently to take the next step. He used a burner from the desk safe to send a coded text, then waited for the return call on the encrypted satellite phone.

"I hope you are calling to tell me you've deposited the rest of my fee in the Caymans account," Lasher began.

"Our agreement was that the target would be permanently dealt with."

"You said 'neutralized.' And I did that. The problem has been solved for you."

"That is not why I called. I have another job for you. This target is the one you have been so eager to engage, for so long."

"Really? You want me to do that, now?" Lasher's voice did sound eager.

"It is time."

"Way *past* time, from what I see in the newspaper. Isn't it a bit late?"

"Not if it is done right away."

"I must find him first. That hasn't been going well."

"Rather than do that, provoke him into revealing himself. He has to be stopped, immediately. At all costs."

"It will cost you plenty, then. First, though, you've got to pay me the rest of what you owe me."

Trammel ground his teeth. "All right."

"And then, for this job? How about another ten?" Lasher laughed. "I'd charge more, but I'm giving you a bargain rate because this will be so much fun for me."

"Another twenty-five, total, then? That is quite steep."

"You can afford it. And as I see things, you can't afford not to."

Trammel hated the smug lout. But he had no choice.

"All right. Twenty-five."

"That's better. I'll get on it—right after I see the money you already owe me sitting in my account."

"It is too late today. I shall initiate the transfers tomorrow. You should see the funds Thursday at the latest."

"Great. Believe me, I look forward to this job."

2

Bad as Tuesday was, Wednesday was worse.

It started with an email from his London investment partners. They were concerned over the controversy and what it portended. They wished to meet at the earliest opportunity "to discuss the future of the partnership." He knew what that meant.

The statement he had released the preceding afternoon had done nothing to quash the rumors and speculation, or dampen the steady stream of media inquiries. His secretary continued to forward their call-back requests throughout the morning, until, exasperated, he ordered her to stop doing that, and instead to refer all reporters to his previous day's statement.

He had just sent out several emails and text messages—to Rouse, Cunningham, Spencer, and various business associates—when he paused to field a late-morning call from Carver.

"Avery, some good news. I just wanted you to know I took the initiative last night to post on the private listserv of the Progressive Media Alliance. I told them I'd known you for years, that there was nothing to this, that it was just a smear by the *Inquirer* and the far right to undermine Spencer's campaign. And pretty much everyone was sympathetic. They appreciate all your generosity over the years. Almost all of the print people agreed not to cover the story, and some of the broadcast and internet media actually volunteered to go on the attack against the *Inquirer*."

"Lucas, thank you! That is exactly what I need to hear right now. You truly are the *Maestro.*"

"Of course, *Geppetto*. We've been friends for so long I know you like a brother. I'm confident there can be no substance to this."

But his tone did not quite equal the confidence of the words.

"Meanwhile, we need to get this story out of the daily news cycle," Carver went on. "I suggest you maintain a low profile for a while. We'll steer you away from campaign fundraisers and other public events. You may want to consider getting away from town for a little while."

Trammel felt something sink inside.

"Would that not look like I am running away?"

"No, no, no, I mean for your own peace of mind. Away from phones and cameras and media pests." Carver's voice sounded as if it was exuding forced warmth—like those smiles of his, which never reached his eyes. "You've said your lawyers are on this. Pull back and let them do their jobs."

He knew he was being shunted aside. He would not allow that. Not after everything he had done. Not after coming *this close* . . .

"Lucas, I have a critical role to play in this campaign. In shaping strategy, in raising funds, in rallying support. Were it not for me, Spencer would not have seized the advantage during the debate. I have invested a great deal in this effort, and I shall *not* allow some fake reporter peddling bald-faced lies to run me off!"

"Easy, Avery. I know you're upset, but it will all work out. Look, I have a lot of things to take care of right now—mostly trying to discredit the *Inquirer* before they go to print next week. Why don't we have a meeting of the executive team in a few days—say, late Friday—see where things stand, and decide how to proceed from there."

"Right," Trammel said, trying and failing to take the edge off his tone. "Let us do that."

He cut off the call before any phony exchange of goodbyes.

Once again he checked his email account. A senator had just cancelled a breakfast meeting tomorrow "due to a last-minute scheduling conflict." Ten already-confirmed guests had sent their regrets about their sudden inability to attend a campaign fundraising dinner he was hosting at his estate next week.

With mounting anxiety, he closed his email and scanned the home pages of the major online news sites. Buried among a column of items on a political gossip blog, he found that at noon Wallace Rouse had issued a prepared statement:

> *"We wish to assure friends of the Currents Foundation that our funding sources are of the highest integrity. To underscore that commitment, we are addressing recent media reports proactively, and suspending acceptance of further funding from the Avery R. Trammel Foundation, pending clarification of the issues raised in those reports. Though we retain every confidence in our long-time partner, we feel . . ."*

Trammel stopped reading. He eased his chair back, away from the computer screen.

No wonder the smarmy little ingrate had not responded to his early-morning email.

He felt suspended between rage and raw fear. The latter emotion was unfamiliar, something he had not had to encounter much since his youth. He was accustomed to instilling fear, not experiencing it.

He had to collect himself. His hand sought the anchor of the silver watch in his pocket. Once again he held it beneath the crystal chandelier to read the faded, etched inscription. The faded, etched initials.

No, he would refuse to submit himself to fate. He had to be bold.

Perhaps Lasher would head off the looming catastrophe by ridding him of the reporter. However, he had to weigh other options.

The digital desk clock told him it was almost one o'clock. Hours before the day's end.

He decided it was time to talk to his handler.

3

The offices of Brotherhood Without Borders occupied a fourth-floor suite in one of the many modern, nondescript office buildings on Vermont Avenue. The executive director's office was spacious and plush, with many customized, retrofitted fixtures, including unusually thick walls and a padded leather door, which insured privacy for the conversations held within. Such expenses seemed extravagant for a nonprofit; however, executive director Leon Sokol rationalized it to his staff and board, because he had to host so many impressive and influential guests.

Guests such as Avery Trammel—who also knew his SVR handler by his real name: Leonid Sokolov.

They sipped coffee from delicate china cups, in the soft comfort of the large club chairs next to the large, sunny window. But for this visit, its heavy curtains had been drawn.

"The Center is not pleased about the prospect of this kind of exposure, my friend."

"That is why I am here, Leon. To prevent that, I require some assistance."

"'Require.' That doesn't sound like a request, Avery. You seem to be forgetting yourself."

"I cannot mince words about this. It is a serious situation for all of us. I am on the cusp of losing the influence it has taken us decades to amass. Helping me is in our mutual interests."

"That depends upon the nature of the help—and of course, the costs and benefits."

"The assistance I require—"

"No. The assistance you *request*."

Trammel tried to stifle his irritation. "All right—that I *request* is for the Center to use its many indirect means to rally support to my defense and, simultaneously, to attack and discredit the *Inquirer*. In addition, they need to tangle the financial records of the Gazprom funds going to me for my Berlin speeches."

Sokolov raised his gaze toward the ceiling and began tapping his fingertips together.

"I am sure we can help with the first—getting people to vouch for you and attack the paper. But the second—that is a tall order, my friend. The financial records are what they are. The underlying problem is that the amounts you are paid for those speeches are extraordinary, and that naturally raises questions."

"Leon, you know why that money was authorized for me, where it went, and what it was for. You *do* realize what will happen if the Kremlin is implicated in an effort to determine the outcome of an American election."

"Oh, I don't know. That depends on exactly what is revealed. We can probably absorb any fallout we might receive for using money to buy political influence. Many governments secretly engage in that kind of interference. What we could *not* tolerate is any link to the terrorism. But we see little risk of that happening." His lowered his gaze back to Trammel's eyes. "There *is* no such risk—is there, Avery?"

Trammel understood the threat.

"Of course not. And the Center has *me* to thank for that. My plan went off flawlessly, leaving nothing to tie the attacks to us. And because of how I coached him to respond, Spencer benefited significantly in the polls."

"A benefit that didn't last, though. It's fortunate that someone neutralized Helm, or it appears your plan ultimately would have failed. As things stand now, though, Spencer is a shoo-in to win the election. So, it won't matter if we're seen as having backed his candidacy."

"But if my reputation is not protected, then I shall lose my influence over Spencer."

Sokolov shrugged. "*Your* influence, perhaps, but probably not *ours*. Even without you, we'd find other ways to bring a weakling like him to heel."

Trammel could not believe what he was hearing.

"Are you implying that I am now expendable?"

Sokolov snorted. "We are all expendable, my friend . . . Come on, now, don't look at me like that. *Of course* we want to protect you, Avery, and help you continue to be successful. You have done outstanding work. But if you lose some credibility and your direct, personal influence over Spencer, it won't exactly be the end of the world. There are many other things you can still do for us, whether or not you are the new president's personal puppeteer."

He balled his fists to prevent his hands from trembling visibly.

"Leon . . . you cannot—"

Sokolov's eyes narrowed again.

"What is it that I cannot do, my friend?" Hearing no response, the SVR officer grunted. "Now, if you'll excuse me, I have to get back to work."

4

During the first moments back in his limo, Trammel's thoughts were in turmoil, buffeted by alternating waves of rage and fear. The smirking, arrogant *apparatchik* was pronouncing a death sentence upon his mission.

Instinctively, his hand found the cool, firm, reassuring surface of the watch in his pocket. It reminded him of his father, and of his father's favorite quotation.

He had to get a grip on his emotions. To find a bold path forward. He owed his father that.

He could *not* lose—not now. He was not born to be a loser. He was born and bred to *win*.

It was always inevitable that he would one day break with Moscow.

He had intended to do that after the new president was inaugurated.

Could he do it now?

The thought began to calm him.

Avery Trammel passed through the streets at the heart of the nation's capital, unseen and unseeing, his focus turned inward. From his father he had been gifted with a quick, integrative mind, one that could seize upon disparate facts and ideas, then weld them into a plan. From the torn scraps of his thoughts and emotions, such a plan was coalescing now.

Why did he have to remain at Carl Spencer's side en route to the White House, now that the destination was assured?

In fact, why did he have to be present at the Inauguration? Or even in Washington?

Then another thought struck him.

Or even inside this damned country, for that matter?

After all, he—and *only* he—still had the photos. Those photos were *power.* The ultimate power. They gave him iron control over the next president.

And he could exercise that control *from anywhere.*

In fact, that would be even *more* satisfying—and safer, because he could make sure they would never find him . . .

He indulged himself the sudden fantasy of lying poolside at some remote tropical resort—or perhaps in the lounge of some snow-covered alpine chalet in Europe—Julia at his side, drink in hand, in the other an encrypted, secure phone—and on the line, an obsequious, obedient President of the United States, taking his instructions, just as his own secretary took his dictation.

Yes, he could still accomplish the mission . . . *by remote control.*

He chuckled to himself. Why, he really *would* be *Geppetto* . . .

The fantasy washed over Avery Trammel like a religious epiphany, leaving him quivering with excitement.

5

"Julia dear, I have a surprise for you," Avery announced as he entered their living room, overcoat in hand.

His buoyant manner startled her. The news about him had been ominous for the past two days; she expected anything but this. She had to remind herself to stay in character.

Rising from the chair and smiling, she said, "You look so happy, dear! What is it?"

"I am taking you on an extended trip. To Europe."

"What?"

He dumped his overcoat into a chair, strode over, and embraced her. Then held her at arm's length. She was astonished to see authentic excitement in his face.

"Julia, we both have been under considerable stress for months. And this is the perfect time for a vacation. You are between film roles, and with all this nonsense in the media, I certainly could use some time away, myself."

"But . . . I can't just—"

"Of course you can! And so can I. Who is to stop us? My business affairs and legal matters are in good hands, and you have no pending contractual commitments to hold you here. I should like us to pack minimally, then leave this weekend—Saturday or Sunday, depending on whatever flight and accommodation arrangements can be made on short notice. We shall first have to stop at the house—stay there for the next few nights. I have things to do there, and some items I need to take with me. We can then fly right from Dulles."

"Avery! Really, you haven't even given me a chance to think!"

"What is there to think about, my dear? All you should think about is where you would like to go. I am completely flexible. If you are not in the mood for Europe, we could go somewhere else. And please do not worry about what to pack. I shall buy whatever you need or want when we arrive."

He squeezed her shoulders.

"Come now, I have made up my mind to take a vacation. I would hate to go without you."

He laughed—a sight so rare that she was even more taken aback.

She forced a smile that she hoped looked authentic.

"All right, Avery. Why not? It sounds like fun."

Thirty minutes later, inside her locked office, she extracted Dylan Hunter's business card and the cheap phone he had given her from their hidden place, in a box at the bottom of the closet.

Then sent him a detailed text message about what had just happened.

FORTY-FIVE

He had not been to his Maryland house on Connors Point for a while. On Wednesday evening he decided to check on it, then stay overnight, leaving Luna in the care of the young cat sitter at his Bethesda apartment.

Red Mama had littered the yard near her fox den with two large, half-eaten fish and scattered bird feathers—bounty she'd harvested from the adjacent marsh to feed her growing kits. He was incredulous to find the lower leg of a deer out there, too—probably road kill she'd managed to drag from the highway, a quarter mile distant. He grabbed a shovel from the garage, scooped up her untidy table scraps, and pitched them off into the swamp.

At dawn the next morning, he took a cup of coffee out onto his screened-in back porch. He watched the purple martins and red-winged blackbirds soar and swoop above the marsh, just fifty yards away. Farther out, ducks paddled around in a patch of open water.

He would be a sitting duck for a rifle shot from out there, if Lasher ever discovered where he lived. The man's reputation as a shooter was formidable. Only chance had prevented Lasher from nailing him that day in Quincy Park. He couldn't count on his luck to hold out forever.

Hunter had spent long hours thinking about how to smoke the hitman out of hiding again, but in some way that would give himself an advantage. He was certain that Lasher was pondering the same problem. There was little doubt that at some point, perhaps soon, they would face each other again. The survivor would be the man who did not make a mistake—and who didn't continue to rely on luck.

He felt the chill morning air from the marsh flow through the screened windows, and took another sip. Felt it warm him as it went down.

Then there was Trammel. A problem almost as serious. A Russian spy, planning to leave the country in another two or three days. No doubt to vanish for good, now that he knew he was soon to be exposed.

During many sleepless hours, Hunter wrestled over the dilemma. He had no proof Trammel had Emmalee Conn killed; he had only Julia's suspicion. Without certainty, he couldn't act to stop him. But if he turned over what he had to the FBI, in the faint hope that they'd do something, it would almost certainly expose Julia as the source.

It infuriated him to think that this lifelong traitor and probable killer, smug and self-important, might escape justice.

But he didn't know what to do about it.

It was still too early to hit the road. He wanted to wait for the morning rush-hour traffic across the Bay Bridge to die down before setting out to return to Washington. He packed into "Vic Rostand's" Honda CR-V just a few items that he could use back in his apartment. As usual, he'd drive it to the long-term lot where he'd left Dylan Hunter's Subaru Forester. He'd leave the Honda there in its place, transfer the items into the Forester, then head back to Bethesda. The drive would give him more time to try to come up with fresh ideas.

He was running the dishwasher when his latest burner chirped. He checked the screen, then answered.

"Hi, Wonk. What's up?"

"Dylan, have you watched the morning news broadcasts?"

"I haven't. I'm on the road. What am I missing?"

"It was just being discussed on CNN. They said a police source, unnamed of course, revealed that an analysis of film footage and ballistics from the assassination attempt on Roger Helm suggests strongly that *you* were targeted, as well."

He stood still a few seconds, then moved to a chair in the breakfast nook.

"How certain of that did they sound?"

"Quite certain. Of course, they are now speculating as to why."

He remained silent.

"Dylan . . . do you have any idea why?"

He didn't answer.

"Would this have any relationship to questions about . . . about your identity?"

"No, Wonk. Not about that. I think it's about something else."

"I am sorry to be so nosy. Truly. I do not mean to intrude upon your privacy. I just worry about you. I sense that you are often in danger."

"Thanks. But it's all right, my friend. No need to worry about me."

He heard a heavy sigh.

"If you insist. However, I thought you ought to know."

"Again, thanks. I'm glad you told me."

He went to the TV and turned on CNN. Then spent the next several minutes watching.

It occurred to him someone else might be watching, too. And that gave him an idea.

He found the number for the CNN Washington bureau, then called through a spoof site. He identified himself and asked to be patched through to the show's producer. Within a few minutes, he'd convinced her of his identity.

Three minutes later, he was being interviewed on-air.

"That's right," he said in answer to the host's third question. "From everything I've learned about these kinds of cases, the person who shot Mr. Helm, then tried to shoot me, is probably some disgruntled loser. The kind of loser who thinks the world is treating him unfairly. He probably nurses some kind of long-standing, petty grudge, and thinks it justifies him striking back against the world. And being a total loser, he picks prominent people as his targets. In this case, a presidential candidate. And he probably singled me out because my name has been in the news a lot. So this loser thinks that by shooting prominent people, that would make him a winner. But when they find this guy, they'll discover a nobody—just another pathetic loser."

They tried to ask about his identity, but Hunter deflected.

"Look, I issued a statement about that and have no more to add. I just wanted to respond to your report this morning, with a message for that loser who shot Roger Helm. He probably imagines he's some kind of a big, tough soldier. But he's a coward. He shoots his victims from hiding, then runs away. He wouldn't have the nerve to confront targets like me face-to-face."

"Aren't you concerned that you are goading this individual, egging him on? An unstable person might even try again."

Hunter laughed. "I'm sorry, but that's really funny. As I said, he's a coward and wouldn't have the nerve. A real man would confront me personally. But this loser will never do that. Believe me, I'm in no danger."

In his hotel room, Lasher finished doing his set of one hundred pushups and situps, then went into the bathroom for his shower. He stood for the moment, naked, in front of the full-length mirror, admiring his body. He looked like an Olympic gymnast. His shoulders and abs were especially great. No wonder women went for him. Maybe his calves could use a little more work, but nobody saw them much, anyway. Still, tomorrow he'd have to pick a hotel with a decent workout room and some free weights.

He showered and toweled off, then padded into the living room and turned on the TV. He surfed the local channels, then the cable news networks.

At CNN, he stopped—riveted by the sight of a familiar face.

". . . actual identity has become the source of speculation, called in to our studios about thirty minutes ago, in response to our report that the would-be assassin of Roger Helm had also targeted him. Here is an excerpt of our interview."

Lasher stood there, naked, staring at the stock photo of Hunter on the screen, listening to what he said.

The bastard was just provoking him, taunting him. He knew he shouldn't care. He knew he shouldn't react emotionally.

But every time he heard the words *loser* and *coward*, it felt like a slap. Not a hard slap, just the kind of light slap in the face you do to someone when you're goading him, humiliating him.

After a minute, he was cursing loudly.

He wrapped the wet towel around his waist, stormed over to his jeans and grabbed his burner. He went to his cloud site, then scrolled through the list of numbers stored there. Then keyed in the number.

"This is Dylan Hunter's answering service. May I take a message, please?"

He was pacing the room when the phone chirped fifteen minutes later. He saw that it was a blocked number.

"This you?" he asked.

"The one and only. *Loser.*"

Lasher sat down. Gripped the phone tightly. Forced himself to stay under control.

"You think so? I changed history."

"You mean shooting Helm."

He felt himself grin. "That's right."

"So, that was just an ego trip, then."

"Hell, no. I got paid *plenty.*"

"I figured. But shooting me—that was personal, right?"

"You were right there, so I figured—Why not? Sorry I missed, though."

"You should be, Lasher. You should be very sorry you missed."

"Yeah, well, *that* won't happen again."

"It's too bad it's only personal for you, and nobody is making it worth your while."

He laughed. "Oh, you have no idea."

"Really? Do I command a decent price?"

"Hard to believe, isn't it?"

"Well, you'll have to find me first, Lasher, before I find you."

"Oh, that won't be a problem. I think you'll want to meet me right away."

"And why is that?"

"Because if you don't, I'll track down your hot girlfriend."

Hunter felt everything go still inside.

"Girlfriend?"

"Petite. Short-haired brunette. Big gray eyes. Gorgeous body. Long legs." He heard the snicker. "I envy you. She must be fun in the sack. But maybe I'll get to find out for myself."

How did he know?

Then, a faint memory, nagging at his consciousness . . .

"So, how did you find out about her?"

Lasher snorted. "Because I'm smart. Smarter than you, asshole."

The memory took fuller shape . . .

"But you don't know her name. Do you." Not a question.

He counted seven seconds of silence.

"That's only a matter of time," Lasher finally said, bravado back in his voice. "Because I'm relentless. You know, Hunter, I'm going to really enjoy raping the bitch before I kill her."

And then it all came crashing together . . .

How could I not have seen it?

He saw it now. All of it.

Knew instantly what it meant.

Knew instantly what he had to do.

He heard Lasher laugh.

"So, you don't know what to say about that, huh?"

Hunter did not react as he anticipated.

"Sure I do. Thank you—*Ron.*"

He felt the cold breath of the air conditioner against his damp skin.

"What? What did you call me?"

"Ron. Your real name *is* Ron Larsen, isn't it?"

He was aware of the sound of his breathing. Rising. Falling. Rising. Falling . . .

"You still there, *Ron?*"

"How . . ." He stopped.

"Because I'm smart. Smarter than you, *Ron*. And better than you. To prove it, why don't you and I meet tonight? No weapons, just you and me, hand-to-hand. Only one of us walks away. Just what you told me you wanted—remember? 'Winner takes all.'"

"Sure. I remember. So, where do we do this?"

"I have the perfect place in mind. How about out at the estate of your billionaire boss?"

No. He couldn't possibly know . . .

"What in hell are you talking about?"

He heard Hunter chuckle.

"Please tell Avery Trammel I'm coming for him."

Lasher stood. He had to stand.

He had to reassert his dominance.

"You come after him, Hunter," he snarled, "you'll have to go through me."

"That's the idea."

2

Annie had dropped off the sealed package to her latest target just two hours ago, with the appropriate deference.

"I know how busy you are, but I'll only take a minute. One of our officers has been grooming a Russian diplomat . . . No, not here in D.C.—he didn't say in which country. But anyway, the computer disk in here"—she waved the package—"contains a copy of a new one-time pad NSA prepared for us. The Russian developmental and our officer are using their copies of this pad to exchange coded messages while they negotiate.

"But our officer has to travel over the next few weeks. So we're supposed to keep this backup copy here, to decode any new messages the Russian forwards through the local COS. Grant figured your safe was the obvious place to keep it." She smiled. "Would you mind?"

The ruse was so preposterous she could only hope the target was too unsophisticated to see through it. And she could only pray the target would react immediately, rather than days later, because she had no surveillance team to help her.

But it worked.

The target left work early, at three p.m. Annie knew that, because she had left, too, right after dropping off the bait, and was waiting in the parking lot. She had attached a magnetic GPS tracker under the target's Acura. When the cursor began to move on the tablet screen attached to her dashboard, she wondered if she'd finally hit pay dirt.

Keeping a healthy distance, she tailed the Acura out of the lot from Langley, past the gates, and out onto Route 123. Then east and south—in the opposite direction of the target's home in Fairfax. Then the target crossed the Chain Bridge, heading into the District.

At that point, the cursor movement became erratic. The target vehicle began to make what looked like random turns down side streets, circling blocks, doubling back, proceeding ahead for a while, slowing to a crawl—then speeding up.

Heart racing, Annie hung back a quarter of a mile, not needing or daring to get closer. The target was doing a surveillance detection run. The only time you needed to do that was during an op, when you were trying to spot or elude someone following you. There was no innocent reason for this target to be doing that.

She hit the speed-dial number on her phone.

"Yes, Annie," came the familiar growl.

"Grant, I think I found our mole."

3

At three fifty-five p.m., Leonid Sokolov left his Mercedes in the Georgetown cemetery's lower parking area. Being near the end of the daily visiting hours, only two other cars occupied the lot.

One of them was the Acura belonging to one of the Center's most critical assets: its last mole in the CIA.

He got out, stretched, and looked around. He loved this somber, primitive place. Perhaps it appealed to the moodiness in his Russian blood. An historic tribute to 19th Century Romanticism, Oak Hill Cemetery was rugged, hilly, chaotic—the stylistic antithesis of Arlington National Cemetery, and its endless tidy rows of uniform white headstones.

But it wasn't merely esthetics and a sense of history that made this his favorite spot for personal meetings with assets and the illegals he handled. It offered the security of isolation.

From an abundance of caution, Sokolov always chose to be armed when meeting his operatives. That is why, despite the warm May afternoon, he wore a jacket to hide the Glock 19 tucked into a belt holster at his back. You never knew whom you could trust, whether someone had been turned. And given his preeminent position among SVR officers in the United States, it would be catastrophic for him ever to be taken alive. Before that, he would shoot his way out of any confrontation with the FBI, or die by his own hand.

He set off up a rising pathway from the lot, listening to the birds chattering in the tangled limbs of surrounding trees, looking at the worn inscriptions on the gray headstones tilting in the soft green earth. He reached and entered the Willow Columbarium, a small, circular stone structure whose interior housed rows of niches for burial urns. An elderly couple sat on the central stone planter in quiet contemplation.

He nodded politely and continued on through. A short distance ahead, a rustic old stone bridge arched over the flagstone pathway. Within the arch, wooden benches faced each other from the opposing walls.

On the right-hand bench sat his prize asset.

Leonid Sokolov smiled and approached.

4

Annie followed the Acura into Oak Hill Cemetery. Fearing her car would be spotted, she slowed and kept an even greater distance. On her tablet screen, she watched the Acura circle the periphery of the cemetery. Then it slowed and stopped.

She pulled over and hit the speed dial number again.

"Where are you now?" he said.

"Grant, it looks like the meeting is going down in Oak Hill Cemetery. The car just stopped in the northeast section. It's out of my view. I'm worried I'll be spotted if I continue driving around the road that seems to circle this place. But the car stopped not far from me at all, as the crow flies—maybe a little more than a hundred yards northeast. I'm leaving my car on the side of that perimeter road, about two hundred yards southeast of the East Gate entrance. I'm going in the rest of the way on foot."

"No, wait till I arrive."

She was already leaving the car.

"Not an option, Grant. This could be a brief encounter, even a brush pass. I have to get there in time to see who the handler is, maybe get photos of the exchange with my phone."

"Annie, you can't go in without backup! You—"

She clicked off the call and shut off the ringtone.

"Like hell I can't," she muttered to herself.

She was tired of being told what she could and couldn't do. She had worked this case for a year and a half, starting well before she took down Muller in March of last year. Groat and the FBI took credit for that one. But she had found this one by herself, too. And this time she would damned well *finish* it by herself.

Her nerves were tingling wires as she shoved the phone in her left jacket pocket. Then checked her Glock 27, racked a round, and jammed it back in the right pocket. The gun's grip beneath her fingers suddenly reminded her of the day at the firing range with Dylan. His intrusive image made her even angrier.

She kept her hand on the grip as she left the little road and began to walk slowly, cautiously northeast over the spongy soil between the gravestones. She peered ahead in the direction where the GPS had positioned the Acura. The ground fell away before her into a bowl-like depression of short gray monuments and crosses. Near its bottom a roadway, perhaps the same perimeter one, crossed before her, rising in an arching stone bridge.

Under that arch, she saw a flash of movement.

She froze in place. Then, ever-so-slowly, maneuvered to the side, behind one of the monuments.

The asset rose from the wooden bench with a smile.

"I'm so relieved you could meet me, Leon," he said, his voice low but excited.

Sokolov took Kurt Spitzer's extended hand.

"Lucky for you I was free when you got clear of Langley and could call." He wagged a finger playfully under Spitzer's nose. "Now, this had better be good."

"I wouldn't have insisted, otherwise. Have I ever let you down?"

"No, you have not, my friend." He glanced around the cemetery. "You were careful not to be followed, of course?"

Spitzer laughed. "I probably added twenty miles to my odometer, running back and forth on every street in Georgetown."

Sokolov didn't much like the guy. Tall and cocky, he wore his blond hair too long for a middle-aged man. When he first recruited him, he'd pegged Spitzer as the type that got involved in this business mainly for the adrenaline rush. The type that wasn't satisfied doing important work for his country in a spy agency, but needed ever-intensifying excitement from ever-increasing risks—including the ultimate risk of deceiving everyone around him. The type that, if not careful, could get himself arrested or even killed.

But precisely because he loved taking chances, Spitzer had been a tremendous asset. As chief of the CIA's Office of Russian and European Analysis, he was able to lay hands on mountains of invaluable information for the Center over the past six years, and also exposed six of Langley's NOCs in Europe and the Middle East. In that respect, he had proven to be even more valuable than Muller.

A flash of movement in the corner of Sokolov's eye jarred him. He snapped his head around.

The elderly couple were leaving the nearby columbarium and shuffling their way down the path toward the parking lot. He smiled and relaxed.

"All right, we're alone now. But we have to get out of here before they close the gates in about twenty more minutes. So, show me what you have and tell me all about it."

From her position behind the stone monument Annie was snapping photos with her phone. The late afternoon light under the bridge wasn't good, though, and the angle was bad. She couldn't get both men framed together in the shots. She tried to zoom in, but the images were coming out grainy.

She would have to get closer.

Sinking to her knees, she pocketed the phone and began a slow crawl to her right. After about ten feet, the sharper side angle blocked them from being able to see her. She rose to a crouch and hustled down the hill to the roadway, just to the right of the bridge. She climbed breathlessly to the road surface, wary of dislodging any stones that might attract their attention.

From here she could see the parking lot a bit further to her right—and that she now stood between it and the men. She realized she might block their escape.

Still, she needed a good shot of the two of them together. The best angle would be from inside the columbarium itself—which would also provide her cover, like a small fortress.

But to get down there, she'd have to cross open ground. She'd be in plain sight, if they looked that way in the several seconds it would take to get there.

Her pulse was hammering and her mouth had gone dry. She pulled out the Glock, then began a wary descent down the grassy slope toward the circular structure. Her eyes kept darting from the uneven ground at her feet to the yawning archway just to her left. She glanced down to take a step, then was distracted by a noise coming from their direction. Her eyes shifted that way . . .

. . . and her shoe caught on a root.

She found herself suddenly stumbling, then careening down the slope. She could not keep her feet, and to protect the gun she pulled it across her body and twisted as she fell.

She landed on her right side with a grunt, then continued to skid on the slick grass and dirt. Her gun hand struck a small stone marker and the Glock jolted loose. She came to a stop not thirty feet from where the men stood.

The gun slid ten feet farther down the slope.

Sokolov had just taken Spitzer's package when he heard a thrashing noise outside. Both whipped around to the sight of a body sliding to a halt just ten meters below them.

For a few seconds they stood frozen, too astonished to react.

Then the person's dark head lifted from the ground and met their eyes.

A woman . . .

Sensing a threat, Sokolov dropped the package and shoved Spitzer aside. He saw the woman looking around wildly, then scrambling on her hands and knees. He pawed behind himself, reaching under his jacket for the holstered Glock.

His hand found its grip and he drew the weapon. He stepped forward, out onto the flagstone pathway, as the woman in the grass rolled from her stomach onto her back.

"Don't!" he heard her shout—and he was startled to see she too had a gun, and from down there on the ground she was pointing it up at *him*, and he raised his and sighted down the barrel and was just starting to squeeze when he felt something bang into the front of his collarbone . . .

They had seen her...

She looked around frantically for the gun and saw where it had fallen. She half-clawed, half-dived for it, scooping it up in both hands. Then she flipped over from her belly to her back as her hands slipped instinctively into the grip he had taught her, and she brought the weapon up just as a man with dark hair stepped forward. And then she saw *he* was raising a weapon and she shouted *Don't!* and from somewhere she heard *pressure nice and steady squeeze* and felt the jolt in her hands and one in her left arm at the same time...

... and then her left hand didn't work anymore and the gun wobbled in her right hand, and the man with the gun fell and then Spitzer ran forward and reached down near the fallen man, and she yelled *NO NO NO NO* but he came up with the gun and she didn't wait, *nice and steady squeeze squeeze squeeze squeeze squeeze squeeze* and he jerked like a puppet and fell...

... and then she was on her back looking up at clouds and trees spinning and spinning, and then a noise a motor a car up on that stone bridge, and people jumping out and everything getting bright and dark and bright, and a woman and a man faces she didn't know floating above her saying *No don't try to move you'll be all right just take it easy* and then another face she did know floating there too saying *You little fool I told you wait you little fool...*

FORTY-SIX

Ed Cronin wasn't a dress-up-and-go-out-to-dinner type. But Ellen had been after him. She said the whole family needed to spend some time together, and she and the kids wanted to try Darcy's Steakhouse in Alexandria, and she had no house-showing appointments on the calendar for Thursday night. So why didn't they go early, say six o'clock?

After all the time he'd been pulling, including weekends, Cronin knew he owed them some attention. And he did like steak.

"Okay," he said, giving her a peck on the cheek. "I'll call them and make a reservation."

She grinned. "I already have."

Ellen demanded that everyone look decent, and she managed to get Cronin to wear his best sports jacket and slacks. He was surprised that the kids really got into it. Sarah, even at age nine, was so cute in her little green dress that Cronin realized he was just a few years from facing boy trouble, while Jack tried gamely to look mature beyond his years in his suit.

"Wow. Aren't you two looking spiffy!" he said. They grinned and dimpled up.

Then Ellen came out in a short cocktail dress, jewelry, and her hair up. He shook his head in awe.

"Damn, you are a vision."

"Daaa-ad! You're not supposed to use cuss words!"

"I'm sorry, sweetie," he answered her, while grinning at his wife. "But sometimes, you just don't have the right words."

At five-forty, they all piled into Ellen's SUV and headed off to the restaurant. It was an upscale, standalone place located in the vast parking lot of an area shopping center. The kids were giggling and whispering in the back seat, and he was thankful for the unusual armistice from the usual bickering. They arrived just after six, and he saw that there was no close parking. The place seemed exceptionally busy for an early Thursday evening.

"Why don't you just drop us off in front and go find a spot," Ellen said.

He got out and went around to get her door.

Her eyes were dancing, and she planted a kiss on him.

"This is going to be so much fun."

He watched them go inside, then drove into the lot to claim a place.

Whistling, he walked back through the warm evening air. This was nice. He hadn't realized how much he needed a nice evening. They'd have to do this more often. He pushed through the double-doored entrance and went to the hostess station.

"They've just been seated, sir," she said, smiling. "Just follow me, please."

She led him through the place, which was only half-filled, toward the back.

He frowned. "Excuse me, why are we seated way back here?"

"It's your wife's request, sir."

She stopped at a door at the back, pushed it open and stood aside, smiling even more broadly.

Puzzled, he stepped inside.

"SUR-PRIIIIIIISE!

He stopped dead in his tracks. Scores of people, maybe a hundred, maybe more, were on their feet around circular banquet tables, laughing, cheering, and applauding, all at deafening volume.

Ellen and the kids stood at the front, glowing. Next to them, Paul and his wife. On their other side, the chief and his wife, along with Father John O'Connor from St. Matthew's. A photographer was hopping around like a chicken, flashing a camera at him.

The room was large and decorated with hanging balloons and twisted crepe paper streamers. Candles glowed on the linen-covered tables, casting flickering sparks of light on wine glasses and silverware.

He was stunned. He didn't understand. It wasn't his birthday . . . or anniversary . . .

Then he saw the banner draped across the far wall.

DETECTIVE SERGEANT ED CRONIN
"The Cop's Cop"
20 YEARS OF SERVICE AND INTEGRITY

Then it finally sank in that he had graduated from the academy exactly two decades ago. He stood there, paralyzed, until Ellen and the kids stepped forward to surround, hug, and kiss him. Paul came over and winked and yelled, *"Congratulations, buddy!"* above the noise. Then the chief moved in, shook his hand, grabbed his shoulder, and said, "It's your night, Ed! Follow me."

He led them snaking through the tables. Fellow cops and friends he hadn't seen in years reached out to shake his hand and slap him on the back. They had set up a banquet table at the far end of the room under the hanging banner, and they seated him and Ellen, with the kids on either side, right in the middle. Hanging from the front of the table where he sat was a blown-up photo of his gold shield.

The chief got behind a wooden stand with a microphone and put down his notes. He went through the ritual of greetings, then turned to Cronin.

"You know, twenty years on the job is a milestone any cop can be proud of. But Ed, you have a lot more than your length of service to be proud of." He pointed to the banner behind him. "See that? It says, *'The Cop's Cop.'* And that says it all. A lot of people are gonna say a lot of things about you tonight, Ed. But let me be the first.

"I've run this department twelve years, and I've been with it a lot longer—longer even than you. I've met and served with some of the best cops out there. And after all those years, I can say, without hesitation, that you are the finest officer I have ever worked with. Your bravery, your devotion, your honesty, and your integrity are legendary—not just in the department, but in our community. If anybody ever asks me to name *the* model cop, I'd tell 'em: 'Detective Sergeant Ed Cronin.'"

Everyone leaped to their feet again, to cheer again, to applaud him again.

Cronin sat still, hands clasped tightly in his lap, eyes staring at his empty plate. He couldn't bear to meet the hundreds of eyes looking at him. He was afraid they would look into his, see into his soul.

He realized that they were trying to honor him, and that this was supposed to be one of the greatest nights of his life.

He knew that the coming hours would be torture.

For a while, he was able to postpone much of that torture, because they served the salad and wine almost immediately after Father John's blessing, and the room filled with the distracting buzz of conversation. He felt disembodied. He knew it was his duty to be courteous and friendly toward all these people, who only wanted to show how much they thought of him. He was able to nod, forcing smiles and laughs at words that refused to register in his consciousness. Sitting beside him, Jack kept looking up at him. "Way to go, Dad!" he said at one point. Cronin looked down at his son's face, exuding pride without inhibition or restraint. It made him feel hollow. But he put an arm around him and squeezed him.

He managed to eat about half his meal. People stopping over to share their well-wishing didn't seem to notice anything inappropriate about his reactions or words. Nobody except Ellen. He had trouble looking at her. He knew her eyes were penetrating his phony smiles and empty words, and from his peripheral vision he could see the undercurrent of worry on her face.

He was reaching for the wine bottle when she placed a hand on his sleeve and leaned close.

"You've already had two."

He pulled his hand back from the bottle.

"What's wrong?" she asked softly.

He shrugged. "All this . . . it's a little much. Hard to process."

"Try to relax and enjoy it."

Of course he couldn't. And it got worse when the after-dinner speeches began.

Some weren't bad. An elderly uncle shared funny tales of what a brat he'd been as a kid. An old college pal recounted some of his hijinks from those days, and teased him and Ellen about Ed's period of "sowing wild oats." But it got harder when his fellow officers began to relate their personal impressions and praise him.

It got worse when Father John stood at the mic.

"Most of you know Ed Cronin as 'the cop's cop.' Just knowing what he does for a living—or hearing his colorful language, for which he's spent ample time visiting me in the Confessional"—everyone, even Cronin, laughed—"you might never guess this man is also a true son of the Church. I have had the pleasure of knowing Ed and his lovely wife Ellen for ten years. Their children were baptized in St. Michael's. He sits beside them in the pews every Sunday his job allows. He is a long-time member of our Holy Name Society. And he volunteers to mentor troubled kids.

"That's a part of Ed not everyone sees. But I do. I can tell you he is one of those rare, precious people who *lives* his faith. In a profession that turns so many into cynics, underneath Ed's tough exterior lies the pure heart of an idealist—a man whose moral principles are woven through the fabric of his being. A more honest and honorable man you will never meet. I am proud to be his priest, but prouder still to be his friend. Ed, you have earned this evening's honors. Thank you for your service to this community, to your family, and to your God."

As Father John came over to embrace him, Cronin knew he had more sins to confess to him.

Then the chief, who was emcee, rose again.

"Ed, you should know that this evening was your partner's idea. The guy in the department who knows you best thought you deserved a tribute. Now he's going to tell you why. Ladies and gentlemen—Detective Paul Erskine."

Paul hauled his hefty frame out of his chair and hearty applause followed him to the microphone.

"Folks, you've all been here a while, so I don't want to take more than a minute or so of your time. I have lots of stories I could tell, but instead, I want to focus on why I thought we should do this." He pointed to Cronin. "This guy—"

He stopped. His lips worked. It was obvious he was choking up. He swallowed, grimaced in self-reproach, then went on.

"This guy, Ed Cronin, has been my personal role model. And you need to know why. I've been his partner going on eight years, now. Like Father John said, it's really easy for us on the job to get cynical. Especially with what we see every day. It seems you can't trust anyone or anything anymore. But this is one guy you *can* trust. In all the time I've known him and worked with him, I've never seen Ed do or say anything dishonest. Not once. You can trust his word. You can trust him to act on what he believes . . . You know, the word 'integrity,' it's *only* a word to most people. Noise. It doesn't mean anything. But this guy—he's the walking definition of integrity. That's why for me, for everybody here, he's 'the cop's cop.' Thank you, my friend."

Somehow, Cronin found the strength to rise and meet his partner when he walked over to him. They hugged each other tightly under the roar of the applause.

"Paul," he whispered, "you shouldn't have done this."

"You deserve it, buddy."

"No I don't."

Erskine pushed him back, grinning and blinking his eyes rapidly.

"Bull*shit* you don't!"

The chief settled everyone down.

"Before we make a special presentation, I was told one more person would like to say something. Folks, I'd like to introduce Ed and Ellen's son, Jack."

Beside him, his grinning kid bounced to his feet. To yet another wave of applause, he marched quickly to the microphone. The chief had to angle it down for him.

"I just want to say, my dad might be a great cop and everything. But to me he's a great father. I'm so proud of him, because he's everything I want to be." Beaming, he looked over at Cronin. "Dad—you're my hero, and I love you."

It was too much.

Cronin had to cover his eyes with his hands. He felt Ellen's warm arm around his shaking shoulders and sensed she was crying, too, and she was saying, *It's okay, it's okay,* and then he felt Jack's arm around him, too, and in the agony of the cheers and clapping he clutched them to him tightly, and wondered how his soul would survive this.

2

The Ford E-series van he kept at the Connors Point house was loaded with toys. Items from the arms cache under his tool shed. Other items that couldn't fit down there, and that he kept in the garage attic. He didn't know what he was going to need. But he knew the opposition would be formidable, and he had worked out a plan for the op.

Knowing full well that the best plan never survives its first moment of encounter with the enemy.

As always, he'd have to improvise along the way.

He drove reasonably, keeping to the speed limit. It would be his last day of freedom if a traffic cop pulled him over.

Coming up to the Capital Beltway just after six p.m., his burner chirped. He'd risked keeping it on in case Julia sent him any more text messages. But glancing at the screen, he saw the numerical signature that identified a caller he didn't expect right now.

"Yes?" he said, not identifying himself.

Garrett replied, "Stay calm and don't say anything. Your lady . . . she's been shot."

The impact of the word almost caused him to swerve off Route 50.

"Listen, it's okay, she'll be fine, don't worry—one shot, it just grazed along her forearm and into her shoulder, missed the bones and anything vital. She did lose blood and we treated her at the scene and hospital for shock, but—"

"How? Who did it? Was it—"

"No! Not him—stop talking, don't say anything more. Not on this line."

He fought down the wave of panic, then realized he had accelerated. He took his foot off the gas.

Hold it together . . .

"She's being treated at the usual place for you two. They ought to name the wing after you. I've arranged for you to be passed right through the gate and security to her room; just show your ID. How far away are you?"

He calculated, knowing he *had* to stay below the speed limit.

"Without any traffic tie-ups, twenty minutes, give or take."

"As I say, she's fine. So don't drive like a maniac. Oh, and one more thing."

"What?"

"Before you see her, you and I need to talk. And that is *not* a request."

"You need to know something."

Garrett stood in a little waiting area just down the hallway from her room.

"I'm listening."

"She told me about your breakup. Don't say it's none of my damned business, because what happened tonight has now officially *made it* my business."

"What do you mean?"

His cold stony features and tone matched the ice in his eyes.

"Dylan, what she did was goddamned crazy. Certifiably nuts. She tracked the mole to a meet with his handler, then went in after them, alone. She violated my direct order to wait for me and backup to arrive. *No way* she had to do that. We were only a few minutes out. She could have waited. Hell, if niceties mattered, she could have turned over what she had to the FBI. But she didn't. She's taking crazy risks now. Want to know why?"

He shrugged.

"Because of *you*. Because without you, she doesn't feel like she has much of anything to live for."

Hunter moved to a nearby window. Stared out into the near-darkness.

"Look, about the breakup—I get it," Garrett went on. "You want to protect her. You don't think you'd have a future, you think it's your responsibility to shield her from whatever she'll face with you. You think if you let her go, she'll eventually find someone else and have a happy life. At least, maybe a longer one.

"But here's what you *don't* get. That's not what she wants. She wants *you*. For God's sake, don't ask me why. I've never understood women. But she does."

Garrett walked over and stood behind him. Hunter saw his reflection, dark gray, in the glass.

"Son, you want to go play vigilante, that's fine. And believe it or not, *she's* fine with that, too. She told me. But just accept something. Even if you leave the girl, you'll never be able to protect her, anyway. Because without you, she's empty. She'll stop caring about what happens to her, because she'll think she *has* no future. She'll start taking foolish chances, like tonight. Which will make her worthless to the Agency. Worse, I think she'll just lose interest in life."

Atop a distant electronic tower, a red warning light flashed in the gloom. Hunter drew a slow breath.

"Sounds like she's damned if I'm with her, and damned if I'm not."

Garrett's reflection put its hands on its hips.

"Then for God's sake, man, *stay with her*. At least make her happy. Give her something to live for."

Hunter said nothing. He just stared at the red blinking light.

"One more thing."

"Yes?"

"If you are really going to go through with this vigilante nonsense, and you want to accomplish anything by it, you'll never be able to do it without her. Because deep down, you're the same as she is. Without her, you won't have anything much to live for, either. You'll only have your anger. I know that about you, Dylan. When you're angry, you take stupid risks. You need something more. Something to live for. Something that will make you want to get back home alive."

The reflection moved close. Raised its hand.

He felt its weight on his shoulder.

"Son, Annie is the only thing in your life that will keep you sane. And maybe alive."

He sighed.

"At least for a little while longer."

3

The bandages began above her left wrist and grew thicker around the shoulder. On the right side of the bed, an IV drip bag hung on a metal rack behind her head, and a clear plastic tube snaked into the back of her right wrist. Her hair was an unruly mess on the pillow. Her eyes were half-closed, from the shock and the painkillers.

She was the most beautiful woman he had ever seen in his life.

He sat on the left side of her bed. She rested that hand on his big palm.

It felt too smooth, too cool. She looked too pale.

But she was smiling now.

"So. Do you think he's right about us?" she said.

Fishing, he knew. It made him smile, too.

"If he weren't such a good spymaster, he'd be the world's greatest shrink."

"Maybe he's the world's best spymaster *because* he's the world's greatest shrink."

They sat in silence, growing comfortable with each other again.

"Well," he said, "if the old man is right about us, maybe I should take back the things I said to you last time." His thumb ran over the engagement ring.

She closed her eyes.

"So, you mean you don't want to take it back?"

"Nah. I guess you can keep the silly thing." He raised his big left hand, wiggled the pinky. "Besides, it would never even fit the little finger on this catcher's mitt."

She opened her eyes and laughed.

Then he stood, leaned over her, and they kissed again.

His phone chirped. He checked the screen.

Read the text message from Julia.

"What's that about?"

He told her.

"Then you'd better go."

He shook his head. "I don't have to."

Her eyes no longer looked quite so sleepy.

"Yes you do," she said. "You have to finish this."

He stood there, bent over her face.

"I suppose I do."

"Then what are you waiting for, Dylan Hunter?"

"Another kiss, Annie Woods."

He got it. Then straightened.

"See you tomorrow."

She smiled.

"I know."

Garrett stood at the window. It was his turn to stare into the blank darkness. He saw Hunter's reflection in the glass and turned.

"So, how did it go?"

Hunter told him.

Garrett grunted—his all-purpose substitute for pleasure.

"I can't tell you how relieved I am."

"It wouldn't have happened without you, Grant. I owe you . . . again."

"Oh, I suspect you two would have come to your senses soon enough."

"I have a bit of unfinished business," Hunter said. "You'll read about it in the *Inquirer* tomorrow."

Garrett grunted again. "Lasher."

"And Trammel."

He raised a brow. "Oh. Of course, I didn't hear that."

"Of course. I didn't say that."

"And you plan to go out there alone."

"There's no choice. You know that."

Garrett's gaze returned to the window.

"You do realize if terrorism in Washington and the hit on Helm is tied to the Russians, we'll all be staring World War Three in the face. That is unacceptable."

"True. And unless he's stopped, right now, Trammel disappears. He'll take his billions and go live like a king in some mansion on the Riviera. That is unacceptable, too."

Garrett faced him. "Entirely unacceptable."

"Just wait for my call later, after I'm clear. I think you'll want to get out there, do some housekeeping before anyone else arrives. Make it look like something else."

"I'll do that. I may call on the assistance of a few retired guys who owe me."

The wintry eyes narrowed.

"Watch your six, Dylan."

Hunter flicked a glance back toward her room.

"I have good reason to do that, Grant."

FORTY-SEVEN

From the elevation of his solarium, Avery Trammel gazed out across the rear lawn, watching the last sliver of the sun sink behind the trees beyond the borders of his estate.

A poignant moment—likely the last night he would spend here. For years, it had been his private castle and sanctuary, the site of so many grand events and so much important work. But after tomorrow, when their afternoon flight left from Dulles for London, he would have to seek another home elsewhere. Given the grandeur of this one, he would take plenty of time to vet and select one. Whatever he chose had to be this estate's equal, at the least, if not its superior.

He checked the time. Eight twenty. It would be dark soon. Lasher had told him what to expect. Which meant that, within a few hours, another of his problems would be solved.

He watched two of his guards out there, patrolling the grounds—two of the five he kept on staff. For an estate this large, that was more than justified—in fact, barely adequate. Sokolov, who had secured them for him, had given assurances that, as former officers in Russia's military forces, these men were first-rate professionals. With Lasher, that would make six present tonight. Their combined skills, experience, and arms would be more than sufficient to deal with that *faux* reporter.

When Lasher arrived in the afternoon to tell him of the man's threats, he was at first incredulous. After all, Hunter had been present here, had seen his security team, had to know there would be electronic security measures, too. The man had to be deranged to imagine he could simply come in here and harm him.

He had summoned and informed the team, ordering them to be especially alert. His only concern was the bickering among them, which arose when Lasher insisted on being put in charge of security for the evening. It was clear he was not popular with the others. Probably because he was not Russian. Probably because he was so condescending to them, too.

It did not matter. Lasher had personal experience with Hunter the others lacked, and so was best suited to anticipating what he might do.

The sun had now disappeared behind the tree line, leaving only its residual golden glow. It reminded him he still had considerable packing to do. The next priority would be the items from the safe in his office. They would be added to the other critical items he had brought from the apartment desk. For security, these had to be the last items to be transported into the car in the morning. Each piece of luggage, obtained for him by Sokolov, had a special compartment that had repeatedly foiled electronic inspection. The Center was ingenious about such things. But because he had chartered a private jet for this trip, he would not have to worry about luggage inspections, anyway.

Trammel took a last look at the tidy, sweeping expanse of his lawn—at his trees and flower beds, at his tennis court and greenhouse, at his pond and gazebo. Sighing softly, he turned away to spend another bittersweet moment in appreciation of the tasteful elegance of his solarium.

So many fond memories in this grand home. He would miss the place.

2

At eight forty-five, Hunter drove the Ford van up the road past the estate from the south. He already had studied the layout and details for many hours, using satellite imagery from a government archive to which Wonk had provided access two years earlier. But he wanted to get a last brief overview himself, to commit to his visual memory an awareness of things that could be seen only at ground level.

Hunter passed the entrance to his right. The gatehouse interior was faintly lit, and a solitary man was in there. The man's car was parked off to one side. The long driveway behind the gates provided the only vehicular access into the estate's walls. He knew that the passage of his van was being observed by the security cameras posted at the entrance, and periodically along the brick walls of the estate. He also knew that infrared thermal cameras and detectors dotted the interior grounds; he had spotted those, too, during his earlier visit here.

He continued just past the northern border of the estate, around a bend in the road. Then killed his lights and engaged the night-vision camera and screen on his dashboard. He turned right, down a dark, narrow, rutted dirt lane. It ran through thick woods for about a hundred yards, then crossed a small, one-lane bridge over a creek. The trees thinned and the road dead-ended in a broad clearing next to a farmer's field. Years earlier, it had been a campsite for the Boy Scouts, until they found a better location. Now it was just a spot where hunters parked in deer season.

It also was within two hundred yards of the northern wall of Trammel's estate.

He got out, went around to the back of the van, and began hauling out and assembling his items. They were things he had been buying and storing since the previous year, during his vigilante operations. He had always thought they might come in handy one day. This was that day.

Hunter kept an eye on his watch. Nine fifteen, now. Timing was everything. This op had to be conducted strictly by the numbers, and this time some of those numbers were out of his control. Because he had to throw this plan together on such short notice, he couldn't follow his usual and preferred policy of operating alone. He had to count on some inside help.

Things would end very badly for him tonight if Julia didn't do her part.

3

In her early years onscreen, she'd had some parts in romantic suspense and action films. She had to keep telling herself that this was just another screen role she was playing. She had memorized her lines, and her director had told her where she had to be, what she had to do, and when. She had rehearsed it all in her mind. Now she just had to follow his script and hit her marks.

Julia Haight also tried to tell herself it was only the usual acting jitters when the clock on her bedroom wall showed it was nine twenty.

Show time, she told herself with forced bravado, trying to forget why these jitters were almost unbearable.

She left her open suitcases and scattered clothes on the bed, retrieved the phone he had given her, and moved to the door. Peeking out into the hallway, she saw no one. The house staff had been sent home at six; they were to return at seven a.m. So now it was only herself, Avery in his office, the guards outside, and that big scary blond guy, Lasher, who was wandering around, all in black—jacket, jeans, and boots.

Her destination now would be the garage under Avery's office. Right beneath his feet.

Even though she felt like creeping down the hallway on tiptoes, she knew furtiveness would look suspicious to anyone who might spot her. *You're his wife, Julia. This is your home. Act like it.*

She walked casually, unhurriedly down the hallway, then took the elevator, rather than the more conspicuous stairs. She stepped out into the foyer, glad she had worn soft-soled shoes that didn't resound off the marble. She crossed over to the corridor door leading out into the garage, flipped on the light, then entered, closing it behind her.

The place was chilly and smelled faintly of oil. Avery's Cadillac limousine, gleaming like a black mirror under the fluorescent lights, filled the nearest bay. Three other vehicles occupied the bays beside it, with the two farthest bays empty.

Her heart was throbbing in her throat and her chest felt tight. Trying to master her breathing, she moved away from the door, toward the center of the garage, where she could not be heard as easily. Huddled between two of the cars, she powered on the phone and tapped in the number he had given her.

"I'm here." His voice soft, barely above a whisper.

"Me too. In the garage."

"Great. How are you holding up?"

"I'm managing. Okay, now what do I do?"

"Just to make this easier, are there any tools in the garage?"

"I think so. Yes. There's a bench over here along the back wall."

She listened as he described what to look for. The closest thing she found was a pair of short pruning shears.

"That'll do. You told me earlier you located the electrical boxes out there. That's our next stop."

She went over to the wall adjacent to the limo.

"Okay. I'm next to them."

"Now, describe them for me."

"One is just a metal box with cables going into the bottom. The other has a row of lights on the front."

"That's the one we want. That houses the automatic transfer switch for the house's backup power generator. Now we're going to disable that generator."

She followed his instructions, tugging a bunch of little plastic plugs out of their tiny sockets. Then he had her use the shears to cut those plugs off the ends of the wires they were attached to. He told her to take those plugs with her, so she stuffed them into the pocket of her sweater. Next, he had her snap off a couple of other little parts, then close the box again.

"Very good, Julia. You're doing great. Now the only thing left for us to do is make sure the cars won't work. Let's start with the limo."

That took longer. She was able to get inside the limo and open its hood, then followed his instructions about cutting some wires and hoses and belts inside. He told her to lower the hood very slowly, leaving it ajar rather than slamming it shut.

"The other cars are locked," she reported to him, alarmed.

"That's okay. Let's just let the air out of some of the tires, okay? That will slow them down enough."

He told her what to do about that. The loud hissing made her nervous. He had her find a rag and lay it over the tire valve while she used a nail to deflate them.

"All right, Julia, it's nine thirty-seven, and we've got to let it go at that."

"But I flattened only two tires on the Mercedes."

"That's okay. We're out of time. The last thing I want you to do before you leave the garage is open up the back of the phone, remove the battery, then remove the SIM card. Do you know what that is, and how to do it?"

"Yes. I think so. I did that once."

"Good. Next, wipe your fingerprints off that card with the rag, then smash it into little pieces before you leave the garage. Kick the pieces somewhere out of sight. After that, wipe all your fingerprints off the phone, too, and hide it somewhere hard to find—maybe under the tool bench or in a cabinet. But don't waste much time doing it. Can you remember all that?"

"I'm good at remembering lines," she said, forcing a chuckle she didn't feel.

"I know you are. Okay, do what I said, very quickly, then go straight to your basement and lock yourself in the room down there you told me about. All your phones and electricity will stop working very shortly. So when you get there, switch on the battery backup power so you'll have light and fresh air. Under *no* circumstances are you to come out—no matter what you hear or see—until I come and get you. Or the other person I told you about comes and shows you an ID. *Only* for us. Do you understand?"

"I understand."

"Okay. I've got to go."

"I'm scared."

"It will be all right." His hard voice was suddenly gentle. "After tonight, they won't hurt anyone else. And they won't hurt you. I'll make sure you're safe. You have my word on that, Julia."

"Thank you," she whispered.

"Thank *you*. You are doing a great thing tonight. You'll realize that very soon."

Then he was gone.

She followed his instructions about the phone, jamming the pieces into a large bag of salt for their water system. Then she went to the door, put her hand on the knob, and shut off the light.

Standing there for a moment in the dark, she suddenly felt on the edge of tears. She didn't know exactly what he was going to do. She didn't want to think about that. She only wanted this nightmare to be over.

She carefully turned the knob. Poked her head into the hallway. It was empty.

You are his wife. You own this place.

Julia Haight took a deep breath, drew herself up like a queen, and strode out toward the foyer.

One of the guards, the dark Slavic-looking one, was standing there with a holster on his hip, facing away, toward the front door. He heard her approach and turned, a bit startled.

"Oh. Hello, Ms. Haight."

"Good evening, Dimitri."

He glanced down her body quizzically.

Her eyes followed his. She saw the dark oily stains on her fingers. Her heart skipped.

You belong here. He's the hired help . . .

She held up her dirty hands and laughed.

"You can see why I hate packing," she said.

He grinned and nodded.

"*Da.* Me too."

She continued past him, to the elevator.

Rode it down, this time, to the basement.

She got out, turned on the basement lights, and hurried straight to the back, to the blocky room protruding from the rear wall. Years ago, Avery explained he wanted to make sure he'd never be vulnerable to kidnappers. So he had this "panic room" constructed with reinforced concrete. He had its heavy steel door lined with the stuff they use in bulletproof vests, and the square window next to it made of thick bulletproof glass.

Julia pulled open the heavy door, went inside, shoved it shut, then threw the twin deadbolts behind her. She flipped the switch that started up its self-contained power supply—a series of twelve-volt batteries stored in the base of its large interior closet. These powered the lights and, as needed, external security cameras, ~~a land line~~, an amateur radio set, an alarm, and an air-filtration system. Also in the closet were emergency tools and supplies, a portable toilet, and—attached inside its door—a gun rack.

Trembling and tense, she sat in a chair.

The only sound she could hear was the faint hum of the air blower.

The battery-powered digital clock on the wall said it was nine forty-six.

4

Nine forty-six.

From the clearing, Hunter launched the first drone, a foldable octocopter carrying a thermal-imaging camera, toward the rear of Trammel's estate. Its powerful battery gave it an impressive flight time of twenty-five minutes, and an operating range of two thousand meters—well beyond what he'd need tonight. Guided by GPS, the speedy drone was in position in just fifty seconds, hovering above five hundred meters, just off the back of the property. He rotated it and let it hover there, the camera aimed at the estate. On his cell phone, he saw three glowing silhouettes of guards in various places on the back lawn.

Nine forty-seven.

Time to create a diversion—for those on the estate, but also for anyone in the area.

He pressed a button on a handheld remote device. It activated one of several firing modules, connected by wires to bays of tubes he'd spread out on the bare ground. With a rushing sound and a trail of sparks, the first aerial rocket speared skyward, and three hundred feet overhead it exploded with a colossal flash and thunderous *boom*.

That should get their attention.

Hunter knew little about fireworks, but some time ago he realized they might one day come in handy for a purpose like this. Last summer he located a licensed pyrotechnics expert willing to bend the rules and put together a professional, ready-to-launch show for him—including the fireworks, the necessary equipment, timed-event scripting software, and a crash course of instruction—all in exchange for an amount of cash hard to turn down. The program the guy prepared would run automatically for the next half-hour. With its flashes and bangs, the display would provide Hunter the ideal camouflage, offering the surrounding community a perfectly mundane and entertaining explanation for what was about to go down on the adjacent estate.

Nine forty-eight.

Using another phone, Hunter launched his second drone. This system had set him back another twelve thousand bucks. It combined a heavy-lift octocopter carrying a high-powered, sophisticated communications jammer Wonk had customized for him. As another rocket soared off over the field, he guided this drone low above the trees, to the boundary of Trammel's property, then across the yard and over his house. He settled it down carefully on a flat portion of the roof, then killed the drone's motor.

Those on the grounds didn't know it now, but except for their walkie-talkies and earpieces, their wireless phones were now blocked for a circumference of one hundred fifty meters.

Nine fifty.

Leaving the fireworks equipment, he carried the phones back to the cab of the van and placed them on the passenger seat, next to his silenced Sig P-228.

He couldn't go in heavy and start a firefight against a half-dozen men. Using an automatic rifle might reveal his positions, let them converge on him. And slow him down, make him less maneuverable. No, success tonight—even survival—would depend on speed and stealth. He'd have to get in close to them, take them out one at a time.

He started up the van and headed back along the dark dirt road, bright and easy to follow on the night-vision screen. Reaching the intersection of the main road, he turned back toward the estate's entrance. As he neared it, he picked up the Sig and laid it in his lap, along with a leather, lead-weighted blackjack.

FORTY-EIGHT

"What was *that?*" Trammel called out to Lasher as a loud explosion shook the house.

Lasher, who had been informally standing sentry outside the doorway of Trammel's inner office, had seen the flash in the window of the main office, which faced north. He drew his Glock instinctively and ran to the side of the window, peeping around quickly then ducking back. Maybe Hunter was somewhere out there with that Barrett sniper cannon of his, trained on this place.

Trammel came rushing out of his office. "What in the world?"

Lasher motioned him to stand back. "Don't get near the window. If Hunter's over there, he could have a rifle and be waiting for us to come to the window so he can pick us off."

Trammel scrambled back into the office doorway. "He could do something like that?"

"Like I said, he's a pro. And sneaky."

Another flash filled the window and Lasher took another fast peek, pulling back again. "I'll be damned. Fireworks." He snorted. "Got to hand it to the bastard, he's full of tricks."

Over his walkie-talkie he heard the Russians babbling excitedly. He grabbed it from his belt and raised it to his lips.

"Hey out there!" he snapped. "Heads up! I think our guy is making his move." He gave them quick positioning orders.

"Well, if you think he is out there with a rifle, then that changes things," Trammel said, his voice nervous. "I am not about to be shot right here in my house." He stormed back into his own office.

Lasher wondered what he meant. Keeping away from the window, he followed Trammel through the doorway. He found him behind his desk with his cell phone to his ear, frowning. He looked at it and tapped the screen. Put it to his ear again.

They heard another bang, followed by a *rat-tat-tat-tat* of smaller explosions.

"This thing does not appear to be working," Trammel said. "Let me have yours."

The pompous prick's tone irritated him.

"Who are you trying to call?"

"The police. We need to get them here to stop him."

Lasher felt his ten million dollars about to slip away.

"No! I mean—we've got this. Seriously, sir. You have just one guy against me, and five other pros backing me. He'll be dead inside a half hour."

"So you say. But as long as *I* am paying the bills for security, *I* shall be the one to decide about such things. If you expect to be employed one more minute, *give me your phone.*"

He held his hand out, palm up.

Lasher wanted to pull his Glock and *waste* the son of a bitch right there. But the thought of the ten mill forced him to swallow his pride. For now.

He strode over and handed over his phone.

Trammel tapped in the number. Waited. Then frowned again. Looked at it again.

"What is going on here?"

"May I have a look, sir?"

The billionaire handed it back to him. Lasher tapped a few times. Then realized.

"He's blocking our commo."

"What do you mean?"

"He's jamming our cell signals. Probably wi-fi, too."

Trammel blinked. "He can do *that*, too?"

"Apparently," he answered, for the first time feeling a hint of uneasiness.

"Well, there is a land line on my secretary's desk," Trammel said, storming around his. "I shall—"

Then the lights went out.

2

Hunter cut his engine fifty yards from the driveway entrance and let the van roll forward silently, lights off. It was fortunate this isolated country road was so lightly traveled. During his recon, sometimes fifteen minutes would pass without any traffic.

He steered to the berm on the left side of the road and allowed the van to drift to a stop. He'd already unscrewed the dome bulb, so when he exited, no light showed.

He was dressed entirely in black; a hooded ski mask now covered all of his face except his mouth and eyes. He crept up fast and silently along the side of the road toward the gatehouse. Its bright security lights illuminated the immediate area.

It was almost too good to be true. The guard was standing outside the structure in the middle of the driveway, his back to the road, watching the fireworks. He was conversing with someone over a walkie-talkie, held in his left hand.

Hunter knew the security cameras would reveal his presence if anyone were monitoring them inside the house. He had to hope they were distracted. He vaulted the low brick wall to get inside the gates, then paused behind a tree next to the driveway, waiting for the next diverting burst of light from the area north of the house. As the flashing and echoing thunder cracked the air, he pounced across the pavement like a cat, covering the distance to the guard in under three seconds.

With his right hand he swung the blackjack hard against the guard's skull. Simultaneously, he snared the guy's walkie-talkie with his left, then wrapped that arm around the falling body. He dragged the stunned man back inside the gatehouse and dumped him on the floor, face down. Setting the walkie-talkie on the small counter, he grabbed plastic zip ties from his pocket and quickly bound his hands behind his back. There was a corded desk phone in there, too. He unplugged the modular ends of its handset cord and used it to tie the man's feet together; then, using the wall cord, he hog-tied his feet up behind him to his bound hands, forcing his back to arch like a bow. The guard started to moan, so he yanked off the guy's clip-on tie and jammed it into his mouth. He flipped him over onto his side, to take a little of the strain off his back and hands. Then he splashed his face with the contents of his water bottle.

"*Slushai' menye vnimatel'no!*" Hunter spoke in Russian. "Listen to me! Nod if you hear and understand."

The man whined behind the gag, but nodded. Tears of pain streamed from his eyes.

"I am going to do you the great favor of letting you live, my friend. You will be the only one who survives tonight. That's because I want you to tell all your friends that *this* is what happens when you work for someone like Trammel, who tries to cheat the *Solntsevskaya Bratva*," he growled, referring to the most powerful Russian crime syndicate. "Did you hear me? Did you understand what I said? Nod if you did."

The helpless man nodded.

"You tell your friends. And you tell the American cops, too, they should stay away from the *Bratva*. Da?"

The guy nodded again.

Hunter left him like that. He shut off the interior light and floodlights around the booth, then took the walkie-talkie and slid the door shut.

He listened to the confused, anxious Russian chatter among the guards.

One down, five to go.

He trotted back to his van. From the back, he grabbed a coil of thin detonating cord and plastic igniter cord. He ran to the nearby utility company pole and wrapped the detonating cord around the electric feeder wire conduit attached to the pole. The conduit carried electricity underground, from the pole over to the house.

Thirty seconds later, there was a bright flash, and the electrical conduit had a sizable gap blown in its middle.

3

"But I have a backup generator!" Trammel shouted in the dark room. "Why is there no power?"

Lasher didn't know, but he had a strong feeling Hunter had somehow knocked it offline.

They bent over the secretary's desk, illuminated by the faint light from their cell phones, only to find it was a cordless phone system, knocked out of service along with the electric power.

"Any of you fellows have a flashlight I might borrow?" Hunter's gruff baritone voice crackled over the walkie-talkie.

A series of flashes cut colored swatches across the walls and their faces, followed immediately by an explosive staccato that made Lasher flinch. Trammel's eyes were barely visible in the faint light from his phone, and only because they were so wide with fear. But he could hear him breathing heavily.

So he's gotten a walkie-talkie. Which probably means one of the men outside is down.

"What's the matter, Lasher? Cat got your tongue? Or are you waiting for Trammel to tell you what to think?"

Don't be baited.

"I've been looking forward to our meeting, Hunter. And thanks for the fireworks. I'm enjoying the show."

"Savor it. It'll be the last thing you enjoy."

Suddenly Hunter launched into fluent Russian.

"What is he saying?" Trammel whispered.

"I don't know," he replied, puzzled. Then it dawned on him that whatever he was doing, it had to be spread confusion and demoralization among the Russian guards.

"Security team! Whatever he's saying, don't listen! He's lying. Fall back from the grounds and get inside the house for close protection."

"Give me that thing! I must talk to them!" Trammel demanded.

Seething, Lasher complied.

"Listen to me. This is Mr. Trammel. I shall give a one hundred thousand dollar bonus to the man who kills Dylan Hunter."

"Just a goddamned minute!" Lasher exploded. "Hunter is *mine*. He was *my* assignment."

"I accept offer, Mr. Trammel," one of the guards said over the speaker.

"Me too."

"Same here."

"Mr. Trammel, sir, this is Yuri. That is good for me, too."

Hunter laughed. "Finders, keepers. But remember—I warned you."

"If you want *your* bonus, Mr. Lasher," Trammel snarled, "then join them out there and earn it."

"Don't you see? That's exactly what he wants! He wants us all outside, where he can pick us off. If you want close protection, the men should come in here."

"I am not going to wait here while you argue with each other. I am going to protect myself." He groped his way back into his darkened inner office.

Lasher couldn't believe this was happening. He followed. He saw Trammel's silhouette behind his desk, and he heard the familiar sound of a round being racked into a handgun.

"Don't tell me *you* are going out there," he said.

"Of course not. I am heading to my safe room in the basement, while you people deal with him. Come and notify me when it is done."

4

Trying to remain invisible, the security team prowled the yard taking cover behind trees, walls, and large decorative planters. From the way they signaled each other, he could tell they had night-vision goggles.

But he was doing the same thing—using the cover provided by the grounds. The difference was that he had the advantage of infrared thermal imaging goggles. Their heat signatures registered whenever the slightest part of them was exposed, and they even left heat prints on the ground where they had stood.

Hunter had given them a chance to flee. Over the walkie-talkie, in Russian, he spun them the same yarn about the Russian syndicate he'd given the guy in the gatehouse. However, the prospect of a big payday proved to be irresistible to them.

Now it would prove to be costly to them.

He was lying prone behind a flower bed not far from the greenhouse. Thirty yards ahead, he could make out the flickering heat signature of a figure hiding behind a tall shrub. The distance was a reasonable challenge, and the bush might deflect the round, but it was time to cut down the odds. He aimed carefully, a little high, watched his breathing, and squeezed off a round.

Then watched the flickering through the branches melt into a bright puddle on the ground.

Through the suppressor, the nine millimeter gunshot sounded not much louder than a set of car keys dropped onto a floor.

Two down.

Seeing no heat signatures nearby, he rolled away, rose into a crouching dash and stopped behind a human-sized garden statue. This position afforded a different vantage point—and another target. A covered gas grill sat on a patio area near the house. The blocky shape provided good cover, except that someone's feet were visible as bright blobs beneath the cover. He decided to circle behind the small greenhouse and approach through some trees, from the target's side.

Again spotting no other bright glowing heat sources, he sprinted from the statue to the side of the greenhouse. No response. Good. He moved along the glass wall, to the rear corner. Paused. Poked his head around the back . . .

. . . and was confronted by a dazzling blob, right in front of him.

The guard fired—just as Hunter jerked his head back, dropped to one knee, then rolled onto his side. Continuing to fire, the guard came whipping around the corner, expecting to find Hunter standing there against the glass wall. But before the guy could react, Hunter fired four times into his face and upper body. The man crumpled to the ground right beside him, his left arm landing across Hunter's legs.

Hunter had forgotten, nearly fatally, that glass usually blocks infrared images. The guy had probably seen *him* with night-vision goggles right through the windows, while to Hunter the guard was invisible.

Now it was *three down,* but his position was blown. Going forward behind glass walls was a non-starter. He'd have to retreat toward the rear of the yard.

He kicked away the shooter's arm, rolled to his right and then to his feet. Within a few yards he heard gunshots and the whiz of bullets flying past. He veered to the left, then almost immediately back to the right, trying to keep an erratic, unpredictable course. He heard yelling behind him, the shooter summoning others, as he approached the pond. The shots seemed less accurate now—the combination of distance, his movement, and perhaps the shooter in motion, too, making a hit a matter of blind luck. He found himself nearing the willow tree where Trammel had fed his fish, so he zig-zagged again, then darted back toward the tree.

A final shot nearly clipped his shoe as he spun around the tree. Panting, he looked back and saw his pursuer running left, toward a tree of his own. Hunter crouched, braced himself against the tree, and trained the Sig's sights at a spot two feet from that tree trunk, trying to time his shot for the guy's arrival. He fired and the shooter ran right into the bullet, spinning and falling right past the tree trunk into a motionless heap.

Four down.

Instantly a chunk of the willow exploded above his head, followed by a much louder report.

Somebody had a rifle—and that changed everything.

5

Glock in hand, Lasher stumbled his way through the dark hallways to the sweeping staircase at the front of the house, then clung to the railing as he clambered down, trying hard not to miss a step. He made it to the bottom then turned and ran straight back through the foyer, then the corridor into the drawing room, then on into the solarium.

Silhouetted against the moonlit sky on the balcony outside the windows, a man stood with a rifle at his shoulder, firing repeatedly, methodically, out into the yard. Lasher stopped running and moved forward cautiously. To his left, fireworks lit the tall, curving windows like colored strobe lights, and the thunder of the blasts reverberated around the semicircular room. He moved to the French doors and, very quietly, out onto the balcony.

He saw that the man with the AK-47 was one of the pair he'd confronted when he first visited Trammel here—the dark-haired guy who had searched him.

"Vitaly, do you have him?"

Startled, the guy flicked a glance toward him, then turned back to his target, chuckling.

"Oh, I have him, all right. Behind that tree." He fired again. There were colored decorative lights out there, around the circumference of the pond, and Lasher saw the shot chip splinters off the willow tree.

"Where are the others?"

Vitaly grimaced. "Bastard down there got them. When I go get AK from room, I come back and see Arkady go down, over there. Then I see others down. But he's dead meat now. He can't run from tree because I nail him." He flicked another grin. "Looks like I get hundred thousand tonight—huh?"

"Don't count your chickens before they hatch."

"What's that mean?"

"It's an American expression—Boris."

Lasher saw the scowl, and waited for Vitaly's head to turn his way. He wanted to see him grinning as he did it.

He watched the Russian's eyes widen with the alarm that was just about to turn into terror when he fired into his gut. Vitaly's knees buckled, but he kept his feet and then screamed. He was swinging the AK around when Lasher shot him again, a little higher. The rifle muzzle sank in arms grown slack, and Vitaly's mouth fell open and his head turned upward, toward the night sky.

Lasher stepped forward and shot him in his open mouth. He half-heard the AK clatter to the balcony as the fireworks boomed and flashed behind him and he fired again and again into the man's falling body . . .

Hunter had squeezed himself in tightly behind the tree trunk. He couldn't move. The grounds around the tree were wide open. He could try to dive into the pond, almost twenty feet away. But even if he made it, the guy would take him out the minute he came up for air. The shooter could just sit there with the rifle and wait him out. Meanwhile, his return fire with the pistol could never reach that balcony accurately. He'd merely empty his weapon, pointlessly.

He had gambled by not bringing his own rifle—and apparently lost.

Another shot chipped splinters and sawdust less than a foot away.

The thought flashed through his mind that he might never get either Lasher or Trammel . . . and then he thought of Annie and what he had told her about coming back . . . and then another shot rang out—but much softer . . . and then he heard a blood-curdling scream, and yet another shot . . . then another . . . another . . .

He dared a fast look around the tree—to see two men on the balcony, one shooting the other, who was tumbling backward, down the stairs, then falling off them and into the yard.

Somewhere, something automatic in him registered and said: *Five down.*

The man stood looking at the fallen body, then turned to him and called out.

"So now it's just you and me, Hunter. Winner takes all."

Then he laughed.

6

Trammel stumbled forward in the near-darkness, holding his .45 caliber Sig-Sauer. He called out for Julia, wondering why he had not seen her in hours, wondering if, hearing the frightening racket, she had hidden herself in her bedroom. He paused in the hallway going back to their bedrooms and yelled several times, but got no answer.

Well, it was too volatile and dangerous now to go searching for her in the dark. After all, she could be *anywhere*. The flashing of the fireworks helped a little as he felt his way down the staircase. Then, to reach the basement, he had to grope his way down the Stygian blackness of the interior stairwell, next to the useless elevator.

Opening the door there, he was surprised to see a square of light ahead in the darkness. Then he realized what it was—and also realized that the clever girl had beaten him here. He hurried across the floor toward that square, a bright beacon promising safety in the madness. They would wait it out together in here, then forever leave behind the hell-hole that was the United States of America.

He reached the three-foot-square window and looked inside. There she was, slumped in one of the chairs, head down, looking lost.

He tried the door. Locked, of course. He moved back to the window.

"Julia!" he shouted.

Her head snapped up. But her wide-eyed expression was one of *fear*.

"Julia, dear! Let me in. Quickly. Nothing to fear—I am alone."

But she just stared at him, looking as if her breathing had quickened. Then she gave her head a slight shake and rose to her feet. She narrowed her eyes and raised her chin, as if gathering herself for something.

"No!" she shouted, suddenly looking defiant.

He stood there, unable to believe it.

"What . . . what are you saying? Let me in!"

She took a step forward, her eyes glittering, her head slowly shaking back and forth.

"No, I will *not!*"

For several seconds he could not speak. Then, bewildered, he asked:

"But *why?*"

She took two more steps, right up to the glass. Their faces were only a foot apart.

"Because you are a *fraud*—Avis Tremills!"

It was as if he had been smashed by a fist. He actually wobbled and recoiled a step back, staring at her, unable to believe it.

"You are a total fraud. You lied to me for twenty years. You lied to everyone. Your entire *life* is one goddamned lie. You have betrayed me. You have betrayed friends. You have betrayed your country—the country that gave you *everything.* And I know it *all.* I know everything about you. I know about your communist parents. I know about your secret life as a spy for Russia. I know about Emmalee Conn, and that she was sleeping with you, and I also know what you *did* to her. You are a fraud, Avery—and a traitor, and goddamn you, a *murderer!*"

This could not be happening.

"How . . ." he gasped, realizing it was the wrong word.

"How? That day when you ran out of the apartment. Remember? You accidentally left your study door open. I knew for a long time you were hiding something, and I knew you were having an affair. So I went in to see if I could learn the truth. And I did. Did I ever! A truth about my own *husband,* worse than anything I could have imagined."

"No," he said hopelessly. "You have gotten it all wrong! Julia, we must talk about this. We—"

"There is no 'we' and *nothing* to talk about. Tonight, Avery, you face reality. Tonight it all comes crashing down on you. Tonight you begin to pay for all the evil you have done. And the worst thing about you is that you did it all of it in the name of your mother and father!"

"Shut up!" he shouted, banging his fist on the glass.

"Can't face it, can you? The fact is, your traitor parents turned you into a twisted mess."

"Shut up, you bitch!"

"Tomorrow, the world will know *everything* about you and your traitor parents. They'll—"

He made an inarticulate growl, pointed his gun at her face, and pulled the trigger.

In the confined space of the basement, the roar of the .45 was deafening. The bulletproof glass shattered—or the outer glass layer did. The ballistic, glass-clad polycarbonate did not break through.

She staggered back, stunned.

He stepped back and fired again. And again. And in blind rage kept firing. The entire three-by-three-foot square became completely opaque, like a pile of snow. But Trammel, who had always taken pride in buying only the best, was thwarted. After nine shots, the gun was empty.

He went to the door and in raw fury pounded it with his fists and the gun, screaming for her to let him in.

After a minute, dizzy and panting, he stopped. He leaned his forehead against the cold steel.

Heard the faint sound of her crying.

The empty gun hanging in his hand, Avery Trammel shuffled slowly back toward the stairs, the darkness deepening with every step away from that bright square.

7

"Hunter, you can come out, now. I'm not going to shoot you. See?"

He snapped a glance around the tree. Lasher held the rifle by its barrel, and swung it forward, pitching it into the grass. He held up his Glock.

"See? I'm leaving it here."

He squatted and put it down on the balcony. Raised his hands, palm outward.

"All I want is what I said before. We meet, hand-to-hand, no weapons. If you toss your own weapon out there, we can do this. The winner walks away. Deal?"

Hunter thought about it. Of course he didn't trust him. But Lasher was out of the effective range of his Sig. He could never get away from this tree still carrying the pistol, not without Lasher retrieving the rifle and gunning him down. So he was trapped here and would eventually die, unless he played along.

And then there was something more primitive to consider, too. Something more elemental.

The prospect of dealing with Lasher up close and personally.

Of looking into the killer's eyes as he died.

"All right," he shouted. "You step away from those weapons, I'll toss out mine—and we can walk over into the middle of the yard and meet there."

"Great. I'm coming down now."

Lasher trotted down the stairs, then moved forward, putting distance between himself and the rifle.

Hunter stepped away from the tree and pitched the Sig and ski mask aside. Then walked out into the middle of the yard. He watched as the killer came to meet him.

He assessed what he could of Lasher's physical and fighting abilities. The man had about thirty pounds and two inches on him, and the battered knuckles of a boxer or MMA guy. With his shoulders and legs, he obviously was a lifter. The big legs didn't seem to move particularly fast. So, all in all, probably MMA, but not a kicker. He'd likely come straight in, try to rush you and get you on the ground, where he could overpower you, break limbs, choke you out, pound you.

It would be a good idea to stay off the ground with this guy.

And finish him fast.

"Gee, Hunter, we both look like Ninjas. All in black," Lasher chuckled. He moved in deliberately and unhurriedly, flat-footed, not bouncing. He raised his fists, boxer-style, left fist forward.

Hunter knew the guy was right-handed. He didn't need to be tagged by a haymaker, so he started to circle to his own right, away from Lasher's power punch. He made no moves to reveal what he knew.

"You still have your jacket on," he said.

Lasher smirked and shrugged, bulging his trapezius and neck muscles. "I like this jacket. Besides, I don't think I'm going to break a sweat."

It made no sense for him to keep the jacket on.

"Don't you want to lose the jacket so you can show off your manly muscles?"

A fleeting movement passed over Lasher's face. He was hiding something under that jacket.

"You want it off me, you can try to take it off."

Hunter watched his eyes and body language. Sensed that the fist movements were just feints. Lasher was preparing to rush him, put him down, then pound him.

Hunter saw the legs tense, so when the lurch forward started he was ready, leaping to the right, leaning, then snapping a hard left kick to the side of Lasher's left knee. The guy's bulk and inertia continued him forward, like a bull passing a matador, but the knee gave way and he went down in the grass on his knees and arms.

Lasher's arms were straight and propping him up from the ground. Hunter hopped forward and snapped a right side kick toward Lasher's rigid left elbow, which would have snapped it at the joint had it landed. But still off-balance, Lasher toppled forward farther, and Hunter's kick just scraped his triceps. Lasher immediately rolled onto his back, cocking his right leg to kick out and his big hand to grab. Hunter thought better of it and started circling the fallen man. Slowly, gingerly, ready to grab, Lasher regained his feet. However, he was limping from the kick to his knee, which probably came close to dislocating it.

There were no more taunts now; both were serious and focused—so much so that the fireworks were almost pushed out of awareness. While Hunter watched Lasher's movements, little snippets of memories about his killings kept returning.

Arnold Wasserman . . . the Chechen . . .

They were moving by degrees toward the south end of the pond area. Whenever Hunter made a move to come back, Lasher stepped over to cut him off. He became aware that this was deliberate, that Lasher was trying to corral him into a narrower area, where it would be harder to maneuver and escape—like a boxer cutting off the ring. They were drifting inexorably toward the pathway that led up onto the little bridge that went out to the gazebo.

Lasher did something else. He started to unbutton his right jacket sleeve. Hunter glanced there, wondered why alarm bells were going off . . .

. . . then, in a series lightning images, he saw Lasher's hand drop with a jerk—the glint of pond lights on something metallic dropping from his sleeve—his hand closing on a cylinder and then rising with a stiletto, rising too high, rising in front of his smirking mouth and mocking eyes that began to squint down its length . . .

. . . and then knowing, Hunter snapped his upper body and head to the left in time with a loud *ping* and the draft of the ballistic blade whizzing past his cheek.

The reactive move threw himself off-balance, sent him stumbling into a flower bed—and Lasher, showing but a second's surprise, lowered his head and charged him. Hunter's foot caught on something, and the momentum spun him, and suddenly he was going down—face down—and feeling Lasher piling right on him, and knowing he was in trouble.

He landed on his forearms and knees in the soft earth, with Lasher's full smothering weight crashing down upon his back—and he felt the man's thick, powerful left arm snake around his neck as his big right palm slapped against the back of his head to add to the pressure, and he knew Lasher was going for the choke, and he knew then how Arnold Wasserman had died . . .

And in that instant's awareness he lowered his chin and hunched his shoulders to protect his neck and throat, and turned his chin left, into the crook of Lasher's arm—and at the same instant he tucked his right arm under him and twisted his body right, and pushed up hard with his left leg, throwing Lasher off his back before the man could wrap his legs around him. And in the next split second before Lasher could move, Hunter shot his left elbow down into the man's groin, not once, not twice, but four times, fast and hard, and heard him gasp and then groan explosively as his body curled and his arms jerked down from Hunter's neck.

And pulling free, Hunter leaned forward, then whipped back around, shooting the elbow down again, this time into Lasher's jaw. He felt and heard something crack there and the man's body went soft.

And seeing his face he thought of all the malignancy of this monster, all the horrors he had committed, all the innocent lives he had destroyed, and he remembered their names and faces, and he knew what he had to do, and how.

Lasher moaned and writhed helplessly; his glassy eyes bulged and jaw hung twisted and slack. But as Hunter rolled to his feet, he knew that was not enough for him—not nearly enough.

"Are you still with me, Lasher? Oh, good. Listen up now. I'm going to tell you the story of your life. You wanted to be a winner, right? But to you, that meant being the *only* winner. It meant making everyone else lose. Your victory meant their defeat. Your pleasure meant their pain. Your life meant their deaths. Everything you won was taken from the lives and happiness of others. But you don't get to keep those kinds of winnings."

The fireworks finale was starting as he grabbed Lasher by the ankle and dragged him over to a cement planter. Lasher had no strength to resist. Hunter raised the killer's left leg so that its calf was braced at an angle against the planter.

"This is for the life you took from Emmalee Conn."

He stomped on the shin bone, breaking it. Lasher's scream was drowned out by the thunderous noise just a few hundred yards away.

He did the same with the other leg. Lasher howled again in anguish.

"And that was for stealing the health and presidency from Roger Helm."

He flipped him onto his stomach, twisted his left arm behind him.

"Now, this is for the poor old man you murdered in his apartment that same day."

He kicked the back of the twisted arm at the shoulder, dislocating it. Then did the same with the other arm. Lasher's cries had become more muted, now.

"That was for everyone else whose lives you've wrecked. The girls you raped in the military. The people you assassinated. The ones you've terrorized and threatened. Including me, and people dear to me."

Lasher passed out from the pain. Hunter let him have a minute, then fetched and splashed some water from the pond onto his head, bringing him around.

The fireworks were constant flashes and explosions now, ripping the sky apart.

He squatted down. He had to get right in his face to be heard.

"There's one other person to remember, Lasher. One more innocent person you killed. A dedicated young reporter named Arnold Wasserman. He was the best friend of a buddy of mine. When I figured out you killed him, then how you did it, I decided there was only one fitting, final punishment for you."

He grabbed Lasher's jacket and dragged him to the pond's edge.

"You rendered Arnold helpless, and then you drowned him. I bet there was a point when he knew exactly what was happening. When he couldn't breathe and was swallowing water and knew he was dying. Well, I thought maybe *you* should know what that feels like, *Ron.* That's why I just took away your use of your arms and legs."

He grabbed the murderer by the collar of his jacket, then heaved him upright. Held him over the pond, suspended and screaming, as the fireworks finale pounded the air. To be heard, he had to shout it.

"You lived by the rule of 'winner takes all.' Now die by it. Ron Larsen—you lose."

He dumped him into the shallow pond.

The big fish scattered to a safe distance to watch an alien spectacle. The colored lights at the pond's edge and the last seconds of the fireworks revealed a human form flailing and twisting helplessly in barely three feet of water, limbs bending, allowing the man no ability to stand, to grab, to crawl.

For a brief, final instant, the killer somehow managed, despite his agony, to raise his head above the water, just once. His skin was white and, like the fish, his lips pursed and puffed and his eyes bugged out as they fixed their last living gaze on the face of Dylan Hunter.

8

He sat alone, in a small puddle of light at the desk in his office, surrounded by darkness and, for the past moments, merciful silence.

He had found a flashlight in Julia's nightstand, and then a small battery-operated LED lantern out in the garage. He had gone to the garage to try to escape by car, only to find that his last way out had been cut off—that he was, for now, condemned to remain for at least a while longer in this vile country, and sentenced to ponder how so much had gone so wrong.

That she had sabotaged the cars, there was no doubt. Just as there was no doubt that she had betrayed him. She had violated the inviolable trust between a husband and wife, revealing sensitive secrets that any partner had a right to regard as private and privileged. He would never forgive her for this. Nor for the unspeakable insults against his parents. No one could be permitted to say such things and get away with it.

And to do it while hiding behind a wall *he* had provided for her safety.

Well, she could rot in there.

He looked at his watch. Ten forty. He was relieved now that everything had quieted down outside. Obviously, the threat had been eliminated. Lasher should be reporting back at any time.

For a time, he had had his doubts about the man; but his courage and skills in these matters was unquestionable. He had taken on all his big assignments: the actions against Muller and Helm; the neutralization of Emmalee Conn when she had become a threat; the hiring of Shishani for the terrorism actions; now, the elimination of the enigma operating under the alias of Dylan Hunter. As annoyingly arrogant as the man could sometimes be, Lasher had been a reliable contractor. In exchange for everything, he probably deserved the additional ten million.

If there were a lesson here, it would be to entrust one's security to the vetted professionals—to Lasher, and to the team hand-picked by Sokolov. He hoped none of them had been injured this evening; he would like to keep some of them around, wherever he wound up living.

Once settled, he would phone Leon and thank him for his splendid recommendations.

He did not relish staying up hours more, especially in the absence of electricity, to finish packing. This lantern was woefully inadequate. Well, he would have to make do. It was important to salvage his critical and confidential papers and decide which would be of future use, and which should be burned in the yard.

Trammel's eyes rested on the envelope at the corner of his desk.

Those photos were the source of his future power. The keys to the kingdom. His Declaration of Independence from Moscow. The Golden Fleece in his quest to vindicate the legacy of his father and mother. Pick your metaphor, however strained or grandiose; but it nonetheless remained true that the Conn/Spencer photos had been *the* turning point during a bleak period. He had been strategically brilliant to take that otherwise useless Conn whore and sublimate her base inclinations for the benefit of a greater cause. Just as it had been strategically brilliant, as well as courageous, to know the proper time to take decisive action, remove Roger Helm, and salvage once and for all the Spencer candidacy.

When one thinks of the pivotal moments in history, one invariably finds a pivotal man. Future historians would find in him such a bold, seminal figure.

The thought reminded him . . .

He took the old silver watch from his pocket. Gazed upon its cracked crystal—damaged during his father's arrest. It brought him back to that terrible night. He flipped the watch over in his hand, seeing the worn inscription once again.

"I *have* been bold, Father," he said softly. "And fortune *has* favored me."

He heard steps in the outer office and glanced again at at the working watch on his wrist. Ten fifty, now. Well, it was about time. He looked up and saw the man's figure approaching in the shadows and called out.

"I am in here, Mr. Lasher. I have finally managed to find some illumination."

"So have I," said Dylan Hunter.

He walked into the surreal atmosphere of Trammel's office. The billionaire sat behind a massive desk with a stupefied expression. The electric lantern on his desk lit him from below, making him look the very image of some madman from a Hollywood horror film.

If only all this had been a movie.

"You're devastated to see me," Hunter said. "I'm so glad."

Trammel could not speak. A silvery object in his hand clattered to the desktop.

"I know, I know: It wasn't supposed to turn out this way, was it? You being Master of the Universe and all, reality was simply going to obey your orders."

Trammel tottered to his feet. Looked around wildly.

"I think this is probably what you're looking for," Hunter said, picking up the handgun from the chair where Trammel must have tossed it. "But that wouldn't have done you any good, anyway."

He left the gun there and slowly approached the desk, moving into the pale halo of light.

"Of all the evil creatures I have ever encountered," Trammel croaked, appraising him with unvarnished hatred and loathing, "you are without equal."

Hunter sighed. He felt terminally weary. Dealing with Lasher moments earlier, he had learned something important.

Now he needed to clarify it aloud, for himself.

"You know, Trammel, all of us grow up believing some story, some narrative about how the world works. A story about why things are the way they are, why people do what they do, and what is right and wrong. It becomes our private morality play. We cast its heroes and villains, and we make ourselves the featured character, because the story is really about us. About our role in the world. And that story gives our lives meaning and purpose and identity."

"What are you talking about?" Trammel demanded, looking bewildered.

Hunter ignored the question. "And I've found two really interesting things about that story. First, most of the things people argue about is really, at root, about that story—the master narrative of our lives. And second, whatever else changes about us, that narrative almost never does. It's interesting that the most important thing that defines us, that makes us who we are, never really changes."

He half-turned and gestured vaguely behind him.

"Out there in your yard I left a lot of dead men. The worst was the monster you know as Ray Lasher, but who was really a malignant sociopath named Ron Larsen. I hated him like I rarely hate anyone. Before I killed him, I decided to explain to him exactly what a monster he was. So I catalogued all the horrific things he had done. And I administered great pain to him for his crimes, before I gave him his final poetic justice."

He chuckled to himself. It sounded as hollow as it felt.

"But you know something? I could see that Lasher didn't understand, or care, or believe me. Because that wasn't *his* story about himself. He was living in his own fairy tale—the one where he had cast himself as a 'winner,' in a world where 'winning' doesn't mean creating and gaining good things for yourself—but instead means beating and defeating and dominating other people, and depriving them of what *they* have. So as I told him about his crimes, I suddenly realized he didn't think they were crimes at all. In *his* story, his victims all had it coming to them. They were losers, and he was the winner, and that was that.

"I could see in his eyes that my litany of his crimes had zero impact on him—even though I *wanted* it to. Because I wanted him to understand *why* I was punishing him. But he was beyond understanding. Because it didn't fit his narrative, the one where he was the hero. He simply couldn't fathom why I was hurting him and just wanted it to stop."

"How you *do* go on," Trammel sneered. He was trying to rally from his fear, to reassert himself. "I suppose there is some grand point to what you are blathering about."

Hunter grunted. "See? That's *exactly* my point. None of what I just said fits *your* narrative. In your story, Avery Trammel is the avenging angel, righting all the wrongs committed against his heroic parents and himself."

He paused to consider the vicious nihilist posturing before him.

"Trammel, I came here tonight intending to tell you what a monster you are, to make it so clear that you'd understand why I came to kill you. But after my experience with Lasher, I realize the futility of explaining. So instead, I just have to do it."

Trammel's condescending expression eroded as Hunter reached into the paper bag he had brought from the van.

He gently lifted out the head of the doll. The one with the long, jagged metal shard in its face.

He held it up in the halo of light.

"I'm not saying this for you. I'm saying it for me. Because my own moral clarity requires it. That truck bombing you arranged in D.C.? Just before the bomb went off, I encountered a lovely young mother and her adorable baby girl. The woman's name was Patricia Wright. Her little girl was named Allison. They were young, happy, and full of life before your bomb blew them to pieces. They left behind a grieving husband and another grieving child, a little boy.

"And that baby girl, Ally, was carrying this doll. Besides pieces of themselves, your bomb left behind pieces of this doll."

He slowly pulled out the metal spike from the doll's head. By now he was sure Trammel noticed he was wearing gloves. He placed the doll's head gently back into the bag. Set the bag gently onto the desk.

He gripped the spike like a knife.

"Avery Trammel, you left this thing in Ally's doll," he said, walking around the desk. "I'm here tonight to give it back."

Dylan Hunter took no satisfaction or pleasure in what he did then to Avery Trammel. In the years to come, he would feel only a small measure of relief from the agony of remembering the little girl with the golden curls who waved the doll at him.

9

He carried the lantern to the basement and walked toward the boxy structure she had described. Drawing closer, he saw the shattered window and glass fragments on the floor. Alarmed, he ran to the door and knocked.

"Julia! Julia, it's Dylan Hunter! Are you there?"

He heard the noise of bolts being thrown.

Then the door was open and she stood there. Looking as if she had endured a long ordeal. Looking as if she had aged ten years in a week.

"Are you all right?" he said softly, not knowing whether to approach her.

She shook her head slowly. Raised her hand to her mouth.

"I'll never be all right."

He shut off the jammer and phoned Garrett, who was on his way with a couple of "cleaners," plus some appropriate stagecraft items they had discussed by phone.

"Bring some food, too. And hot coffee, tea, whatever."

"What do you prefer?"

"It's for her."

Hunter assured Julia he'd stay with her till they arrived. Then he'd have to go outside and retrieve all the items he'd used in the assault.

They sat waiting in the now-unnerving silence of the drawing room. Faces of Roman warriors on ancient battlefields looked down upon them from the huge paintings on the walls. The faint odor of gunpowder hung in the air.

"He's dead, isn't he," she said, her voice flat.

He nodded, glancing at his hands, hoping he had washed them fully.

"You did it, didn't you."

He held her eyes. "Yes."

"Did you have to?"

"I think so."

"Why do you get to make decisions like that?"

"It's a question I ask myself every day."

"And you can live with yourself?"

"So far."

"What am I supposed to tell the police, then?"

"That's entirely up to you, Julia."

"Do you want me to tell them the truth?"

"About what?"

"About all of it."

"I think you should ask my friend Grant that. He may have things to say about some of it."

"About you, then. Should I tell them what you did?"

"I can't answer that for you."

"How am I supposed to answer it?"

He offered a little smile.

"Ask yourself how you can live with yourself afterward."

FORTY-NINE

At the gatehouse, Cronin badged his way past the yellow tape and perimeter cops and into the estate, using his D.C. Vigilante Task Force affiliation. Almost nobody knew what the task force's authority or reach was, so its credentials usually allowed him to Pass Go and Collect Two Hundred Dollars.

He hiked in to the mansion and first approached the people standing around out front. He talked to some CSIs who told him about the five stiffs they'd found out back, and the one upstairs in the house, who was Trammel.

A sergeant from the Virginia State Police told him they'd found a guard hogtied in the gatehouse, babbling about a Russian mob hit. The cars in the garage had been disabled to prevent anyone from escaping. And they'd found traces of drugs in Trammel's open office safe. So, at least at first glance, it looked like an epic drug gang battle, like they have south of the border. Maybe a cartel turf war.

"But isn't this Trammel a billionaire investor?" Cronin asked.

The grizzled veteran rolled his eyes and nodded toward the mansion. "How the hell you think anybody gets this rich, anyway?"

Cronin nodded. But of course a drug war made no sense, not in this case, not from what he had read and heard about Avery Trammel. And his wife was a famous actress.

Yet only recently he had investigated another hit on a fortified place, where a single man was able to defeat a different group of armed men.

Cronin stood near the central fountain, hands on hips, incredulous at the apparent sophistication of the assault and related weaponry and technology involved. Then he overheard a group of detectives talking about a body just found in the pond out back.

He hoofed it around the massive house, past knots of techs and cops hovering over bodies scattered around the giant lawn, out to where they'd set up lights near a gazebo sitting in the middle of a substantial pond. At the pond's edge, the body had been laid out on a white plastic sheet. A big blond guy in black. His arms and legs were twisted and bent in all the wrong places, and somebody had beat the shit out of his face.

Cronin approached a detective squatting over the corpse.

"Looks like a broken arm and leg," he ventured to the cop.

"Both arms, both legs. And look at his face. Busted jaw, looks like. No apparent fatal wounds, though. So I'm thinking, whoever did this to him dumped him in here afterward while he was still alive. Drowned him like a rat."

"Damn," Cronin said, bending close. "This dude looks too big and tough to take this kind of beating."

"Somebody's always bigger and tougher," the detective responded, not bothering to look up.

Cronin suddenly remembered Orlando Navarro. A massive bodybuilder and gangbanger, also taken apart by somebody late last November. Fractured skull, snapped elbow, crushed throat. Next to his body, his dead Doberman—whose neck had been broken.

The vigilante had done that, then left behind a Dylan Hunter newspaper clipping on Navarro's body.

Cronin straightened. Looked down at the stiff.

Knew the same vigilante had done this, too.

Entering the mansion, he paused to admire the interior. Then shook it off, knowing vast wealth hadn't been enough to protect its owner. He trotted up the spectacular staircase, following the sound of voices. He turned left down a hallway, where two uniforms stood talking. Hearing more voices beyond, he followed them into a business office, then farther on, into an interior office.

He recognized Julia Haight, the actress, instantly. She sat on a small leather couch in the middle of the room, absolutely still and staring blankly into space. Two suits stood nearby, speaking to each other, not her. One had Lead Investigator written all over his face and manner. Cronin approached and introduced himself. They stepped away from the woman and lowered their voices.

"Aren't you a little out of your jurisdiction? And what's this got to do with your investigation?" The guy was a Lieutenant Edwards, Virginia SP, Homicide.

"Trammel also lives and does business in D.C. A few months ago, somebody we think is with the vigilantes blew up his jet at Dulles, left one of their signature calling cards at the scene."

"No shit. Hey, right, I think I remember reading about that. So you think *they* did this?"

Cronin shrugged. "Won't know till we see the evidence, talk to witnesses. So where's Trammel's body?"

"Over there—behind his desk, under a sheet." He gestured to the actress. "Naturally, we didn't let her see that. But she wanted to come in here. Said she needed to 'experience his office' and try to understand what happened."

"She see anything that happened?"

"She says no. Says she was hiding out in the basement. She really hasn't said much at all. At least she hasn't asked for her attorney, though. I think she's close to being in shock. We were about to call the EMTs over to take look at her, maybe transport her to a hospital."

"Can you give me a few minutes with her first? Alone? Maybe with a little quiet, she'll open up."

The guy thought about it for a few seconds.

"I suppose so. But she tells you anything, play nice and share—okay?"

"Happy to."

Edwards moved the investigators away, gave them some space. Cronin sat across from Julia Haight. From a distance, she had still looked like the famous, flawless babe in the movies. Up close, though, he could see the strain and shock on her face. It made her look a lot older. Maybe she was.

He introduced himself, talking quietly and gently. Her eyes blinked, and her head turned his way.

"You say you're with the vigilante investigators?" The familiar voice sounded empty.

"That's right. Listen, I know you've been through a horrible experience, but maybe you can help us."

"I already told them. When everything went dark and the shooting started, Avery made me go hide in our panic room, down in our basement. I locked myself inside. I had battery power there, but my cell couldn't get a signal. So I couldn't see anything. Or call anyone. Then somebody tried to get in and shot at the window. I was too afraid to come out, even when the shooting stopped. Not for a long time."

"Do you have any idea what this might have been about?"

"Not until the detectives told me they found drugs over there, spilled inside his safe, along with money. Now it all makes sense."

"What do you mean?"

"My husband—he had all these tough-looking Russian guys working here. I never understood it. He said they were for security. That being wealthy, he had been threatened. But now I think I understand. They were all involved with drugs, I guess. Smuggling. I've read about Russian cartels. That's probably why he had the panic room installed." Her voice caught. "I . . . just can't believe he was involved in drugs . . . I mean, I *can*—but I *can't*. It does explain all his secrecy, the mysterious, sudden travels. And the Russian guards and their guns."

She began to stare into the distance again, eyes unfocusing, slightly shaking her head, over and over.

"So you didn't know anything about that? Or suspect anything? How's that possible?"

Life came to her face. She looked back at him, indignant.

"My God! I had no idea! Avery's business interests kept him traveling constantly. I never knew what his deals were about, it was all too complicated. And he was a very private man. He never explained anything." She look down and shuddered. "Now I know why."

Cronin kept watching her, nodding in sympathy. But none of this made any sense.

He reminded himself that this woman was one of the greatest actresses in the world.

Knowing he might not get another shot at her, he decided he had nothing to lose. He got up and moved to sit beside her on the small couch.

It shocked her, as he knew it would. She shifted away. He leaned in.

"Listen, Miss Haight," he said softly, to keep her calm and so no one around them could hear. "I'm going to be straight with you."

He swept his hand around the demolished office.

"I'm not buying this. This whole 'drug cartel' scenario."

"What . . . what do you mean?"

His eyes drilled into hers. He added an edge to his quiet voice.

"Because I have another theory that fits a whole lot better. I told you I'm with the Vigilante Task Force. I've been following somebody for months. A killer who takes out people he thinks are bad guys. And to tell you the truth, they are. I've been to all the crime scenes, including one up in Baltimore not long ago. You know what? This looks a lot like that."

She broke eye contact and looked away. Her mouth tightened.

Which told him he was on the right track. She was hiding something.

"I don't want you to say anything right now," he said, making his voice less harsh again, more sympathetic. "Just listen. I know you've been through hell. But I don't think that started tonight. And I think you know the truth about what happened here, and I don't think it was about drugs. I'm betting something like this happened. Your husband is a—was a very rich and powerful man, involved in politics at a very high level. And—sorry—but I suspect he was up to no good. Something really bad, really serious, or else the vigilante wouldn't have targeted him."

Her face remained averted from him, eyes looking rigidly forward.

But even from the side, he could see her eyes narrow, her jaw set. She was closing up fast.

He had to gamble.

"Miss Haight—do you know Dylan Hunter?"

She was good. If he hadn't gotten this close, he would have missed it. But he watched the flicker of shock pass across her features like a small wave.

"You do, don't you."

Not a question. She didn't respond or protest.

Keep talking.

"Okay, here's what I know. Hunter has been investigating your husband for illegal stuff involving the election. I read his articles about it. Mr. Trammel was apparently pouring money into the Spencer campaign in ways he shouldn't. And something else, something really, really serious had to be at stake or going on, too."

Great actress or not, she couldn't stop herself from turning pale.

Time for a Hail Mary.

"I want to tell you something confidentially. I have been investigating Hunter for a long time," he said softly. "You've probably read or heard that nobody knows anything about his background. But I do know several things about him. I know he has an obsession with justice. I know he is capable of violence—and that he's very skilled at it, because he killed a man who was also extremely skilled at violence. And you know what else, Miss Haight? I know damned well that Dylan Hunter is the vigilante we've been looking for."

She pressed her lips in a tighter line.

Yes.

"Here are a few other things I know about him. He has a code, his own code of honor. He won't hurt anyone who hasn't hurt someone else first. And he won't kill anyone except people who have been involved in committing murder."

Her eyes closed.

"Miss Haight, here is what I think happened tonight. I think Dylan Hunter came here and did all this—then arranged the scene to look like something else. Like something involving drugs. I also don't think you were hiding in your safe room. I think you were here, at least long enough to see him. Maybe you even saw him kill your husband. And if he did that, it was because he believed your husband was involved in murder."

Her shoulders quivered.

"Miss Haight, I want to promise you something— something none of these other cops here will promise. I absolutely promise you that anything you tell me will go no farther than my ears. That is my solemn promise, on my wife and kids' heads. I don't want to bring down Mr. Hunter. I don't want him in a cell. I just want him to *stop*."

A tear formed in the corner of her eye and crawled down her cheek.

"Please look at me, Miss Haight."

It took a few seconds. Her eyelids fluttered, and more tears fell. But she turned to face him.

"Thank you. Here," he said, offering his handkerchief. She dabbed her eyes with it.

"Look at my face. Look in my eyes and see if I'm lying to you. I am promising you that whatever you tell me about him won't get you in any legal trouble, or be used against him, to arrest or prosecute him. You know, the other cops here would arrest me if they heard me saying this to you. My own partner, Paul, would turn against me if he knew I was doing this.

"But I'm making you this promise because a part of me actually admires the guy—even though I hate his methods. Look around you . . . That's right. You see what I mean? Hunter has been leaving bloody scenes like this since at least last September. Nine months of killing. Of slaughter. And it's got to stop. You *do* see that, don't you? Maybe you and I, together, can convince him to stop. Will you help me do that? Can I count on you to help me, Miss Haight?"

She searched his eyes. Swallowed. Cleared her throat.

"It's Julia, Detective Cronin."

He felt a surge of relief. He smiled.

"Then call me Ed." He held out his hand, immediately feeling stupid about it.

But she took it. It was the first time he'd ever shaken hands with a gorgeous movie star. He thought of his wife. Ell was a big fan. She would kill to be here. Or maybe she would kill *him* if she knew about this. He would never tell her.

Julia looked at the other cops working the crime scene.

"We should go to my office to talk privately," she said, keeping her voice low.

"Yeah, let's do that."

She stood. "I have a great deal to tell you about my husband, and why this happened, Ed."

He rose to his feet, too.

"I bet you do, Julia."

2

Garrett entered the hospital room just after ten a.m. He nodded at them, a twinkle in his eyes.

"You look like the bearer of news," Annie said.

"Yes, indeed," he said, taking a visitor's chair and crossing his long legs. "Good news and bad news. As soon as you finish healing, you'll be getting a medal in a special ceremony from the deities in the front office."

"I assume that's the good news. What's the bad news?"

"As usual, you won't get to wear it home. It stays locked in a vault."

"So I can't even sell it on eBay?"

"No. But by tradition, you get to keep any cake you eat at the party."

She laughed, and Hunter clapped. "*Brava!* Since I won't be allowed there, I'll give you your round of applause now."

"Is that all?" Garrett asked. "I can do you one better."

He got up, walked to the bed, leaned over and kissed her forehead.

"I can't tell you how proud I am of you, my girl," he said softly, pushing an errant lock of her hair aside with his forefinger.

"Thank you, Grant. That means a lot."

As he was settling back into his chair, Hunter asked, "Will she be charged with failing to let the FBI handle the takedown of Sokolov and Spitzer?"

"Even if they wanted to, nobody in the Agency or Bureau wants the embarrassing details of this fiasco to come out in a courtroom or congressional hearing. Besides, I told them Annie was simply following Spitzer and got involved in a firefight accidentally, in self-defense, when they spotted her. Naturally, the new FBI guy running CIC's counterespionage didn't buy it, and the Bureau is fuming that she stepped on their turf. But this will blow over. Everywhere in the Agency, you're a heroine, Annie."

She grinned. "I'm just glad I didn't become another star on the wall in the lobby."

"Me too," Hunter said, raising and kissing her hand.

"As for you, mister, how in hell did you ever figure it all out?" Garrett glanced at his watch. "I've got some time."

"With a little logic and a lot of dumb luck," Hunter began. "For a long time I was confused. So I had to start with what we already knew. I knew the Russians wanted desperately to stop American fracking. Lasher unknowingly supplied me information linking that fact to other things. He admitted he was a contract killer hired to silence Muller. So, whoever hired him had to be working for the Kremlin. He also boasted he was the guy shadowing me that day outside the EPA. Which meant two other things: first, that his Russian boss knew about my meeting schedule that day; and second, that his boss had to be somebody high up in the anti-fracking network I was investigating."

"Reasonable logic, so far," Garrett said. "But there had to be lots of suspects in that network. How did you figure out the Russian agent had to be Trammel?"

"By degrees. First, when I visited his home, he had a security team of Russian contractors. Hard guys, pros. That was bizarre. The second big clue was when I uncovered his connection to Gazprom."

"The Russian energy company?" Annie asked.

"Majority owned by the Russian government," Garrett interjected. "Putin cronies are in charge. So, how did you find out about that?"

"I learned Trammel had been making annual trips to Berlin to speak at 'alternative energy summits' hosted by a German environmentalist organization. When I researched the group, I saw its officers included Russian oligarchs tied to Putin—and one of them was a top Gazprom official. I dug deeper and found the group was getting huge donations from Gazprom. It wasn't a leap to deduce the organization was just a front group for Moscow."

"Lots of people besides Trammel attend those conferences," Garrett pointed out. "That doesn't seem particularly suspicious."

"True. But in every investigation, I create a timeline of events, and I noted the dates of Trammel's conference appearances. Later, while checking out federal financial reports, I noticed an interesting thing. He gave big, annual, tax-deductible donations—about a half-million dollars at a time—to his Trammel Foundation. He listed them as income derived from 'speaking and consulting fees.' The dates of the donations rang bells for me. I checked the timeline, and sure enough: He made those contributions to his foundation immediately after his Berlin speaking engagements.

"So I had Wonk sift through federal grant forms, and he noticed another intriguing coincidence. Within a week or so of receiving each of his donations, his Trammel Foundation turned around and made their own huge grants of nearly identical amounts to the Currents Foundation. The grant forms listed their purposes as 'energy awareness advocacy'—a euphemism for propaganda and activism against fracking.

"But a lot of that activity was really run by groups working against Roger Helm. Currents money funded outfits running pro-Spencer voter registration drives. Groups holding protests at Helm's headquarters, rallies, and the homes of his top donors. And something called the Progressive Media Alliance—a network of press shills who colluded online to push daily anti-Helm narratives. Oh, and guess what political communications outfit the Currents Foundation hired to coordinate all those efforts?"

"Let me guess: Lucas Carver's company," Annie said.

"What a coincidence, huh? Carver is Spencer's chief communications strategist, while his Vox Populi company—funded by Currents, with money supplied by Trammel—runs the national campaign to smear and destroy Helm."

"So the Russians were laundering millions of dollars through Trammel into those Currents groups—"

"—which, in turn, funneled those millions into the campaign to elect Carl Spencer and defeat Roger Helm. That's the bottom line, Annie: illegal Russian interference in an American presidential election. *That* is what Arnold Wasserman discovered. Somehow, he picked up a loose thread and followed it through the network right back to Moscow. As a good reporter, he would have interviewed people inside that network, maybe Trammel himself. When Trammel realized he was getting too close to the truth, Wasserman had to die. And when CAP followed in his footsteps, they had to go, too. Eventually, so did I."

Garrett squinted. "That's a lot of conjecture. The Russian funds were laundered and co-mingled, so you still had little hard evidence of their direct involvement."

"There was more, though. Trammel's wife—Julia Haight, the actress—found out Trammel was having an affair with someone. So she started checking up on him and managed to sneak into his office. That's when she found out the ugly truth about Avery Trammel."

He picked up a thick file folder.

"And it's all here."

Over the next ten minutes, with the aid of the photographed documents supplied by Julia, Hunter told them the story of little Avis Tremills—son of the infamous Soviet spy John Avery Tremills. He explained how, motivated by obsessive hatred of America, the country he blamed for his parents' deaths—and for his own traumatic childhood—Tremills became Avery Trammel, a KGB sleeper agent. Then, with their secret backing, a billionaire investor, and finally a politically powerful Kremlin agent of influence.

"I first met Julia when I visited his estate. I could tell she was troubled about something, so I left my card and told her to contact me if she ever wanted to talk. But when she found and photographed this stuff, she was too scared to tell anyone.

"That changed when the cops visited their apartment to question him after the murder of Senator Conn's widow. That's when she realized his secret mistress had to have been Emmalee Conn."

"*What?*"

"Just wait, Annie—it gets better. Anyway, Julia knew her husband was lying through his teeth to her and the cops. She was certain he was behind Emmalee's murder. So she decided to give all this to me."

Garrett was still frowning. "But how did you figure out Lasher was working directly for Trammel, as his hired assassin?"

"Because being an arrogant psychopath, Lasher couldn't stop boasting and also unwittingly revealing things."

"Such as?"

"Such as being a hired hitman—going after Muller at the safe house—following me at the EPA. He admitted all that. And when I was targeted during the hit on Helm, that told me *he* had to be the shooter—which meant the assassination attempt had to be an SVR op, contracted by his boss. Without realizing it, Lasher was sketching for me a map of Russia's involvement.

"But his worst slip-up was threatening to come after my 'girlfriend.' He was able to describe Annie, yet he didn't know her name. Only one other enemy of mine had seen me with her: Avery Trammel. He knew what Annie looked like, but didn't know her name, either. That was just too great a coincidence. I knew right then Lasher could only have learned about her from Trammel."

"Which meant Lasher's boss *had* to be Trammel," Garrett interjected.

"Exactly. And if that were true, then everything else made logical sense."

"So Avery Trammel was behind everything," Annie said. "Protecting Russia's CIA moles. Promoting Moscow's campaign to stop fracking.

Throwing the election to Spencer. And killing anyone who became a threat."

"But there's one last thing I cannot understand," Garrett said. "You say Trammel was a megalomaniac, playing a double game even against his Russian handlers—that his plan was to take over the country, first by throwing the election to Spencer, then by controlling things *himself*. How in the world did he ever expect to manage that?"

Hunter had been holding back the last item in the folder—a large manila envelope.

"This is how."

He opened the envelope, slid out the photos, and spread them on the blanket covering Annie.

"Oh my God," Annie whispered.

"Just to reassure my disbelieving eyes—that *is* Emmalee Conn and Carl Spencer, right?"

"Grant, I didn't know about this until after the firefight, when I tossed Trammel's office. They were inside a briefcase he meant to take with him in his getaway—probably as his insurance policy, to force Spencer to protect him in the future. I think he'd already used the photos to blackmail Spencer and get him under his control.

"But when Trammel later had Emmalee murdered, these would have become even *more* devastating. Imagine: A presidential candidate has kinky sex with a woman not his wife, and scandalous photos are taken. That's bad enough. But the woman is the widow of his recently murdered political rival—and then *she* is murdered, too. Now, this candidate is in the White House, and he's the most powerful leader on the planet."

Hunter tapped one of the photos.

"Except he *isn't*. Avery Trammel is. These photos could be used to frame the President of the United States for two murders. Holding these over Spencer's head, Trammel could have forced him to do pretty much *anything*. He could have caused the nation catastrophic harm."

He looked off into the distance.

"So yes—I think Trammel actually might have been able to pull off his insane, lifelong revenge fantasy against the United States."

Annie broke the long silence that followed.

"Would you *please* get those disgusting pictures off my blanket?"

"Sorry." Hunter slid them back into the envelope, and shoved it back into the file folder.

"Goddamn," Garrett said at last. "Dylan, I still can't believe how you figured out everything."

"Not everything." Hunter said, nodding toward Annie. "What I couldn't know was who was running the moles in the Agency. Nor could I possibly know that their Russian handler, Sokolov, was the same SVR illegal also running Trammel. They were all part of the same cell. And *you* cracked that part of it, Annie."

"That she did," Garrett said. "Brilliantly, too. This past year she took off the board *three* Russian illegals doing tremendous damage to our country."

He looked at them both with a mixture of disbelief and awe.

"I have seen a lot of incredible things during my years wandering in the 'wilderness of mirrors,' but this tops them all. Here you are, Dylan, unmasking Russian manipulation of the election. Meanwhile, Annie is uncovering Russian moles in Langley. We assume you're conducting totally unrelated investigations. But they turn out to be different parts of a single conspiracy. You two were just following all the links from opposite ends of the same chain."

"And we met in the middle," Hunter said, turning to her and laughing.

"I hope so," she said.

Not laughing.

Apparently noticing, Garrett plunged back in.

"We've stopped the immediate threat. But others remain. The public questions about your real identity, Dylan. The investigations into the terrorist attacks, Helm's shooting, Emmalee Conn's murder, the firefight at Trammel's estate. The Russians will pull out all the stops to whitewash themselves."

"Of course," said Hunter, "because what they did is an act of war."

"And to avoid an unthinkable war," Garrett continued, "a lot of Americans—probably starting with Spencer—will *want* to believe those lies. Truth is likely to be another casualty." He looked away, then added: "However, given the stakes, maybe that's not such a bad thing."

"Well, what can be proved, anyway?" Hunter asked. "I can prove the Russians ran and funded Trammel. I can make a pretty persuasive case that Russian money went into the election campaign, using Trammel as the conduit. Those things will go into the *Inquirer* articles next week.

"However, I—we—also know a lot of things we can't prove—not beyond a shadow of a doubt, anyway. We know the Russians ran Shishani, and that Shishani organized the terrorist conspiracy in Washington. But the terrorist I questioned has lawyered up now and isn't talking. We know Lasher worked for Trammel—his body was even found on the estate. We know Lasher murdered Wasserman, Shishani, Emmalee Conn, and the poor old man who owned the apartment overlooking the park. We know he shot Helm, and tried to murder me. And we know Moscow was behind all of that."

He shrugged.

"We know it—but we can't prove *any* of that. Trammel kept no incriminating records anywhere about his actual ops—only his fake IDs, tradecraft items, some stuff tying him to Sokolov, and sentimental family albums showing his background with communism and Russia."

"We know Trammel blackmailed Carl Spencer," Annie pointed out.

"But we can't prove that, either," Garrett replied, "because Dylan took the blackmail photos from Trammel's briefcase. If he hadn't, when investigators found them there, that would have incriminated Trammel and his Russian handlers—and also knocked Spencer out of the race. Hell, Dylan, that would have been a trifecta. But you blew it by taking away the photos."

"No, I took them on purpose," Hunter said. "Think it through. Imagine what would happen if these got out. The country has already lost two candidates to violence: Conn and Helm. Losing Spencer now would turn the election into a one-man race with Tom Waller the sole candidate—a total farce. The chaos would destroy the last bit of confidence people still have in our political system."

He tapped the envelope.

"When I saw these, Grant, I realized that nightmare would be everything Avery Trammel ever dreamed of. Even after death, he would have won his final victory over America." He shook his head. "No way I was going to let him win it all."

Garrett grunted. Then said, "You're right. Moscow would have loved it, too."

They sat reflecting on it for a while.

"Meanwhile, what about you and me, Grant?" Annie interrupted. "Where does all this leave us?"

"It's total bedlam at HQ now. They've been penetrated by moles and failed to foresee terrorist attacks on Washington. There will be congressional investigations, finger-pointing, heads rolling, and more reshuffling of our organizational chart. There's a ton of work to do."

"That's for sure," she said. "I honestly don't know where we begin."

Garrett fixed her with a cool, unblinking stare.

"*We* don't do anything. You, both of you, have done quite enough. Now it's my turn. My top priority will be to stop World War Three with the Russians, which just might happen if their role in all this is unmasked. Second, to make sure Carl Spencer, as president, won't cause us future grief, now that he's unleashed from Trammel. Third, to try to salvage what is left of the Agency. But fourth—and hardly least important—to protect you, Dylan."

"Me? Look, you don't—"

"Shut up, son. These past few months, you've managed to keep the White House out of the hands of fanatical killers, not once, but twice. It's criminal that the nation can never be allowed to know that. But it would be far more criminal if you're harassed and punished now, after everything you've risked and done. I am not about to let that happen."

He stood. "I am dying for a smoke, and I've got a big to-do list, in that order. So I'd better get going. Before I do, I have only one request."

He held out his hand toward Hunter.

"Please give me those photos."

They locked eyes.

"What for, Grant?"

"As I say: You need to be protected. So does Annie. So do I. So does the country."

Bitter experience had taught Hunter not to trust easily, and over the years there had been only a handful whom he'd trust with his life. Two of them were in this room.

He wanted to ask his old boss exactly how he intended to use the photos. But in Grant Garrett's clear gray eyes he saw a rare man he could trust to do the right thing.

Without a word, he withdrew the envelope from the folder and handed it to Garrett.

Who actually smiled. Just a flicker. But a smile.

"Grant, you can't possibly deal with all of that 'to-do' list alone," Annie protested.

He raised a brow. The wintry eyes seemed to twinkle.

"Never make the mistake of underestimating me, my dear."

3

Hunter stayed with her through much of the day. They had lunch together in the room, and talked about small things for a change—their homes, their pets, the foxes in his yard out at Connors Point—trying to reclaim a forgotten sense of normalcy.

Occasionally, they tuned in to the news channels on the room's TV. There were the inevitable stories about the terrorism, Trammel, and Emmalee Conn. Then they were relieved to hear that Roger Helm's condition had been upgraded from critical to serious, and that he appeared to be on the slow road to recovery. A reporter said the bulletproof vest he'd been wearing had partly deflected the rifle shot.

"It was just when he turned to wave at me," Hunter said. "It hit him at an angle. If he'd taken that bullet straight on, he'd be dead, vest or not."

"So your presence there actually saved him," Annie pointed out.

"I guess." He thought about Helm, how he'd looked on the platform. "I'll have to visit him, when he's up to it. It's so tragic. He would have made a great president."

Around three-fifteen, a handsome Fox News anchor's face hovered over a chyron that read: *Who Is Dylan Hunter?* He turned up the volume with the remote.

". . . adding another layer of mystery to the stunning events of the past months. Our Washington bureau's Ashley Dunn has been following this part of the story. Ashley, what can you tell us?"

A pretty blonde reporter appeared onscreen standing outside the door of the Capitol Inquirer Building.

"Bill, in response to our repeated questions and, frankly, questions from all the rest of the media about the mysterious background of the *Capitol Inquirer's* controversial investigative reporter Dylan Hunter, this morning they issued this statement written by him." She held up a sheet of paper. "Let me read it:

"'Recent circumstances compel me to reiterate my previous statement. I have demonstrated to the satisfaction of law enforcement investigators and governmental agencies that I am indeed Dylan Lee Hunter, a freelance investigative journalist. However, for reasons of personal safety, I am unable to respond to questions in any greater detail than that. I shall have nothing further to say on this subject.'

"That was this morning, Bill. But just moments ago, this statement"—she waved another sheet of paper—"was put out by the media office at the CIA. As many viewers know, some speculation swirling around Hunter is whether he ever worked for the CIA or other intelligence agency, and if he has undergone a change of identity. So let me share this CIA statement:

"'Given recent events, our agency has been asked to comment about a certain member of the news media, and his possible involvement or history with our Agency.

"'We understand the interest of the press and public in such matters.

However, like all federal intelligence agencies— as well as law enforcement agencies such as the U.S. Marshals Service, which administers the federal witness protection program—the Central Intelligence Agency never confirms or denies the possible affiliation, either past or present, of any specific individual. This policy is necessary to protect our national security, the safety of individuals involved with our activities, but also the privacy of individuals who have no connection to our activities. Nothing should be construed from this statement other than a reiteration of our long-standing official policy.'"

"That's fascinating, Ashley," the anchor said. "What are we supposed to make of that?"

"Bill, for me, the most intriguing part is the reference to the U.S. Marshals Service and its witness protection program. It raises the possibility that at one time Dylan Hunter may have been a government witness or informant, who had to go into hiding and was given a new name and identity. If true, that might explain why no one can find out anything about his past. I can think of no other reason for including that particular reference, since no other government agency was mentioned in the CIA's statement."

"I can't either. It only thickens the cloud of mystery surrounding this maverick reporter, who has broken a lot of big stories. But you have to wonder why he would choose such a high-profile career if he wants to hide his past . . ."

"I have to wonder about that, too," Annie said.

"No comment." Hunter clicked off the TV. "I don't know how Grant got the Langley press office to go along with it," he added, "but his statement is perfect. It will send reporters off on a different wild goose chase."

"So, you're going to let them believe whatever they want to believe," she said.

"They will anyway. But now their inquiries have hit an official brick wall."

"They'll try to dig deeper, you know."

"And only dig an empty hole."

"But the 'man of mystery' hook will keep a spotlight on you."

"Maybe they'll pay more attention to what I write."

"Seriously, Dylan. What happens when they find out about *us?* Maybe about where I work?"

He brightened. "Hey! If they do, they'll realize I have insider access to secrets they don't." He looked off into space. "You know . . . having CIA officer Annie Woods as my secret intelligence source might even give my reporting more credibility."

"So you're just going to *use* me."

He looked around furtively, then reached over and slid his hand inside her hospital gown.

"Just watch me."

4

It was four in the afternoon and she was tired. Hunter gave her a kiss and promised to return at seven, after she'd had some sleep.

He left the room and nodded to the young, tough-looking Agency security officer seated right outside the door.

"Take good care of her," he said.

The man stood. "It's my honor, sir."

Hunter offered his hand. The young man took it.

Reassured, he headed down the hallway. He pushed through the door and continued on, into the crowded waiting room.

"Hunter."

He stopped and turned at the sound of the familiar voice.

Cronin rose from a seat in the corner and approached.

"How is she?"

"She'll be okay. Thank you."

"Glad to hear it. She's tough like you, I guess."

Hunter thought about it. "In her own way, she's tougher than me or most men."

"To put up with you, she'd have to be." The tone was sharp.

"I won't argue. I appreciate your coming here to check in on her."

"It's not just that. We need to talk. You and me."

"Again?" He rolled his eyes.

"Yeah. Again." Cronin looked around. "I think I saw an empty meeting room or something down the hall."

Hunter wondered what this was all about. On the way to the room, images from a host of ops flashed to mind—killings Cronin had tried to pin on him. Maybe this was about the hit on Dixon's gang in Baltimore. He felt tired, mentally fuzzy. He would have to be careful.

They entered the room, and Cronin found a light switch. The place held a small, narrow conference table surrounded by molded plastic chairs, and smelled faintly medicinal. Cronin gestured to the chairs and they took seats facing each other. He got right to it.

"I've just been to see Julia Haight."

"The actress?"

"Don't play dumb. Avery Trammel's widow."

"Oh. Right. You know, I met her once. She has to be devastated over what's happened. How's she holding up?"

"What if I were to tell you she fingered you as Trammel's killer?"

It caught him off guard, which was just as well. Surprise could indicate innocence. Hunter allowed his mouth to fall open. Then he slowly smiled, leaned back, and laughed heartily.

"You *wouldn't* tell me that, because we both know it didn't happen."

"No?"

"You're bluffing, Ed." He grinned, hoping it was true.

"It's 'Detective Cronin.'"

"Sorry."

"She's truly a great actress. So great, in fact, for a moment she nearly even convinced me her husband was killed by a drug gang, and not you."

"What in hell are you—"

"Stop. Just shut up and hear me out."

Cronin looked away, as if gathering himself for this. Then bent forward, resting his elbows on the table.

"Hunter, she *told* me. Don't blame her. She didn't want to, and I got her to do it only because we worked out a deal. I promised her that whatever she said, I wouldn't use it against you. And unlike you, my word means something. I keep my promises. I *won't* use what she told me against you. But she confirmed what I already knew for months. And what Adair and the Jacksons also confirmed."

He paused. Then said it with unstressed, quiet certainty.

"Hunter, you're the vigilante."

They sat there like that, silent, looking at each other for long seconds. Cronin spoke first.

"Let me reassure you that when anyone else questions Haight, she'll stick with that bullshit fairy tale you two cooked up, about Russian drug cartels. The other cops seem to be buying it. And I'm content to let them believe it. But you know *why* she told me? You know why I'm here? Because I promised her I'd try to get you to stop. Not arrest you. Just get you to stop murdering people."

He tapped his fingertips on the table. He seemed to be weighing his next words.

"Everything you did before—those people had it coming. All those killers you whacked. And now—from what she told me, you just stopped some kind of a big conspiracy to take over the country. Maybe more than one conspiracy. I'd already figured you for killing that scumbag senator, Conn. Now this Trammel character. From what she says, he was involved in the terrorism in Washington, maybe working with the Russians, too. Which is just . . . unbelievable."

He lowered his eyes and his voice, sounding pensive.

"Except somehow, I *can* believe it. These days, things have gone so bad I can believe anything. If what she said is true, then they've just about hijacked the election. Even if they don't get away with it, they've thrown the whole country into chaos. Maybe that's what they were really after all along. What is it they say? 'Divide and conquer.' It seems to be working, too. Nobody trusts anything or anyone anymore."

He stopped again. Ran a hand over his bare scalp. Raised probing eyes.

"I've been doing a lot of thinking about what to do. If I push this, and it all blows up and gets out in the open—with you killing not just punks and scum, but politicians and leaders—it'll only add to the chaos. The investigations into all these conspiracies, the terrorism, Conn blown up, Helm shot, your killing spree, whether you got help from inside the government. God help us, this thing with Trammel and the Russians might be the last straw. It might tear apart what's left of the country."

Something changed in his eyes. Like some creature from the depths surging to the surface.

He slammed his fist down on the table.

"But how do I look myself in the mirror, now? It's either 'Ed Cronin, the guy who single-handedly pushed America off the edge of the cliff.' Or 'Ed Cronin, the cop who violated his oath, didn't do his job, and let a murderer walk.' So, what do I do? And how the hell do I live with myself, either way?"

He stopped. Whatever had surfaced receded back into the depths. His eyes were no longer fierce, but sad. Helpless-looking.

Hunter was faintly aware of hospital noises outside the room. He tried to keep his breathing steady, his hands still.

He waited to learn his fate.

"So here's the deal. Here's what I've decided. All those crime victims, and Julia Haight—they've been through enough. I don't want to force them to turn against you in court—though I doubt they would. So I'm going to wipe the slate clean with you. I'm not coming after you anymore for anything you've done in the past. I haven't shared a lot of what I know, or even suspect about you, with anyone else on the task force. Not even with Paul, my partner. And if I they start looking at you, I'll do my best to throw them off the scent."

Abruptly, another mercuric mood change. The sad blue eyes grew cold again, then clouded over, like an approaching storm.

"But—here's the other thing. All bets are off about anything you do from here on out. No, I am not going to ask you to promise to stop shooting people, because there is no way I'd believe you. You've lied to me from the first day we met. But I'm not going to let you keep pulling this vigilante shit and think you're going to get away with it forever, either. You're not above the law, mister. So I'm going to stay on your ass. If you ever—*ever*—do so much as jaywalk or break the speed limit, I'll be right there. And I'll nail your head to my wall as a trophy. You hear me?"

Hunter realized that he had stopped breathing. He inhaled slowly to steady himself before speaking.

"I hear you."

Cronin's hands balled into fists. Incredibly, the stormy eyes now seemed on the verge of tears.

"I'm a cop; you're a criminal; my job is to nail guys like you. But I *can't*. And I *hate* you for that, you son of a bitch. I *hate* you for putting me in this position. You've turned me into your accomplice, in murder and too many other crimes to count . . . You know, when I was a kid in the academy, I knew the temptations I'd have to face on the job. I took a vow to myself, way back then, that whatever else, Ed Cronin would never be corrupted.

"But now, look at me. I'm corrupt. Because of you, I'm breaking that vow and my oath. And I honestly don't know how I live with this. I don't know how I can look my kids in the eye. Especially when they tell me how proud they are of their dad. Now I have to worry for the rest of my life that someday they'll find out their old man sold out his principles. And for what? To protect a serial killer. Because technically, that's what you are. You feel proud of yourself, Hunter?"

He didn't answer.

"Your father still alive?" Cronin demanded.

He felt his jaw tighten.

"No."

"Lucky him! Lucky for my father, too, because he's also dead. Thank God they didn't live to see how their sons turned out. They don't have to wonder where they went wrong."

"Ed—"

"It's *Detective Cronin!*"

"Right. Sorry. Detective—whatever else you may be right about in what you just said, you're dead wrong about one thing. That you're corrupt. You're not."

"Right." It sounded like a growl.

"I mean it. And here's the proof: No truly corrupt man would care so much about losing his integrity."

Cronin blinked. Hunter went on.

"You may not believe me, or care, but I know exactly what you're going through. Whatever you think of me, don't be hard on yourself. It's a morally impossible situation. There are no good options. A good man can only choose the one he thinks is least bad. As for your kids—"

Cronin launched himself across the table at Hunter, grabbed the front of his shirt, and fired a hard right into his face.

Hunter made no effort to block it; he just turned his head slightly so that Cronin's fist smashed into his left cheek. The shock of the powerful punch stunned him; he felt himself toppling off the chair, onto the floor. His head was spinning as he lifted it and turned his blurred gaze at Cronin.

The detective had come around to loom over him, fists clenched, shaking, blinking rapidly to clear the tears forming in his eyes. He pointed an accusing finger.

"Don't you *dare* mention my kids! Or talk to me about integrity! How can you live with yourself? How can you do this to your girlfriend?"

Ed Cronin stood there, torment on his face.

Then spun and stalked out of the room.

Hunter lowered his aching head to his forearm.

Closed his eyes.

Thought about what Cronin had said.

Remained there, on the cold hard floor, not moving for a long time.

FIFTY

Garrett met the two of them in the director's conference room. This time, alone.

Houk was in his chair at the head of the long, empty table. Burroughs was at his right.

Garrett sat across from Burroughs.

"So, what is this all about, Grant?" Houk asked. The words were a demand, but their delivery conveyed a tone of uncertainty.

Garrett folded rough hands atop the polished table. Looked from one to the other as he spoke.

"You've seen my full report. Just the two of you. Right now, we are the only people at Langley that know who was really behind the terrorist attacks in Washington and the assassination attempt on Roger Helm. Thanks mostly to my stagecraft, everybody has now concluded that radical Islamists attacked the capital; that two guys visiting a mutual friend's grave in a cemetery were shot to death in a random gang initiation rite; and that financier Avery Trammel, a secret SVR agent of political influence, moonlighted by developing a side racket with Russian drug cartels, and died in a feud between two warring factions. And we are still trying to figure out who shot Roger Helm. All horrible, yet completely unrelated acts of violence, so sadly typical of life in America today."

He grunted. Then coughed.

"Those are now the official stories. For the most part, the press is buying them, and so are most people. And we want to keep things that way—right? Because gee, fellows, if the nation were ever to find out the Russians were behind *everything* in order to control our election outcome, why, that just might be considered an act of war. And we certainly do not want to go to war with Russia, now, do we?"

They frowned at each other, looking uncertain.

"Of course we have to keep a lid on the Russian angle," Burroughs ventured.

"And of course it would be even worse for *you* two, if the country were to discover that there was a second Russian mole in the agency; that you tried to stop me from investigating him—"

"Now, wait a damned minute—"

"—and that Wesley here helped this traitor rise through the Agency ranks. And that Spitzer spied for the same Russian handler who also ran Avery Trammel. And that Trammel, in turn, helped Russia plot both the terrorism and the assassination attempt on an American presidential candidate."

He stopped. Gave them a few seconds to exchange nervous looks again.

"Just where are you going with this?" Houk's voice was low, his face pale.

Garrett laced his fingers across his stomach. Began to rock back and forth in his chair.

"You know, there are an awful lot of dead people because of what happened these past few weeks. Of course, you two are not responsible for *all* of that carnage. But you are certainly responsible for some of it. Maybe if you hadn't interfered with my hunt for Spitzer—or if you had actively supported it—we might have unraveled the SVR network far sooner. Maybe flipping him would have led us to Sokolov. And without his handler, maybe Trammel would have been stopped, too. That means his involvement with Lasher, Shishani, the terrorism, Helm's assassination—who knows what could have been prevented?

"But let us not speculate on what *might* have been prevented. Here is what I am in a unique position to prevent *now*: a lot of embarrassing questions sure to come back here, directed right at you two. Because a great many angry people correctly see this as a massive failure of our intelligence community. There will be investigations galore. However, I am in a position to guide the direction of those inquiries. I can point them away from you." He stopped rocking and glared at each of them in turn. "You know I can."

Burroughs's Adam's apple bobbed. "What do you want?"

Garrett reached into his gray suit jacket and withdrew an envelope, along with his steel-gray pen. He opened the envelope, extracting two sheets of paper. Then he separated them and slid them in front of the two men.

"In exchange for doing you this enormous personal favor, I think some resignations are in order."

For a moment, they looked like mannequins, speechless and immobile.

"I have even spared you the bother of drafting your own letters of resignation. These say the usual bland, even noble-sounding bullshit about 'assuming full responsibility for unacceptable intelligence failures,' and 'hoping to restore the full confidence of the American people,' blah blah blah."

"So *that's* it, then," Houk said, a bitter grimace twisting his lips. "You're after my job."

"Oh, God no. I am quite happy in Ops—at least the Ops we used to have before you came along. But I am confident the nation can find someone better qualified than you. Than either of you. Hell, they could do that by covering their eyes and pointing at random names in the phone book."

Garrett was too sickened by them to take pleasure from their stricken looks. He laid his pen atop Burroughs's letter. Nudged it around with his forefinger so the barrel was within his reach.

"You first, Wesley."

The man stared at the pen as if it were a poisonous reptile.

"If you don't—or if you attempt to retaliate against me, or Miss Woods—then I'll dump to the media all the sordid details about Spitzer, Trammel, the Russians, and how you were their enablers."

"Can't I please—"

"No, you can't, Wesley. Stop stalling and whining. I don't have all day." He glanced at the silver watch on his wrist. "I have an appointment in forty-five minutes with our next president."

2

"I appreciate your volunteering to give me an early national security briefing, Mr. Garrett."

"And I appreciate your willingness to meet me alone for this discussion, Senator Spencer."

They were meeting in the candidate's suite at a downtown hotel, where in two hours Spencer would give a luncheon speech to a major business group. They faced each other across a small dining table. At Garrett's request, Spencer had banished his aides and security people to a closed, adjoining room.

Garrett opened his slim briefcase, withdrew a sealed envelope, removed a file folder from it, then slid it across the table.

"I believe you have seen the contents of this folder before."

The candidate's cheery, boyish look melted into a look of puzzlement. He opened the folder wide—then his eyes—then his mouth. He gasped and slammed the folder shut. Garrett watched the color drain from the man's panicked face. He didn't say a word.

Garrett reached across the table, retrieved the folder. Slid it back into the envelope.

"Senator," he began, "my job is to protect the security of the United States. I take that responsibility more seriously than you can imagine. I believe these photos already have been used against you to compromise national security. But the good news is, I am reasonably confident I have managed to close that security breach. For the time being, at least.

"However, looking ahead to your likely presidency, I see other kinds of threats on the horizon. Threats not just to our country, but specific threats to certain individuals. To myself, for one. And to certain of my associates."

He picked up the envelope. Bounced it in his hand.

"I want to promise you, Senator, that these photos will remain securely in my possession, out of the reach of anyone who might wish to harm you. And they will never see the light of day—as long as your presidency never threatens the safety of America, or the safety of those individuals I just referred to."

He slid the envelope back into his briefcase, then stood.

Spencer remained seated, trembling and staring up at him.

"What individuals?" His voice was a soft rasp.

"Oh, I'll be in touch about that," Garrett said. He nodded. "Have a nice day, Senator."

He turned and left.

3

"I can't believe how big and strong this pup is getting," he said.

Cyrano was tugging on the leash, his nose to the road, trying to accelerate the excursion to new aromas.

"Yes. Well, you would notice if you saw him every day. But instead, you dumped him with me."

"Now, that's not fair. I figured since you are confronting the bad guys so much, you needed a guard dog."

"Sheepdog."

"Same thing. Something to keep the wolves away. You *do* know I have a vested interest in keeping the wolves from your door."

"Do I have a say in that?"

"No."

"You have it easy with Luna."

"True. She doesn't require walks. But there's the litter box. It's all trade-offs, you know."

"Oh, look who's here. Cyrano is going to love this."

Up ahead, Jim and Billie Rutherford, "Vic Rostand's" next-door neighbors, were heading their way, walking their golden retriever,

Happy. The second they spotted each other, both dogs began tugging at their leashes.

"Annie!" Billie said, giving up on the job of holding the two dogs apart. "It's so nice to see you again!"

"Well, it's nice to get out here. I can't make the trek from D.C. as often as I'd like."

"It sounds terribly inefficient," Jim said, winking at Dylan. "You ought to consolidate households."

Hunter looked at Annie. "A topic under ongoing review."

"If you do, I hope it's you coming out *this* way, Annie, not the other way around. We'd hate to lose Vic, and we'd love to have you as a neighbor."

"How's the fox situation doing?" Jim asked.

"I can live with all their dead animal carcasses in the yard," Hunter said, "as long as they don't burrow under my porch or inside my shed."

"Oh, the shed," Annie said, eyes twinkling. "Now that would be a disaster."

"Looks like Happy and Cyrano are already pals," Hunter said. "We should try to coordinate our walks."

"We should coordinate our *meals*," Billie said. "We keep saying we'll get together and never do."

"I'll be here over the weekend. Why don't we do it then?"

"Oh, Annie, that would be great."

After conversing about food and wine preferences, they retreated to their respective houses.

At dusk, they were on the porch sipping wine when Annie noticed the mother fox trotting at the edge of the marsh. They got up to watch. Then, as the darkness deepened, the kits emerged from their den and began chasing each other in the yard, rehearsing their little power rituals of dominance and submission, heedless of their human audience.

"They don't care that we're here," she said.

"But I care that we're here. I like it here."

"I'm glad. You belong here, Dylan, with your foxes. You remind me of that famous American Revolutionary War general, Francis Marion. He also hung out in marshes and used guerrilla warfare tactics against the enemy. They called him 'the Swamp Fox.'"

He chuckled. "I like that symbolism. I do belong here." He glanced over at her. "*We* belong here."

She turned away to hide her smile. "So you changed your mind about selling this house?"

"I guess so."

"Even though you have to live under a different name here, and wear a stupid disguise in public?"

"I'm used to living under different names, you know."

They were quiet for a while, sipping the wine and watching glow ebb from the sunset sky. There was something left unsaid. She felt she had to say it.

"You know . . . we could keep things just as they are."

"What do you mean?"

"I'm saying that we make a good team . . . just as we are, Dylan Hunter."

"Yes, I'd say we do, Annie Woods."

"We don't have to think about the future. We have the present. We have now."

"It *is* a pretty good now."

"So, going forward, I don't see any irreconcilable conflict between our relationship and our respective . . . missions and priorities, after all."

"What about those dreams you talked about?"

She lowered her eyes, hesitating. Felt him watching her closely.

"Frankly, after everything I've been doing at work, I don't think I'm cut out for a white picket fence, raising two-point-three children."

"No?"

"Not really . . . So I guess we could just stay 'permanently engaged,' then."

Her breathing stopped and she stared at the ring, waiting long seconds for his answer. She heard his slow intake of breath. Heard its slow release.

"Possibly." There was amusement in his voice.

Something danced inside her. She looked up and grinned.

"It will be a 'win-win' relationship, right?"

A crooked little smile played at the corner of his mouth.

"Oh, I'm not so sure. I think *I* am the winner here."

She held his hazel-green eyes. "And 'winner takes all,' huh?"

The eyes narrowed. "Pretty much."

"Well, in that case . . ."

She began to unbutton her blouse.

A few seconds later, he approached her.

Wearing nothing but the crooked little grin.

4

Sunday morning was sunny and cool. They stayed in bed till ten, then got up and made breakfast.

"Well, Dylan, what's on our agenda?"

"It's such a beautiful day. Why don't we go for a ride?"

They drove across the Bay Bridge, past Annapolis, toward Washington. The hum of the car and the warmth of the sun made her feel sleepy.

"Anyplace in particular you have in mind?"

"As a matter of fact, yes."

"Aren't you going to tell me?"

"As a matter of fact, no."

"So it's a surprise, then." She yawned.

"Only if I don't tell you. Look, I didn't allow you much sleep last night. Why don't you take a short nap. I'll wake you when we get there."

"Okay."

Sometime later, she felt the car slow. Her eyes fluttered open.

Before she could figure out where she was, he turned into a driveway.

"Dylan! What are you doing? Why are we here?"

He turned off the car and the radio. Then turned to her.

Took her left hand.

"Annie Woods, you said we could just stay 'permanently engaged.' Well, I decided I don't like that idea. This ring means something. A promise."

Holding her eyes, he raised her hand, leaned over, and kissed the ring. As he had once before.

He said, "It's time he knew."

She couldn't speak. Her eyes filled with tears.

"Here," he said, offering his handkerchief. "You don't want to make him think I've been abusing his daughter, do you?"

She laughed. Then stared at him in wonder. Then laughed some more.

"You are really something, mister."

"Oh. Well, then—if you're not sure you want to go through with this . . . *Ow!* Damn it, that hurt!"

"The next punch will be on that big nose of yours."

"So, Annie Woods," he said, smiling, "I gather you are ready, then?"

Not smiling, she looked deep into his hazel eyes.

"I've been ready since the first day I met you, Dylan Hunter."

She would always remember and treasure what was in his eyes at that moment.

Lying at his feet, Gracie, his old Irish Setter, suddenly perked up her ears and barked. Seconds later the doorbell rang. The dog clambered awkwardly to her feet.

"Easy girl. Stay."

Ken MacLean put down the entertainment section of the *Post* and his reading glasses. Rising on stiff knees, he went to the front door, wondering who it could possibly be on a Sunday afternoon.

Opening it, he was startled to see his daughter with a man.

"Annie! What a nice—"

Then he recognized the man.

"You," he said, his voice tight.

Annie reached out to take his hand.

"Dad . . . I need to speak to you."

"We need to speak to you, sir," Dylan Hunter said. "We have a great deal to talk about." Hunter then looked at his daughter. "And I have something to ask you. May we please come inside?"

Ken MacLean looked at them for a long moment. Felt his daughter's hand tighten on his forearm.

Looked down at the hand.

Saw the diamond ring.

Everything stopped inside him.

He looked at each of them, in turn, for long seconds.

Then sighed and closed his eyes.

When he opened them, he realized he was smiling. And he knew that his answer to them expressed a sudden realization of the inevitable.

"Of course."

***

READ THE BESTSELLING THRILLER THAT INTRODUCED
DYLAN HUNTER — *THE NEW FACE OF JUSTICE*

HUNTER

#1 KINDLE BESTSELLING THRILLER
A *WALL STREET JOURNAL* "TOP 10 FICTION EBOOK"

Two people, passionately in love.
But each hides a deadly secret.
He is a crusading vigilante, on a violent quest for justice.
She is tracking this unknown assassin, sworn to stop him.
Neither realizes the truth about the other.
And neither knows that a terrifying predator is hunting them both.

A spy mystery — a crime thriller — a passionate romance . . .
and a suspenseful parable of justice that has readers cheering.

"Robert Bidinotto has crafted a masterwork of thrills and suspense."
—Gayle Lynds, *NYT* bestselling author, *The Assassins* and *The Coil*

"*HUNTER* delivers in a way few thrillers do. A fantastic debut thriller."
—Stephen England, author, *Pandora's Grave* and *Day of Reckoning*

"A terrifically paced suspense novel with a killer premise. If you're a fan of Lee Child's Jack Reacher series, I suspect you'll like *HUNTER*."
—Randy Ingermanson, author, *Writing Fiction for Dummies*

BUY IT NOW ON AMAZON!

Kindle ebook: http://amzn.to/1iZ241a
Trade paperback: http://amzn.to/TiuTkt
Audiobook edition: http://amzn.to/1sHnK7E
iTunes audiobook edition: http://bit.ly/1jISteU

The Second DYLAN HUNTER Justice Thriller

BAD DEEDS

CLFA "BOOK OF THE YEAR" 2014
#1 AUDIBLE "POLITICAL THRILLER"

He sought peace in the tranquility of nature.
But can he tame the violence in his own nature?

At a cabin in the Allegheny National Forest, Dylan Hunter and his lover, Annie Woods, seek to heal the wounds from their ordeal at the hands of a twisted psychopath. And to build a life together, Dylan promises Annie that he'll abandon his violent ways. But ideological zealots and Washington's political elites have conspired to terrorize and plunder the hard-working locals. These victims have no protector against the bad deeds of the powerful and privileged—

—except for one man.
A man as ruthless and violent as they.
A man committed to absolute justice.
**Because Dylan Hunter cannot walk away—
not even if it costs him the woman he loves.**

"I loved Bidinotto's first novel, *HUNTER*, but *BAD DEEDS* just might be better."
—Shawn Klein, author, *Harry Potter and Philosophy*

"A plot which could be ripped from today's headlines."
—Erika Holzer, bestselling author, *Eye for an Eye*

"Filled from prologue to epilogue with tricky twists of plot, passionate ideals, and characters that you love—or love to hate."
—Rose Robbins, author, *In From the Cold* and *The Accidental Dragon*

BUY IT NOW ON AMAZON!

Kindle Ebook: http://amzn.to/1kX03bC
Trade Paperback: http://amzn.to/1lr3E2L
Audible Audiobook: http://amzn.to/2zlZK4U

IF YOU ENJOYED *WINNER TAKES ALL*,

please take a moment to go to the *WINNER TAKES ALL* page on Amazon or Goodreads, and share your opinion with other readers. Reader reviews and ratings are critical to the success of this novel. Thank you!

JOIN THE DYLAN HUNTER EMAIL LIST:
http://eepurl.com/xObUz

We will notify you whenever a new Dylan Hunter thriller is released.

Your email information will be used *ONLY* to notify you about the latest Dylan Hunter books, news, and author appearances by Robert Bidinotto.

To learn more about Dylan Hunter, author Robert Bidinotto, and how to obtain personally inscribed copies of these books,

VISIT "THE VIGILANTE AUTHOR" BLOG:
http://www.bidinotto.com

Do you have questions or comments for the author?

CONTACT ROBERT BIDINOTTO

RobertTheWriter@gmail.com
On Facebook:
https://www.facebook.com/RobertBidinottoAuthor

ABOUT THE AUTHOR

Robert Bidinotto is the author of *HUNTER*, a #1 Kindle bestseller in "Mysteries & Thrillers," and a *Wall Street Journal* "Top 10 Fiction Ebook." *BAD DEEDS*, the second book in the Dylan Hunter thriller series, won the CLFA "Book of the Year" award in 2014, and became an Audible #1 thriller bestseller. *WINNER TAKES ALL* is the third installment in the series.

Robert earned a national reputation as an authority on criminal justice while writing investigative articles as a former Staff Writer for *Reader's Digest*. His famous 1988 article "Getting Away with Murder" stirred a national controversy about crime and prison furlough programs during that year's presidential campaign, and it is widely credited with having affected the outcome of the election. It was honored by the American Society of Magazine Editors as one of five finalists for the National Magazine Award for "Best Magazine Article in the Public Interest Category."

He is author of the acclaimed book *Criminal Justice? The Legal System vs. Individual Responsibility*, with a foreword by John Walsh of the "America's Most Wanted" television show, and of *Freed to Kill*—a compendium of horror stories exposing the failings of the justice system.

His many articles, essays, book and film reviews also have appeared in the *Washington Times,* the *Boston Herald, Success, The American Spectator, Writer's Digest,* and other publications. Robert was awarded the Free Press Association's Mencken Award in 1985 for "Best Feature

Story," and he has been honored by the National Victim Center and other victim-rights organizations for his outspoken public advocacy on behalf of crime victims. As an editor, in 2007, he won the magazine industry's top honor for editorial excellence—the *Folio* gold "Eddie" Award. A popular speaker, he has appeared as a guest on scores of major talk programs.

With his wife, Cynthia, and their stridently individualistic cat, Luna, Robert makes his home on the Chesapeake Bay, where he is working on the further adventures of Dylan Hunter.

BEHIND THE SCENES

It took me three years—from 2008 till 2011—to write and publish *HUNTER*, the first book in this Dylan Hunter thriller series. Then it took me almost another three years before I published its first sequel, *BAD DEEDS,* in 2014.

Which is ridiculous. That's *way* too long to write a thriller, right? Some prolific authors crank out several decent books each year. But at my pace between projects, even Dylan's diehard fans can forget about him and lose interest.

So I vowed things would be different this time. After *BAD DEEDS*, I'd get cracking right away on the next book, and rush it out within a year.

Well, three-and-a-half years after *BAD DEEDS*, the third episode in the Dylan Hunter saga finally has been published. During that period, I cringed almost daily at questions from Dylan's multitude of fans about my many missed deadlines. I tried to explain, then gave up, because it sounded like excuse-making. Maybe it was.

And we all know how Dylan deals with excuse-makers, right?

So, for the past year, I pretty much stopped communicating publicly about the book. I didn't want anyone—least of all my long-suffering wife—to know I'd reached the point where I met each morning with paralysis and dread, staring at a plot structure that had sprouted and spread like kudzu, harboring within its half-dozen subplots a proliferation of unruly characters who were multiplying like horny bunnies.

How did that happen? It happened because, for me, this single book had to accomplish so many different objectives.

For one, the story had to harvest seeds planted in the first two installments of the series—resolutions about Dylan's future course, where his relationship with Annie might be headed, and the ominous threat looming over them at the end of *BAD DEEDS*. More fundamentally, I had to confront and answer the questions:

How can I realistically sustain the "career" of a vigilante assassin over the long term? What could plausibly motivate Dylan to continue on that course? How could he possibly keep his identity secret from the world—especially from the ever-suspicious cop Ed Cronin, hot on his heels? What would it mean for Dylan's relationship with Annie?

Not only does *WINNER TAKES ALL* have its own deviously complicated tale to tell; it also had to answer all those *series* questions, too. So, though I never planned things this way when I began to write *HUNTER*, this third book had to give readers a satisfying resolution to everything implied and left open in the first two books—in effect becoming the third installment of a self-contained opening trilogy. (More about that in a moment.)

Secondly, I want my Story World to remain tied at least loosely to things going on in the Real World. But complications arose because of unanticipated Real World events. Upheaval and reorganization at the CIA, and the unexpected outcome of the 2016 presidential election, considerably affected my planned "series arc." In the middle of writing, I had to rework the plot of *WINNER TAKES ALL* so that future books in the series would remain anchored to reality, rather than go off into total fantasy.

Thirdly, the writing challenge was made much greater because my stories are "theme-driven." Rather than start out with a character or a situation and build from there, I start instead with some abstract premise or "moral of the story." My characters tend to embody "variations on the theme," taking opposing sides, and the story events grow organically from their basic conflicts. This approach adds a much higher level of complexity to the plotting, because I am trying not only to write compelling thrillers; I'm also trying to write "thrillers for thinkers."

While the primary goal of my thrillers is to give readers grand entertainment, those familiar with my previous novels—and with me as a person—know that my books' themes and settings are rooted in the serious issues of our times. These are topics I've written and spoken about for decades. They're unavoidable in my fiction.

WINNER TAKES ALL draws upon many controversies you've been reading and hearing about in the Real World. The threat of terrorism. Russian meddling in our elections. "Fake news" and media bias. Sex scandals among the rich and powerful. Government harassment of private citizens. Leaks of classified material from our spy agencies. Border security. The influence of money on politics. The controversy over fracking and energy production . . .

But in this story, the glue holding all of it together is a theme: *the psychology of power-lust.*

Why do so many people crave power over other people? Why do they *enjoy* bending others to their will, through manipulation, intimidation, humiliation, or brute force? Why do they believe they can only achieve their own success and happiness if they make others fail and suffer? Why do they believe their gain requires someone else's loss?

Though the lust for power is an epidemic in our political lives, the disease certainly isn't confined there. We find it everywhere in our society: in our families, schools, social and cultural institutions, churches, businesses, and personal relationships.

So, while the main villains in *WINNER TAKES ALL* are enmeshed in political conspiracy and conniving, I wanted to show how the lust for power permeates all other aspects of their lives, too: their workplaces, friendships, sexual relationships, and social interactions. For me, one of the most interesting contrasts is between Dylan and Annie's passionately romantic relationship, rooted in mutual admiration and respect—and the crude, superficial, manipulative, and abusive sexual relationships of the various villains. If you were uncomfortable reading about the latter, rest assured that I was uncomfortable writing about them. But the book's theme made it unavoidable: As Henry Kissinger notoriously said, "Power is the ultimate aphrodisiac." Here, that is depicted literally.

I also wanted to dramatize the critical role excuse-making and rationalizations play in enabling and perpetuating power-lust. *WINNER TAKES ALL* surveys a large cast of characters in that regard, but for clarity, it focuses on a few.

The two primary villains—Trammel and Lasher—share a well-nurtured sense of personal grievance and victimhood, as well as narcissistic grandiosity. In their fantasies, the crimes they commit are righteous revenge upon their (symbolic) victimizers. But as a sadistic sociopath, Lasher's rationalizations are simplistic and shallow; they amount to a personal Narrative in which he casts himself as an entitled "winner" in a world of pathetic "losers." By contrast, Trammel, being far more intelligent and self-aware, requires more sophisticated psychological excuses. In his Narrative, he is an avenging angel on a mission fueled by nihilistic revenge fantasies, but rationalized by ideology. In Avery Trammel we see the role that religion, philosophy, and political ideology too often play in providing quasi-intellectual excuses for appalling evil.

Julia Haight and Emmalee Conn provide an interest contrast, too. Each suffers from a deficiency of self-esteem, which allows them to be manipulated by powerful men. However, Julia is more of an authentic victim, trying to reclaim her sense of self-worth, while Emmalee blithely uses her sexuality as a tool to manipulate men. Readers may find a parable of sorts in how I made things turn out for these two women.

Squeezing *all* of these elements into a single, fast-moving, page-turning thriller became a mind-boggling challenge for me, at times an overwhelming one. But slowly, somehow, it finally all came together.

Early readers are already guessing which Real World individuals and organizations I must have had in mind as I wrote. Let me say emphatically that my Story World characters are completely imaginary; they are not meant to "represent" any specific individuals—though Real World people definitely gave me *ideas* to incorporate into my characters' personalities. Some of my characters are hybrids of the styles, attitudes, and values of several people, poured into the faces and bodies of certain actors or celebrities—and mixed well with ingredients from my own imagination. The only Real World characters in the book are Luna (our cat), Happy (our neighbor's dog), and—by occasional reference only—Vladimir Putin, who never appears on-stage. Given this book's theme, I couldn't resist taking a few shots at Vlad, although he is treated completely fictitiously here: He didn't actually do *all* the nasty stuff attributed to him in the novel.

Or at least, not most of it.

Or at least, not to my first-hand knowledge . . .

As for the fictitious organizations mentioned in the book: The Trammel Foundation, the Currents Foundation and Currents Center, Vox Populi Communications, and the Center for Advocacy Profiles *do* have real-world counterparts. No, I was not making that stuff up: The actual groups function pretty much as I describe them in *WINNER TAKES ALL*, with a few artistic liberties taken. No, I won't name them; perhaps curious readers will do some homework online and find out what the real groups are up to.

I offer an apology only to one actual organization: the Capital Research Center (CRC). CRC was the inspiration for my fictional Center for Advocacy Profiles (CAP), although the personnel described in this novel are completely imaginary and bear no resemblance to CRC's staff. The group does great investigative work to expose the trails of money and political influence in the world of foundations and nonprofit advocacy groups. In the Real World, CRC is headquartered in the very building that my fictional terrorists in this Story World blew to bits. It's a fine old building, and I'm happy to report that in the Real World, it still stands. I know all this because I used to work there. (I suppose I should also offer apologies to the occupants of the surrounding buildings, including the Methodist church across the street, for the terrible collateral damage my Story World terrorists inflicted.)

As I mentioned, with the publication of *WINNER TAKES ALL*, I have completed an initial self-contained trilogy of Dylan Hunter stories. That was not my plan or expectation when I began to write *HUNTER*. I had no idea that subsequent books would grow from it as they did; nor did I have a clue what directions these stories would take.

Even during the writing of this one, my characters surprised me constantly. I had no idea the relationships of Dylan and Annie, or Dylan and Cronin, would go where the characters hijacked them. I didn't know Wonk had a pet. I didn't know the foxes that are digging up my Real World backyard would take up residence at Vic Rostand's Connors Point home, too. I didn't know Julia Haight—who began in *BAD DEEDS* as a character I didn't much like—would redeem herself here to play such a pivotal, positive role in the outcome. I didn't know that mother and baby would be on the street that terrible day of April 20th. I didn't know what Roger Helm's fate would be.

Dylan, Annie, Luna, Cyrano, Wonk, Garrett, Cronin, Erskine, Trammel, Lasher, Emmalee, Julia, Helm, Spencer, Wulfe, Boggs, MacLean, Adair, and the many other inhabitants of this Story World simply showed up in my office, often unannounced, and invited me to spy on them. Sometimes, over glasses of wine, they told me their life stories and revealed what they were thinking and feeling, even in their most private moments.

I have spent the past decade sitting here spellbound—listening, watching, and taking notes.

They are so damned *interesting*. And I bet some of them have a lot more to tell me.

I promise to share.

—Robert Bidinotto
November 27, 2017

ACKNOWLEDGMENTS

WINNER TAKES ALL was the hardest, most exhausting writing project I've ever undertaken. My brain was completely fried at the end of the process, and I was incapable of giving the manuscript the kind of close, objective scrutiny it required before publication.

That's where over two dozen volunteer "beta readers" stepped in to save me from eternal public embarrassment. These talented people include writers and editors, as well people with backgrounds in many of the specific topics in the book. My beta readers always have been critically important to the process of editing, revising, and proofreading my manuscripts—but never more so than this time. I can't begin to catalogue the numbers of errors they caught, or the number of brilliant suggestions they made to improve the writing and the story.

I don't know what "perfection" would be in any piece of fiction. Whatever it is, I know that *WINNER TAKES ALL* falls far short. But my dedicated betas helped make the book far less *im*perfect. Blame any of the remaining flaws on me—not on these wonderful volunteers:

Liz Baker, Caroline Joy Barnhart, Kathy Barnhart, Joani Barr, Jonas Barr, Bill Brent, Pramod Challa, William Dale, Tyler Donoghue, Roger Donway, Stephen England, Mark Gardner, Greg Gerig, Ian Graham, Dan Harrison, Robert Jones, Claudia Leone, Jason Lockwood, Steven Lord, Kenneth Miller, Henry Scuoteguazza, Hendrik Sharples, Jason Stotts, Gabrielle Suglia, Gary Triplett, Gregory Wall, and Thomas Weller. A handful of additional volunteers could not participate due to medical and other personal issues, but I am indebted to them for their support and enthusiasm.

Next, my deepest thanks to those professionals in the "I.C."—the intelligence community—who generously reviewed the portions of the book dealing with the CIA, NSA, and related agencies and matters. Precisely because the activities of these agencies are highly classified and take place in restricted places, it's difficult for any outsider to present them plausibly, let alone realistically. It's impossible to capture solely from books, articles, and online sources the ambiance, jargon, procedures, and "you are there" feel of authenticity that only insiders can provide. For self-evident reasons, these individuals have asked not to be named. But I'm profoundly grateful to them for any credibility my book has about intelligence-related matters, and for the invaluable services they perform to keep our nation safe and secure.

One of the fun aspects of writing a novel is inventing the names of characters. Early in my writing, I invited recipients of "Bullet Points"— my free email newsletter to Dylan Hunter fans—to participate in a "name the character" contest. I was looking for an appropriate name for the Independent candidate for president, and a number of folks offered great names. I finally selected "Roger Tyler Helm."

That winning entry was suggested by Tyler Donoghue, a dedicated fan of the Dylan Hunter series. Tyler also is one of the most courageous men I know, who has faced cruel hardships with extraordinary grace and spirit. Thank you, Tyler, for suggesting to me the name of your beloved grandfather. I hope he likes the great character wearing it and is relieved that I let that character survive. Thanks also for serving as a beta reader.

Other participants who offered fine suggestions are: Patti Blask, Roland Breault, Bob Bryant, Nellie Guthner, Samantha Hallock, Kay Harms, Tracy Harris, Lori Larsen, Marilyn Mann, Tim McSherry, Jason Monaghan, John Pardee, Shawn Reynolds, Mickey Rudolph, Mike Stephenson, Rosemarie Wilhelm, and Vicki Williams.

Among other indispensable members of the Dylan Hunter support network whose contributions to the success of my books can't be adequately measured:

My talented cover designer, Allen Chiu (http://allenchiu.com), once again hit it out of the park. His covers draw thousands of browsing Amazon customers to my books, and I can't thank him enough.

Jason Anderson of Polgarus Studio (www.Polgarusstudio.com) is responsible for the formatting and layout of the ebook and print editions of the books, including this one. Jason takes my words and makes them *readable.*

Everyone asks me, "When is Dylan Hunter going to become a TV or movie?" If it happens, it's likely going to be because of the efforts of two fine thriller authors who are also Hollywood entrepreneurs: Matt Cook and Jeff Edwards of Braveship Entertainment (www.braveshipentertainment.com). These gentlemen (Matt is CEO, Jeff runs the book division) *love* Dylan Hunter, and their company is developing thrillers into feature films, video games, and related projects. Our fingers are crossed. Stay tuned.

Thanks also to entertainment attorney Kevin Koloff (http://www.kevinkoloff.com), for his efforts to give Dylan Hunter additional attention in Hollywood.

Joshua Zader (www.atlaswebdev.com) did fabulous work designing my blog, "The Vigilante Author" (www.bidinotto.com). Visit it and see for yourself—and while you're there, sign up for my email list, okay?

My terrific agent, Sarah Hershman (www.hershmanrightsmanagement.com), landed *BAD DEEDS* a nice audiobook deal with Audible. She'll be handling foreign and audio publishing arrangements for *WINNER TAKES ALL*, too.

Once again, let me sing the praises of Rob Walton, designer of "WriteItNow," the fantastic novel-writing software I have used to write all three books. If you are a fiction author, check it out here: (www.ravensheadservices.com). You'll be amazed.

Writing is a solitary pursuit, and the community of authors is tight-knit and mutually supportive. Without the following fabulous writers communicating with me by email, phone, and sometimes—happily—in person, I would be a pathetic recluse in a bathrobe with six-inch fingernails: you know, Howard Hughes, but without the money. Here are just a few of the terrific authors who share their insights, advice, feedback, marketing tips, and platforms with me—and who have generously promoted my books to their own readers:

Stephen England (www.stephenwrites.com),
Edd Voss (http://eddvoss.com),
Ian Graham (www.iangrahamthrillers.com),
Rose Robbins (www.roserobbinsonline.com),
Steven Konkoly (www.stevenkonkoly.com),
Gary Ponzo (https://www.garyponzo.com),
Robert McDermott (http://www.remcdermott.com),
Allan Leverone (http://www.allanleverone.com),
Martin Crosbie (http://martincrosbie.com),
Michael J. Sullivan (http://riyria.blogspot.com),
J.Carson Black (http://jcarsonblack.com),
John Clarkson (https://www.johnclarkson.com),
Neil Russell (www.neil-russell.com), and
Wayne Stinnett (http://waynestinnett.com).

The writers named include some dear friends who contribute to my life in ways beyond our professional interests. But in addition to them, no list of thank-yous would be complete without mentioning my close family and friends.

To my many friends and fans at Kent Island United Methodist Church, Shore United Bank, and Queen Anne's Chorale, whose support has been unwavering and heartfelt.

To long-time and beloved friends Steve and Cindy Lord, Henry Scuoteguazza and Claudia Leone, Hank and Erika Holzer, Gene and Sally Holloway, the entire Slate clan, and the entire Bidinotto clan. Love you all.

To my brother Ed Bidinotto, whose love and loyalty has been steadfast for over six decades. Hope you enjoy this one, Brother.

To my daughter Katrina, and granddaughters Doria and Enid: three amazing young ladies whom I love and admire beyond words. And to Margaret, for so many things, including the gift of our daughter.

To my best friend, Alan Paul—who has endured my soliloquys,

rants, brainstorms, joys, and sorrows with infinite forbearance, steady encouragement, and unflagging humor; who has fixed my computers and my attitude, as necessary; who has enriched my life with his brilliance, wisdom, wit, knowledge, and character. Alan, I am truly blessed by your friendship.

Finally, to my wife Cynthia . . .

When I was a younger man, I fantasized that I would find a woman of great soul and grand talent, of intelligence and beauty, of sensitivity and passion. However, I've been far luckier than that. I found one with the patience, understanding, generosity, and love to accept life with a difficult, often-distracted man.

I couldn't have written this trilogy without you, love. You've helped me fulfill my dreams.

Now, let's go chase a few of yours.

***

CPSIA information can be obtained
at www.ICGtesting.com
Printed in the USA
LVHW020848070421
683685LV00009B/398